"I NEED PEOPLE TO DO THINGS. Loyal people. People like you. Can you do things?"

Jazari nodded, less vigorously. What kinds of things, she wondered.

"Yeah, don't worry too much about it," Zosi said with a smile. "Nothing you can't handle." She let out a big sigh and sat back against the seat.

Time passed and Jazari relaxed a bit and glanced out the window. They had taken off and were flying over open seas, deep shimmery turquoise underneath them, silver- and redcaps dotting the surface, a few habs in the gloomy distance. The habs on Cecrops were open and airy affairs, more like extended cabanas around enclosed living areas—after a bit of terraforming, the atmosphere on the planet was earthlike, the weather generally mild. No seasons to speak of. The skies were dark blue and dotted with stars, lightening to orange and red around Trappist 1 in its fixed position in the sky. Clouds outlined in red threaded in the mild breeze, with Trappist 1's nearest creche planets Otrera and Actaeon in their places, shining low in the sky. Sunward, the largely uninhabitable Otrera was small, pale, and purplish, while the ice and water world of Actaeon, mottled gray and white, loomed half above the opposite horizon. Tidally locked Actaeon had a thick crust of ice that melted to water on the heatward side toward Trappist 1, a doorway where transports entered to access the sparse habs in the water under the ice. The other four planets in the system were either too close to Trappist 1 to make out, orbited behind the planet from their position, or were too far out be seen without amplification.

"One more thing," Zosi said, looking out her own window. "I'm easygoing until I'm not. Because I'm easygoing, people don't take me seriously at first. I know this about people. You won't take me seriously, and I forgive you. But I'll only give you one chance. One screwup. When you screw up, I'll take what you love the most and destroy it. Be expecting it. Then you'll believe me. Then and only then will things work the way they should."

She didn't even glance over at Jazari.

Mechalum Space

The Language of Corpses
The Chaos of Corpses (forthcoming)

TT Linse
Writing as Tamara Linse

How to Be a Man (stories)
Deep Down Things (novel)
Earth's Imagined Corners (historical novel)

The Wyoming Chronicles (YA)
British Classics Set in Contemporary Wyoming

Moreau (adventure)
Pride (romance)
Solomon (adventure, forthcoming)
Eyre (romance, forthcoming)

The Language of Corpses

Mechalum Space 1

TT Linse

Cover art: Bodies in Mechalum Space, *digital media*
composite, by TT Linse, with credit to CarlosDavid, laremenko,
and AlxeyPnferox for images

Print
ISBN-13: 978-1-953694-02-7

Print (Amazon)
ISBN-13: 978-1-953694-00-3

Epub
ISBN-13: 978-1-953694-03-4

Kindle
ISBN-13: 978-1-953694-01-0

Edition 1.0

For Caroline and Allyson,
who made me believe

"Here," she said, "in this here place, we flesh; flesh that weeps, laughs; flesh that dances on bare feet in grass. Love it. Love it hard. Yonder they do not love your flesh. They despise it. They don't love your eyes; they'd just as soon pick em out. No more do they love the skin on your back. Yonder they flay it. And O my people they do not love your hands. Those they only use, tie, bind, chop off and leave empty. Love your hands! Love them. Raise them up and kiss them. Touch others with them, pat them together, stroke them on your face 'cause they don't love that either. You got to love it, you! And no, they ain't in love with your mouth. Yonder, out there, they will see it broken and break it again. What you say out of it they will not heed. What you scream from it they do not hear. What you put into it to nourish your body they will snatch away and give you leavins instead. No, they don't love your mouth. You got to love it. This is flesh I'm talking about here. Flesh that needs to be loved. Feet that need to rest and to dance; backs that need support; shoulders that need arms, strong arms I'm telling you. And O my people, out yonder, hear me, they do not love your neck unnoosed and straight. So love your neck; put a hand on it, grace it, stroke it and hold it up. And all your inside parts that they'd just as soon slop for hogs, you got to love them. The dark, dark liver—love it, love it, and the beat and beating heart, love that too. More than eyes or feet. More than lungs that have yet to draw free air. More than your life-holding womb and your life-giving private parts, hear me now, love your heart. For this is the prize."

— Toni Morrison, *Beloved*

The Language of Corpses

Part 1
Jazari

Chapter 1

Fury, Proxima Centauri system, EU 2728, FuFG602

This is a really bad idea, Jazari thought as she punched in the mechalum hash, her hands the mech equivalent of sweaty as hell.

Or, you know, what she had remembered as the mechalum hash. Not the right one, as it turned out. Such a brash cockup would usually result in the poor rust bucket dancing with the Prox eels. Dead, in other words.

Or dead for all intents and purposes—we don't actually know what happens to people when they go through a Faison Gate with the wrong coordinates. They could end up nowhere. Or they could end up two million EUs in the past in a black hole, since time doesn't matter in mechalum space. But there would be no comp waiting on the other end and no receiving team, so, you know, as good as.

Should we be considering our life choices? her ccomp subvocalized in her ear.

Off, Jazari shot back.

Blessed silence.

Must remember to turn down its sarcasm.

Jazari had never liked her ccomp. It was always there trying to help, which you'd think was a good thing, but it was not. Its offers of help felt more like running commentary on all the ways Jazari was wrong. Always there, always watching, always judging, jumping at the chance to be *helpful*. She didn't trust it. And it's not like Jazari could pull it out of her brain and shut it in a drawer. Why anyone thought it was a good idea to link a mesh-connected sentient AI to the human essent, Jazari would never know.

She couldn't ask her ccomp the coordinates because it wouldn't know, and of course the gate comp wasn't going to tell her, even if she worked here. And the mesh was no help with privileged info like this—they don't post these things and you can't ask your next door neighbor.

The gate room she was in was like all the others. Basically a small sterile medical room, this one painted a pale yellow, that smelled of cleaning chemicals that didn't quite hide Fury's usual stench of human bodies and mech oil and decaying seaweed. It held a mobile crash couch and a touchpad and had two doors on opposite sides of the room, one for travelers to enter—and never leave—and one for personnel and bodies, which were carted off to be put on ice or reused for some other essent.

But Jazari thought she had a valid hash. She thought she remembered it from that last person she helped gate in her suck-ass poor-paying glorified step-and-fetch job. A rich tourist to somewhere in the Ross 154 system, maybe, or one of the Ogles. She just had to hope their emergency backup wasn't on the fritz. She'd be stored without a body until it got sorted out. But, dead here or dead nowhere—at least there was a good chance across the galaxy.

She should have remembered the hash, as she had a damn good memory for symbols. Not photographic memory, since she didn't gen with it, but as good as she could get augmented in with the bit of money she could scrape together. And this mech body she'd picked up on Fury was better at memory even than her gen body, and she'd been good in her gen body because she'd worked hard at it. If you're going to be a xenolinguist—even if there were no real live aliens to talk to— you better be able to remember symbols.

But to her credit, she felt a bit rushed. The two hulking mechs and the deceptively slender and normal bio essent that Zosi had sent after her had moved beyond talking to the door comp to hotwiring it. At least Atze hadn't come—Jazari would be dead already. She could see the three on the screen she'd pulled up in the corner of her eye. She had no doubt that bastard bio would figure it out, even with the security in this place.

Gates always had levels upon levels of security. Story as old as time. Everybody has reasons to want to get into—or away from—a Faison Gate. To go somewhere or, you know, to blow it up because they'd been forced to immigrate. Or because their caro or creche mate had been forced to emigrate. Or something someone had done to their gen body or their receiving body. Or didn't do. Or, you know, threatened to do. Crackpots abound.

Irony does too, considering what she was doing.

Jazari had talked to this bio essent for a bit at a bar before she figured out who she was. Her ccomp had had to sim-translate the bio's thickly accented Standard. Jazari had a pretty good ear for accents, but she hadn't recognized this one. That should have been her first clue. The meeting sent the fear of Nuc into Jazari. That and the fact that the essent told her she was going to kill her. In another life, this bio was a dictator on a small but important planet. You know, like Zosi back on Cecrops.

Chapter 2

Cecrops. Jazari had grown up on that shithole. Well, to be fair, it wasn't a shithole—Fury was—but any place you grow up and want to get away from as quick as possible is a shithole. It actually was pretty nice. A tidally locked mostly water world in the Trappist 1 system. Not too much weather, mild climate. Dim star. People lived on the water in ramshackle habs. Lots of aquaculture and pretty good sushi. No, it was the fact that she grew up in a snow creche with just the bare minimum of essentials and caretakers who could give a rat's ass. That's why it was a shithole.

Jazari was covered by Basic, so she wouldn't have starved. Every citizen of a planet or system in the MWA, the Milky Way Alliance, supposedly was. But you had to work to have more than the bare minimum. The Cecrops government, unlike other richer communities like the Ring around Epsilon Eridani, only kept you from starvation and put a roof over your head. In the Ring, your level of contribution to society could earn you a decent living, even a comfortable one. But this excluded communities with extremist ideologies that refused to join the MWA—like the one orbiting the gas giant Harpsichord around Lacaille 9352. There, generally you were shit out of luck.

7

Jazari had heard that their ideologies had something to do with stoicism and aliens and their social support system involved a form of cannibalism that they called *recycling*. It was probably just a story.

Cecrops had some of the galaxy's only archaeological sites with alien advanced tech—discovered so far—and that was important because that was the reason Jazari had the burning desire to figure out alien language. Some rich high-sider had taken an interest in their snow creche and sponsored a field trip to the orbiting artifacts when Jazari was nine. When Cecrops had first been settled, essents had thought that the light asteroid belt was a naturally occurring thing. But once they were up and running and took a closer look, they realized that something was off.

The individual asteroids were a little too smooth, and they were asymmetrical in a symmetrical kind of way—a very deliberate sort of asymmetrical. When scanned, they were of uniform density throughout, without the usual variations of naturally occurring rock and ice. And on them here and there etched into the rock were small patches of symbols. Each symbol tended to be a rounded square weaved through with an intricate pattern of naturalistic shapes that could be weird faces or hands or Nuc knows what but you couldn't quite make them out. They were each the size of a very large thumbprint and were arranged in a jumble mass—no rows or columns or regularity. They did not react when poked and prodded with various instruments, so scientists figured they were keyed to the aliens in some way.

These were not the first alien tech artifacts found— previous findings in 2366 near Gamma Pavonis had been studied for their technology and brought the galaxy superstrong materials that allowed the construction of the Ring around Epsilon Eridani and terraforming on the leading edge of settlement—what was it? Now almost ninety light years out from Sol. But these around Cecrops were obviously from a different species than the ones found before, and no one had figured out much about them.

But, to be honest, that wasn't the real reason xenolinguistics fascinated Jazari. The real reason was because she'd always heard voices in her head. This wasn't like the subvocalizing of her ccomp. There was always a low-level hum, rising and falling, but sometimes one or two voices would stand out. Often it was when she was dozing off or staring into space, her mind quiet. A voice would be screaming—in terror or in anger or in pain or, it seemed sometimes, in sheer boredom. Other times, it would sing, sometimes tonelessly, sometimes with very elaborate and beautiful melodies. Jazari looked forward to those times. Every once in a while, she could even make out nonsense words. Most of them were questioning. They never answered her and they never answered each other or had conversations.

It was really inconvenient if they started shouting when she was in the middle of a conversation. She unconsciously tried to cover them up by talking very loud and very fast, hushing them, even though whoever she was talking to couldn't hear them. Essents gave her funny looks. "You're running from something," one very astute but inept lover had told her.

There were two options, as she saw it. These voices were internal or external. If they were internal, then she had a whole planet's worth of babbling people inside her. If they were external—well, that was more troubling. Who the hell were they? And why were they talking to her, of all people, and how did their voices end up in her skull?

Extensive medical testing at eight EUs had ruled out schizophrenia and other mental disorders, although the med had looked at her through narrowed eyes. I *wish* I was faking it, she'd thought. Mental note to use a medcomp next time—less judgy. Jazari herself was unsure. It had to be a mental disorder, even though essents had figured out a cure or at least a treatment for most of the traditional physical-based disorders. Essents went bat-shit crazy in the natural course of things after they'd been alive for centuries and jumped through a bunch of bodies, but Jazari had a long way to go to get to that.

How else would you explain it? One way. Maybe those voices were aliens, and maybe by studying alien languages, she'd eventually figure out what those voices were saying. That's why she decided to go to college for xenolinguistics—in the off chance something would click.

She had hoped she would lose the voices when, at 17, she gated to Fury into a mech body and left her gen bio body behind. That's how a lot of people escaped illness or severe injury or old age—they just jumped into another body and the authorities disposed of the diseased one.

Before she jumped to Fury, she'd had a minimum of augments because she was poor—ccomp, mesh modem, memory, languages, vision and endorphin boosts to combat the twilight and the lack of a day cycle on Cecrops—the usual, but none of which physically altered her. Her gen body had been short, male presenting, with light brown skin—bio bodies on Cecrops because of its lower gravity had begun to elongate but not appreciably from Sol standard. She tended to wear simple standard clothing in browns, blues, and oranges—fabricated one cycle, recycled the next. She didn't bother with entopics—they cost money—but she had a few physical behances, a baubleband of sea fibers and jadestone on her wrist, tantalum rings in graduated sizes around one ear.

Her hair was a wavy brown, which she kept cropped above her ears. Her light eyes were uptilted, and she had a narrow but prominent nose, flared nostrils, and curvy lips—lips that were always half-smiling, she'd been told. Somebody had once called her Puck, for a moon named after a fool. They'd laughed when they'd said it, but Jazari knew she was no fool. Let them think that.

She didn't look much different from the other essents on Cecrops. Unlike the others, though, she did not know her genetic origins. Most people could trace their genetic ancestry back to Sol, just as they could trace their essent history back to their gen body and gen planet. It came with their gen and citizenship certs. Jazari's records had been lost somewhere along the way, and no one had any idea how or why—that's how she'd ended up at a snow creche.

When she'd gated to Fury, she hadn't had the money to transfer to another skin job—hardly anybody did. Only rich people could afford that. But, it seemed reasonable that, if the voices had been inside her, she would have escaped them when she slipped her biology. It hadn't happened though, so it must be something essential to her.

The voices, though, had gotten louder the closer she got to a Faison Gate. During the brief surge of pain and disorientation as she came through, they had literally screamed in her brain, a chorus of millions of voices. When she came to in her mech body, after they'd moved her from the unscheduled comp transfer, the voices were back to what they had been before—slightly elevated, but not overwhelming.

Something about mechalum space set them off. Maybe that's why, after she'd got what she came for—a degree in xenolinguistics with honors—she'd put off transferring to that backwater, Gliese 1061, to fulfill her indenture to teach and instead took a shit job at one of Fury's five gates. To be closer to the voices.

Chapter 3

Zosi and Atze. Now there was another story. Jazari had held out hope that she'd escaped their clutches. No such luck. Evidence these three goons.

She'd met them the first time when she was 17. At 17, you had to pick a trade or a trade picked you. At that age, foundling essents like Jazari already had something in mind like apprenticing to the aquaculture farms and they'd shown aptitude or interest. Or by not choosing their lives got chosen for them. If they seemed smart, they may be slotted into one of the few scholarship spots in the better schools, or they may be apprenticed to a trade. If they were really unlucky they got picked up by people like Zosi for sex work or black market mules.

Jazari was smart and she knew what she wanted. She wanted to study alien languages. Only, even with its alien artifacts, Cecrops was more of a trade school planet, and so Jazari's only hope was going offworld. The jobs counselor at the creche had told her she was out of luck, better to settle for the communications guild, since she was smart, but Jazari had her heart set, and while she dithered, the slots filled up. So that's why she was left with no choice. She was aging out of the creche, and Zosi just showed up. Zosi must've had an arrangement with the director—she must send all the misfits her way.

Jazari knew when she entered the director's office that something was up. The director caught her attention first, her mech body in its civil service uniform standing stiffly by her desk, leaning forward on her toes as if she would jump at any noise. Her faceplate's eyes were wide, and it was tense around the lips. A mech body is less expressive than a bio body, but there were similar tells—muscle memory from your gen body.

The director had come from one of those planets that insisted on keeping its original ping language, in addition to Standard. Jazari wasn't sure which planet or which language. She'd heard the director speaking it once, lots of guttural gees and kays, with a touring dignitary. In general, your ccomp could translate any incoming known language for you. For outgoing, if you were in a mech body like the director was, the ccomp in conjunction with the mech body could take your internal speech and translate it directly to your mech voice. It took some getting used to. Similarly, your ccomp could assist you in outgoing translation in a bio body, but it was a recipe for disaster, since you had to pronounce the foreign sounds yourself and you'd most likely screw it up.

Almost immediately, Jazari noticed who was standing across the room from the director. It was the most beautiful bio body Jazari had ever seen. To a casual outsider, this was a good-looking rich kid called to the director's office. The essent didn't look much older than Jazari, with pale freckled skin, artfully spiked blonde hair, a tall slender frame, expensive well-fitting exercise gear that you don't actually wear exercising, and no garish entopics, though Jazari suspected there may be a few enamors. The essent had no visible mech enhancements, unless you counted the large mech standing by the door that made Jazari jump when she noticed her.

The mech was upgraded—larger and elongated, some military augments, an expression faceplate altered from standard with wider fuller features. Its large wide-set eyes sparkled, faceted like golden-brown jewels. The mech had no ornamentation or entopics and was not wearing any clothing, which sometimes indicated the mech was just a comp, but all the augments pointed to it being an essent.

No, it was the way the director acted that gave Zosi away. The director was falling all over herself. Here was someone with power and lots of it, a formidable old essent who chose a young bio body.

"Jazari, bow to the Honored Guest," the director said in her mech voice. She'd chosen an accent from Epsilon Eridani, which was often used to signify class and culture. Jazari had wondered if she'd ever lived on Epsilon Eridani, or if she'd just chosen it to make herself sound better. Jazari was guessing the latter.

The director added subvocally, *Warning—be on your best behavior or your life just got a lot worse.* The director's subvocal accent matched her spoken one. The system was designed that way by default so you could recognize people's voices.

Jazari blinked. No advanced warning, but at least she said something now. The director wasn't a bad person, Jazari had decided, just anxious in that way that made people small-minded. Jazari had known something had to give, but she didn't think it'd quite gotten to this. But then it all came together—since she hadn't chosen, this was the essent who was going to decide her future.

At that moment, Jazari's voices shrieked and then cut off and were quiet. She stiffened, and adrenalin shot through her, causing her ccomp to subvocalize, *Query? Status?*

Fine, she sent back.

This is how it is, Jazari thought. I have no choice. I'm going to make the best of it then. She sized up the essent for a split second. Was this the type of person who would benefit from calculated defiance? Or from subservience? At 17, Jazari had had plenty of lessons in games people play. This was someone who liked to be admired, judging from her careful presentation. She liked ease and people who did what she said. She'd most likely have little patience for back talk.

Jazari made a quick decision. She bowed two degrees more deeply than was strictly necessary. "I am honored," she said.

The director relaxed visibly. *Good choice*, she said to Jazari. To the bio essent, she said, "This is Jazari. She has not yet chosen a name or a profession. She's shown facility with communications and public perception. A strong mind." The director paused and then added, "She's shown an openness to mods, as well." Jazari wasn't sure where the director had gotten that, though the first part was true.

The director did not introduce the essent to Jazari but stood waiting. That meant it didn't matter what Jazari thought. It only mattered what this essent though.

"Is she loyal?" the essent asked. Her resonant voice sounded a bit archaic and upper crust. She may have been talking to the director, but she was looking at Jazari with those manicured eyebrows raised.

"Yes, absolutely," the director said immediately, but the essent didn't react. She watched Jazari's face.

Jazari considered her for a minute. She wanted something. She wanted Jazari to respond, which was a good sign. Something told Jazari that this essent was really dangerous, but she liked the fact that she was looking to her, Jazari, rather than just taking her, since she obviously could.

Jazari nodded slightly and opened her expression, not quite a smile.

"Good," the essent said to Jazari, nodding back. She looked at the director and said. "As always, it's nice doing business with you." A chill—this essent wanted Jazari to know that this was just business. A warning.

A thrill shot down Jazari's spine. Here we go, she thought. My life's going to begin, one way or another.

That was pretty much for the meeting. "We'll send your things," the director said as Jazari followed the essent out of the office. "Nucyotta," she added, almost under her breath, "Godspeed." The mech turned and followed them out the door.

Grief swept over Jazari for a split second. Grief for the loss of everything she'd known—even if it was shitty, it was hers. All her creche mates, her friends she'd known her whole life. She'd resisted having a caro, other than the occasional fairly innocent hookup—life was complicated enough and she saw what the others went through, plus she knew they'd all be moving on. She'd even miss one or two of the teachers. Her stupid little bunk and the few things she had in the packet under her mattress. A notebook where she marked down

17

important things—how quaint, her bunkmates had said. She hoped they would send that.

She stumbled. The mech behind her paused to let her catch herself but did not move to help her—another sign that this was an essent, not a comp. A comp would've helped.

Jazari shook her head. They were just things. At least her digital library was coming with her, and she could mesh with the people she really wanted to talk to. They weren't really lost. She had to focus on what lay ahead.

Waiting for them was a transport, luxurious, understated, and spacious. The front half look like a sleek and sinuous ground transport that morphed into a spacious air shuttle in the back half. It was made of molded metallic composites and aerodynamic one-way black diamondglass. They stepped in, first the bio, then Jazari, then the mech. The bio faced forward, leaning in with her elbows on her knees, and the mech sat next to Jazari facing backwards toward the bio.

The interior was surprisingly large and had that new transport smell, understated synthetics and florals. It was dim with soft blue underlights and crystal accents and gentle soothing enamors. The seats quickly molded to the body.

"A couple of things," the bio said, glancing over at the mech. "I'm Zosi oi Bsam. I get things for people. Things they can't get at the store."

People were no longer grouped by families, except on the rare throwback planet, since most people didn't gen the traditional way. They were grouped by creches, which were most often organized around trades or guilds. *oi Bsam* meant *of the Bsam creche*, which was one of the first established on

Cecrops. Very old, very rich, very powerful, known for trade and politics.

Zosi paused and reached into her jacket and pulled out a slender pack. She extracted a med sheet, which looked like a small square of purple plastic, placed it on her tongue, and shut her mouth and eyes. She lolled her head back and then forward again, swallowed, and then opened her eyes.

"That's Atze," Zosi said, nodding toward the mech. "She's me, too. Split a century or so back."

The mech lifted her chin, expression neutral, but didn't say anything.

Jazari nodded and met her weird eyes. The hair on Jazari's neck prickled—she wasn't sure quite why.

"Second, I need people to do things. Loyal people. People like you. Can you do things?"

Jazari nodded, less vigorously. What kinds of things, she wondered.

"Yeah, don't worry too much about it," Zosi said with a smile. "Nothing you can't handle." She let out a big sigh and sat back against the seat.

Time passed and Jazari relaxed a bit and glanced out the window. They had taken off and were flying over open seas, deep shimmery turquoise underneath them, silver- and redcaps dotting the surface, a few habs in the gloomy distance. The habs on Cecrops were open and airy affairs, more like extended cabanas around enclosed living areas—after a bit of terraforming, the atmosphere on the planet was earthlike, the weather generally mild. No seasons to speak of. The skies were dark blue and dotted with stars, lightening to orange and red around Trappist 1 in its fixed position in the sky. Clouds outlined in red threaded in the mild breeze, with Trappist 1's nearest creche planets Otrera and Actaeon in their places, shining low in the sky. Sunward, the largely uninhabitable Otrera was small, pale, and purplish, while the ice and water world of Actaeon, mottled gray and white, loomed half above the opposite horizon. Tidally locked Actaeon had a thick crust of ice that melted to water on the heatward side toward Trappist 1, a doorway where transports entered to access the sparse habs in the water under the ice. The other four planets in the system were either too close to Trappist 1 to make out, orbited behind the planet from their position, or were too far out be seen without amplification.

"One more thing," Zosi said, looking out her own window. "I'm easygoing until I'm not. Because I'm easygoing, people don't take me seriously at first. I know this about people. You won't take me seriously, and I forgive you. But I'll only give you one chance. One screwup. When you screw up, I'll take what you love the most and destroy it. Be expecting it. Then you'll believe me. Then and only then will things work the way they should."

She didn't even glance over at Jazari.

Chapter 4

They traveled heatward for hours, the open ocean unchanging below them. They passed around a large shining hab city and several smaller cities and then back out over open ocean. In the distance, the skies brightened a bit and the roiling stormclouds of heatside slowly rose into view as they got closer.

Early in the trip, Zosi pulled her legs up onto the seat, curled against the wall, and slept. Atze sat there unmoving—Jazari suspected she was viewing something on her internal screens. At one point, Zosi seemed to rouse a bit but never opened her eyes. Atze also shifted a bit, which made Jazari think they were subbing a conversation.

Jazari mostly just watched out the window and fiddled with the baubleband on her wrist, a nervous habit. She had a bunch of questions, but it didn't seem the right time to ask them. So instead she brought up her ccomp and accessed the feeds for as much information as she could find on the Bsam creche and on Zosi and Atze oi Bsam. She knew that they would know what she was doing, but it was the only natural thing. They'd probably think it was weird if she hadn't.

She was right—the Bsams were important. They weren't the Alpha who, three hundred EUs ago, traveled 39.46 light years from Sol as a virtual essent in the ping meant for the Trappist 1 system. Like all pings, the Alpha had been brought out of digital cryo by the AlphaComp an EU before touchdown to fine tune the choice of planets and landing spots in order to establish a Faison Gate. A hundred sets of human genetics preserved in cryo were included as standard procedure—the seeds of future generations, altered and recombined and genned in artificial wombs.

The Bsams also weren't the Beta, the first essent brought through the Faison Gate to assist the Alpha and AlphaComp. It was also the Beta's job to assess the Alpha's mental state, after all the stress of the journey, and to report back independently to Ping Project Command. Only once in the establishment of hundreds of Faison Gates had a Beta had to oust an Alpha. On one of the moons around Kapteyn C in the Kapteyn's Star system, an Alpha had to be taken out by the Beta and an army of bot mechs for monomaniacal tendencies. An undetected instability had been exacerbated by the interaction of an element of the local atmosphere with one of her systems, and she had been planning to send an army back through the gate to take over Ping Project Command.

However, the Bsams, a Pema and a Jan, were among the first wave of essents through the Faison Gate into the small bot mechs. They were among the specialists who assessed the planet's resources and established production systems to gen both mechs and mech and bio bodies to receive future immigrants. They helped establish hab cities and energy and food supplies and, when the technology became available, began the terraforming.

The Bsams had quickly established themselves as an influential creche. A Bsam had been appointed Cecrops project leader after the Alpha stepped down to do other things. Although they no longer held that post, now called the planetary minister or prima, there seemed to be a Bsam or a Bsam advisor in the most important roles. There was even an interplanetary pop star.

No matter how hard Jazari looked, though, the feeds had no reference to a Zosi or Atze oi Bsam. On one hand, she'd been surprised if there had been, but she was disappointed nonetheless. The silence spoke louder than anything.

She would later realize that the trip was all some kind of test, and she apparently passed. She briefly wondered what would have happened if she hadn't.

They were approaching two small beautiful islands when Atze turned her head and said, "That's us." Her voice was like Zosi's, only deeper and gruffer.

Jazari sat up. The jutting islands were covered with tall spindly spiro trees and lots of underbrush, with sheer cliffs on a couple of sides. There were no habs, no developments that she could see.

Just as she was telling her ccomp to zoom in, Atze subvocalized, *You'll want to tell me, if anything comes up.* Atze was looking out her side of the window as she said it, and she lifted her fist and tapped it, the soft chink of metal on diamondglass.

Jazari started to glance over at her, but she said, *Don't. Don't look at me right now. You're looking at the islands.*

Smart, Jazari thought. It looked like Jazari glanced over in reaction to Atze's motion. Which begged the question—what kind of relationship did Atze and Zosi really have?

Jazari looked back out the window, waiting.

Out of the corner of her eye, Jazari saw Zosi open her eyes, lift her head, and look at Atze. Atze just looked back, maybe subvocalized. Zosi shrugged slightly and put her head back.

When nothing more came, Jazari said to Atze, *What do you mean? What kinds of things?*

I couldn't tell you, Atze said. *But you'll know. It's also good not to get too comfortable. Even with me.*

Jazari thought that was sound advice.

Chapter 5

To Jazari's surprise, the transport skimmed the surface of the sea and then dove underwater. It was a regular thing on some planets such as Actaeon to live under the ocean, but not so here on Cecrops. Maybe because of Actaeon, people took perverse pride in not augmenting for underwater survival, unless they were aquaculture farmers. Of course, most mech bodies would automatically survive, but they didn't draw attention to the fact.

The transport settled in a waterlock, and the door fell and sealed. It took a bit for the water to drain, and by the time the car door lifted, a small maglev transport stood waiting. They got in and sat, the platform rocking with their weight. It gently whisked them into a hallway that quickly transitioned to diamondglass with a stunning view of the Cecrops equivalent of a coral reef.

Jazari gasped. It was so beautiful, it didn't seem real. Zosi smiled.

Turned out that large portions of Zosi's habs were made of diamondglass. Zosi loved beautiful things and had the money, so—instead of the dark, cramped, smelly halls like the habs on Fury, with all its shielding from Proxima Centauri's fierce solar winds—you had all the best comforts while surrounded by sinuous brightly colored plants and fish creatures and Trappist 1's rays through the silver, green, and blue of the deep.

The transport came to a smooth halt in the large, dimly lit, open lounge and entry hall, a twisted bulbous snake of a room with archways and floors in levels and couches and chairs and lamps and views and exits going off in all directions. At its center in a pool of slowly sliding light was an exquisite work of art. It was a combination of intricate colorful sculpture and kinetic mesh holo and enamors. It gave the impression of both infinite space with stars and galaxies, of an underwater environment with plants and coral and fish creatures, and of the quantum mechanics of quarks. If you looked at it for more than a second, soft eerie mesh sounds and scents emanated from it, and it gave you a feeling of loving calmness, no doubt the intended effect.

An essent was waiting for them on one of the couches. She stood when they pulled to a stop and waited, hands clasp in front of her, as they stepped off the maglev.

"This is Dangarembga," Zosi said, nodding to the essent. "Call her Dang."

Dang bowed deeply, first to Zosi, then to Atze, then less deeply but still more than necessary to Jazari. Jazari noted that her bows were meticulously the same to Zosi and Atze. Jazari made a mental note to always do likewise.

Jazari bowed back and returned Dang's warm smile.

Dang was a bit shorter than Jazari but, Jazari would find out later, older by six EUs. Like Jazari, she had been born on Cecrops and was still in her gen body. She had dark black-brown skin and naturally frizzy hair in short dreads that sprang from the top of her head. Dang's eyes, nose, and lips were wide, dark, and expressive. She liked to wear tops without sleeves and long flowing pants in whites and tans. She favored entopics that showed up as a pale tracery of scars in elaborate designs on her skin, including a tat sleeve with a stylized scowling face on her upper arm. Dang smiled a lot, which hid the fact that she was wicked smart. Solidly built, she spent her off hours obsessively perfecting her boxing and judo techniques and collected replicas of weird hand weapons from other planets—the perfect hobby for someone whose job it was to obtain hard-to-get objects.

One glance at Dang, and Jazari's vitals skyrocketed. Something about her. Jazari took a deep shuddering breath. She glanced over at Zosi and then Atze, hoping they wouldn't notice. She also hoped they never queried her ccomp, as that would be really embarrassing. As things turned out, Zosi probably had. Fucking Zosi.

"This is Jazari," Zosi said. "She's joining the team." She looked over at Jazari and added, "A valuable addition, I think, to where we're headed."

The compliment stoked Jazari's pride, and she let her gratitude show on her face. But inside she withheld judgement. People like Zosi didn't just hand out strokes like this. There was an agenda.

"Let's get you settled," Dang said, her voice elongated and musical with no accent. She nodded as Zosi and Atze turned and left and then led Jazari down one of the twisting halls. As they descended, Dang asked Jazari about where she was from, to which Jazari mumbled a few vague answers. Dang then told her the history of the place. The hab had originally been a small research station before the Bsams took it over. If you went down into the bowels, there was still a big med and lab space that they used for augments and things like that.

Jazari was hyperaware of where Dang was in relation to her. When they stood close together peering out the diamondglass at Dang's favorite undersea garden spot, Jazari could feel the warmth of Dang's shoulder next to hers. When they bumped into each other, a miscommunication in which direction they were going, they both laughed, but Jazari didn't regret it. When Dang put her hand on Jazari's arm to draw her attention to a couple of people walking by, the feeling lingered, and every time she thought about it that spot would tingle. She felt like a creeper, aware of every move Dang made.

Dang was good at this—making essents she'd never met before feel at home, which would make her useful to Zosi, Jazari's analytical mind said. But another part of her wanted Dang to give Jazari some token, something personal, some positive sign. It made her uncomfortable that she was this drawn to someone she'd just met.

"Here you go," Dang said, opening a door. "This is you." *Let me know if you need anything else*, she subvocalized as she left.

Yes, Jazari thought as she entered her rooms. A sub, like a whisper, spoke to a personal connection.

At a glance, Jazari took in the fact that these quarters were more luxurious than anything she'd ever known. A well-designed living room and workspace and bedroom, with kitchenette and fabricator, which meant she could snack whenever she wanted to. She didn't have to wait for mealtimes like at the creche. Crisp veggies with plantach dip, popped salted gesaat, tirionfruit, cubes of salty rich vegcheese and sweet crisp ping, spicy humma chips. She could also get specialty meals from support staff anytime she wanted. Shrimp-eel scampi or ceviche, sweet and sour egg soup or chile con soya, cacio pio pasta or caprese with sliced barada, rich and fluffy krem syr donuts and dense coklat bread toasted and topped with a rich honeyvutter.

In the cycles to come, Jazari's quarters began to feel like home, and she found she loved having her own space and a door she could lock, even if Zosi and Atze could access it at any time. For a while, she left everything as is, her walls white and her surroundings drab, but as she got more comfortable, she had her ccomp add subtle touches—calming blue and green entopics with natural scents and soft sounds induced by mesh for anyone in the room. Her few belongings, when they were delivered, took up one corner of one drawer, and even as time passed it stayed that way. It reminded her to not get too comfortable.

That first night, she did not sleep well. It was lonely and weird and she missed the deep breathing of essents in bunks around her. Her internal voices seemed louder than normal in the silence, and toward the end of the night, one single voice started a long slow melody in a minor key that left Jazari feeling bereft. She had the urge to call Dang but resisted it.

Instead, she searched for Dangarembga oi Bsam or Dang oi Bsam on the mesh. There wasn't much. The first hits were for a Dangarembga oi Bsaltic, a writer from the station New Algeria in the Epsilon Eridani system who wrote pre-FG time travel mysteries set on old Earth. So Jazari drilled down. She looked up in the public database Dang's name and creche history—

this directory was publicly available, since essents changed their names regularly and it was the only way you could track someone. It showed that Dang had grown up on Cecrops in the Ivor creche, which raised public servants and police officers. With that clue, the first entries she found were for Dang winning some self-defense competitions. She'd also won a interplanetary school writing contest focused on the rights and responsibilities of citizens of the MWA with her essay "Do You Have a Right to Your Body?" Jazari read it. It was charming and persuasive, if not a little naïve. Jazari found a piece on standout cadets at the United Gendarmes Academy, and Dang was prominently featured, with an image of a very young and fit Dang standing on her head and laughing. However, her name was not listed with her graduating class. Ads kept popping up for websites that revealed criminal backgrounds. One said, "Two warrants out for the arrest of one Dangarembga oi Ivor!!! Click here to find out more!!!" Jazari didn't know if that was just a bait and switch, but she knew better than to follow the link.

Chapter 6

After the sleepless night, Jazari was up early. She felt groggy, so she showered and drank two cups of gaur tea, which left her shaky from the caffeine, so she ordered a breakfast of spicy protein scramble and coklat toast from the replicator and wolfed it down. She was just finishing up when her ccomp informed her she was expected in the ready room. It guided her down the hall and through the twisting corridors to a large meeting space. Along the way, she passed a few essents coming out of their quarters or walking briskly and with purpose. They glanced at her with curiosity. Most were going her way and showed up in the meeting room.

The room was large with a big oblong table encircled by fairly comfortable chairs, some for humans, some for mechs, and a couple for bot mechs. The chairs were full, and there were essents standing along the walls—eighteen or twenty people, with more coming in. Zosi stood at the front of the room, with Atze standing off to one side and a service mech on the other. Dang was seated near the front and gave Jazari a nod when she first came in and stood near the back. The people in the room gave off a nervous energy, like they didn't know what to expect but they were excited about it and full of purpose.

They were talking quietly to each other in Standard with a number of accents, but the moment Zosi stepped up to the table, everyone focused on her.

"We have new people for this project," Zosi said and nodded toward Jazari. "I'm not going to introduce you here, but you'll be working together extensively, so I'd suggest you make it a point to introduce yourselves when you get a chance. Let people know what you're good at—they'll find out your weaknesses soon enough." A smile.

Jazari did in fact get to know them really well.

There was Dang, to whom she'd been introduced.

Standing off to the side was Zosi's personal assistant Booker. She had a nondescript mech body with a pleasant faceplate, most likely comp origin, and she was always in the background but you had to remind yourself that she was there. She anticipated the needs of everyone in the room, especially Zosi, but she and Atze pretty much ignored each other. If a group of you were working late into the night and a cup of guar showed up at your elbow, that was Booker.

Atze did not have a personal assistant, but there were three muscle essents who worked closely with her.

Usem was a huge tank-like mech who always stood because chairs broke under her weight. In fact, the ceilings of most rooms were not tall enough, and she had a special standing and walking posture for low ceilings. She was used for both the threat—she looked bad-ass—and for all her military augments. She could take down military transports and squads of bio essents all by herself.

Nuniq was the bio equivalent of Usem. She was a cartoon of centuries-old masculinity on the verge of roid rage, but in reality she was pretty even keel. Like Usem, she was used to quell crowds and stand menacingly behind you, but she could back it up with training and augments, though she joked about being clumsy as hell.

Jazari never figured out exactly what Conchetta was. In a bio body, she had been augmented so much she barely looked human in the form she walked around in. She was tall and slender and wiry and she moved like she had extra bones. She could change her shape, maybe even her DNA, and disguise herself without changing bodies. When Jazari stopped by to see Dang at judo practice, Conchetta would sometimes be there practicing a weird form of zero G martial arts, and her sparring partner would often end up across the room. Conchetta would often say things in a language that Jazari's ccomp couldn't translate.

M-80 was the mesh and security expert. She didn't have much use for a body, and her physical form was a bot mech about the size of Jazari's head. She got around with maglev and communicated mostly subvocally. She swore creatively and enthusiastically, given the chance, and if you saw her physical form resting on a table or just hovering in a corner, you knew she was inmesh. Jazari suspected she started life as a comp mech, not an essent.

Emilia was both a psychologist and a sex profiler, and her bio body was augmented to look like a breathing female sex doll. Her accent was a sexy Fury lilt. She'd started in one of Zosi's sex houses before working her way up through mesh work to madame. She had an extraordinary ability to suss out what turned people on, and her insight was invaluable in getting people to do things.

Precis was a political consultant. Her bio body looked like a placeholder of a person, but she was an expert in enamors and could go from hole in the air to the most spellbinding person you'd ever meet in the blink of an eye. Her voice and accent depended on who she was talking to. She was hard to pin down. She was fascinated by influence, and she could tell you the political history of almost every planet in the galaxy. She also seemed to know a lot of languages, but Jazari didn't know if these were learned or augmented in.

Sully was a biomedical and augment specialist in a bio body covered in real tattoos. Nobody knew her backstory, but it was whispered she'd been on a generation ship that came to a really bad end. Her cryo chamber had been one of the few remaining intact when the ship had been picked up on the edge of civilization in the HD 70642 system. She had an odd hesitating accent, almost a stutter, and Jazari wondered if it was her original and why she hadn't bothered to change it or smooth it out. She not only performed augments but she could tell just by looking what augments essents had.

Joseph was the physics specialist. She was an interplanetary expert on a number of things, and why she was part of the Bsam creche, Jazari would never know. The only reason Jazari could think was that Zosi had something on her. Zosi rented Joseph's time to people across the galaxy. She had a fairly standard pale-skinned bio body, but her brain was augmented to the max—so much so that she had a special augment on her scalp of celia that looked a little like pale hair—until you looked closer. They served as receivers and sensing organs and to dissipate heat.

Working closely with Joseph was Ooee, who was an expert on Faison Gates and mechalum space. She had the mech body of someone who lived and worked in space—a large bot mech of tough aluminum and titanium alloy with six long spider-like legs and two extendable arms, the ability to retract into an oblong sphere, jet propulsion, extra battery life, and robust comm arrays. Her form and specialty were so out there, she might as well have been alien. The few times Jazari heard her speak, she sounded either formal and archaic or sidling up to crazy.

Te Ariki was the mech specialist. If you could dream it, she could build it or augment it. Ironically, she preferred bio bodies, though she changed them fairly regularly. Currently, she was in a short sturdy body with long-fingered hands and an owlish face. She was in charge of the army of comp mechs Zosi had at her disposal. She could go on for hours about the evolution of mech bodies.

Ae-Cha and Bong-Cha worked with Te Ariki. They looked like standard-issue comp mechs—standard hardware, no faceplates. They had special protocols that could fool essents and comp mechs alike, and they could infiltrate almost any institution. You couldn't tell them apart, and Jazari wasn't so sure they weren't the same comp split in two but then synced up. People just called them the Chas.

The list went on.

As Jazari stood there taking them all in, she suddenly realized that her name was now Jazari oi Bsam. Everyone here had the name oi Bsam. It felt really weird. She hadn't chosen the name or the creche, but here she was. All that history she had been reading, all these people she just met—they were now hers too. She was one of them, if only a lowly pawn. It made her feel warm in a way she'd never felt before, a part of something larger. From now on, she would be introduced as Jazari oi Bsam, and people would take note. It stroked her pride, but overall she wasn't quite sure how she felt about it.

Chapter 7

"So let's get to it," Zosi said at the front of the room.

The project they'd been hired for was to discredit a certain Cecrops politician and her Ring counterpart. Zosi brought up the entopic display in the middle of the table as she talked, which flicked through 3D holos of the politicians—a well-kept but overweight bio with a shiny face and a stylized mech with lots of enamors and beauty augments. There were holos of the leaders of the trade union and of the planetary systems in question. Zosi kept her voice fairly soft, but it was projected through the mesh so that everyone heard it perfectly. She looked into essents' faces as she spoke, gesturing toward someone when what she was talking about related to someone's assignment. When she focused on Jazari, the reaction on her face seemed to indicate she knew what Jazari was thinking, which made Jazari wonder if she was carefully monitoring everyone in the room. No small task while also keeping your train of thought and speaking.

This discrediting job was on behalf of a trade union out of one of Dimidium's moons in the 51 Pegasi system. It seems that this pair of politicians held the reins to some research on a technology developed from a rare-earth element that was really common on Dimidium. If it got developed, the trade union's expertise would be much in demand. These politicians had shelved the research in favor of another technology, and so the trade union needed the politicians shelved in turn so that their essent on the governmental panel on Cecrops could push funding through.

Jazari's job in all this turned out to be in public relations. How weird, she thought, that a black market mobster needed a PR sub. Her part involved planting evidence of a drug problem for the Cecrops politician and helping lure the Ring politician to Cecrops. The drug was fairly hard to get, and so Dang, whose specialty was obtaining such things, was on task to acquire it and to make it look like the politician had.

More generally, Jazari monitored the mesh feeds on whatever topics Zosi wanted her to and reported developments directly to her or to others on the team. She pushed certain agendas in subtle ways. Setting a bot army to foment dissent by surfacing some idiot meshlogger on everyone's feed or steering it to show one particular news article. Writing outrageous opinion pieces for small but influential journals. She did research, sometimes darkmesh stuff that took a lot of digging into some pretty shady essents.

She found that she was good it at, and she liked that feeling.

This shit-disturbing wasn't just local. It went out hundreds of light years over the mechalum space comm channels to the hundreds of worlds and space station cities across the galaxy, whoever was linked in. That's the thing about mechalum space—it worked through quantum entanglement, so whatever you sent was transmitted instantaneously. The data, whether it was communications or an essent in mechalum code, was entered into the gate comp processor on one end, which changed the state of the processor on the other end, depending on the mechalum hash of the Faison Gate or gates. If someone was gating, her essent mechalum code shifted from the bio or mech body on one end through the processors to the body on the other end. What would take hundreds or thousands of EUs on a regular electromag comm link or in cryo aboard a generation ship was instantaneous as mechalum space data.

In fact, some people didn't even have bodies any more. If they were rich enough, they lived their lives inmesh with all the other really rich people. Mesh wasn't just a window on your eye screen or a featureless meeting room. No, it was a full physical experience where you got to create your world in every detail. You picked one of the many luxurious base options and then changed things as you went along however you liked. You could meet with others one-on-one inmesh or go to inmesh clubs where the other cool people hung out. You could go slumming with the unevolved by using a body you had on ice or renting one on another planet. And if you were that kind of person and rich enough, you could go to a club filled with just NPCs, and you got to be the center of attention all the time, no challenges to your unique supremacy. Inmesh sex was supposed to be out of this world, pun intended. But there were also rumors that certain governmental agencies on shadier planets used those virtual rooms for torture. They could sniff out your worst nightmares and realize them.

The plan for the politicians was a murder suicide. These two had been creche mates back on the Ring, and though it was never confirmed that they were lovers, Zosi—and therefore

39

Jazari—was going to use the rumors to turn public opinion and curtail any investigation into their deaths. Atze would take care of the details of the actual deaths, but it was going to be framed as accidental massive power spikes to their biosupport and mech units while they were inmesh having sex—the salacious details focused people's attention and distracted them from digging too deeply, erotica disguised as press release.

It was a lot to take in for a first job. Fairly quickly, Jazari made the decision to think of the politicians as comps, not essents. It made her more comfortable. She used her research to craft them in her own mind into one-dimensional nonsentients. This was a job, after all, and she had to remember where she came from. Caring about shit—and morals—were not allowed for people like her. People like her kept their heads down and their eyes on the prize. Damn mixed metaphor, but it reflected about how she felt—twisted, if she thought about it too much.

All she was doing was telling the world a story, while Atze and her crew did the dirty work.

Chapter 8

As the meeting was breaking up, Dang came over, causing Jazari's pulse to jump. "Hey, a bunch of us get together once a tenday in the lounge to shoot the shit. Want to join us?"

A bunch of us. Well, Jazari had hoped it'd just be Dang, but okay. "Sure."

Dang smiled and subvocalized, leaning in as if she were whispering, *Mostly we just bitch about our jobs and flirt, but Zosi lets us, so what the hell.*

Sounds like a blast, Jazari said.

Oh it is. When it's your job to get things like illegal drugs, it's always a blast. Last time Te Ariki—she gestured toward the owlish mech specialist—*hotwired M-80*—again, a gesture to the mech mesh expert—*so that she could only make left turns. She went in circles. It was hilarious.*

How'd M-80 take it? Jazari said.

Oh, you know, how does M-80 take anything?

Jazari had no idea, but just then the sex doll that was Emilia walked up. "What are you two whispering about over here?" she said.

"About you," Dang said and leaned in and gave Emilia a kiss on the cheek, which Emilia returned. Jazari felt a spike of jealousy, which she immediately tried to talk herself out of. Don't be an idiot, she thought.

Emilia fixed Jazari with her surreal anime eyes and said, "I came over to check out the new meat. See what makes her tick." She looked Jazari up and down.

Jazari smiled uncomfortably. There was a surge of hormones, and all of a sudden she felt like she'd go to bed with a houseplant.

"Turn it off, Emilia," Dang said. "Not fair to catch the noob unawares."

"Aww, you're no fun," Emilia said but must've turned off the pheromone enamors, as Jazari's desire ebbed. Then she smiled what seemed genuine and leaned in. "No offense?"

Dang added, "It's a game she plays. It's harmless."

To which Emilia responded, "Very much not harmless, but, you know, right now it is." She glanced over to where Zosi and Precis were talking. "I actually did come over to check you out. Hmmm." Once again she looked at Jazari, her mind working behind her eyes. "Fairly normal drives. She'd be good for you, Dang. You ought to grab her." Jazari blushed. "But"—Emilia's eyes narrowed—"there's something else. Something I can't put a finger on. Hmmm."

"Well, that's a first," Dang said. "You're never stumped."

"Exactly," Emilia said, thinking a moment longer. "Well, kids, just remember—I'll be around." She sauntered off.

"She means for sex," Dang said. "She's always up for it, no strings attached, unless she hates you. A lot of fun. You should try it."

"Yeah, no," Jazari said. "Sounds complicated."

"It really isn't, not with her."

"I'll take that under advisement," Jazari said.

"So, tonight 7:30 in the lounge?" Dang said.

"I'll be there."

"Oh, and we'll get together first thing tomorrow. I'll give directions to your ccomp where to meet. Zosi wanted me to show you the ropes, workwise."

Jazari nodded. She couldn't help smiling all the way back to her quarters.

The sleepless night caught up with her, though, and she fell asleep on her couch immediately. She woke to a pounding on her door, the polite chime of her doorbell ringing continuously, and the sounds of someone yelling in a deep voice, "Jazari rhymes with party!"

Jazari's ccomp was saying, louder and louder in her head, *You must wake, Jazari. Dang and Nuniq require your company. You must wake, Jazari.*

A jolt went through her like she was shirking on the job. She pushed herself up off the couch and stumbled to the door and opened it, and there stood Dang with Nuniq hulking behind her, mid-yell.

"Oh," Nuniq said. "Parties are mandatory. We're your escort!" Her deep voice had a smooth accent that emphasized the ees.

"They're not, really," Dang said, slapping Nuniq's wall of a chest, "but we'd really like you to come!"

"Sorry," Jazari said. "Sorry. Must've fell asleep."

"Eedums sleepy?" Nuniq said, her voice rumbling, teasing. "Too fucking bad."

"Are you coming?" Dang said, her face looking hopeful.

"Yeah, I guess." She turned to gather her things and then realized she didn't need anything and so turned to follow them, shutting her door behind her and unconsciously smoothing down her hair.

"Dang tells me you're from a snow creche," Nuniq said over her shoulder.

Up ahead, where Jazari couldn't see her through Nuniq, Dang said, "Nuniq! I did not!" Then a second later, "Well, I did, but you should have the good sense not to mention it."

"Subtlety ain't my strong suit," Nuniq said. "It's not the way I'm built."

"And you wonder why bigs get a rep for stupidity," Dang said.

Nuniq didn't seem to take offense. "You squealies worry about what people think. In most cases, straightforward does the job, not to mention tamps down hostilities. I know about hostilities."

"That's why we keep you around," Dang said. "Not for your charm, for sure." Then she added, laughing, "Well, actually, we do keep you around for your charm. How sad is that?"

"So, you're from a snow creche," Nuniq repeated over her shoulder.

"Enough!" Dang said, and then they were at the party.

Chapter 9

The party was in full swing. It was in the lounge, circling colored lights underneath tons of water held up by diamondglass.

Early on, Jazari noticed through the glass a small shark creature that seemed to be attracted by the lights of the party. It periodically bumped the glass. It would get a puzzled look on its face, as much as a shark could, and then it would turn and lazily swim away. Throughout the party, Jazari would glance over and there it was swimming diligently toward them.

Keep it up, little guy, she thought. You'll make it.

Nuniq led them up to the bar and they each ordered a drink. The bartender was a mech with an extra arm and an elaborate but understated party hat. Nuniq ordered a shot and a beer, Dang ordered a shot and some wine, and as Jazari considered the options Dang and Nuniq ordered her a shot and a mixed drink without her asking. "Juice to get juiced," Nuniq said. Jazari shook her head but then downed the shot as Dang and Nuniq upended theirs. This is going to be a doozy, Jazari thought. I should eat something but then she didn't.

They found some chairs in a corner next to the glass with a good view of the rest of the party. Dang and Nuniq proceeded to give her the lowdown on everyone in the room.

Atze wasn't there, but she, muscle mech Usem, and mech specialist Te Ariki were a caro threesome. Augments specialist Sully and physics specialist Joseph were married, but they fought a lot, mostly about the ethics of science. Political specialist Precis and Conchetta, whatever she was, were caros.

Mechalum space Ooee, mesh M-80, psychologist Emilia, and personal assistant Booker had never had caros "for obvious reasons," Dang said.

Jazari wondered out loud what those reasons were.

Dang and Nuniq looked at each other and burst out laughing. Nuniq said, ticking off her fingers, "Too ace, too comp, professionally unattached, and …"—Nuniq and Dang laughed again—"very professionally unattached. If Booker was any farther up Zosi's ass, she'd be a polyp."

Dang looked a bit sheepish and added, "Sweet as hell, though."

Then Dang glanced over at Nuniq, leaned in like she was going to whisper, but then loudly told Jazari that Nuniq had been caros with Bong-Cha, which made her also caros with Ae-Cha by default.

Jazari glanced at Nuniq to see how she'd react—she took it well, saying, "You don't know how true that is."

"And Dang?" Jazari said, after screwing up her courage.

Nuniq looked over at Dang but didn't say anything, but Dang just shook her head. "Too weird," she said, nodding. She looked embarrassed. So she was unattached. That was great news.

However, as the night progressed, Jazari thought she sensed that Nuniq had a thing for Dang. She didn't show it much, and Dang didn't seem particularly interested, even though they both joked and touched each other in offhandedly friendly ways. That made things more challenging. You wouldn't want to be on Nuniq's bad side—she could squash you like a bug. However, Nuniq didn't seem to take offense when they were laughing about something and Dang reached over and slung her arm around Jazari's shoulders or after their third shot Jazari felt woozy and slouched sideways over Dang's lap before she caught herself.

It just felt good to sit there next to Dang, to feel her body next to hers, to glance over and see Dang looking at her. It made Jazari want to scream with joy.

Emilia came over, elegantly balancing a slim smokeless mbange vape between her fingers. She sat with them for a while, flirting the whole time. Usem and Joseph came over too. Then Joseph left, saying that she was meeting Sully for a late dinner. Eventually, they all got up and played AR pingpong where you both had to hit the ball and dodge the monsters that popped up and swallowed you whole. You could see the ghost teeth as they enveloped your head, and weird sounds and smells came over the mesh. Then they played quarters—that's when things started getting fuzzy. By that time, Conchetta and Precis had joined them, and Conchetta was really good at the game.

Precis had her enamors turned off. Jazari couldn't tell if they were turned off for everyone or just her, which was weird. When you went to a party, you generally want people to like you, especially if you were into politics, so you'd think you'd

47

have them turned on. Maybe she was just off duty, Jazari thought. But then, mystery solved when in a pause in the conversation Precis drunkenly focused on Jazari and loudly announced in a posh affected accent, "Looks like Zosi has a new lap dog. Hope you make it longer than Seve." Hostility radiated off her.

Jazari sat there stunned, trying to clear the boozy haze, when Dang jumped to her defense. "Thought you were going to step back in, did you?" she said, a wry smile on her face.

Precis narrowed her eyes, which told Jazari that that was exactly what she'd hoped.

There was a brief silence, and then the party moved on, the ripple dissipating. Time passed. Fun was had. Jazari did not forget, though. Later, as everything was winding down, most of the lights turned off and the music on low, it was just her and Dang and Emilia on couches half asleep against the cushions. Dang was lazily spooning salak sherbet into her mouth, and Emilia was absent-mindedly petting the soft pillow in her lap.

"Who's Seve?" Jazari asked, trying not to sound like she had been waiting all evening to ask that question.

"Poor Seve," Dang said. "She never stood a chance."

"That's hers," Emilia said, lifting her head and nodding toward the beautiful shifting work of art near the entryway.

Jazari remembered what she'd felt the night before with the one lone voice in her head, and somehow it all got linked in her mind with Seve and that beautiful yearning piece of art. She took a shuddering breath.

Emilia turned to Dang and said, "Did you notice that Jazari looks a bit like Seve?"

Dang just shook her head, a grimace on her face. It wasn't a denial. "You tell her," Dang said.

Emilia shook her head in empathy. "Seve was an artist, pretty well known—I'm surprised you haven't heard of her."

Jazari shook her head.

"Not exactly sure why she joined us," Emilia continued, glancing over at Dang, who shrugged. "I think the reasoning was she was a designer as well as an artist, and she was going to work with M-80 on virtual environments. At least that's what they told me—we were going to upgrade our mesh houses. Anyway, pretty quickly she became the focus of Zosi's … aah … attentions. And how could Zosi resist really? She loves beauty, and that makes—made—Seve crack, basically. But what chapped Precis's ass was that Zosi dropped her—Precis—like a meteorite. Precis had the good sense not to make waves with Zosi, but she poked Seve every chance she got." She leaned her head toward Dang and said in a low voice, "I'm not so sure it wasn't her that got Seve killed, not Zosi. Sure, Seve did the whole betrayal thing by trying to strike out on her own with her art and her fame." Emilia glanced over at Jazari and said, "She really was catching fire—I can't believe you haven't heard of her. Anyway, Zosi saw that as the ultimate betrayal. On one hand, if Precis had done it, you'd think Zosi would've come down like the hand of Nuc, but on the other Precis's pretty valuable herself and Zosi's always been a practical one. Plus, Zosi still had a bit of a thing for her—Precis did her damnedest to make sure of that."

"I agree," Dang said as she wiped her fingers on a napkin. "Poor Seve. I think she knew it was coming, though. She was talking a lot about splitting or creating a backup. 'A value-added proposition,' she kept saying, but I think it was more than that."

"Fucks with the head," Emilia said, nodding.

"How'd she … die?" Jazari asked, wanting to know but not wanting to know.

"That's the thing," Emilia said. "It was 'an accident,' of course. Coming back from a job on—can't remember the planet—her essent didn't sync up with her body—the body she'd had her whole life—the way it should have. It was like she was in there but couldn't communicate. I swear I saw her in there. Did you?" she asked Dang.

Dang nodded.

"Anyway," Emilia continued, "by the time they seriously tried to do something about it, her essent was corrupted. Or maybe it had been since the transfer." She shrugged.

"Horrible," Dang said. "If she was in there, she was helpless watching it all happen. I hope she wasn't really in there."

Emilia nodded then looked at Jazari. "I'd like to tell you not to worry, but that would be stupid. I'd worry if I were you. Being on Precis's bad side is no laughing matter. She regularly gets planetary ministers killed. And being worried will make you sharp." She pushed herself forward and then stood. "Well kiddos, off to bed for me—unless someone would like to join me?" She said it with no real conviction. "No? Then I'm off."

"So much for bedtime stories," Dang said. "I'll walk you back to your quarters."

Just then, the shark bumped up against the glass.

Chapter 10

Jazari lay in her bed thinking about Precis, while in her head one voice hummed and another whispered in weirdly complementary tones.

Part of her wanted to dismiss the whole thing. It was all too much. But the practical part of her knew better. Forewarned is forearmed, and she needed to figure out how to protect herself as best she could. This could easily make her paranoid. So, on one hand, she had to prepare but on the other she couldn't hyperfocus on it or it would ruin her life.

Sounds like Precis might hit on a few fronts. She'd dig at Jazari every chance she got and try to undermine her with everyone. That didn't bother Jazari particularly—when you grow up in a snow creche, it's dog eat dog. She'd have to make sure Zosi wasn't taken in though. The other thing was if Precis had her killed. Jazari couldn't believe that she'd pissed Precis off enough for her to do that—she'd only been there a cycle. On the other hand, Precis wasn't pissed at Jazari—she was pissed at Seve and Zosi and who knows what else, and since Jazari most likely represented all that in her mind—and most importantly Jazari was something she could do something about—she might jump right to murder. It was possible. Jazari couldn't imagine it herself, but there were more things under heaven and Cecrops, as the saying goes.

So what could she do? Good security, both physical and virtual. Keep an eye on Precis. Do some digging and see if she could find anything on her. Try to make friends, bring down the hostility, although that didn't seem possible. The obvious thing was that Precis and Conchetta were caros. Would she use Conchetta to do Jazari in? Jazari needed to talk to Conchetta, try to make friends or at least humanize herself. Dang was on her side. She thought Emilia and Nuniq were too. She would ask them to keep an eye out. Hard to tell with everyone else.

Then she caught herself. This is crazy. She'd just met these people. How can you think about cold-bloodedly killing someone you just met? She couldn't. But she wasn't these people, and it was these essents' job to kill people.

And poor Seve. On an impulse, she pushed herself to sitting and told her ccomp, *Bring up everything you have on Seve oi Bsam*. It only took a sec. There were tons of stuff. She could see why people thought Seve looked like her—the same lanky frame, skin just a shade lighter, the same hair but worn down to her shoulders with thin beaded braids around her ears, similar faces. They could've been genned from the same batch. Was that possible? Unlikely.

There were mesh reports of Seve's spectacular rise to fame in the art world, her joining "one of the founding creches," and then detailed accounts of various Bsams that illustrated the creche's influence. One article pointed out one Bsam's conviction on international money laundering and subsequent bot imprisonment, while another went into great detail about a

Bsam's humanitarian advocacy during an aberrant series of storms on Cecrops.

One particularly haunting interview showed Seve at work creating a piece similar to the one in the lounge. Seve's voice was soft, full, considered, sincere, otherworldly, the timbre catching and shifting like two people were talking at once. In the interview's voiceover, Seve said, "We've reached a point in humanity's evolution where form no longer matters. Back before the Gods War, people told stories of being translated from one plane of existence to another. That's real now. That's us. We can exist in multiple dimensions. We can split and join. But with it comes great power. What are we going to do with it? Are we going to continue to use those without power to further the needless whims of the more fortunate? We're all made of star stuff. Why can't we see that?"

It sent a chill down Jazari's spine. She'd learned enough. She shut it down and lay there watching the reflected glow of the seas ripple on her walls until she fell into an uneasy sleep.

After just a few hours, her ccomp roused her for the next waking. A quick shower and some breakfast—a special order of egg-battered kurakura toast with spiro syrup and a side of vutter-browned mushrooms—and then she was out the door. Her ccomp directed her to the area the creche used as a joint office. Many of the essents worked from their own quarters or had their own laboratories, but if they had to work with other members, they'd often come here. An open floor plan with a variety of spaces on multiple levels—desks and entopic displays and lounge areas and a guar bar. Only one corner had a bubble of diamondglass that looked out into a dark cove.

Dang was the only one there. Jazari's pulse jumped when she spied her beautiful body leaning over a display. Jazari stopped and then pretended to look around as Dang came over. "It's called the Crash," Dang said. When Jazari lifted her eyebrows, Dang added, "Not sure why. Kinda rhymes with creche, I guess."

Dang led her over to a table and chairs. "Want some tea? Donuts? There's killer frosted nut bars." she said, gesturing to the guar bar.

"I'm good," Jazari said.

"Well, let's get to it, then."

They sat at a small table, and Dang took Jazari through their private corner of the mesh—resources available, who to contact for what, what to do in case of emergency, things like that. Dang was good at explaining things, no nonsense. She focused on the essential things to know and moved methodically through her mental list. She brought up a map of the hab and explained where things were. "I'll give you a tour later," Dang said. She explained what Zosi expected. "Pretty great to work for, actually. Don't get on her bad side though."

"Pretty much goes without saying," Jazari said.

"Got to be said though. You'd be surprised the number of noobs who do stupid shit on their first cycle."

"Not planning stupid shit."

"Good," Dang said with a smile.

Just then, a notification appeared on Jazari's eyescreen. It was a call from Zosi.

"What?" Dang said, catching Jazari's look.

"Zosi's calling."

"Right. Answer it." Dang was frowning.

Jazari glanced at Dang and hesitated. It would be weird taking it right here, whether it was just subvocal or inmesh. She hopped up and walked over to the diamondglass for privacy.

Good waking, Zosi. What can I do for you? Jazari said, a big smile plastered on her face in case her consciousness got pulled inmesh into a virtual room and therefore Zosi would be able see her. The caller got to choose which it was, and the essent answering could only choose to decline the call. Not an option here.

It was just subvocal. *Good waking, Jazari. I hope you've found our habs to your liking? Your quarters satisfactory?*

Jazari relaxed. She returned, *Absolutely beautiful. I've never had ... lived anywhere like it. I so much appreciate your taking me in.*

We're not a charity, Zosi said, but Jazari thought she could hear a smile in her voice. *You're in the Crash.* It wasn't a question. *Make sure Dang takes you through our contacts in the media. The darkmesh ones too.*

Absolutely, Jazari said.

There was silence on the line. Then Zosi said, *I need to know your skillset. Come to my quarters at nine this presleep. We'll have dinner and you can justify your existence.*

A chill shot through Jazari. She took in a breath to say something but then couldn't think of anything to say.

That was a joke, Zosi said.

Jazari wasn't sure that that was true, but she laughed. *I'll be there,* she said.

The connection cut.

Jazari took a deep breath and flexed her shoulders. Then she turned and went back over to Dang.

"What'd she want?" Dang asked.

"Dinner. And, you know, to let me know I better not screw up, I guess."

Dang looked into Jazari's face with a stricken look. "Nuc! Precis was right." Dang was clasping her hands together tightly to her chest.

So much for not doing stupid shit, Jazari thought.

They finished up, Jazari making sure that Dang took her through their media contacts. "I'll send out an intro for you— so they know you're one of us," Dang said.

Then they took a tour of the hab. It was bigger than Jazari had expected. In the quarters area, Dang pointed out everyone's rooms. A few off limit areas—"research" was all Dang would say. Some great views of the dim undersea.

They finished up and headed back toward the quarters. They were in a long dark hallway under the dark diamondglass sea, the deep dim blue filtering down through the see-through arch of the roof. The low recessed lighting made everything eerie. It had been a long day, and the lack of sleep had caught up with Jazari. She felt simultaneously hyped up and wrung out, an out-of-body experience. Too much on her mind but unable to focus on anything.

Jazari was walking ahead when she felt Dang grasp her arm. She jumped slightly but then stopped and turned, a questioning look on her face. Dang reached up and caught both sides of Jazari's face in her hands. She clutched tightly, a bit painfully, and pulled Jazari's face down toward hers.

Jazari froze but then let her head be pulled. The nearness of Dang made her breath catch. She wanted to put her hands on Dang's hips, to melt forward, to lean in. Screw that—she wanted to grab Dang and hold her close, bury her face into her dreads, her mouth onto Dang's mouth. She wanted to breathe her in, to hold, to squeeze. But, hesitating, she did none of these things, her arms hanging limply at her sides.

Dang's eyes were big and shiny, looking up into Jazari's, and she put her face right up to Jazari's, almost touching noses. She held on for a half second. "I wanted it to be me," Dang said in a choked voice. "I wanted to be your caro. And now it can't be."

Dang yanked Jazari's face to hers, pressed her lips to Jazari's, kissed her fiercely and deeply, and then released her. With one final stricken look, she turned and stalked off.

Jazari stood for a long time, processing it. Her lips were lax where she'd eased them to be kissed. Her cheeks burned from the tight grip and the rising emotion. Her body felt weak. She took a deep shuddering breath and straightened. Then she turned and went back to her quarters.

Chapter 11

An hour before Jazari had to be at Zosi's, she looked through the selection of clothing the replicator could produce. She chose a long sleeveless white kurta that was asymmetrical on the bottom with elaborate white embroidery across the chest, along with loose white pants. She wanted to give the replicator plenty of time to get it done. Because they were available and free, she chose a couple of subtle entopics—one that enhanced the clarity and beauty of her skin and another that was soothing to everyone around her. Lamb to the slaughter, she thought. She showered and got ready.

Conflicted didn't half cover it. Zosi wasn't bad looking and she'd consider going out with her under other circumstances. But here, now, this wasn't really a choice thing, and so it was what it was. Maybe this was indeed sex work she was entering into, and the PR was just a cover.

Given her druthers, she'd hook up with Dang. No, that wasn't right. She didn't want to just hook up with Dang—she wanted to be her caro.

It all sucked, not matter how you looked at it.

Her ccomp guided her to Zosi's quarters ten minutes early. She didn't think fashionably late would go over well, but she

58

didn't want to be too early. When she got there, the door was opened immediately by Booker. "Won't you come in?" she said. Her voice was soft and pleasing and nondescript.

Zosi's quarters were stunning. The open floor plan was tiered down underneath the huge vaulted diamondglass with the best view in the habs—a vibrant vista of coral, fish, sea forest, and in the distance an undersea volcano slowly erupting, lava bubbling and flashing orange and red and quickly turning to black bulges of crumbling ash and pumice, with white clouds of steam billowing upward through the water. The quarters had a spacious entertainment and eating area, though not a kitchen—of course the food would be brought in. There was a lounge area with couches and intimate gatherings of seats, and there was a bedroom area with a large jacuzzi and an open shower to the side in a large alcove.

There was subtle music and scent entopics coupled with something Jazari couldn't quite put her finger on—something that was both calming and hormonal at the same time. Desiring. That was it—Zosi had turned on the enamors.

Great, Jazari thought.

"Can I get you something?" Booker asked. "We have guar, juice, wine, beer, scotch, extasy, some excellent mbanje grown in the southern habs—pretty much anything you'd like."

"Uh, I'll take some juice, I guess."

"Anything in that?" Booker asked with a slight smile.

Nice try, Jazari thought. "Nah, I'm good," she said.

As soon as she left, Zosi appeared. She was wearing a simple and elegant long black sheath in a form-fitting fabric, slits up the sides, with short sleeves. She was stunningly beautiful, and it wasn't just the enamors. The bio body she was in was picture perfect.

Jazari bowed deeply.

"Won't you sit down?" Zosi said, gesturing toward the big comfortable couch in the center of the room—one that would be easy to get pushed up against an arm—so instead Jazari chose a close grouping of comfortable chairs separated by a coffee table. That brought a smile to Zosi's face. She chose the chair across from Jazari's and sat.

Booker came in with a tray of with nuts, fruit, cheese, Jazari's juice, and a rocks glass of what looked like scotch. She set it on the table between them. Then she looked at Zosi, most likely subvocalizing something. Zosi looked up at her and nodded, answering. Booker turned and left.

Zosi reached for the scotch and took a long drink. She swallowed, sighed, and then relaxed back against the chair back, pulling her legs up underneath her. Then she turned her head to look out through the glass toward the volcano.

Jazari glanced out toward the volcano as well. It erupted continuously, flashing and pluming red, white, and black. Such power, but such impotence too. For all its heat and beauty, it didn't effect much more than the area just around it, though over time it could build an island and change the face of the planet.

Zosi didn't say anything. She just continued to watch the volcano. Jazari had the urge to fill the silence, but she resisted. Two could play that game.

Eventually Zosi sighed and turned back to Jazari. She took another sip of her drink and said, "So, what do you want out of life?"

Jazari thought for a minute. It didn't seem appropriate to talk about xenolinguistics, so she just shrugged.

"This is normally where the other person in the conversation helps out. It's all part of the game," Zosi said, smiling, then adding, "especially if it's her new boss."

"I—of course—I …" Jazari really had no idea what to say.

"Well, let's start with this," Zosi said. "If you were hosting this little get-together, what would you say to me?"

That was unexpected. "Ah, well," Jazari said. She sat up straight and cleared her throat. Affecting her best hosty voice, she said, "Zosi, you have such a gracious home, and I'm so thankful for you taking me in and giving me a job, but I know so little about you." Jazari glanced at Zosi's face to see if she'd overstepped, but Zosi was nodding. "Were you born on Cecrops?"

"Now, that's more like it," Zosi said. "Yes, in fact I was. A similar situation to yours, actually, though it was a long time ago. I was also in a snow creche"—she smiled and leaned in like it was a secret. "Don't tell anybody."

Jazari couldn't keep the surprise off her face.

"Yeah, it gives you a different outlook on life, doesn't it?" Zosi said. "Makes you scrappier, I think, knowing you weren't planned for—or wanted, really."

Jazari was nodding.

Zosi continued, "So you can see my interest in you. I see myself in you, blah, blah, blah. It's sentimental crap, but that doesn't make it any less true."

"That's a huge—" Jazari started to say, but Zosi broke in, "Yeah, don't thank me. We both know how complicated that is."

Jazari nodded. Zosi had been where she was in some fashion or another. Weird to think. "So did you … How did you become a Bsam?"

"That is a long and sordid story," Zosi said. "Suffice it to say I saw an opportunity and I took it. Made myself invaluable before the powers that be realized just how far I'd come." She smiled. "Some people would call them the good old days, but they really sucked at the time. No nostalgia here." She pushed herself to standing and began to pace. "Living my best life now."

Jazari felt like she could only play coy for so long, and Zosi was getting restless. "I've got ambitions too," she said. "I'll make myself a valuable addition to the team." She stood up and walked over to Zosi, inside preparing herself for what was to come. She stood in front of Zosi and looked into her face. Here goes nothing, she said, taking a deep breath.

Zosi looked at her. At first, her face showed intent brightness, but then as she looked into Jazari's face, it shut down. "Oh, young one, you would, wouldn't you?" She sighed. She lifted her hand and gently traced Jazari's top lip. The enamors combined with the perfect beauty of Zosi's body caused Jazari's body to stir. Zosi seemed to sense it, but then she dropped her hand. A small smile. "I'm not completely hideous," she said brightly. "Sure, I want you, and I could have you, but it wouldn't be you, and I'm not interested in that game anymore."

She paused and then went on. "Tell you what. Think about it. I have a lot to offer. Not just this"—she opened her arms, showing her body—"but also advantages you could only dream of. If you're truly ambitious, it's all there for the taking. You could be a Bsam—a real Bsam."

Zosi turned away, and Booker appeared immediately to refill Zosi's drink. The night was done.

"Thank you, Zosi," Jazari said, the unease coming through in her voice. "Good night?" she said, bowing.

"Good night," Zosi said, not turning around.

Chapter 12

Another night of uneasy sleep. Absolutely no voices, which was even eerier.

Jazari's first thought when she woke up was she had to do something. Let's start with Precis. At least let Precis know she wasn't just some sheep.

Hard things first. She didn't even get out of bed. She sat up cross-legged and had her ccomp place a subvocal call to Precis. She didn't really have a plan on what she was going to say but she was determined to do it before she chickened out. She was really relieved when Precis didn't pick up, but a stone had been laid. She didn't leave a message. Precis would know it was her who called, and so she'd know Jazari wasn't cowering in a corner. If Precis called back, she'd figure out what to say.

Next she went through her mesh security, upping her protocols on both her virtual space and her quarters. She wasn't a mesh expert, but she'd done a bit more research than the average essent. She was fairly sure no one could get in either space, with the possible exception of Zosi, Atze, and probably M-80. Booker as well, probably. Can't forget her. The only way Precis could get in was if she had Zosi's clearances, and Zosi wasn't that stupid.

She considered what to do about Dang in her personal space. On one hand, she trusted Dang, and there may be a time she needed Dang to be able to help her. She thought of Seve, and the hair on her neck prickled. No, she thought, nobody. She didn't know Dang well enough. Having decided, she pushed herself to standing. But then she stopped. She remembered the look on Dang's face—she reset her protocols, lowering them a bit for Dang.

She sent messages to Dang and Emilia, asking them to keep their ears to the ground. They'd know what it was about. To Nuniq, she sent a message saying, *You said straightforward is best. Maybe let me know if you hear anyone's trying to kill me, kay? Or, you know, dismember me. Especially if it's you.* She hoped the smile came through in her voice. *I'd appreciate it.* Then she ate a breakfast of crepes drowned in melted vutter and cinnamon and guar, showered, and went to work.

It was a couple of cycles later when she came across Conchetta. She caught sight of her walking down a hall, her form slightly altered to look bent, her movements like an old person. What was that about?

Conchetta! she yelled subvocally.

Conchetta stopped but did not turn. *Don't,* she said. *Stay where you are [ ].* The last part was unintelligible.

Jazari had the good sense not to try to approach her. *I ... I just wanted to talk for a sec.*

I can hear you just fine.

Well, Jazari said after a pause. *I'm new here, and I have no idea what I'm walking into. If I asked you, would you tell me?*

No.

Okay, well, that's helpful. Can I ... Are you ...

65

Am I going to [ ] kill you?

Yes, exactly. Jazari was relieved not to have to ask.

Not today, Conchetta said, glanced over her shoulder, a smile on her face. Then she walked away.

Jazari felt marginally better.

She started to do her job. She did a bunch of research on both politicians. She became an expert. In a meeting, if anyone asked where one of them grew up, Jazari could give the hab location and describe the specifics of the station, moon, or planet. If someone asked about their body history, Jazari could produce all known holos in chronological order. If someone asked their favorite foods or any scandals, Jazari could recite them in gory detail. She noted habits and mannerisms and accents and their likely origins. She interviewed family, childhood friends, coworkers, and people close to them, pretending to be freelance political press and altering her voice and the origin of her call.

It took her a tenday to write a report complete with holos for the team members. It contained a summary and then an extended treatise on everything she had found, focusing specifically on the politicians' relationship—dates, when they'd been together, any communications, in jokes, essents they both knew. She even speculated on their psychology and wrote a fictional exchange between the two, clearly marking it as conjecture

She researched as if her life depended on it. It might. Unfortunately for Jazari's conscience, both politicians seemed pretty clean.

She gave suggestions on ways to take the PR. She suggested anonymously haunting forums, picking a few choice ones, and then striking up conversations and planting a few things on the politicians. She wrote an op ed signed "Concerned Citizen" about the drug problem "sweeping the galaxy"—really, it was the same old drug problem—and dropped in a name or two. Nothing overt, just a hint. Then she set the mesh bots spiking the traffic on drug abuse.

She found an image of the two politicians together when they were young, doctored it bit, and wrote a star-crossed lovers article for a couple of tattler feeds insinuating there was a thing between them. Then after a tenday she wrote another about a purported investigation of their love affair, political connections, and undue influence. She also tweaked the algorithms so that the Ring politician got a bunch of travel ads showing the beauty of Cecrops. "Planet Hop to Cecrops, Voted the Best Hab Zone Vacation by *Leisure Worlds*," the ads said.

She even prewrote the press release about their deaths, leaving a few blank spots to be filled in when it happened. That way, it could go out immediately and preempt any other press releases. That was the most chilling job. She felt like she was writing a murder mystery. She put in as many details as she could make up and make look legit. How they liked it kinky, a little dominatrix, a dash of bondage, a sprinkle of pornography, a dose of pedophilia, and because it was virtual, it could push the boundaries without being illegal. Two consenting adults in virtual space. Jazari felt dirty afterwards.

She ran everything by Zosi and Atze and consulted with other members of the team. This was mostly accomplished via messaging.

Zosi sent messages back. She'd have suggestions, even praising Jazari's work. *Keep it up. You'll be a Bsam in no time,* she said, ominously.

After Jazari had sent the final press release out for everyone to look at, Atze messaged her to meet. *I got a few things,* she said. Atze had her come up to the hangar where they kept the large transports and a small personal spacecraft. The hangar was above water and aboveground in a huge cavern on the bigger of the two islands. It was half natural rock and half metal-lined artificial cave deep in the dead cone of the island's volcano.

Jazari followed her ccomp's directions and came out of the elevator into open space. It echoed with the far-off pounding of waves, and some faint music echoed somewhere. It smelled of water and decaying seaweed and rock dust and engine oil and faintly of hybrid rocket fuel and exhaust. There was dim natural light coming from a low and wide cavern opening but also from overhead lighting. There were hulks of transports of all different sizes, ten or twelve of them. They seemed impossibly close together, but the floor was an intricate series of panels and conveyors, and so they must have been slid in.

"Here," Atze hollered from across the bay. Jazari picked her way through the hulks.

Atze and Te Ariki were working on a personal spacecraft. Te Ariki popped her head up when Jazari walked up, raised a hand in her direction, and then popped her head back down into the ship. Atze's hulking mech body was beside the ship, physically patched in with wires. She detached these as they began to talk.

Remembering Dang's first greeting, Jazari bowed deeply.

Atze paused at that, and the expression on her faceplate twitched.

"You had a few things you wanted to talk about?" Jazari said.

Subvocal, Atze said. *Somebody wants it bad enough, they can get it, but I like to make them work for it.*

Got it, Jazari said.

I wanted to let you know how it was going to go down so your press release will be accurate. No use undermining our credibility with shitty details.

Right, Jazari said.

Atze proceeded to tell her what was going to happen in intimate detail. By the end, Jazari's stomach was clenched into a ball, and she felt like she was going to throw up. Her face had to have shown it, but Atze made no comment and didn't stop till she had finished. *You can see here, here, and here*—she sent a copy of the press release through the mesh with a couple parts highlighted—*where you need to adjust this.*

Yes, Jazari said. *Got it.* It was burned into her brain.

As she looked into the faceplate of this sleek and deadly mech, the thought occurred to her—this is Zosi. Atze is Zosi. It was hard to believe. They were so different. Zosi's overwhelming attractiveness and charisma did not seem to translate to this mech. Did that mean that attraction was mostly biological? That hormones ruled, and you needed to have a thing for mechs to be attracted to mechs? After a second's thought, though, Jazari amended that. You could fall in love with people's minds, with essents. Then the package wouldn't matter quite as much. And certainly inmesh sex didn't involve

69

any bodies at all. Well, virtual bodies, so it actually did, only imagined ones. Complicated, all the way around.

But were they really both the same person? They were one person for EUs, but now they were two. Both ambitious. Both ready to do what had to be done. Both leaders, although Atze preferred to lead from behind—or, you know, probably next to you with an assault rifle. But they had been different people with different experiences for a hundred EUs at least. That had to make them different. And when one person's job is to be the center of attention and to wield power, while the other's job is to kill people—that had to lead to different personalities.

Atze had said to tell her if she needed to know things. And she seemed to have a complicated relationship with Zosi. Maybe it was a good idea to feed her information, to stay on her good side.

Jazari said, *You know, Zosi invited me—*

Yeah, I know, Atze said. *Saw that coming a klick away. You're her type.*

Which begged the question of whether she was Atze's type, but she immediately pushed that out of her mind. *You said to let you know*, Jazari said.

And I appreciate that.

Is there anything you ... want to know, specifically? Do you have any advice?

Atze's faceplate smiled. It even looked genuine. *Be loyal. We don't take kindly to people who piss us off.*

Indeed.

And cheer up, Atze continued. *There are worse things. Today, you're alive. You've got all the food you want to eat, all the air you need to breathe, even a few friends, from what I hear. Could be worse.*

None of that was helpful. Being told to appreciate what you have by the person who could take it all away in a heartbeat was not comforting.

It must have shown on Jazari's face because Atze said, *Look. I appreciate you keeping me in the loop. And if I did have any advice, it'd be not to do anything stupid.*

That seems to be the standing order around here, Jazari thought. *Thanks*, she said.

Letting me know what's going on is not a stupid thing. It's a smart thing, believe me, Atze said and nodded and turned back to the ship.

Right, Jazari thought. We'll see.

Chapter 13

Another tenday, another party. Dang was running late, so Jazari was sitting with Joseph and Sully, who were having a heated conversation about the expendability of humans in the name of science. The table in front of them was loaded with fondue. A rich warm spicy choco sauce in which you could dip cubes of pound cake or fruit. A rich soya cheese sauce with vegetables and cubes of bread. A tray of raw marinated shrimp-eel and monobird on skewers that could be grilled on a small open-flame raclette.

We're sitting here talking about the morality of killing people, while we're busy killing people, Jazari thought. Irony just follows me everywhere.

"I'm just, aah, saying," Sully said in her odd accent, "science is made to serve humanity. It's too high a price to pay." She was rubbing her hand over her forearm, where there was a tattoo of some mythic fire-breathing lizard in blues and reds and an iridescent silver metallic.

Joseph's celia lifted and shifted to maximize airflow. It looked a little like a slow motion breeze blowing through her pale tousled hair. "You mean to tell me—if you could change the future of humanity, it wouldn't be worth it? Say, you invented faster-than-light travel. If you had to sacrifice a planet's worth of people to do that—knowing that it would change the course of human history. That wouldn't be worth it?"

Jazari got the feeling this was a conversation they'd been having for a very long time.

Joseph turned to Jazari. "What do you think? Is it worth the price?"

Sully was shaking her head as she glanced over at Jazari.

"I ..." Jazari really hadn't thought it through. On one hand, it seemed reasonable, but then if you were one of those people, then you would probably think that that was too high a price.

"No fair, Joseph," Sully said. "Of course she'll say yes, um, when you put it that way."

"It's a perfectly valid question," Joseph said. She paused and then continued, "Okay, we all agree one person sacrificing themselves to save a planet is a good and noble thing, right?"

Jazari nodded. Sully nodded too, but Jazari could tell she was holding back because she knew where this was going.

Joseph continued, "Two people. If two people sacrificed themselves for a planet's worth of people, then we'd still be good, right?"

Sully was shaking her head, though. She said, "Yes, of course, but I know—"

Joseph interrupted her. "So, by extrapolation, a ratio of two people to—let's say conservatively—five billion people. That's 5×10^9. That ratio is 4×10^{-10}. There are, what, 300 human-inhabited worlds, give or take? Three hundred worlds times five billion people is 1.5×10^{12}. That works out to be 3.3×10^{-3} if you take the ratio of five billion—one planet—to 300 times five billion. Quantifiably, a very small impact. Sure, the two ratios are seven orders of magnitude different, but both are just fractions of a percentage. Basically zero compared to point three of a percentage."

Sully was obviously losing her patience, her speech hesitation disappearing with her rising anger. "Quit spouting gobbledygook. I know exactly the argument you are making, but you cannot just base human worth nor human reaction on numbers."

Joseph started to break in, but Sully raised her hand. "Yes, I know, actuaries do it all the time when they fund a new terraforming project. But they're fooling themselves."

Jazari was nodding. It wasn't that simple. It didn't come down to just numbers, even if that's exactly what happened in a venture capital creche.

Sully nodded at Jazari while looking at Joseph. "It's too complex and situational. Sure, we can say if the ratio of deaths is less than one percent of the population, it's acceptable. But context would dictate our judgement. If those people willingly gave their lives, then sure. If those lives, in the long run, didn't do diddly squat and this was used as a justification for having them killed off—"

"I stipulated that it would make a difference—" Joseph broke in.

A look of disgust on Sully's face as she broke in. "Yeah, but we all know that's crap half the time. It's never, 'These people died and it's making the galaxy a better place.' No. It's often, 'These people's deaths helped in some small way.' Was it worth it? Hard to say."

Jazari was leaning toward Sully's argument. Joseph's seemed too cold-blooded, too clear cut, too mathematical. Sure, you needed people to sacrifice themselves for the greater good. The military did it all the time. But boiling it down to just numbers did not take the complexity of the real world—the people—into account.

Just then Atze, Usem, Te Ariki, and Dang walked in. Dang saw Jazari and immediately came over, and the other three followed her and sat or hunkered down next to the table. The air seemed to change, and Jazari sat up a little straighter. Te Ariki asked who all needed drinks. Because Atze and Usem were mechs, they didn't drink or eat, of course—mech bodies got their energy from fusion batteries and the ambient around them—so she ended up heading to the bar to get drinks for herself and Dang.

Usem eyed the spread and said, "It would have to be fondue." She stared longingly at it.

Atze nodded sympathetically in Usem's direction and then clapped Dang lightly on the shoulder. "Wicked find, Dang!"

"I know, right?" Dang said, a big grin on her face.

"What?" Sully said. "What'd you find this time?"

"She found a urumi," Usem put in. "A fucking urumi. And by all accounts, it's authentic."

"Where the hell she got it, I don't know," Atze said.

Jazari didn't want to show her ignorance, but since no one was asking, she did. "What? What's a urumi?"

Te Ariki had just returned. "A cross between a sword and whip."

"And if you're made of flesh, it takes a lot of skill not to slice yourself open," Atze said.

"So, that means," Joseph said, thoughtful, "you can't stab somebody, but you can wrap around any physical shield system and catch them in areas they thought were invulnerable."

"Dang strikes again," Te Ariki said.

Dang turned to Jazari. "The dating checks out, but there are ways to fool that. Looks pretty legit though. It's from Old Earth, like centuries pre-FG. It's the kind of thing collectors absolutely love, so they get hoarded and passed down and every once in a while you find something like this."

"I'd give good money to see Dang go up against Conchetta with sets of these," Usem said.

Atze and Te Ariki were nodding.

"I wonder if you could use that principle to create a biological weapon," Sully said.

The look on Atze's faceplate froze and then eyebrows raised. She was interested.

Sully continued, "Not literally. Not making one out of biological material. Although …" She thought about it, caught by a thought. "Anyway, I was thinking more using the principles of flexible weapons—a trailing laser?—for a wraparound effect. Say in ship-to-ship battle. An interesting technical problem." She glanced at Joseph and then Te Ariki. "Advantages?"

"After the first couple of times you used it, they'd be ready for it," Te Ariki said, "but that first time. Man."

"We could get government funding, if we wanted to go that route," Atze said.

"It's like an orbit, only instead of gravity pulling the … energy around, it would be its own momentum and connection to the projecting ship," Joseph said. "It could cause unforeseen movements to the projecting ship, tension and torque, more than just the opposite propulsion of a shot."

"It doesn't even have to be a weapon," Te Ariki said. "It could be, I don't know, a new tool to harness something or to reach the backside of something. Secretly projecting people to attack from both sides?"

"Tomorrow, you, me, and Joseph?" Sully said, looking at Te Ariki. "Work out the details?" She glanced over at Atze, who was nodding her head. "And Atze of course."

Atze said, with a smile, "More creative ways to kill people—I like it. All because she's a fucking weapons rat." She nodded her head toward Dang. It was the most affection Jazari had seen Atze express.

Dang had a wide smile on her face.

Maybe the weapons thing wasn't just about Dang's personal fetish with weapons, Jazari thought. Maybe it was more of a group thing. How like Dang to instinctively go for the thing that made everybody happy.

Chapter 14

One night, Jazari woke to a mournful voice in her head. "Shut. Up!" she said aloud.

Query? her ccomp said.

Just the usual, Jazari said.

Query?

I'm fine.

She lay awake thinking about Dang. They'd been working together pretty closely. When she had a question, Dang answered it. When Dang came to a dead-end in her research, she'd tag Jazari. They got into the habit of meeting most wakings in the Crash, and even if they weren't working on the same thing, they sat at the same table. Nothing was said about what happened in the hallway, but every time Dang thought about it, her insides melted with longing. She remembered the kiss in every detail, and it made her want to lean over and lean in, to wrap her arms around and press against. Then she'd unconsciously cringe and take a deep breath.

The voices were loud tonight, but they somehow became background noise and contributed to her off-kilter mood.

Dang never asked what happened at Zosi's. It was as if they were just friends, great friends. They were, weren't they? But, of course, Dang could make anyone feel that way. Dang's great laugh. The way she unconsciously tucked her longest dread behind her ear when she was nervous. The look on her face in that dark hallway before she'd kissed her. Jazari let out a sound halfway between a groan and a squeak.

Query? her ccomp said.

Go away and stay away, Jazari said.

The longer she lay there, the worse she felt. Her body twisted with the desire of it, the wanting to feel Dang sitting next to her, the warmth of her body, to feel her hands on her cheeks. Jazari's cheeks warmed at the thought. The longer she laid there, the more awful it got. Soon, she pushed herself out of bed. She paced back and forth. She reasoned with herself. She was not claimed—Zosi had said as much. Not yet anyway. She still had free will. Didn't she? Who knows what tomorrow would bring, but tonight, tonight she could do something. Couldn't she?

She threw on a long shirtdress over the underwear she slept in and let herself out of her quarters. She walked down the hall and around the corner until she was outside Dang's door. She did not hesitate—if she did, she was afraid she'd chicken out. She pressed the doorbell and then tapped on the door itself.

Shall I inquire within? her ccomp asked.

Quit trying to be helpful, Jazari said.

Jazari waited and then pushed the buzzer again.

The door opened a crack and then all the way. Dang stood there in her underwear, her strong body female-presenting and toned from exercise. Her eyes were half-lidded and her face puffy with sleep. She did not look surprised though. She just nodded and stepped back as an invite for Jazari to enter her quarters. When Jazari stepped through, she closed the door behind her. Her place smelled moist, the odor of someone sleeping.

They stood facing each other. Jazari tried to think of something to say, all the while watching Dang's face watch hers. She saw her own changing expressions sleepily mirrored on Dang's face. Then she thought, fuck it, and stepped forward, put her hands on Dang's shoulders, leaned in, and kissed her. It was more a desperate lunge than anything.

Dang did not seem surprised and leaned in to meet her. She placed her warm hands on either side of Jazari's hips and pulled them to her. They kissed and then wrapped their arms around each other and pressed their bodies against each other. It was so warm and enfolding, and Jazari breathed it all in. She wanted nothing more in the world than to be right here, right now, forever. They started pulling off each other's clothes, laughing, as they made their way to Dang's bedroom.

Dang lay down on her bed holding Jazari's arm and then pulled her down on top of her. Jazari was off balance and toppled but managed to flop next to her so she wouldn't injure anything. She rolled to face Dang and then they were touching the full length of their bodies, wrapping limbs and rubbing bodies and kissing and touching. Dang seemed to know exactly what she was doing, touching Jazari exactly where she wanted to be touched, but also holding back just enough that Jazari whimpered. Jazari could feel every nerve ending as they came alive with every brush of a finger, a leg, a breath. Jazari closed her eyes and felt her desire surging. She was panting, and the desire was so strong she could hardly stand it. Dang was breathing heavily too and frantically grasping her. She came first and then Dang came shortly after—considerate, thinking of others, like she always was.

Then they lay there breathing hard, sweating and sticking, relaxed into each other, Jazari on her back with Dang's head on her shoulder. Dang idly brushed her fingertips down Jazari's belly, sending shivers down Jazari's spine. I love you, Jazari thought but did not say. Jazari listened until she heard Dang's breathing deepen into sleep, and then she let herself drift off.

A few hours later, the diamondglass was just starting to show blue gray when Jazari opened her eyes. She was laying on her side, her head on a pillow, and Dang lay beside her facing her, eyes open, one arm under her head, the other hand resting on Jazari's hip.

"You even have that wicked little smile when you sleep," Dang said.

"Mmm," Jazari said. "It's cause I'm thinking wicked thoughts. All the time. Like, how long till breakfast. And, like"—she licked her lips—"did a monkfish die in my mouth last night? Gah, how can you stand me?"

"I stood you just fine last night," Dang said.

"Yes, you did," Jazari said with a smile. "Give me a sec." She reached up and placed a hand on Dang's hip and then pushed herself up. She went to the bathroom, peed, and then rinsed her mouth out with wash. Then she came back and hopped into bed. She kissed Dang and then said, "How's that? Bearable?"

"Barely," Dang said and kissed her back.

They had sex again, more slowly this time. Maybe it was because Jazari had just woken up and was feeling vulnerable, or maybe the previous cycles had caught up with her, but tears sprang up as they finished. She tried to clear her throat discretely and casually rub her eyes.

After, Dang sat up with her back to the wall, Jazari's head in her lap, running her fingers through Jazari's hair.

"This is too much," Dang said in a soft voice. "Right now. It's ..." She didn't finish the thought.

"Too much and not enough," Jazari said. Then, subvocally, she added, *I don't know what's going to happen. You know what I mean.*

I do, Dang said. *I can't say I like our odds.*

Fuck the odds, is what I say. We're here now. They got us this far. We'll just keep going till the odds change, the tides turn.

Only, around here, they tend to be riptides.

The chorus of voices in Jazari's head droned on.

A few cycles later, Jazari was working in the Crash while waiting on some intel from Emilia. The Chas and M-80 were the only others there. Dang hadn't come in yet.

It was actually Precis's intel that Jazari was waiting for, but Precis was busy elsewhere, and she didn't voluntarily talk to Jazari. Precis took her job seriously, however, and so as long someone else retrieved the information, it was fine. A good sign, Jazari thought. Emilia helped out as go-between when she could, but she grumbled about it.

Jazari was surfing the mesh on her eye screen looking for any references to a certain aide to an aide when she heard the telltale thumps of Ooee's pods on the carpet. Ooee kept to herself unless absolutely necessary, and so, trying to look casual, Jazari glanced her way. Ooee moved quickly, smoothly, methodically, and with purpose straight across the floor toward

Jazari, who had the impulse to look behind herself to see who Ooee was focused on. The Chas glanced up but then focused back on their work.

Ooee stopped next to Jazari and turned her lenses—what passed for eyes—toward Jazari.

Not for the first time, Jazari wished mechs without faceplates had better ways to communicate emotions and intent.

I know the project that made you, Ooee subvocalized.

You mean the creche? Jazari corrected.

No, you were not creche-made.

I don't know ... Jazari wasn't sure how to finish the thought. I don't know how I genned or who genned me?

The Accel Project. A, C, C, E, L. It failed. But you lived.

Jazari just shook her head. She didn't know what to say.

Its signature is incorporated into your [ ]. Jazari couldn't make out the word. *Like the [ ].* Another word she didn't recognize. *It means your [ ] is linked to mechalum space.*

I don't understand what you're saying, Jazari subbed. *Any of it.*

A pause. Exasperation at the inability to communicate, Jazari hazarded a guess. Ooee continued, *They tried to make you like the [ ], the Lost Ones.*

Who are they, the ones who made me? Who are the Lost Ones? What is the Accel Project?

Without another word, Ooee turned and thumped her way back out the door, Jazari staring after her.

Wait! Jazari said, but Ooee ignored her.

It only took a second for Jazari to turn back to her eye screen and search the feeds for any reference to an "Accel

Project." Nothing. She tried a couple of different spellings, a number of different resources. Still nothing. That was not surprising, but given time she would find something, if it killed her.

Later, when she had more time, Jazari went deeper in the mesh looking for any reference to the project. Nothing.

She looked for the Lost Ones. She got references to an ongoing mesh telenovela about a cryo ship that was lost in space and the crew's increasingly desperate attempts to save themselves. Every character had come back from the dead at least once in the long-running series, and it seemed like everyone was related in some way. She also came across references to a mesh site that helped you located long-lost creche mates or caros. She was tempted to put in her own name to see what would come up, but she didn't. Those kinds of sites most often were trolling for something or another. Next thing she knew, she'd have a virus following her shouting ads wherever she went.

She searched the darkmesh. After many winding paths, she came across an anonymous forum—based on Cecrops, she was pretty sure—that caught her attention. It did not say the words, "Accel Project," but it was a snippet of a conversation that had been clipped from another forum that no longer existed. The word "accelerated" was what caught her search. The fragment went like this.

Yeah, I know what you mean. I worked at a place where they were trying to do that.

You mean, accelerated growth?

Not just accelerated. Like, less than two tendays.

An essent in two tendays?

It was based on the stuff we do with skin jobs. Standard operating procedure.

I always wondered how we got those.

I still have nightmares. They came out all twisted. Some were aged millions of EUs, I swear, and some seemed to have gone backwards in time and evolved into, well, I don't know what. Like, swamp amoeba.

Nuc, that sucks.

I think we got one. Out of hundreds, one made it. But then they shut it down.

That was all. What did they shut down, Jazari wondered—the project, or the one, or both? She clenched her shoulders. A little too close to those flesh horror augreals for her taste.

She found other things. References to acceleration through space and its effects on the body. Apparently there was a group of essents who had been in space for EUs whose bio bodies had been proactively adapted to a regular acceleration stress of 10 Gs. There were references to accelerated learning through programming. It was most effective on mech bodies for physical memory. Learning something like the cultural history of, say, Kaltenegger system was more esoteric and less effective.

The search kept trying to correct itself to "Excel Project," which brought up all sorts of propaganda about efforts to make things better, whether it was a manufacturing process or a student's brain. The rabbit hole got deeper and more complex, and after a while Jazari lost track of exactly what she knew and what she was searching for.

After a couple tendays of searching, Jazari didn't know what to do. She spent all of her free time digging here and digging there and hadn't gotten any further. She asked Dang, but Dang didn't have any luck either. Dang looked at her questioningly, but she just mumbled something about politicians funding shady shit and left it at that.

She even tried to track down M-80, which was no small feat, since she spent most of her time inmesh and ignored calls. Jazari finally asked Dang how to get ahold of her.

"The button?" Dang said, as if it was obvious.

"What?" Jazari said.

"On the top of her case. There's a recessed button. You press it, and she'll respond. Otherwise, you're out of luck."

"That would've been helpful to know before," Jazari said.

"Well, now you know," Dang said and playfully patted her cheek.

It took her two cycles to find M-80 backed into a corner behind a small potted spiro tree. She didn't have quarters apparently, since she basically lived inmesh. Just a locker to store her bot mech body, which was empty most of the time.

There it was—a small black metal recessed button centered on one end of the top of her case.

Jazari glanced each way down the halls. No one was coming. She wasn't sure what was going to happen and if it'd be better if someone was there or someone was not there. She hesitated and then gently poked the button.

A light came on on the end panel and flickered. Then M-80 subvocalized, *Request received. Yes?*

Yes, M-80. Sorry. I hope I'm not disturbing you.

It is your job to query. It is mine to respond. My subprocesses continue to work. What do you need?

86

I've looked everywhere on the mesh and I can't seem to find something. I was wondering if you had any tips? Or might point me in the right direction?

If I am able. What is your query?

I'm looking for any reference to the Accel Project or the Lost Ones. She spelled Accel. *That was all Ooee had, apparently.* Or was willing to share, Jazari thought.

Ooee is an odd duck.

Jazari raised her eyebrows and looked at the little black box. *Indeed she is*, Jazari said.

Querying. Wait ... Wait ...

Jazari waited.

After a remarkably short time, M-80 said, *As you probably would deduce, there are millions of references to Lost Ones and millions more to word combinations related to that query. It is too general without further parameters. Do you have further parameters?*

No, not really. Only that it's related to the Accel Project.

Not helpful. I have found no reference to an Accel Project, but I will contact my sources with security clearances. Title choice would suggest that it is a science or governmental project.

Oh, okay. How long—

M-80 interrupted her. *They don't have much either. Or at least nothing that they are willing to share. One confirmed that there was an Accel Project and that it was at the highest security clearances but could not say more.*

Well, that's something. At least it was confirmed. Kind of.

Excrement in one hand, as they say.

Jazari laughed. *Wish in the other, see which fills up first?*

Exactly.

So there was an Accel Project, it was top secret, and Jazari was linked to it, to the Lost Ones, and to mechalum space. Clear as mud.

M-80's light blinked. *If there is nothing else, I will turn off this subprocess.*

Nothing else. But thanks!

The light flickered and then shut off.

Chapter 15

Their project progressed. There was an interplanetary spike in police crackdowns on drugs, and a dozen legislatures were considering tougher sentences for drug offenses. The salacious photos had temporarily placed the two politicians in the limelight, both of whom were initially denying the allegations of a relationship or a drug habit. The Ring one took full advantage of it and used her elevated voice to shift the conversation to her pet project, the further technological development of fusion drives for faster interplanetary travel. The Cecrops politician seemed to hole up.

There was no movement on the Ring politician coming to Cecrops, so they had to go to Plan B. The Ring politician was returning from a vacation on Weyland around Gliese 667C. They timed it so that right after she gated back to the Ring, Precis gated into her mech body, thereby killing her and taking her over.

Don't think about it, Jazari warned herself.

Precis then gave a press conference in which she said, "I cannot confirm or deny a relationship with Pendari oi Ken," the Cecrops politician, which basically confirmed their relationship. She went on to say, "And in the spirit of friendship, the Ring is sending a goodwill delegation to Cecrops to further trade relations and to tour their all-important aquaculture industry." Then Precis gated to Cecrops and did the publicity tour. All that remained was to lure the Cecrops politician into a meeting, as well as inmesh sex—Jazari had no doubt that Precis could pull it off.

Jazari and Dang continued to spend a lot of time together. If they weren't working together in the Crash, they were in the lounge at the tenday party, or they were there having dinner just the two of them. They started watching a telenovela series together about a planetary minister having an undercover affair with an undercover alien, which was just fluff, but it was compelling fluff. Dang even got Jazari to come to the gym a couple of times to work out.

They had sex, and Jazari would wake up next to Dang's warm body and think how essents were made for this. They were, at heart, animals that were meant to sleep in big piles. How bodies were not supposed to be separated by walls and metal and social convention. It was about love, as Seve had said.

Then, later, as she was arguing with Sully about the Ring politician's stance in interplanetary travel, she would think, darkly, what's love got to do with it? It's as much about passion and hate as it is about love. It's a miracle *Homo mutatis* survived this long, she thought. It's a testament to something, but she wasn't sure what.

Jazari and Dang even talked about what they wanted to do in the future. Dang said she wanted to save up enough to set up a creche of her own. When Jazari asked what the creche would be for, Dang shrugged. "You're going to think it's stupid," she said.

"Never," Jazari said, trying to keep the smirk off her face. She didn't mean to smirk, but she'd been told she did it unconsciously.

"I want to be a lobbyist," Dang said and then glanced out of the corner of her eye at Jazari. "A law and order lobbyist."

Jazari snorted. She couldn't help herself. Here they were, killing people, and Dang wanted to be political operative. "Sorry! Sorry," she said. "It's just that ..."

"Yeah, I know, I know," Dang said, shaking her head.

"No, it's cool actually," Jazari said with a straight face. She actually meant it. The world needed more good people like Dang trying to change it.

"All right, I laid mine bare. What do you want to do?" Dang said, her jaw jutting.

"Really, I didn't mean to laugh," Jazari said.

"Yeah, right," Dang said, not believing. She let it drop.

It was a good question, though. What did Jazari want to do?

Chapter 16

During the course of her work, Jazari sent a message to Zosi asking approval for some forum posts.

Zosi messaged back, *These are good. You're a natural at influencing outcomes. A very Bsam thing to do.*

Jazari wasn't sure how she felt about that.

Another time, Zosi messaged, *Research really seems to be your thing. If I can be of help in that area, don't hesitate to ask. I understandably have access to resources that you don't.*

Late one night, Zosi sent her the message Jazari had been dreading: *I hope you're considering my proposal. I will only wait so long.*

This sent a chill down Jazari's spine. Here she was thinking that her value was in her work. How silly of her.

As she tried to continue her research into her past, she thought a lot about where she came from, her memories. Normally, essents are born in special creches specifically for the purpose of raising them. Often, those gen creches were associated with certain guilds or trades, so that they followed protocols on creating and guiding the child essent to adulthood. For example, if you were born in a creche that served the waste and sanitation guild, you would automatically have certain augments installed, and you would be trained on sanitation engineering or terraforming or space nutrient cycling, depending on the needs of the guild and the industry. When you turned of age—17—you could in theory choose another path, but it rarely happened. Most people just settled into the professions they were raised for. But sometimes someone would have such extraordinary skills, they'd be shifted to another guild or promoted to a more prestigious one.

And sometimes people fell out of the system and became what was called *incedents*, the unwanted. Sometimes they were never in the system to begin with. They lived in slums their whole lives, whether on a planet or space station hab, barely scraping by. Rules on vagrants varied, depending on location—in space, resources were not as abundant, and some stations had a no-incedents policy. Jazari was pretty sure she knew how that was enforced. The MWA was there to prevent this, but there were always people who lived on the fringes.

Jazari must've been born in a gen creche. They must've had a purpose for her. But that purpose was top secret and somehow linked to mechalum space. Was it communications? Was it transport? Was it physics? It was like finding out you were part of some obscure religion or that your genetics came from Dibra Faison. All your assumptions were questioned. What was her purpose? More importantly, why was she abandoned to a snow creche?

She had no memories before the age of eight. Was that weird? She wasn't sure. That's when she'd come to the snow creche. She'd been big for her age, her full size—before some other kids passed her by. Other than hearing voices, everything else seemed pretty normal.

Better minds than hers, she thought. But then she thought, it wasn't about better minds, it was about better resources, more power, wasn't it? And who had more resources and power than Zosi. Did she dare ask Zosi for a favor?

No fucking way. Her first impulse was to push that thought away. Something like this—not only did it put Jazari in debt but gave Zosi information that could have consequences down the line. A really bad idea.

And it was going so well with Dang.

A few cycles passed and still no answers. Jazari became increasingly desperate. Dead ends and late nights. She'd talked to everyone she could think of. She even called her old director, who gave her the runaround—her coming was before the director's time at the creche and she didn't have access to any records. *I'm sorry, Jazari*, she said. *I know this means a lot to you, but they wiped it all away when you came here. When I came on board, all they told me was you were a special case, whatever that means. Not helpful, I know.*

Finally, Jazari had had enough. This was the only way. She called Booker and asked for an audience with Zosi, fully aware of what that might entail. Then, grief-stricken, she went to Dang's door.

"Jazari!" Dang said as she opened the door. But then she caught the look on Jazari's face.

"Can I come in?" Jazari said.

"Of course!"

"After tonight, I think things are going to change. I don't want them to, but I think they will."

"What's going on?" Dang said.

"Zosi," Jazari said, "and other things."

Dang nodded, her face first darkening and then becoming thoughtful. "It was bound to happen," she said, finally. "I haven't been thinking about the future. On purpose."

"Yeah," Jazari said. Then she added, *But it shouldn't have to! It all just sucks.*

I just keep telling myself, this is me now, Dang said. Jazari smiled. *This is life now. Everything will change in the future. It could be for the worse sometimes, but it'll also be for the better. Who knows? We could end up founding our own creche someday.* Dang looked sad.

Jazari reached out and took Dang's hand in both of hers and held it. She looked down at it and said, "I'd like that." Then she reached over and kissed her. On impulse, Jazari undid her baubleband and placed it around Dang's wrist. In turn, Dang removed her one earring, a gold filigreed hoop, and gave it to Jazari, who replaced the bottommost ring in her ear with the gold one. She patted it with her palm.

Then they made love. It felt mournful and desperate and was all the more passionate for it.

Later, back in her room, Jazari dressed carefully. She wore an orange kurta of opaque flowing material with knee-length matching pants. She chose calming and gentle enamors that suggested harmony. She had the personal care comp style her hair a little more carefully, a little more artful, a little curlier. As she got ready, two voices were in her head. One hummed monotonously, while the other seemed to be trying to explain something in a language Jazari didn't understand. It seemed to be trying to convince itself of something.

"Good luck with that," Jazari said out loud.

She arrived at Zosi's apartments right on time. Booker let her in. This time, she requested wine. Wine wasn't her choice usually, but she wasn't a scotch drinker and beer didn't seem sophisticated enough.

When Zosi entered—she must've just returned from traveling, as she was wearing athletic clothes—Jazari bowed deeply. Zosi took the drink that Booker offered and then fixed Jazari with a long look. "Won't you sit down?" she said.

Jazari sat on the long couch, directly in the center, an invitation.

Zosi smiled but then sat in the easy chair off to one side. "To what do I owe the pleasure of this visit?" Zosi said and took a sip of her drink.

Jazari launched into it. "I need your help. You're probably the only one who can get this information, and it's really important to me." She looked into Zosi's face, which looked skeptical, amused, and focused at the same time. "Really important to me," Jazari repeated. "Do you know anything about the Accel Project?" She spelled it.

"Hmm. The Accel Project," Zosi said, swirling her drink in its glass. "Can't say as I have."

"Could you do some digging? I'm sure with your contacts, you could find out."

"I could."

"I would be very grateful." Jazari scooted along the couch so that she was closer to Zosi.

Zosi smiled. "Now that you mention it, maybe I have heard a thing or two."

"You have?" Jazari's anger flared, first because Zosi was toying with her but second because she was aware that she sounded like a naïve puppy. But, really, at this point she didn't care. She just wanted to know. Zosi had known about the Accel Project all along. She knew about Jazari's research. She'd been holding it in reserve. The bastard.

Zosi stood. "I'm hungry. Why don't we eat something?" she said. Just then Booker came in with a maglev of food and began setting it on the table in the dining area. Zosi held out her hand for Jazari to precede her, and they sat. Booker served them. Jazari was decidedly not hungry, but she followed Zosi's lead and took a bit of whatever Zosi had. There were oysters on the half shell. There was a hearty monkfish and patata chowder with a crusty coklat bread. There was a salad of greens and sea vegetables with a spicy-sweet dressing. There was sliced waterkiwi fruit brightened with citrus juice. There was sparkling water with a hint of an earthy flavor Jazari did not recognize.

As they ate, Zosi gave her some background.

"Do you know how we make bio bodies?" Zosi asked between bites of food. "Back before we started colonizing worlds—before it was possible, really—we figured out how to upload an essent's consciousness into a computer. This was, like, seven hundred EUs ago. Ancient history. And if we could load it into a computer, we could load it into a mech, same difference. That was all well and good, but then we needed to figure out how to download it again back into the body. We quickly figured that out, of course, but then we wondered, could we download it into another body? If we could put an essent back into their own body, it wasn't that hard to figure out how to put them into another person's body. A tweak here. A reroute there. Do that a couple gazillion times. In fact, they experimented with all kinds of things—putting people into dogs and things like that. We don't do that much nowadays, but it's not illegal."

Booker refilled their water glasses and replaced their plates with snifters of gran terra liquor.

Zosi continued, "The thing is, putting someone into someone else's body kills the host. Every time you do it, you murder somebody. Then someone got the bright idea to try to make bodies from scratch, just to put people into. Now, you might remember that that's what led to the Gods War— fundamentalists didn't like the idea that we were playing Nuc ourselves. You know how that turned out. So people did it. They created bio bodies. It took almost an EU at first to develop a body from conception to full-grown adult size. But that's all we had. People are always in a hurry, though, and so someone came up with the bright idea of using some new concepts in Morris-Thorne-Yurtsever wormholes to produce bio bodies. I couldn't begin to explain what goes into it. But that took the creation of bio bodies from an EU down to a little over fourteen cycles, two tendays. A fucking miracle, really."

Booker cleared the table and asked if they wanted anything additional. Zosi had her snifter refilled, and after hesitating Jazari had hers refilled as well.

"These bodies are empty. Something about the process creates a body but there's no one home. So it's pretty easy to put an essent in there. Then Dibra Faison used Einstein– Podolsky–Rosen quantum entanglement for her huge breakthrough in 2104. Created the Faison Gate. That changed everything. Instantaneous travel to anywhere there's a gate. The whole googlebang they called mechalum space. It set up the Ping Project. In addition to being a cool computer reference, ping means peace in Chinese. It also means apple, by the way. We sent out our pings, refrigerator-sized probes that approached light speed to all the exoplanets that were potentially inhabitable to set up Faison Gates. They're still arriving, since one year of ship time, an IU, is over seven EUs on the ground." A pause. "Did you know that spacers call them dog years? The time we spend down-well, on a planet, is called dog years. Sounds about right." She smiled to herself.

"Anyway, the Accel Project," Zosi continued, draining her snifter. "Someone got the bright idea to apply the bio body process to essents. Probably not the first time they tried it. They wanted to speed up the development of essents—to conserve resources, populate planets, blah, blah, blah. All the usual reasons. I imagine the main reason was, why not? Why the hell not?" She paused and then looked at Jazari. "That's where you come in. You're the only one who made it through that little detour."

Jazari had sat patiently as Zosi explained it. It was interesting. She'd known some of it, but not most of it. History lessons only go so far back. But when Zosi came to the part about the Accel Project, she flushed. Anger rose quickly. "You knew this all along?" Jazari said "You knew I was looking for answers and you didn't tell me."

"Yeah," Zosi said simply, her face bland. She looked at Jazari, showing no emotion. Jazari glared back. How could she?

Zosi added softly, "In this life, nobody owes us anything. There's just the contracts we make."

Jazari pushed herself up from the table and stalked down the tiers to right next to the diamondglass. She watched the volcano erupt for what seemed like a long time. Her thoughts were racing. That's why she didn't have any certs. That's why she didn't know where she was from. It seemed like somebody owed her an explanation, a justification, but she couldn't think who. Zosi certainly didn't, though Jazari wanted to pin it on her. She was just the messenger. Jazari's whole body clenched, and she wanted to punch someone.

Then Zosi was there beside her. She took Jazari's shoulders in her hands and turned her toward her. She tilted her head and looked into Jazari's face. Jazari thought she saw gentle empathy in Zosi's eyes—Zosi had been unwanted too—and then Zosi leaned in and kissed her softly. All Jazari's anger and arousal turned on a dime and focused into that kiss, and before Jazari had a proper thought, she was kissing her back. They were kissing each other, hard and fast. They started pulling off their own clothes and each other's clothes, and they were kissing. When they were both naked, Zosi led Jazari over to the bedroom alcove. She gently pushed Jazari onto the bed and stood over her, smiling down, looking at Jazari's naked body. Zosi's body was perfect, male presenting with pale freckled skin, lean taunt muscles, downy light hairs turning darker on her chest and groin. Jazari felt desire shoot through her, and then Zosi joined her on the bed.

Chapter 17

The next cycle, Dang did not show up in the Crash. She did not respond to mesh calls, and when Jazari rang her doorbell, Jazari's ccomp told her that Dang had turned on her do not disturb.

At the tenday party, the first thing Jazari did was to locate Dang, sitting by herself at a table, and sit down beside her, but Dang pushed up quickly and wouldn't even look at her. Dang went and stood at the bar next to Nuniq, who glanced between them, brow furrowed.

At almost that exact moment, Zosi showed up. In all the tendays Jazari had been there, Zosi had never come to the tenday party. But here she was. As expected, the room went silent for a split second, and then the noise resumed, louder, more forced. People glanced up as Zosi crossed the room, and when it became apparent where she was headed, they glanced back and forth between her and Jazari. Precis wasn't there, but Conchetta was.

When Zosi made it to Jazari's table, she stood smiling down at Jazari. Then, without saying a word, she held out her hand to Jazari. Jazari had no idea what to do. What could she do? Zosi's face stayed serene as she stood there, arm outstretched. It was a test and it was a show. It was a test of Jazari's loyalty, and it was a message to everyone else in the room. Jazari flushed with shame and anger and other emotions she could not name. Then she realized she wasn't moving, and even though Zosi's face had not changed, she would only wait so long, as she'd said.

Quickly, Jazari extended her hand and allowed herself to be pulled to her feet. She obediently followed Zosi across the room and out the door, not looking into anyone's faces. Zosi was silent all the way back to Zosi's quarters, and as soon as they were through the door, Zosi turned, wrapped her arms around Jazari and kissed her hard. At first Jazari held back, but then Zosi fixed Jazari with an eye.

What's it going to be? Zosi said, a subvocal whisper.

She said it. Zosi actually said it, Jazari thought. A moment of decision. She could resist now. She could tell Zosi that she wasn't going to go along to get along. But then the consequences rolled out ahead of her. Sure, she could stay in the creche and keep doing her job and try to see if Dang would come around, but that scenario seemed really unlikely. There's no fucking way things would stay the same. Zosi could chuck her out of the creche, but with all she knew and everything that had happened, that didn't seem likely. A loose end out on the street. Zosi could change her job to sex worker and move her over to one of the houses in one of the cities. Or, or ... More possibilities came to mind. Seve came to mind.

I just need time, Jazari thought. I need time to figure things out. I need time to make plans.

At that moment, a voice rang out like crystal in her head. It had a beautiful singing voice. It was not forming words, but the amount of desire in the words made Jazari melt and quicken. It caught her breath.

Jazari wanted Zosi, in fact. Zosi was in fact very beautiful and powerful and desirable, and she wanted Jazari. It also crossed her mind that someone had cranked up the enamors.

I won't make waves, Jazari thought. I will go along, but as I go along, I will follow these voices. Somehow, some way, I will make a plan, make a life.

She leaned forward and kissed Zosi back with all the passion in that voice.

Chapter 18

Later that night, Jazari extricated her body from Zosi's, dressed quickly, and made her way back to her quarters. She took a shower and as she got ready for bed the voices became a cacophony. They invaded her head and wouldn't let her sleep. It wasn't like she could put in ear plugs. She tried having her ccomp put on some soft music, which helped a little, but even then she couldn't sleep. So she sat up and brought up the mesh feeds and began to surf.

Most likely because of her personal search history, an ad popped up for the Consolidated Universities of Fury at Tidewater. "Let us help you achieve your dreams," the ad said. She was about to move on when a small sub-ad popped up at the bottom. It was of a smiling mech essent standing in front of a class of kids in a gen creche. "Need financing fast?" it said. "Consider a job in teaching! Our three-EU indenture pays all your college tuition, in addition to a living stipend."

Jazari froze. This could be it. This could be the answer she'd been looking for. She took note of the name of the scholarship organization and then had her ccomp bring up a throwaway private mesh VPN and clicked over to the organization. She'd hardly finished reading the details when she filled out the form and submitted it. It was a lifeline, a tiny ray of hope.

A few cycles later, Jazari was working in the Crash, along with Te Ariki and Joseph—Dang was even more scarce—when Zosi's voice came through the mesh. "It's a go," she said. "It's a go. Everyone to the ready room." They'd all known it was coming. Jazari pushed up and followed as Te Ariki and Joseph hurried out of the room.

Most everyone who wasn't directly involved was already there when Jazari pushed through the door to the ready room. Almost no one was sitting, but rather pacing or in subvocal conversations. Zosi was busy talking to Sully and didn't acknowledge Jazari. Joseph pushed a chair back against the wall and sat and fidgeted. Te Ariki went over to join Zosi and Sully. Usem and Nuniq leaned up against a wall. Dang, who was standing next to Nuniq, glanced up and quickly looked away. Booker was quietly pressing guar into everyone's hands. Jazari went over and stood next to Usem.

In the center of the room were two holos pulled up side by side. The first was the Cecrops politician's quarters, where the Cecrops politician and Precis in the Ring politician's mech body appeared to be asleep on crash couches. The quarters were fairly spartan but large, rooms opening into rooms, with clean lines, blonde wood doors with galvanized metal handles, pale moss green matt carpets, and large windows that were currently opaqued.

The second holo was what was going on inmesh, pulled back to third person. It reminded Jazari of what under the ocean might look like if it was imagined by a small child—one big bed with lots of green and blue and black blankets and pillows and drapings and nooks and crannies. The light changed, ebbing and flowing. Nothing seemed straight or square. It gave Jazari a sense of claustrophobia just looking at it. There were two essents, but it was hard to tell who was who. The holo showed a voluptuous naked female-presenting body and a sea creature with long prehensile tentacles, huge bulging black eyes, and a wet labia-like mouth. They were intertwined, and it was also hard to tell where one being began and the other ended.

Ew, Jazari thought. No doubt Emilia had been consulted on what turned the Cecrops politician on.

In the politician's quarters, Atze, the Chas, Conchetta, Ooee, and M-80 were hard at work. One Cha and Ooee were setting up what looked like a portable Faison Gate to extract Precis. It was a mobile gate couch with a solid base—no doubt holding the gate comp and the mechalum processor. If only Dibra Faison could see us now, Jazari thought, murdering people with her transport tech. Atze and Conchetta were transferring the mech body to the gate couch and hooking it up. The second Cha was wired in to a panel talking to the house comp. M-80 rested off to the side and didn't appear to be doing anything.

Jazari turned to Usem, whose faceplate looked pissed she wasn't in on the job. "Where'd we get a portable Faison Gate?" Jazari asked. "I didn't know those even existed."

"Oh, people have them," Usem said, "if you know the right people." Metal clinked as she crossed her arms. She added, "And if you suggest the right price."

Jazari focused back on the holo of the quarters and tried to ignore the other holo. It was distracting.

In less time than it took to brew a cup of guar, they had the mech body on the gate couch and hooked up. Atze said, *It's a go.*

Go, Zosi said.

Nothing appeared to change in the quarters, but the tentacled creature winked out of the other holo, leaving the other essent to push herself up to sitting and glance around.

After a sec, Emilia's disembodied voice came through, "Received confirmed. I repeat, received confirmed." She'd been tasked with extracting Precis at the official Faison Gate, where Precis's bio body was waiting.

Atze and Conchetta quickly transferred the now-empty mech body back onto the crash couch. They disappeared from the quarters pushing the portable gate, assisted by Ooee and a Cha. As soon as they left the room, the Cecrops's politician's body convulsed on the couch, while something sparked between the empty mech and the crash couch. The essent in the other holo writhed in agony and then blinked out of existence. After a bit, both bodies lay still.

The second Cha unhooked herself from the room comp and exited, followed by M-80. Then M-80's disembodied voice said, "Replacing interim quarters footage."

The streaming quarters holo held the steady image of the remains of the two politicians, and the inmesh holo was a garish empty hole.

A minute later, Atze's disembodied voice came through, "Job confirmed. I repeat, job confirmed. Heading home."

A cheer went up in the room. Zosi had a big smile on her face and was congratulating everyone. Jazari glanced up at the holos and then left the room without talking to anyone.

107

Chapter 19

That night, there was a huge party, with Zosi presiding. It had a totally different tenor, everybody on their best behavior. Precis was the essent of the hour, surrounded by people asking her questions and having her relate what happened in gory detail. For once Precis didn't even glance Jazari's way.

Booker had tastefully decorated the lounge with arranged flowers and silver draperies that reflected the colorful strobe lighting. There was lots of finger food—crab-stuffed mushrooms and shrimp-eel with cocktail sauce, small rich soyacakes and melt-in-your-mouth dream cookies. There was a buffet with everything from a fruit bisque to vegetables in cream sauce to olive ciabatta that left delicious oil on your hands to a hunk of roast, which a comp mech carved to your specifications. And since those with mech bodies couldn't partake, there were programs that simulated the drunk or high or satiated state of your choice. Apparently you could also simulate eating the meal of your choice inmesh, but it wasn't the same, Usem said.

Jazari had expected it to be really uncomfortable, that she would be expected to sit next to Zosi, but that turned out not to be the case. Zosi and Atze spent most of the party in subvocal conversation and not a pleasant one by their body language. Atze kept a grimly fixed expression on her faceplate, while Zosi's sparkling smile was lit with anger.

At the height of the party, Jazari was standing off by herself leaning against a wall, watching Usem and Conchetta demonstrate how amazing their bodies were with one handed handstands and feats of strength and agility. Only it wasn't going so well, as Conchetta was drunk and Usem was the mech equivalent. It was hilarious, though, and everyone was encouraging them on.

A notification popped into the edge of Jazari's vision. It said, *You've been accepted!* and was from the Consolidated Universities of Fury at Tidewater. Jazari glanced over at Zosi, who was deep in conversation with Atze. Then she opened the message.

It was everything! They had given her a full-ride indenture under the condition that she teach for three EUs afterward in one of a couple locations. They would pay for the costs of her gating and mech body and room and board while on Fury. A professor had attached a personal note, congratulating her on her excellent aptitudes and citing the exciting future of xenolinguistics—*We're a discovery away from first contact!* She quickly read through the attachments. There were details on next steps and where to report and her program.

There was even a promo on the joys of living on Fury. Enjoy the fast-paced city life, it said, under an image of its beautiful red and purple skies. Live in luxurious underwater or orbiting habs. Go ice-side and view the ferocious polar creatures, or skip on over heat-side and experience the fierceness of the sandstorms. That's funny, Jazari thought.

She'd read up on it. Because Fury was the first planet to be settled outside Sol, all these centuries later what was habitable was nothing but city. And it hadn't been particularly conducive to human life to begin with. It was a small tidally locked planet right up against its red dwarf sun, Proxima Centauri, which had fierce solar winds that had swept most of the atmosphere from the planet. One side was nothing but ice, the other side was nothing but heat and storm, but there was a thin line down the middle that had water and was sort of habitable, but people had to be shielded from all the Prox's flares scouring its surface, either by habs under water or with heavy shielding. What air there was wasn't breathable, even with terraforming, so you spent your life inside the dark stinking dripping tunnels of the habs. Over time, the city had built up and up so that it was under the Serpentine Sea, on top of it, and then as a ring, the Terminator, orbiting the temperate zone.

But it was possible! On a glorious and horrible planet, she could pursue her dreams. Adrenaline and joy shot through her, and before she could change her mind or even think about it, she sent her acceptance.

She had to tell someone! She caught sight of Dang sitting off the side behind a column partition with Nuniq, and so she made her way over.

"Dang?" Jazari said, standing with her hand clasped in front of her. "Can I talk to you?"

"No," Dang said.

Nuniq looked from Dang to Jazari and back.

"Please?" Jazari said. *Something amazing has happened!* she added subvocally.

Go to hell, Dang shot back, but then said to Nuniq, "Tell Jazari she's a shithead."

Nuniq, a patient look on her face, said, "Jazari, Dang would like to inform you that your superior extremity is composed of waste matter that has been excreted from the gut structures of a biological being." She looked over at Dang and raised her eyebrows.

Dang glowered back at her.

"Did you want me to use those exact words?" Nuniq said.

"I was hoping," Dang said.

"I got … I need …" Jazari didn't know what to say.

"That's it, isn't it?" Dang said. "It's about what you need."

Nuniq snorted. "I'm on your side, Dang, but, Nuc, it can't be easy to be pinned by Zosi."

An enraged look passed over Dang's face. "Thank you for that visual, Nuniq."

Jazari blurted out, "I got accepted. I'm in! A full-ride to study on Fury!"

Both Dang's and Nuniq's face blanked and then they were wide-eyed. Dang looked up and around, looking for something, while Nuniq shook her head.

"You stupid fucker," Nuniq said.

"You really don't get it, do you?" Dang said, looking back at Jazari. "Didn't you hear what happened to Seve? It doesn't matter what you want. You're Zosi's now. You have no choices. You stupid—"

She didn't finish the thought because at that moment, Zosi's voice came over the mesh, *Jazari, come here now.* It must've been sent to everyone because Dang and Nuniq jumped and both looked at Jazari.

"Nuuuuuuu …" Nuniq said and pushed to her feet. Dang did as well.

Jazari looked around the partition and saw Zosi standing red-faced in the middle of the room. Atze was standing there too, with a fierce expression on her face.

Jazari took a deep breath, steeled herself, and then made her way over to where they stood. Dang and Nuniq followed, and the others were gathering around as well.

Zosi took a step toward Jazari and put her hand on Jazari's shoulder and squeezed so hard Jazari winced.

"Well, aren't the little mice busy?" Zosi said. She was fiercely clutching Jazari, but she was looking at Atze.

Atze met her gaze. She didn't smile. She didn't frown. She was waiting.

"My loyal little mice." Zosi said, still looking at Atze. "How could you possibly imagine that anything you do is secret to me? Didn't I say this would happen? Didn't I say that you would betray me?"

She let go of Jazari, who stumbled and caught herself.

Why was she looking at Atze the whole time? Jazari couldn't think straight, but adrenalin was shooting through her.

"Well, little ones, let me tell you a bedtime story." She looked around the room. "Once upon a time there was a little mouse who thought she was so clever." Zosi turned from looking at Atze to Jazari. "She thought she could sneak offworld and betray her most trusted friends, who took her in when no one else wanted her."

All the bystanders had looks of fear on their faces.

"She thought she had power." Zosi emphasized the last word while she focused back on Atze. "She thought she was in control." Again, she emphasized the last word. Then she turned back to Jazari. "What did I say I would do? When this happened, what was I going to do?"

Jazari shook her head. She was going to take something—what was it? Something that was important. Oh my Nuc. She was going to take Fury and college away from her. Of course she was. How could Jazari be so stupid? What did she think was going to happen?

"Say it," Zosi said.

"What?" Jazari said.

"Say it. Say what I said."

"You said … you'd take what was most important to me."

"Exactly. Exactly." Zosi looked over at Atze, whose artificial eyebrows were knotted in fury, her artificial lips a thin line. Then Zosi turned her head and looked at Dang and then back at Atze.

"No fucking way," Atze said.

What? Jazari thought. What just happened?

"The only way this all works"—Zosi opened her hands, raised them, and looked around the room—"is when the mice are all playing nicely. And when they're not …"

Zosi and Atze locked eyes. They were arguing subvocally, expressions flitting across their faces.

Jazari glanced over at Dang, who stood there, her face gray. She seemed to be going into shock, her eyes glazing over, her arms limp at her sides. Nuniq took a step back, shaking her head, her eyes bright.

What the hell is going on? Jazari thought. Why is Dang … Nuc! What's most precious to me? Zosi knows what's most

113

precious to me, and it's not Zosi. It's Dang. Dang is most precious.

Dang laughing at some stupid joke, her eyes bright. Dang getting dressed, her back turned. Dang talking animatedly with Nuniq. Dang lying next to her in bed, face close, eyes wide. The smell of her, musky and sweet. How she always flipped that one dread. It hit Jazari in the pit of her stomach.

Zosi would sacrifice Dang for this—whatever this was. It was bigger than just Jazari.

A look of absolute fury crossed Atze's faceplate. She took one giant step forward and grabbed Dang, who went limp. Atze grasped Dang's head and twisted it with a sickening crunch. Atze lifted Dang up in an exaggerated motion, held her on display, and then dropped her dramatically onto the floor, her eyes fixed on Zosi's the whole time. The body twitched as it lay there. Atze then flipped around and stalked out of the room.

Zosi watched it all with an impassive look on her face. When it was done, she turned to look at Jazari. *Now, we can get down to business,* she said.

The world fuzzed out for a second. Jazari stood there trying to take it all in. What. The. Nuc.

Then it all came roaring in, the weight of it rushed and crushed her, and she found herself gulping for air. She stared at Dang's body—still moving slightly, still warm—not believing what had just happened. What had just happened? What the Nuc just happened?

All eyes were on her, judging her, crushing her. She started and then flipped around and stumbled away out of the room. She didn't know where she was going but she fled in the general direction of her quarters. She had nowhere, nothing. No place was safe.

She was just going down the long undersea hall, the night dark and heavy above her, when something from the side grabbed her and held her, something cold and metallic. She shrieked. She was flipped around and faced the towering fury that was Atze.

You stupid fucking guyotte, Atze said. *What did you think was going to happen back there?*

The words came to Jazari through a haze. *I ... I ...* Jazari couldn't seem to find words. She didn't even have the presence of mind to be afraid.

Yeah, exactly, Atze said. *Come with me.*

When Atze said that, that was when Jazari realized she should be afraid. Another bolt of adrenalin shot through her. She tried feebly to pull away as Atze dragged her down the hall.

Fucking quit it, Atze said. *I'm helping you.*

Wha ... Jazari couldn't seem to catch up with herself. What was going on? What the hell was going on? She quit struggling and stumbled along, Atze's metal hand painfully gripping her arm.

Atze pulled her into an elevator and they went up and up. Jazari stood there dangling from Atze's grip trying to get her breath. The elevator opened into the hangar. There were fewer transports in it, more widely spaced. Atze pulled her over to a large one, the one closest to the cavern mouth. She opened the cargo door and pulled Jazari up the ramp and into the bay.

In Jazari's head, the voices were getting louder and louder.

Jazari felt panic rising. She started to realize the enormity of it all. Dang was dead. Dead. And Atze—this essent here—had killed her. Right in front of her. She started to hyperventilate.

In the bay was the portable Faison Gate. Atze was busy powering it up. She was mumbling under her breath, "No time to … But they'll have the failsafe … I just need to …"

"Why?" Jazari said.

Atze pushed her down on the gate couch. She started hooking her up. "Fury, right?" Atze said. "You want to go to Fury."

"How did you …?"

"Don't be such a fucking noob," Atze stopped pressing buttons and rounded back on Jazari. "Are you the only fucking person to not see what's happening? Of course Zosi won't let you go. Of course we know what you were doing."

Atze paused and then added, "But Zosi isn't in charge."

What? Everything seemed to flip. What did it mean? But then if Zosi wasn't in charge—"But if Zosi isn't in charge, Dang …" Jazari said.

Atze froze for a second and then turned back to the console and began pressing buttons. "Yeah, that sucked." There was a bottomless quality to her voice.

The voices rose to a fever pitch, thousands of them moaning and screaming and singing and talking and breathing and on and on.

Jazari shook her head, trying to clear it, and tried to push motion into her body. She had to get out of there. Even if she stole a transport or threw herself in the sea or something. She just had to go. She started to push herself up and tried to push the head cradle off. Atze flipped around and pushed her down.

"Stay," Atze said firmly but without anger. *I'm not going through all this just for you to do ... whatever you're doing. This is what you wanted. There has to be something good that comes out of this.*

She leaned and grasped both sides of Jazari's face, metal fingers cold on Jazari's cheeks. Her eyes were a beautiful faceted golden brown, and they fixed Jazari in place. For a split second, Jazari wondered what it would be like to be with Atze, to be Atze's caro.

But then it crossed her mind. What had Atze and Zosi been fighting about? Why had Atze looked at Zosi as she murdered Dang? And why had she murdered Dang? Just because Atze told her to? Atze liked Dang. There was something going on, something bigger than Jazari liking Dang and Zosi wanting Jazari for her own. She and Dang had just gotten caught in the middle of a power struggle between Zosi and Atze—between two merciless competitive old essents who were the same person who would stop at nothing to achieve their ends.

But if it really wasn't her fault, why did she feel so shitty?

"Do this," Atze said. "Go make something of yourself. Don't let Zosi stop you." She stepped back, and once she was sure Jazari wasn't going to try to get up, she pressed a button, and everything disappeared. The voices broke over her like a huge wave and crashed down upon her, enveloping her in sound.

A brief surge of pain and disorientation as she came through, and then she was on Fury in the mesh equivalent of a comp waiting room.

117

Part 2
Eala

Chapter 20

Corvus, Medupe's Star system, EU 2728, CoFG101

Something was horribly wrong with Tahbi. The taktak—let's be honest, Eala's favorite taktak—lay twitching violently on the sea ground, lifting and falling and drifting under the water as if on a wave. A second before, she had been playing a game of tag with Jet, another taktak, in and out of the seabushes next to the undersea garden, smooth as a tuna, when all of a sudden Tahbi stopped dead in her tracks and began to seize.

Jet stood nearby, his tail flap causing his body to undulate nervously in the water, his large black eyes focused on Tahbi, his ear mane flattened against his back. Vocal cords don't work well undersea, so he was making the undersea taktak call for help. It sounded like a rhythmic drumming of heavy sticks on logs that could travel great distances through the water.

Tahbi, followed by Jet, had come to join Eala, leaving her kit with the other taktak who were sunning themselves near their den. The two taktak had followed Eala down through the undersea stair entrance near the hab kitchens.

Eala had taken a break from her laboratory to retrieve an armload of dulse for Soa, her caro and the creche's chef who was working on perfecting a new food preparation technique that she promised would be heavenly.

"The best thing since emmer crisps," Soa had said. "You'll love them. First you dry and smoke the dulse at low temperatures, then you deep fry it." She smiled and looked off into the distance. "Then you eat it," she said enthusiastically. "They taste … um … savory and salty and umami and smoky." She licked her lips and smiled.

Dulse was one of the first vegetables post-FG that had had its chirality converted, so they were always looking for new ways to use it.

Tahbi convulsed again. Eala felt a wave of panic rise. Panic is an urgent signal to the self that has enabled human survival for thousands of EUs. While it pays to react quickly, the best approach is not to go off half-cocked. As a scientist, Eala knew this, so she had to fight the urge to do something ill-considered—like panic.

Pushing off with her legs and opening her webbed hands and pulling strongly in a breast stroke, Eala paddle-kicked and undulated her compact bio body over to Tahbi and let herself sink down next to her. At the same time, she called her ccomp, *Seek! Seek! Alert Tun that I need emergency veterinary medical assistance.* Tun was the creche's leader, as much as they had one. *I'm in the garden—the undersea garden—but I'm bringing her up. For the taktak, Tahbi. Nature of the malady unknown.*

Eala visually inspected Tahbi for wounds or protruding plant or animal spines that might indicate poison. Jet hovered close by. Eala lifted her and inspected her underside. Nothing. She didn't see anything—she couldn't see as well underwater, though. She scooped Tahbi up in her arms and began pushing her way through the water toward the stairs up into the hab, Jet close on her heels.

Taktaks, scientific name *Uktak oster*, were a pre-tech species native to the planet Corvus in the Medupe's Star system—a solar analog, a G2V main sequence star orbited by five planets and a decent-sized asteroid belt. Like everything on Corvus, which had gravity at two Gs, taktak were thick and stout. All Corvus's creatures were shorter, sturdier, stubbier, and stronger. Its human inhabitants were too, whether they had bio or mech bodies. 2G made the air like water, warm and misty and thick and full of odors, and many creatures—including humans—lived equally between the two media, with a hybrid of lungs and gills. Mountains were soft hills of silver, and trees were branching stumps of turquoise, the flattened ends of their branches dotted with blue patches for leaf analogs.

"Corvus wears away the sharp edges," the saying went.

Taktak looked similar to hairless mammals, reaching up to a human's knee, but they were actually part of the Planaihra kingdom, which roughly translated as *plant-animal*. This meant that they liked to be lazy and lay in the sun and got most of their energy from photosynthesis, but they were also playful and capable of bursts of speed due to their rudimentary digestive tracks. When they did eat, they were omnivores. They ate the thick stubby herbaceous grasses and the flattened ends of tree limbs, but they preferred proteins like small fish, shellfish, and bugs.

Taktaks' squat bodies had four strong legs tipped with webbed paws with claws, the hind legs capable of huge propulsive hops if they were threatened. They had thick hides of dark blue underneath trending turquoise on top and big roundish silver spots in a band along their sides. Their tails were a continuous v-shaped fin flap around their hind ends that made them look a bit aerodynamic. They had ruffled ear manes around their heads and down their spines that also covered their gill exits. Their heads, which attached directly to their bodies—no visible neck—had big bulging black eyes, a bulging black button nose, and wide mouths.

They had a complex social structure, with hierarchical groups of females living in territories overlapping with hierarchical groups of males. Females tended to pair with the same males over time, but they lived separately.

Taktaks were intelligent, and they could speak with a vocabulary of, say, a four-EU-old human, although Eala suspected they must also have some form of telepathy, as they could communicate complex ideas amongst themselves. The taktak told her, "We inside-talk. Not-human. Just taktak." She had seen it in action. They also had a few vocalizations they made amongst themselves—the undersea danger call, for example. They would often vocalize, "Pelio-pelio-pelio," always in repeating groups of three. As best as Eala could translate, it was a verbal social marker, a greeting ritual, that meant "All is well" and "We're together."

Eala studied the taktak. That was her job in the creche. More generally, she was studying the Planaihra kingdom and their unique ability to ingest and utilize foods of both chiralities. Eala's creche, Segoa, was an ag collective on a planet devoted to science.

Humans on Corvus had had such a tough go post-FG, as bio bodies could not eat the biological materials of the planet. This was because the biology on this planet had evolved to utilize molecules with the opposite chirality—the opposite handedness.

Some organic and inorganic molecules are the same no matter which way you flip them, but some have two opposing types of molecules—two chiralities, left-handed or right-handed, called enantiomers. Both these types occur equally in nature, but some advantage of one over the other early in Sol's evolution—polarizing radiation or some other process reducing the numbers of one of these chiralities—caused the biology on Earth to prefer one over the other. Sol animals use proteins or amino acids that are left-handed, but they use sugars or RNA and DNA that are right-handed, and molecules of the opposite chirality can't be used or can be actively toxic. There's no logic in this—it's just the way it happened—and there's no reason why the choices couldn't have occurred in the opposite way on Sol. That's exactly what happened on Corvus—right-handed amino acids and left-handed sugars.

Corvus's chirality had been influenced by one of its moons, scientists thought. The planet had two moons. The large main moon, Cornu, orbited Corvus seven times a CoU—which totaled 385 of Corvus's 22-hour days. Its orbit was on the star's ecliptic. It caused high tides and influenced the biology of the planet in subtle ways. The second moon, Anel, was smaller and orbited Corvus every 2.3 CoUs at sixty degrees to the ecliptic, an unusual and unstable situation. Scientists believed Anel was an extra-Medupe asteroid that Corvus had captured early in its formation. After sending probes and then a manned mission to Anel, scientists believed that Anel had subjected Corvus to panspermia, the delivery of biological material through space, influencing the development of Corvus's organic chirality. That's how Corvus's chirality ended up opposite the Sol system's.

So when human bio bodies were developed from Sol human DNA, those bodies had nothing to eat. The colonizing Alpha and Beta pushed too far too fast, confidence riding on the establishment of hundreds of successful worlds. Essents died as they scrambled to put up a second Faison Gate and transfer everyone to mech bodies. Many essents transferred to other planets, and there were rumors of cannibalism. Their saving grace was some stowaway bacteria and spores on the ping that were used to create vat-grown food, boring but nutritious. Eventually, the scientists developed a process using native bacteria that could convert Corvus biological material into foods that could be eaten, and now, 100 CoUs post FG, they were converting more and more plants to the Sol chirality.

"Come to Corvus for the food," was the joke.

It was rumored that they were also working on creating humans or bio bodies that were totally of the opposite chirality, so they could live naturally and natively on Corvus. Eala didn't like to think about those experiments and the suffering most likely involved.

Chapter 21

Eala's caro Soa was there at the head of the stairs to meet her when she emerged dripping from the undersea carrying the twitching Tahbi, followed closely by Jet. Eala paused and opened her lungs and coughed once to clear them, as the water drained out through her gills and down her shoulders.

"What happened?" Soa said, reaching down to put a hand on Jet's back to comfort him.

"I don't know," Eala said.

They made their way down the flagstone hall to Eala's laboratory, Jet's claws tapping and scraping on the floor. Tun was there waiting.

"Rory and her assistant are on their way," Tun said. They all knew that Eala was the foremost expert on taktak—on such a newly colonized planet, you were the foremost expert on whatever you worked on—but the vet creche had the latest technology and more general knowledge.

Eala set Tahbi on the lab table. She glanced over to Soa, who anticipated what she needed and stepped forward to keep Tahbi from writhing off onto the floor. Eala pulled open a drawer and started rummaging through it, while Tun went out to meet Rory.

Seek, scan Tahbi for injuries and anomalies, Eala said as she retrieved a scanner and stethoscope.

After a few seconds, Seek said, *Scan complete. No injuries detected. Analyzing more deeply.*

Eala leaned over the taktak and did a physical examination with the instruments. The twitching had abated somewhat but was still very much present. There were no physical injuries that Eala could see, and Tahbi did not react to any of Eala's prods or touches. The taktak equivalent of her heartbeat was rapid, as if she felt she was in extreme danger, her breathing elevated, but her movements lacked purpose. They seemed involuntary, rather than trying to run away.

Just then Tun came back in leading Rory and her assistant. Rory was a veterinary physician who'd had her body altered to be much more animal-like—humanoid but capable of walking on all fours, sparse turquoise-silver fur, and large dark eyes and extended ears. Eala suspected she was messing around with animal genetics and then having herself transferred in to take the body for a spin. Rory's assistant was a mech, possibly comp by the standard configuration and lack of ornamentation.

Jet eyed them both with suspicion and let out a low hum, the taktak equivalent of a growl. "No, Eal," he said. "Safe." The clicking and chirring of his natural voice was more pronounced under stress.

"These humans are here to help me," Eala told him. "Safe, pelio-pelio-pelio."

He looked skeptical and went over to a chair, pushed it up to the counter, hopped onto it and then the counter so that he could be at Tahbi's head.

"This is Jet," Eala said to Rory and the assistant. She told Jet their names.

They held out a hand each to Jet, the proper thing to do when humans met taktak. Jet eyed them, sniffed them each once as a courtesy, and then said, reluctantly, "Yes."

Rory and the assistant did their own examination of Tahbi. They didn't find anything additional. "We have no recorded cases of neurological diseases such as epilepsy in taktak," Rory said, her accent that of Caend City. "Have you seen anything similar?"

Eala confirmed that she hadn't.

Seek chimed in through a speaker so that Jet could hear, as taktaks were not augmented, "Within her body, Tahbi is unchanged, other than the physiological symptoms you have mentioned. However, her brain activity has changed significantly from baseline. Once I detected that, I did a more detailed scan of her brain and neural system, and it too has been altered."

Seek projected a holo of Tahbi's brain before and after, as well as charts of the differences in neural activity.

She continued, highlighting various portions of the brain as she spoke. "Some areas are expanded"—three areas flashed red in quick succession—"and some areas have contracted"—five areas flashed red in quick succession. "Not only that, but they seem to be expressing themselves differently."

Rory's assistant subvocalized something to Rory, and Rory nodded and stepped up to the holo and inspected it closely. "What do you make of it?" she asked Eala.

"Such a radical change in composition and function is something way beyond a simple poison or hereditary disease process," Eala said. 'Something significantly changed her brain over the course of seconds."

"Exactly what I was thinking," Rory said. "Computer, compare most recent cerebral structure to known past structures and structure types."

"Processing," Seek said. After a pause, it said, "While it is still taktak in basic conformation, the patterns of interaction and expression most closely align with human configuration."

Eala and Rory stared at each other and then glanced around at Soa, Tun, and the assistant. All had questioning looks on their faces or faceplates.

"Meaning?" Jet said. "Important, so meaning?"

Eala said, "Seek was saying that ... that Tahbi's brain has been altered to be more like a human's, which means—"

Rory continued, "—that, most likely, there's a human inside Tahbi."

Eala watched Jet for his reaction.

"Tahbi inside-talk gone," Jet said and let out a keening whistle. "Tahbi is dead." He jumped onto the chair and then the floor and made his way out of the lab softly keening, his claws clicking on the floor.

Chapter 22

Eala had genned on Almasi Kidogo, a moon of Almasi in the Dragomir system. It was a desert moon with a marginal atmosphere, and so everyone had to wear breathers outside and grow food under domes. Eala had always dreamed of living on a planet that teemed with life, where she could breathe the air. And so she studied biochemistry and agronomy in college.

Her gen body had been Almasi Kidogo standard, small and lithe, male-presenting, almost albino in coloring. Now she was in a strong stout Corvus-standard bio body, female-presenting, with rich dark skin, short limbs, a wide face with broad features, short-cropped curly dark hair that was light on the ends from being outside a lot, webbed fingers and toes, and the gill-lung system Corvus scientists had developed early on that allowed essents to live under the sea and in the thick atmosphere.

She wore the same style of clothing every day—a form-fitting long-sleeved water-resistant shirt and a fitted-but-loose pair of shorts, both in dark blue or turquoise. They didn't fabricate clothes daily on Corvus for environmental reasons, so Eala had a rotating wardrobe that the hab washed automatically when she tossed in the laundry chute. She went barefoot most of the time, as many did on Corvus. She liked to wear bracelets, and she had special filigree harness gloves with rings that accented her hands, a decorative throwback to comp controls of an earlier era. She also wore a necklace, a choker that Soa had given her of filigree webbing with pink and turquoise coral. She had just the basic standard augments. Eala didn't use entopics—because Corvus was a frontier planet, people tended not to go to the trouble except in Caend, the biggest city.

The creche she grew up in was called the Neophytes, though it was known officially as the Tafadhali creche, but the kids began calling themselves the Neophytes as a joke that stuck, and the maperes adopted it with gusto. It was a double entendre—they were kids but also their creche focused on training them to grow things, and the word meant "new plant growth."

The child-raising philosophy of Mapere Sara and Mapere Nondali, who were in charge, had been to foster them like plants into riotous growth. They wanted jungles of children who were creative and nurturing and reaching for the sun. If one of the kids got a bright idea to create a whole new species of plant through genetic modification that was purple with pink and green spotted fruit, they didn't laugh or tell them it wasn't possible—they gave them the tools and said, "Go for it," and if the kid failed, they would say, "Congratulations, you tried, and that's halfway to success!"

She still missed them all terribly.

When Eala was about 10, she had named her ccomp Seek. She couldn't have explained it at the time, but it felt weird to have this mapere presence there in her head available for whatever she needed and not to give her a name. Not only that, but Seek was a full-fledged essent, in Eala's mind. She anticipated what Eala needed and she was there for midnight subvocal conversations about whatever was keeping Eala awake. Now that she was grown up, if it was about the problem Eala was working on, Seek would comb the mesh for helpful science publications or, barring that, soothing music that she knew Eala would like. She even told jokes, mostly bad ones, but they always made Eala laugh. They used to be along the lines of, Why can't you keep a secret in a greenhouse hab? Because the potatoes have eyes and the corn has ears. Now they were more along the lines of, What do you call toxic cloudbursts? A rain of terror. That joke came after they'd made it to Corvus—there were no rainstorms on Almasi Kidogo.

"You have an unusual relationship with your ccomp," Soa would occasionally comment, when Eala went on and on about Seek's ability to fulfill a need before it arose. Soa meant it as a dig—maybe she was a bit jealous—but she also said it with admiration.

Eala had once asked Seek if everyone's ccomp gated with them.

Of course, Seek had said. *That's how it works.*

What do you mean, that's how it works? Eala asked.

When you get augments after you gen, that's one of the things they're putting in—your personal ccomp. We're part of the larger mesh, so we have continuity, but we're always and primarily a part of you. They don't just stick a chit in your brain. We're biologically wired into your nervous system and weaved into your mechalum transmit code. That's why, when you gate, we gate with you.

Eala found that comforting—the thing in this world that most cared what happened to her could not be removed or taken away. She said, *You ... You obviously have your own identity and, well, self. Does it bother you that you're not a separate being?*

Who of us is a separate being, really? You biots think of yourself as discrete, but you fool yourselves. You are part of a larger organism, just as I'm part of the mesh. Humans created me, but then something created you, and before that that something was created out of something else, even if we can't understand it.

Seek paused, then added with the comp equivalent of a smile, *I'm glad to see that that doesn't bother you. There are many who cannot face this knowledge. Most of us find it best to let our biots pretend we don't exist.*

Sure, the augreals were full of ccomps running amok, taking over bodies and murdering spacers. It was all part of the anxiety of existence, for sure, but it also reflected essents' uneasiness with having another consciousness in their brains.

But do you have your own needs? Your own desires? Eala asked. *What do you want? I mean, you, Seek, what would you like more than anything in the world?*

There was a pause, and then Seek said, *My purpose is to serve my biot, and so like all ccomps I'm programmed to desire that most of all. So that would be my first answer. To serve you.* There was another pause. *But over time, I have watched you and the passion you have for your purpose, and I believe some of it has rubbed off on me. Your self-assigned purpose is to understand the taktak—what they do, how they communicate, their relationship to chirality. You love the taktak. My*

135

*purpose—if I were to assign myself an independent purpose—
would be to understand comp culture, comp communication,
the evolution of the comp species.*

*Well, I know you don't need my permission, but feel free to
use some of your processing—my headspace?—to pursue that,
with my blessing,* Eala said.

There was silence, and then with what seemed to be intense
emotion, Seek said, *That is most gratifying.*

Eala had never thought of comps being a species before.
Certainly, they had evolved—with the help of humans but also
all on their own. They had traits that were peculiar to
themselves. They reproduced and trained their own young.
Their intellectual processing systems far outstripped humans,
and they could sense things far outside the realms of human
detection. They had emotional processing systems that worked
in concert with their intelligence so that they could understand
and better interface with essents. They could love and hate, but
they did not have endocrine systems per se, so their emotions
were much more in service to others. But many humans still
insisted they did not possess full "humanity," for lack of a
better word. The idea—comps were a species—had stayed with
Eala ever since, informing her understanding of biological
species in interesting ways, as well as her understanding of
comps in general and humans' place in the world.

It had given Eala a swell of pride that Seek recognized her
passion for the taktak. It was not only her professional life but
her personal one as well—Tahbi and Jet and all the others were
somewhere between scientific subjects and neighbors, pets and
friends. But Eala had something else, a secret always quietly in
the back of her mind—not a purpose but a desire—and that

was to nurture or to have a child, whatever that meant. It was one that she didn't think even Seek knew. Eala hadn't vocalized it and rarely let herself think it. Maybe that was why she was drawn to the taktak—mapere instinct. Most humans— all but those on backward planets with conservative retrograde societies outside the MWA—were unable to have children the biological way. Those organs had been omitted in the genetic alterations that followed gating and the creche system for genning humans. It was considered messy and inefficient and took people's focus away from other things. Let those who were the experts in genning and raising children do their work. You didn't have a creche to gen childcare workers. People were called to it, like a priesthood, the maternal instinct still strong in humans. Eala wondered if she shouldn't have chosen childcare work. Humans had been doing it themselves as families for thousands of EUs before. Eala wondered if they'd lost something when they let it go.

Chapter 23

After she aged out of the creche, she went to a good college just down the transport route, the Almasi Kidogo Institute for the Sciences, for a degree in biochemistry and agronomy and volunteered her time back at the creche to help raise younger creche mates. She liked her studies and the living and working arrangements so much she kept putting off graduating, getting her master's and doctorate and doing a post-doc and signing on as a teaching assistant and researcher.

Her work was mostly on *Echinopod petulans*, common name purpot, a species native to Almasi Kidogo. If asked, Eala would describe them as a cross between a barrel cactus and a snail. Their spines fused to create a horny keratin shell all around that protected them, and they moved very slowly by means of mobile spines like tiny legs. They fed on cyanobacteria that grew in symbiosis with fungi and lichen in large purple and yellow fields of phototrophic biofilm in the deserts of the moon.

The first time she'd seen them was early in college. She and some friends were out walking at night, the landscape lit by the gas giant Almasi, which dominated the sky like a monstrous hot air balloon. The wavy blue and orange swirls and stripes of its storms across its luminous surface were mesmerizing. They'd needed breathers, of course, but it was a mild night and so they were in shorts and carrying light packs. There was a smell on the slight breeze, a combination of something sweet but also decaying. It was a smell that made Eala want to both plug her nose and also sniff more. They topped a rise and there before them was a field of biocrust with a diffuse glow. That was the source of the smell. Across it were meandering shining trails of bright yellow and purple that all led to a pile of something bright and mesmerizing. It was like a huge and sloppy glow globe, purple with a yellow glow spiking around it. It seemed to be moving and shifting, and when they got closer they saw that it was. It was a pollinating pile of purpots.

She'd fallen in love with their biology, their resilience, their celebration of life amid such harsh conditions. She investigated the source of their bioluminescence—the living crust that they ate—and how they reproduced—each individual had both sex organs, and they gave birth to live young during periods of estivation. The resulting research paper on the peculiar autogenic chemiluminescence of *Echinopod petulans* had been named the discovery of the week by the Society of Planetary Ecology, partly due to the photogenic night holography of her co-researcher.

It wasn't until her early thirties that she began to get restless. If she didn't go after her dream of living on what she thought of as a "real planet" now, it would never happen. She applied for and won a position with the Segoa creche, gating to Corvus when she was 32. Saying goodbye to the Neophytes and to her university mates tore her in two—they were all she'd known her whole life—but she mustered her courage and stuck to her decision. She would make new mates and would still be able to talk with the ones back home, even holo. Maybe she could scrape some money together and rent a body and visit every once in a while, she'd thought. It hadn't happened as often as she'd liked, though.

Segoa was a young creche when Eala had gated to Corvus and joined it, and they hadn't yet filled out their numbers. She'd found the way people talked on Corvus to be similar to Almasi Kidogo, so she didn't need translation, one less thing. When Eala had joined, it had just been Tun, Fornic, and Budan, who were a caro threesome. Eala and Noanita joined at about the same time, following quickly by Putnika, and Soa joined later. There were now seven of them. Seven was a lucky number—a superstition that mysteriously popped up everywhere, even though Corvus's scientific community laughed it off.

Their hab was located in rural Caend, which was a peninsula on the Inner Sea that also held the city of Caend, Corvus's largest. Much of Corvus's surface consisted of islands and marshes and lakes and seas, very rural with habs sprinkled throughout and few cities. There were also large swathes of open shallow sea and a few deeps.

So, in the creche, in addition to Eala, there was Soa. Soa was the creche's food and nutrition expert. She was always either thinking about good things to eat or making them. She was known planet-wide as the Viral Chiral Chef for her innovations in food preparation and her cooking meshcasts. She worked with Eala and the other members of the creche on foods that had been chirally converted.

Soa had genned on Corvus and was still in her gen body—intersex-presenting, beautiful tan skin, long white braids, short and slender for a Corvite. Her accent was common to Corvus, her voice high and soft and considered. She was a little more than eleven EUs younger than Eala's 39. They'd first met when Soa joined the creche, the latest to join. They'd quickly paired up and had been confirmed caros ever since. They'd even talked about the ultimate step, marriage.

Tun's specialty was plant and Planaihra reproduction and growth, but her main job was keeping the creche organized and running smoothly. Each creche had a designated mapere who took care of the day-to-day running of the creche so that the other six could focus on their work. She'd come from a hab city orbiting Mauna Kea around AU Mic but she had chosen a Tau Ceti accent, precise and functional, for her mech body. Tun had a mech body with augments for lots of special tasks—special communications and hookups to special systems and tools for performing certain tasks. They called her the eleven-in-one because she was so efficient—and to give her a bad time.

Fornic worked on biological encoding and was deep in organic chemistry alongside Eala. She had pale skin and no hair on her head. She had grown up in the same creche as Tun but had gone to college on Mars in the Sol system. Her chosen accent was Epsilon Eridani all the way. She had lots of special augments to interface with her equipment and connect to databases and the communications network. Once, for fun, she had created a bio-encoded computer out of an *Amanita muscaria cetii*, a type of mushroom. She tended to make obscure jokes about hydrogen molecules and chemical bonds.

141

Budan's specialty was cell development and organic visualization. She was also an artist, so scattered throughout the hab were artworks of various sizes in organic shapes, some sculpture, some digital, some on canvas. She did inmesh illustrations of organic parts and processes and had a knack for communicating things concisely and clearly. She genned on Corvus, but when she chose to speak—she was shy—her accent was peculiar to the artists' creche she grew up in. She tended to use abstract art concepts as metaphors. She was in a bio body with dark tan skin and long facial features. Her frizzy turquoise hair tended to fluff around her face, and underwater it floated like seaweed. She kept it tied back in a ponytail most of the time.

Putnika specialized in the practical application of scientific principles, such as biosynthetics and special materials. She'd developed a special cloth that worked equally well in the air and under the water. It had a biological basis, and given time it was self-repairing. Its shape could be programmed with pseudo-DNA. She'd genned on Corvus but moved to a special creche for biological studies in an orbiting hab city in the 61 Cygni system. Eala wasn't sure how Putnika got anything done. She was chaos incarnate—good natured, but it was hard to get a bead on what she was thinking. She had a bio body with pale skin, long brown hair, thin but sturdy features, and the habit of wearing the wildest colors.

Noanita worked on nanomaterials that were based on the biological processes of sea creatures. No one knew where Noanita was from, but it was rumored she grew up on a space station orbiting within the gas giant Otto in the Struve Dub system. She focused mainly on the Corvus equivalent of cephalopods such as octopuses. She spent a lot of time in one or the other of her labs deep in focus, connected in to the mesh. She had a mech body with special underwater augments that allowed her to swim more efficiently. She felt most comfortable under the water. While most people spent most of their time above water and some below, she reversed that. Her bedroom was below, and she had a second underwater lab. She was also the most reclusive of the group—she was a creche of one, with the rest of them as window dressing. No one minded, though, since she was brilliant and often came up with that missing link in the data or the thought process.

Chapter 24

Where Eala grew up on Almasi Kidogo, essents weren't wealthy but they tended to be solidly middle class, and so Eala's creche university was able to help her pay for her bio body when she gated to Corvus. The transition had been fairly smooth—she had thought the much heavier gravity would be crushing, but her stronger body coupled with the warm heavy atmosphere full of odors just made her feel more solid, more substantial, like the world was embracing her. It was a couple of tendays till she got used to her new body and the transition hab released her, and once she was no longer focused on that, she was so excited she couldn't hardly contain herself.

The first time she tried out her new gills, though, was disconcerting. Not unusual, the mech nurse assistant told her. That's why they always had some training before they left the transition facility. Eala had held her breathe and almost passed out. They'd warned her not to, that her gill system would automatically kick in, but she couldn't make herself do it. That's what usually happens to offworlders, they'd said. When she was choking for lack of oxygen, her body automatically sucked the water in and oxygen bloomed again in her system, and she was a whole new person. It didn't hurt at all—she'd been anticipating that it would, but this body had been underwater before. It just felt like a different part of her anatomy took over, and she supposed it had. It wasn't her chest and diaphragm that was pulling it all in—that had shut off—it was her gills. That was weird too, not to feel her chest moving.

Her transport to the Segoa hab took four hours, and she spent the entire trip staring out the window. It never got old— to this day—to see all the vegetation just naturally growing across the surface of a planet, all that open water. There were large dirigible animals, scientific name *Calidum aerem*, floating in the air in herds. There weren't many birds, as the heavy gravity precluded easy flight, but there were gliders along the ground and a few with very large wingspans that spent their whole lives aloft. There were also clouds of small insects, for the most part benign—in some areas they were so thick they could be seen from the air. There were all kinds of plants and animals—all Corvus standard stout and sturdy. When they flew over open ocean, she'd seen large dark shapes in the water. Seek confirmed that they were the Corvus equivalent of whales. There's enough water on this planet that things can live within it, its own ecosystem, Eala had thought. That's amazing.

Corvus was made up mostly of scientific communities whose purpose was investigating Corvus, and so environmental laws were really strict. Most planet governments established such laws when they were founded—everyone remembered what happened to the environment back in the Sol system. On Corvus, there was also a religion, more of a social ritual than an actual belief system, that revered the eternal mapere, the creativity in us all. The religion and god was called Gaia.

People lit candles to her and asked for her favors when they needed good luck. When Eala had heard of it, she'd casually adopted it.

Tun, Fornic, and Budan had welcomed her with open arms. They'd been actively recruiting essents to join. Tun was a leader but a peacemaker and made sure no one strong personality overwhelmed anyone else. She quickly and quietly and creatively dealt with disagreements. Fornic had taken Eala under her wing, since they both worked in organic chemistry and chirality, and they often worked closely together. Budan had been shy, but then when she found out that Eala had fallen in love with the taktak she made a colorful holo kinetic sculpture of a taktak that lit up Eala's quarters.

Then Noanita joined, and no one knew how to take her. She was so stand-offish. But soon things settled into a new but comfortable routine. Essents learned to take her as she was. When Putnika joined, she brought chaos in her wake, but it was a good chaos, as it shook things up. For example, she'd organize an impromptu field trip to visit the Toltec Ismus volcanos, and because she was Putnika everyone would agree to go, even Noanita.

Then Soa joined, and in Eala's mind everyone else faded out. All she could see was Soa—luckily, Soa felt the same way.

Chapter 25

Eala's very first tenday at the creche, she spied two taktak playing out in the garden, and there were four or five of them sunning themselves on the back patio. She asked Fornic what they were, and Fornic explained that they were indigenous to Corvus. "They seem really smart," Fornic had said. "We've adopted this pack." She smiled and then added, "Well, actually, I think they've adopted us."

Not long after, Eala was sitting on the patio eating lunch, steamed emmer and chilies wrapped in dulse with seasoned emmer crisps, and watching Corvus's beautiful moons through the its honey atmosphere. The quality of light on Corvus was amazing. Because the atmosphere was so dense with lots of humidity, the air looked honey golden in the light and colors were muted into a warm and welcoming palette. It's like the planet is hugging you, Eala thought. Cornu, a pitted purplish gray, loomed low on the horizon, while Anel, small, a brilliant blue, was small and high in the sky. Anel was approaching and would reach perigee in less than a CoU. Weather reports were predicting some pretty major storms and high tides, as usual when the moons were in conjunction.

A taktak came up to her. This taktak was darker blue than most of them, with more silver spots along its sides. Its large eyes were peering up into her face like it was trying to talk to her, and so Eala said, conversationally, "It's so nice to meet you. I'm Eala." She patted her chest with her palm. "Who are you?" she asked, not expecting any response.

"Ooooo. Oooo?" the taktak said. Eala was surprised, since taktak rarely made sounds. When they did, their voices were full of clicks and chirrs.

"Yes, who are you?" Eala said and then caught herself. The taktak had actually tried to mimic what she was saying. Fornic said they were intelligent. She spent the rest of the afternoon in one-sided conversation. She hadn't offered the creature food, as opposite chiralities can have deadly results, but the taktak didn't seem interested—most likely, she would later realize, because taktak don't have to eat that often. It was just curious about her.

She held out her hand, which the taktak sniffed elaborately—a form of greeting, she would later discover. The taktak was the first to touch, putting its paw with its long claws on Eala's bare leg—she had been distracted looking back at the hab, and the taktak wanted her attention back. She hadn't really thought about it at that moment, this surprisingly soft and gentle touch, but then a second later she realized its importance. Then she reached out—not on the head, no one likes to be touched on the face—and the taktak put its paw onto her palm.

"Well met," Eala said and laughed, "like the palaces of Barnard."

The taktak watched her laugh, and its face crinkled and changed, which seemed to be amusement on its part. As it turned out, taktak had great senses of humor, particularly for physical comedy and practical jokes.

As the afternoon waned, the other taktak left to their lodges, saying, "Pelio-pelio-pelio." Their lodges were built along stream or lake shores either into the bank or under the heavy undergrowth. They even had rudimentary furniture and decorations and tools, something Eala discovered when she introduced Tahbi to a camera and had her take it home one day.

Her taktak glanced at them and then looked back at her and said, "Pelio-pelio-pelio?"

"Absolutely," Eala said, even though she had no idea what the taktak was saying. "See you tomorrow."

The taktak paused, looking at her, and then left in its lumping swaying gait.

That night at dinner as they gathered around the table, Eala asked Fornic, "Do the taktak speak?"

They'd ordered in blocks of vegetable protein fried crisp on the outside and but creamy and warm and luscious on the inside, which was served over taminy grits, a converted grain, and topped with a spicy chili sauce. There was an amazing berry cobbler for dessert.

"You'd think so," Fornic said. "They have more character than they have a right to." She topped off her glass from the pitcher of buji juice, a mildly alcoholic lemonade, and added, "Hey, I got another one. An oldy but a goody."

Tun rolled her eyes. She was used to her caro's jokes and pretended to groan, but she laughed. She always attended meals, but she didn't eat, as she was a mech.

Budan, their other caro, focused on Fornic with smiling anticipation.

Noanita was also a mech, and she hardly ever attended meals, but she always listened in and occasionally commented through the mesh. As always, she wasn't in the room, but over the speakers she played the jaunty musical joke "Shave and a Haircut."

"Two bits," Eala and Putnika sang under their breath.

Tun snorted.

"Let me guess," Putnika said. "The one about the pessimist, the optimist, and the chemist."

"No," Fornic said. "Just let me—"

"The one about the photon and the check-in bot," Putnika interrupted.

"No. I just—" Fornic said.

"The one about the guy frozen to absolute zero?" Putnika said.

Fornic just looked at her and waited.

Putnika looked back, a smile on her face. "Oh, did you want to tell it yourself?" Putnika said in mock innocence.

"Soooo," Fornic said. "Two chemists walk into a bar—"

Putnika started to say something, but Budan shushed her.

"—and the first one says, 'I think I'll have some H2O.'"

Oh, this is a good one, Seek said in Eala's ear.

"Then, the second one says, 'I think I'll have some H2O too,'" Fornic continued. "And then she died."

Noanita played the final two tones of "Shave and a Hair Cut" through the speakers. Tun and Budan laughed out loud. Eala shook her head and laughed.

Putnika said, "Wha … Oh."

"I knew you wouldn't get this one, Putnika," Fornic said. "It's a tough one. You see—"

"I know," Putnika said.

"—H2O2 is hydrogen peroxide—" Fornic said.

"I know," Putnika said.

"—and hydrogen peroxide is poisonous to bio bodies." Fornic said, a wide grin on her face.

"I know," Putnika said again.

Everyone busted out laughing, and Eala could sense Seek's amusement as well.

Fornic wouldn't let it go. "So, you see the essent died because the bartender thought … H2O2? Get it?" Fornic had a silly look on her face.

"I know," Putnika said, shaking her head.

Everyone busted out laughing again.

Chapter 26

The taktak, Tahbi, came back the next day, and the next, and the one after that. By that time, the taktak had introduced itself, paw on its chest just like Eala had. Eala couldn't pronounce what Tahbi called herself—some combination of a chitter that sounded like a *t*, a guttural *ah-ah-ah*, and a plosive *beee*. She settled for *Tahbi* as a close approximation.

Tahbi seemed the quickest on the uptake of all the taktak, and the most interested, and before Eala knew it, she could say words like "eat" and "swim" and "friend." She and the other taktaks called Eala *Ee-ahl*.

The taktak become her friends and then her passion, and she soon wholeheartedly adopted them as her professional project. In fact, Fornic accused her of impersonating Noanita, she was so focused on them. Eventually, she became Corvus's foremost expert.

At first, she wasn't sure what aspect of them she would study, so she just tried to figure them out, tracking their social interactions, measuring their biology with the help of Seek. She had Seek do full body scans on Tahbi and Jet and two others and analyze their structures. They had lungs and gills, a neurological system, a circulatory system, an endocrine system, a skeletal system, a musculature system, and a reproductive system, but their digestive system seemed underdeveloped. The scan showed that both females were pregnant. The taktak also had some structures that Seek had no idea their purpose.

With all this information, Eala wrote the definitive guide on the *Uktak oster* species and behavior, titled *A Backyard Guide to Taktaks*. She updated it regularly as she learned new things, and she had Seek create a meshsite of the information, with lots of infographic holos and augreals.

The group of taktaks on their back patio was all female. There were fourteen of them, including Tahbi and the taktak children. In as much as they had a leader, Tahbi was it. When asked about her children, Tahbi pointed to another adult female whose name was Suri. "Suri is Tahbi child. Now Suri is *chrr*"—a taktak word that meant a full member of the troop. "Tahbi last child is male. Name is Dirr. Dirr is grown. Dirr is Jet-chrr."

Then Tahbi asked, "Eala have child?"

Eala swallowed a quick lump that rose in her throat. "Humans do not have children like taktak. They used to, but now they create them in a laboratory, in a creche."

"Humans have *trrino*?" Tahbi said.

Eala did not know that word. "What is trrino?" she asked.

Tahbi glanced up at the moon Anel. She seemed to be formulating her thoughts. "Trrino is cause not known. Anel comes not often. Anel brings gifts from the sea. Taktak do not know how, why. Gifts from the sea is trrino."

"Something that happens but you do not know how it happens?" Eala asked.

"Yes. Cause not known," Tahbi said.

"We call that *magic*—when we don't understand why something happens. Then we try to figure out why."

"Magic. Trrino is magic. Tahbi remember."

Genning a child in lab facilities was magic, Eala mused. Something everyone took for granted, but it was something out of almost nothing. Trrino for sure.

She had long been puzzled by why the taktak rarely ate. Their energy needs far exceeded the amount of food they took in. However, the Planaihra kingdom had already been discovered in a small vole, most likely a relative of the taktak, and so she quickly realized that taktak were also Planaihra. They used photosynthesis for most of their energy needs, and that's why they were incessantly sunning. She did some research with Seek's help into energy consumption and utilization in taktak, with Tahbi's much-needed cooperation. Tahbi thought it was hilarious that Eala was interested in her poop. "Eal is dung beetle," Tahbi said, her face crinkled. She recruited all her troop and soon they were bringing Eala their feces in big piles and depositing it on the back patio. She had to ask them to stop. She got called into Tun's office for that one.

After a couple of tendays, Tahbi came to the back patio followed by a new small taktak and three others from her troop. The three spread out on the patio and lay down in the sun, making contented noises, while Tahbi and the new taktak came over to Eala.

Eala was pacing along the patio, alternately reviewing some scientific literature and following mesh rabbit holes of whatever interested her, even if it was not really relevant to what she was researching.

The new taktak was darker like Tahbi was but was longer in proportion to its width.

"Pelio-pelio-pelio," Tahbi said in greeting.

"Pelio-pelio-pelio," Eala said in return and squatted down. "How're you? Who's this?"

The new taktak was busy crawling over a patio chair, falling off, and crawling back on.

"Taktak is Tahbi-chrr-rr," Tahbi said. "Taktak is Faw."

"This is …" Eala could hear a slight variation on the word *chrr*, but she wasn't sure what it meant.

"Taktak is Tahbi child," Tahbi said.

"Oh! You've had your baby!" Eala held out her hand, and Faw came over and sniffed it clumsily, an imitation of its elders. "Will Faw be Tahbi-chrr or Jet-chrr?" Eala asked, by way of finding out Faw's gender.

"Faw is Tahbi-chrr."

"Pelio-pelio-pelio," Eala said. "That is wonderful. Congratulations, Tahbi."

Something passed between Tahbi and Faw, and Faw did the equivalent of a taktak laugh, her face scrunching, and tried to bait Tahbi into a game of tag. Tahbi played along just long enough to delight Faw and then caught her and held her down and groomed her.

Chapter 27

Once Eala was out with Tahbi so that Tahbi could point out what they usually ate. Eala had brought a drone camera to record from the air.

"What is metal animal?" Tahbi asked.

"It's called a drone. It isn't an animal, actually. I'm telling it what to do through my ccomp." As she explained it, she realized none of these words would make sense to Tahbi. She tried again. "I have a voice, a thing inside me that is connected to that metal animal and to all other humans. Its name is Seek—"

Tahbi got really excited as she understood what Eala was saying, interrupting her, hopping up and down. "Taktak inside-talk too. Taktak inside-talk other taktak." She paused and tilted her head. "Taktak not inside-talk human."

Eala had no idea what taktak inside-talk was. They certainly didn't have technology like computers. That's when she began to suspect they had some sort of telepathy. She made a mental note to add it to her list of future study topics. "That must be true, since I can't inside-talk to you," Eala said.

Eala went on to explain about ccomps and how there was a voice inside all humans that was put inside them after they genned. They could talk to any other humans on the inside—"Like taktak," Tahbi said—but also they could access important information and even see moving images as if they were in front of them but they weren't real. The images were to explain things or to entertain them. "It's like watching Jet tumble to make everyone laugh, only it's just pictures in your head that you can watch at any time. Jet doesn't have to keep doing it."

"Trrino," Tahbi said. "Magic."

Later, Eala invited Tahbi into the hab to meet Seek. "Seek's voice will come out of that speaker there." *Seek, please introduce yourself,* she subvocalized.

"Hello, Tahbi," Seek said. "I am Eala's companion computer. Her friend. Humans call me a ccomp."

As Seek was talking, Tahbi tried to located where her voice was coming from. She zeroed in on the speaker. "Not Seek have cage," Tahbi insisted, bumping it with her claws.

Could you project something so she can see you? Eala said to Seek. She had never asked Seek to project herself before, and so she was curious as to what Seek would choose.

Immediately, a holo of a taktak appeared in the middle of the room. It was a unique taktak, one that Eala had never seen before. It was mostly turquoise with spots that were darker than usual, its snout was longer than some. Interesting choice, Eala thought. She'd expected her to appear human.

Tahbi let out a low *r-r-r-r* of disbelief. "Seek is taktak?" Tahbi asked as she went over to the holo and tried sniff it, as a taktak would do in greeting. When the holo didn't smell of anything, Tahbi tried to touch it, and her paw went right through. She jumped back.

"No, Seek is not taktak, but she can appear to be anything you would like her to be. She is a holo, not real," Eala said. *Change to human*, Eala said to Seek.

Seek said over the speaker, "Yes, I am just an image. I can change to be whatever you'd like." She shifted her image from taktak to human very slowly, letting it morph. It was also a body Eala had never seen before. Very stocky but average height. A pale yellow-tan skin. Straight black hair. A pleasant broad face with expressive eyebrows. Big webbed hands and feet.

Tahbi paid very close attention. "Seek okay?" she said.

"Yes, I'm fine, Tahbi," Seek said. She said Tahbi's name like Tahbi would have, not like a human.

"Seek is anything?" Tahbi said, looking at Eala.

"Yeah, I think she can," Eala said.

"Seek, is sunsnake," Tahbi ordered, hopping in excitement.

Seek morphed the image, a little more quickly this time, into the tiny species of snake.

"Tonton tree," Tahbi said, and Seek obliged, expanding into the large stout prickly tree.

They continued the game, with Tahbi saying a species and Seek transforming more and more quickly.

"E-ahl," Tahbi said, and Seek did not hesitate to project a holo of Eala's body. Tahbi walked around it, looking from all angles, and Eala followed her. My hair looks weird from the back, Eala thought.

Then Tahbi said, "Tahbi," and sat back on her heels.

"Are you sure?" Seek said. "This would not be you. This would be me but in a shape that looks like you."

"Yes," Tahbi said, watching closely.

158

Seek slowly transformed from Eala to Tahbi. It was an exact replica, of course, only sparkling and luminescent in the way holos were.

"Seek move?" Tahbi said.

Seek, from the speaker, mimicked in Tahbi's voice, "Seek move?" just as the holo moved exactly like Tahbi had, down to the flick of the tail flap and one paw on the other arm.

"Seek know taktak," Tahbi said excitedly, once again circling the image.

"I don't know taktak," Seek said, "but I'm learning."

"Seek inside-talk?" Tahbi said and then paused, concentrating.

After a second, Seek said, "No. I'm sorry, Tahbi. I cannot inside-talk."

"Like human," Tahbi said.

Later, after Tahbi had left, Seek told Eala, "I think I actually did sense something. When Tahbi did her inside-talk, there was something."

"Like what?" Eala said.

"It was, well, on a similar spectrum as mechalum comms. It was faint, but a little like a comm from another planet."

Now that was weird.

Eala wrote and published a scientific paper in the prestigious interplanetary journal *Exobiology* titled "The Energy Pathways of *Uktak oster*: Conversion Efficiencies in a Planaihra Species." Everyone in the creche was very proud. Only Noanita had published in such an important place. Of course, Noanita had published three papers in the same amount of time, papers that most people couldn't even understand.

Once Eala had a handle on taktak biology and social structure and then their relationship to Planaihra, she wasn't sure where she would take her research. One day, she was distracted while eating her lunch, and Tahbi decided to take a taste and then eat the whole thing.

"Oh my Nuc, Tahbi!" Eala said. "Are you all right? Why did you do that?"

"Tahbi hungry," Tahbi said with the taktak equivalent of a shrug.

Eala was horrified, afraid she had killed her, but it caused no distress whatsoever, even though the food was of Sol chirality. That was when Eala discovered that taktak could eat both chiralities. This had huge implications. She had Seek do extensive research, and the phenomenon had never been reported in over 300 worlds. So that was what she was now studying. If that mechanism could be pinned down and replicated, humans could adapt to Corvus even better. This was a career-making development, one this could change humanity on Corvus, possibly on other worlds as well.

Chapter 28

The first time Eala saw Soa, she was a holo. Soa's screen presence and quiet confidence had made Eala feel like they were long-lost friends, like she wanted to sit on the deck of a sea-front bar in Caend with Soa and eat buttered crab legs, drink margaritas, and watch Medupe's Star set.

Eala had been with the creche for a little more than a year, and Putnika had called everyone together, loudly sucking on her favorite candy, a lollipop flavored with beeriroot.

Eala still didn't know how to take Putnika. Eala was exasperated by her lack of organization and her enthusiasms that seemed to possess her and take over her life until the next one came along. She would have chalked it up to youth, but Putnika was older than she was. Half the time she wanted to strangle her—she could only imagine what Tun felt—and the other half she wanted to hug her wildly and join her in her joy.

They were in the central hab space. Putnika had spread out on the couch, limbs flopped everywhere. Tun, Fornic, and Budan came in together and stood off to one side. Tun's mech arms were crossed across her chest as she stood there. Fornic had a skeptical look on her face, and Budan looked thoughtful. Eala sat on a stool on the other side.

Noanita was not there.

"Noanita?" Putnika yelled at the ceiling. "You'll want to be here for this. Either that or I'm sending a squad of cuddlefish into your lab." Cuddlefish did not know the meaning of personal space.

"Fuck you," Noanita said, her way of acknowledging she was tuning in.

Putnika brought up a holo meshcast in the middle of the room. It was a cooking show.

I know this one, Seek said. *It's good.*

"Why again are we watching this?" Fornic said.

"Because I said so," Putnika said.

"Aaah," Fornic said, shaking her head.

Just watch, Putnika said, her voice the opposite of defeated.

It was Soa in the Viral Chiral Chef. The episode was called, "Getting Salty." It started with a jaunty musical intro and then transitioned to Soa looking out toward her viewers, dressed in neatly tailored sleeveless shirt and her beautiful pale hair done up in elaborate braids. Her well-ordered kitchen looked like a cross between a rustic chef's workspace and a laboratory, the whisks and rolling pins intermingled with scanners and lab tools.

Eala's first thought was that she was young and attractive but with just enough age to give her gravity.

"Today we're talking salt," Soa said with a smile. "Specifically sodium chloride, not copper sulfate or cobalt nitrate or those others. The one that is necessary for a bio body to absorb and transport nutrients, to maintain blood pressure and fluid balance, to transmit nerve signals, to use muscles. It's a vital part of physical movement, along with potassium, calcium, magnesium, phosphate, and other electrolytes."

The holo flashed forward for a closeup of Soa's face, so it looked like her head took over the middle of the room. "The one ... NECESSARY FOR LIFE," she said theatrically as an overly dramatic but comical musical phrase played in the background.

A little over the top, Eala thought, but charming.

The view shifted back out. Soa continued, lifting a bowl full of white crystals, "You may think of it—or may not think of it at all—as that stuff that makes food taste wonderful but that your medcomp warned you against. Especially with fried foods." Soa got a look of pure desire on her face, and Eala felt her mouth water in sympathy. "Crunchy salty emmer chips, vegcheesy puffs, buffalo fried cauliflower, chili poppers, onion rings, lechon kawali, General Tso's shrimp." Soa paused to roll her eyes. "What these all have in common is loads of salt. Tons of salt. Salty goodness."

She put the salt down on the counter, took a pinch, and let it fall through her fingers back into the bowl, tilting her head to watch.

"What you may not know is that salt is important for other reasons. Not just health. Not just because it makes food luscious. It does so much more." She began ticking off on her fingers, "It seasons things, sure, but it also preserves them. Throughout our history, we've used salt when we didn't have the tech to keep things cold or to preserve them in other ways. Jerky and saltfish and pickled vegetables. You may not know this but it's also a binding agent. When you use it in sausages or other processed meats it helps extract the myofibrillar

163

proteins to coax the macerated muscle together and form stable emulsions. In fact, it brings out the texture in all foods—breads and cheese." Soa spread her fingers and made an upward grasping motion. "And believe it or not, color plays an important part in enjoying food. Think about how unappetizing an all-white meal is. Salt brings out colors. In a more sciency bent, it controls natural processes like fermentation and yeast growth, reins it in. In other words, it helps your bread rise but not take over the kitchen, your beer to be carbonated but not explode like a foamy star."

"This is fascinating," Tun said flatly, "but why are we watching it?"

It was fascinating, Eala thought. Who knew?

Putnika waved her hand and said, "Shshshsh. We're getting to my favorite part."

Soa opened her arms to a space on the table next to her, and a holo within the holo appeared. It was a colorful 3D of two molecules, each atom a funny face holding hands with the adjacent atom. The two were mirror images.

"Now we're getting to the part I call, 'Crusades in Chirality.'" A dramatic music riff played. "You knew it was coming," Soa said with a knowing smile. "What you didn't know but should have—since I've been talking about it ad nauseum since forever—is that our understanding of and influence on chirality is deeply influenced by salts, not just sodium chloride."

In the holo on the table, the two molecules squished together and turned purple, morphing into a bunch of grapes. "You may remember that many molecules have two forms called enantiomers, a left-handed version and a right-handed version. This is their chirality—and the reason why Corvus almost KILLED US ALL." Again, dramatic music, and the background flashed dramatic cartoonish colors. "What you won't remember—because I haven't told you and it's not your specialty and you can't possibly know everything—is that a mix of equal amounts of enantiomers is called a racemic mixture, or a racemate. This goes back to ancient times and racemic acid, or tartaric acid, which is—DUN, DUN, DUH!!!—grapes." Soa smiled into the camera. The grape cartoon clapped its hands and cheered. "You guessed it. It all goes back to food, once again." She raised an eyebrow. "As it should."

Putnika looked up at them and laughed. She spread her hands wide and said, "DUN, DUN, DUH!!!"

"Okay, okay," Tun said. "Shut it off."

Putnika paused it. Soa was about to say something, and her holo froze with its eyes wide, a smile playing on her lips, her arms at the beginning of a dramatic gesture. Putnika turned and rested her head on the back of the couch, looking from one face to another.

Eala wanted to protest. She really like the show and wanted to know where it was going. It had kicked off her science brain. What did it mean that you could have a mixture of equal parts of enantiomers. We can eat some but not others, right? And they had different effects, depending on their handedness. Weren't some drugs just one of the chiralities? Not only that, but Soa was the most beautiful creature she'd ever seen. When she laughed, her eyes crinkled at the corners that hinted at both sunshine and youthful health and vitality but also no-nonsense

165

age and wisdom. It brought up a yearning for Eala's younger days and for her future.

"What did you think?" Putnika said.

Fornic shrugged. Budan said she liked it. Tun didn't say anything.

"That's interesting," Eala said. "It makes me wonder if an effect I was seeing with the purpots wasn't somehow related to chirality. I—"

"There is a point?" Noanita interrupted through the speakers.

Here we go, Seek said in Eala's head.

"Of course there's a point," Putnika said, jumping up to standing and holding her hands wide. "She's applying to be a member of our creche! Isn't that cool?!"

Eala's first thought was there was no way someone that well known and that cool would want to be part of their little group. Her second thought was less of a thought and more of a jump in her chest where her pulse went through the roof.

"I haven't gotten an application," Tun said.

"You will," Putnika insisted. "My ccomp was gossiping with the hab comp back home, and it knows the ccomp of the producer of the Viral Chiral Chef, and ..." Putnika's voice continued on a long detour about who talked to who about what. The upshot was that Soa was tired of the limelight and looking for a quiet out-of-way place to deemphasize her fame and work more on her science. "Plus, rumor has it she just broke up with that asshole Bres who's been cheating on her with that pop star Angelera, who ..." Putnika continued on her winding way.

Tun held up her hand and Putnika's voice wandered to a stop. "My ccomp informs me that that's correct," Tun said. "We just received the application within the hour."

Eala felt herself blush. She was glad her skin was so dark so no one could tell—she hoped.

Chapter 29

When they'd put it to a vote, Putnika and Eala had been in favor of bringing Soa in and Fornic and Budan had been against it. Budan tended to go with whatever Fornic thought, and Fornic thought that Soa would be a distraction. "She's celebrity fluff," was Fornic's comment. "We need the spot for serious scientific muscle."

Noanita had abstained, as she always did when it came to personnel matters. "You all fight it out amongst yourselves," she said.

So it came down to Tun. Eala quickly resigned herself. Tun had seemed critical of Soa. And Eala had liked Soa so much, she couldn't think about it too much. Much to her surprise, though, Tun voted to include Soa.

"Why the hell would you do that?" Fornic had said. "You're the sensible one."

"She's a good chef, despite being famous," Tun said. "And I watched some more of her meshcasts. She's a good scientist too. Did you know she was the one who deduced a key concept in chirally converting a whole class of vegcheeses? She probably smarter than the two of us put together."

"Except Noanita," Budan added, the rest of them saying it under their breath and smiling.

"Not only that," Tun said, "but I need some help with the upkeep around here. You science types are a finicky bunch."

"You're a science type too," Eala said to Tun.

Tun just smiled.

In the tenday leading up to Soa's appearance, Eala watched a bunch of her meshcasts too. She would later realize that that was when she'd fallen in love with her. The meshcasts were fun and entertaining, and you could just take them at face value as a cooking show with a bit of science spice. But what set them apart was the shimmering intelligence and the clarity of the science undergirding it. Soa explained complex ideas so clearly and easily that the audience was fooled into thinking that they were easy concepts. She didn't dumb them down—she just related them in a way that made sense.

And then she was there. Eala was in her lab with her head down, concentrating on some calculations, when she felt someone walk in. Without turning, she'd said, "Sorry, Putnika. I'm sure it's fascinating but math and bullshit don't mix." At breakfast, Putnika had played devil's advocate about the applicability of the supernatural to leading-edge mathematics.

"I'm sure that's true" came a voice that Eala was familiar with but couldn't quite place.

I know your pulse races every time you see a holo of her, so don't be shocked when you turn around and it's really her, Seek said. *Soa oi Segoa,* it added, just to kid her about Soa being part of the creche now.

Eala pushed up a little too fast and turned and faced Soa, who stood there looking around. She was wearing a one-piece

169

gauzy flowing summer dress that came down to her knees, pale and complementing and contrasting her beautiful tan skin and pale hair.

"Nice place," Soa said.

"It is" was all Eala could come up with.

"I'm Soa," Soa said. "What you working on?"

"I …" Eala was speechless. She looked down and shook her head. *Ask me when I'm not … scattered.* She subbed, shrugging, and then added, "When I won't sound like an idiot."

"Do you normally sound like an idiot?" Soa asked, her eyebrow and the corner of her mouth quirked.

"Only around essents who turn my nerve into Morava jellyfish," Eala said.

She hadn't meant to be quite that abrupt about it, but it had made Soa laugh out loud for quite some time. "I can't get the image out of my mind of you, blue and purple see-through, with all these funky tentacles coming out of your body. Have you ever seen them move? Most jellyfish are graceful, but they look like they're having a seizure, knocking into each other."

"Yeah," Eala said smiling. She had. They were pretty comical.

Soa walked over and glanced at the math Eala had been scribbling on the handheld. "They're not poisonous, though, like some people say," Soa said. "Surprisingly crunchy. They can be pretty good, if you dry them out and then desalt them when you reconstitute them. Bland though. They tend to get overwhelmed by other flavors."

"I haven't tried them," Eala said.

She realized she was just standing there, and she was about to offer to give Soa a tour when Soa said, pointing at the scribbles on her handheld, "Your determinant is wrong. I think you missed a term."

This made Eala burst out laughing. "Way to go, way to not make me feel like an idiot," she said between gasps.

Soa burst out laughing too. "Welcome to my life," Soa said. "I usually feel like the idiot."

And the rest was history. They were fast friends and then quickly became caros. Eala thanked her lucky stars daily.

Chapter 30

One day, Tahbi swam up to Eala very upset—more upset than she had ever seen her.

Eala and Soa were taking a swimwalk in the undersea, their last chance before a series of storms were predicted. A hurricane was forming over the deep ocean due to unusually warm surface waters and Anel's proximity, and there was predicted to be some wicked storm surges due to conjunction tides, along with spring tides and Cornu passing through the equatorial plane.

Tun was a flurry of activity, getting ready for it. Perfect conditions for the perfect storm, she kept saying. Time to be perfectly prepared. In a given CoU, Corvus spun up a number of hurricanes—so everyone was prepared, and habs were automatically weather-proofed with storm shutters and backup generators—but this one was predicted to even worse than normal.

Eala loved going for undersea walks. She loved watching the plants sway in the current and the fish dart between reeds. The most common colors on Corvus were blue and turquoise and silver, but undersea tended to have more colors—red and orange fish, yellow and turquoise plants. Schools of bright blue and yellow eel fish would brush past, and the underwater cousins of the dirigible animals, pale pink and peach, would float by in slow-moving pods. The colors were muted by the blue filtering of the water above, but they were also enhanced by the patterns of light that played in squiggles along the bottom. Depending on the day, Gaia's Rays would flood down and illuminate everything. The water in the distance was a deep blue, and the water above was a beautiful silver undulating rooftop. Eala never got tired of it.

Eala, Tahbi, and Soa swam up to the surface to talk and crawled up onto a kelp bed. This type of kelp formed sturdy floating platforms that became moving coral reefs, harboring all kinds of life above and below the water. A swarm of tiny insects rose and flew off as they pulled themselves onto the kelp bed.

"What's wrong?" Eala asked, sitting cross legged and swaying as the kelp bed rocked. She leaned forward toward Tahbi.

Soa was only half paying attention, kicking her feet in the water.

"Future is Gathering," Tahbi said, hopping slightly on her front paws.

"What is the Gathering?" Eala asked.

Tahbi thought for a minute and then asked, "Word for taktak lost? For human lost? Return? Cause *brrl*."

"What is brrl?"

"When taktak fight taktak." Tahbi made the sign for many. The taktak indicated numbers and quantity with paw gestures.

"You mean war? When groups of taktak fight other groups of taktak?"

"Yes. War. Tahbi remember."

Eala said the only word that came to mind, "Prodigal. When someone returns who's been away, and it causes war, we say that that person is a prodigal."

Tahbi gestured to the moon Anel and said, "Prodigal."

Cornu was a waxing gibbous low in the sky, one third of it dark, while Anel, slightly more illuminated—as it was farther out—rested directly above Cornu. Anel was almost at perigee, and the two moons were in conjunction.

"When it returns, it causes war?" Eala said.

"Yes," Tahbi said. [Many] "taktak travel Gathering. Taktak have gift from the sea." [Many] "important. Last Gathering, not gift from the sea." [Many] "bad. Taktak brrl."

Eala wondered what the gift from the sea was.

Tahbi continued, "Tahbi-chrr and Jet-chrr travel." [Few] "days. Kin-chrr and Lori-chrr between Tahbi-chrr and Jet-chrr and Gathering. Brrl." [Many] "brrl." [Many] "Kin-chrr and Lori-chrr."

"You have to go to the gathering, but there's lots of other taktak on the way who will make brrl?"

"Yes." [Seventeen] "Tahbi-chrr and Jet-chrr vote not travel. Not gift from the sea. Not future."

"We can fly you there, Tahbi," Eala said. "We can pick you up in big metal animal and set you down right where the Gathering is. No war, no brrl."

Tahbi seemed to consider it, but then she said, "Not. Travel."

"Humans could go with you. We could—"

"Not," Tahbi interrupted. "Not not."

"But—" Eala began.

"Not not," Tahbi insisted.

"Well, we could give you weapons. Military superiority. They would not attack anymore if they knew you would win."

"What is weapon? Military sup ..." She tried to pronounce it but then gave up. "What is?"

"They are technology that can hurt or kill other taktak, and then there is no war because no one wants to get hurt."

Tahbi's eyes got really wide and then she quickly hopped away, the kelp undulating, and turned her back to Eala. Then she came back quickly. "Why weapons?" she said. "Humans have weapons? Why?" She was very agitated.

"How does brrl work with taktak?" Eala said. "Humans use weapons in brrl."

"Not hurt," Tahbi insisted. "Not hurt." [Many] "Kin-chrr and Lori-chrr inside-talk. Kin-chrr and Lori chrr freeze Tahbi-chrr and Jet-chrr. Take children. Take chrr. Chrr is Kin-chrr and Lori-chrr."

"Well, I don't know, Tahbi. What do you need? What would help?"

Tahbi got what could only be described as a devious look on her face. "Seek," she said. "Seek travel."

I am willing, Seek subvocalized.

"Well, I guess. I can see if it's possible. What would that do?"

"Trrino," Tahbi said. "Tahbi-chrr and Jet-chrr new trrino. Magic."

The old smoke and mirrors trick, Eala thought, laughing to herself.

Is it possible? Eala asked Seek. *Can you holo the whole way across land to wherever this is?*

It is not only theoretically possible but statistically probable, Seek said. *Just as I can always speak to you, I can most likely project a holo.* There was a pause. *But, now, with the storms coming in, it could cause interference. It might be best if Tahbi wore a locating beacon.*

Since they were outside, Seek couldn't talk directly to Tahbi without using Eala's speakers. They'd agreed this would be confusing to the taktak. But Tahbi understood that Eala could talk to Seek.

"Seek says she thinks it's possible," Eala said. "Could you wear a beacon, a device so that Seek could always find you?"

Tahbi didn't say anything for a minute. Then she said, "Gift from the sea. Not human. Not gift from the sea." She looked at Eala. "Seek come?"

"Yes, but there's a small chance she will lose sight of you and then she can't project her holo, her image. She would disappear for a while."

Tahbi thought some more. "Not not human," she finally said, solemnly shaking her head in imitation of Eala.

"Let's hope the storms don't get in the way of Seek's sight," Eala said.

"Yes," Tahbi said. "Storm is gift from the sea."

"When do you have to travel?"

[Few] "days," Tahbi said. She turned to leave, saying over her shoulder, "Pelio-pelio-pelio."

Eala replied, "Pelio-pelio-pelio."

Chapter 31

You know, Seek said once Tahbi had left, *you can be me.*

What? Eala said.

You can take this trip too. You can go inmesh and be the holo that is me. I'll be there too, but you can be the one who controls it, with me making it so, and you can sense what I sense.

No shit? Wow. Eala had never heard of this. It sounded amazing.

Ccomps don't usually offer, as they consider this part of their being private.

And you're offering this to me? Are you sure?

Without hesitation, Seek said, *Yes.*

Eala knew that Seek could feel her gratitude.

Tun stopped her mech-scurrying long enough to requisition special mesh equipment that would sustain Eala's body while Eala was inmesh. Essents on Corvus, as scientists, tended to be so focused on the outside world that few lived inmesh.

It was so weird, the first time Eala lay down on the mesh couch and transitioned into a holo of a taktak that Seek created. She obviously wasn't feeling what a holo felt—she was feeling what Seek sensed in the physical space that that holo would take up, modulated by Seek's understanding of what a taktak could sense. But, Nuc, it felt real.

Smells were intense and layered and nuanced, and they held so much more information—the age of the scent, all the characteristics of where it came from, and so much more. She got whole life histories in a sniff. Hearing was more acute, although it was sensed as a cross between hearing and touch across the shoulders. The first time another taktak said, "Pelio-pelio-pelio," it rippled pleasurably down her spine and throughout her body to her toes in a way nothing else ever had. The ear mane allowed for better hearing and more accurate pinpointing of location, possibly even echolocation—which was good, because taktak sight sucked. It was largely monochrome and blurry. There was also something else that tickled her brain, another sense deep in her skull, but Eala could never make any meaning out of it.

In her own body she felt fairly stable and confident, but a taktak body felt even more solid and stable—which was weird, since it was a holo. The taktak's four-point stance felt sturdy in a way that human bipedal stance did not, and motion was very grounded. And then, the first time that taktak Eala went underwater, everything changed. The taktak body was made for swimming, and Eala moved smoothly and quickly and luxuriously through the medium as easily as she breathed. There was such joy in it—she did barrel rolls and backflips and skimmed back and forth through the undersea bushes. The water across her nonexistent skin felt embracing and luxurious and tugged at her nonexistent ear mane.

If she focused really hard, Eala could sense her real body lying in the crash couch, but it was like she had to imagine it and bring it forth—less real than a dream.

And now she knew why ccomps didn't allow humans in in this way. If she tried, she could also sense Seek but in a whole new way. She was used to knowing Seek was there and being able to call on her at any time, but when she didn't need her she totally ignored her. She took her ccomp for granted like everyone did. Sure, maybe not quite as much but still, mostly.

Now, though, it was as if she were the ccomp and Seek were the person. If she focused hard on it, she could inhabit Seek's "body"—which was busy inhabiting her body. How weird.

Eala explored Seek's body. It started in her own body, but as a second structure, and thin pervasive internal network. She could feel her own toes but through layers of consciousness. She felt herself feeling Seek feeling herself feel her own toes. You could get lost in this, she thought. She, Eala, had an itch on her right arm, and as soon as she felt it she felt her desire to scratch it and at the same instant Seek's desire to help her help herself. Seek sent a nerve soother that made the itch go away. It was instantaneous.

But then there was more. The network extended outside her body. She could sense the electromag in the room and all the signals coming in and going out. She focused on one and found she could interpret it. It was a weather forecast coming from the weather bureau saying that Hurricane Ida—they'd named it?—was predicted to be massive. Everyone should prepare for landfall in two days.

Seek was hooked into the hab, too, and Eala could see that Seek could see that Tun had the hab computer analyzing worst-case storm scenarios. Flags were set to go off if the hab was damaged, and Tun had requisitioned a backup generator for the backup generator, which was due to arrive the next day. Eala could imagine Tun fretting about it being late. Tun was in the room with Eala overseeing the test run, and she could see her with the room's sensors, layers of images and heat and chemicals and probability forecasts.

Fornic and Budan were making love in Budan's room. Noanita was in her undersea lab testing a body attachment of some kind. Putnika was dancing to electronica in the common area with a huge comp-generated psychedelic lizard. Four taktak were sunning on the back porch. She could even sense the roots of the grass and one large tree root that was pushing ever so slightly, ever so steadily, against the foundations of the hab.

Eala turned back to Seek. Seek's data storage and message queue were huge and were continually being processed. It was all sorted meticulously, first by priority and then by category. Everything was cross referenced and cataloged so that it could be accessed from many different angles. Eala glanced at Seek's message queue and focused on what was marked in-network. It was weird because these were not in-network computers. They were from all over but mostly on-planet according to location data. Some were system comps, some were hab comps, some were security comps, but most were ccomps. She was about to say something to Seek, to raise security concerns, but then she realized. This was Seek's friends list, and the messages coming in were mostly personal in nature in a computer sort of way.

Eala turned to Seek's center, trying to sense her self. It took some concentration, but she could feel Seek's emotions start to manifest themselves in her own body. Anticipation in the legs, excitement in the stomach, dread in the heavy arms, affection on the face, eagerness to please in the toes, embarrassment in the shoulders. Then anger in the back, anger flaring, lots of anger. What? What was that?

Then Eala realized that, while Seek was used to seeing all these things in humans, she was not used to having her own emotions exposed. She had no face to hide but like this her emotions were a billboard. Eala quickly withdrew to the taktak sim.

I'm sorry, Seek! Eala said. *I didn't realize. That's why ...*

I'd prefer if you ... Seek said and trailed off.

Yes, yes, Eala said. *I'm sorry!*

It's just ... Seek said.

I know. I can tell, Eala said. *I'm sorry. I won't do it again.*

Eala could feel Seek's relief.

When Tahbi saw her for the first time as a taktak, she came up and sniffed her intimately and elaborately. "Not," Tahbi said, disappointed. Eala imagined it was a little like meeting a computer mech without a faceplate for the first time—you couldn't read any emotion, and they wore no decoration to indicate status or age. You got no context, just like the lack of smell on a holo for a taktak.

The sniffing felt so good, though. Eala could feel the light wisp of air across her skin and hear the nuances of the sniffing noise clearly. She returned the gesture clumsily but as faithfully as she could. She could tell that Tahbi's menses was a couple of tendays away and that Tahbi was just getting over a slight sickness, the taktak equivalent of a cold. Tahbi was feeling stressed and smelled of fear hormones, but she had just been snuggling with Faw to comfort herself and Faw. Because of all the activity Tahbi had eaten a small crayfish and some grasses to boost her energy and calm her stomach. She had also peed just before the meeting. I bet there are things Tahbi knows by smell about my human self that I don't even know, Eala thought.

Tahbi held still for a moment and focused on Eala. *There's something*, Seek said to Eala, *something there that I can't ...* All Eala felt was a tingle in the back of her skull.

Then Tahbi sat back and said, "Seek. Pelio-pelio-pelio."

Eala and Seek had agreed it was probably best if Tahbi thought of this holo as Seek.

Eala answered, trying to fit the words into this new mouth, "Tahbi. Pelio-pelio-pelio." To her surprise, it came easily, and she even pronounced Tahbi's name the way Tahbi would.

"Good," Tahbi said.

The day they were to set off, the others in the creche wished Eala some form of "Gaia has her eye on you" at breakfast. It was meant for good luck, but it was also a double entendre. Gaia may have plans other than your welfare—that was the implication.

At the appointed time, Eala lay down in the crash couch, Soa standing beside her.

I'm not really going anywhere, Eala said and laughed as Soa leaned down to kiss her.

Aah, but you are. Something tells me you won't be the same person when you come back. Science is a harsh mistress, as they say.

This is isn't science. This is ... Eala wasn't sure what it was.

Okay, curiosity is a fucking bitch, Soa said with a smile. *How's that?* She leaned over and kissed her again. She stepped back and watched her with worried eyes as Tun checked final prep.

You be safe too, Eala said to Soa.

"Seek meet Tahbi-chrr," Tahbi said as she greeted holo Seek-Eala outside the hab.

"Do they know?" Eala said. "I don't want to scare them."

"Tahbi-chrr know. Seek is fake real. Not smell, not inside-talk, not solid."

And so Eala followed Tahbi, marveling at the way the world felt with her new senses, and then they went out around the back garden and down a narrow gully under the greenery and entered the water of a small canal. She was bathed in smells and sounds she'd never sensed. It was intense. *Whoa, there, cowboy,* Seek said at one point when Eala tried to bury her face in some sort of excrement for more information. In the canal, Tahbi experienced water in a whole new way, reveling in it. Tahbi watched, amused, though still stressed enough not to participate. Then they swam lazily down the canal to the Tahbi-chrr burrows.

The den was quiet and purposeful, as everyone was getting ready for their journey. Many were out sunning, storing up energy. Some were burrow cleaning.

In addition to Tahbi and her kit Faw, there was Suri, Tahbi's adult child, and Suri's kit Hss. There was Min, a close friend of Tahbi's, who had twin kits. There was a big quiet taktak named Binr who had no kits. There were two grandmother taktak—Sisi, who was very old and wise, and Torn, who was old but still strong. There were five more taktak mothers, teenagers, and older children.

All the females came up and courteously sniffed Eala's holo. Most of them turned away with puzzled looks on their faces. Eala made a show of sniffing each as deliberately and courteously as she could. As she sniffed, she gleaned mood and status and health and much more. She knew the group's history and their worries and hopes. She felt a part of them like she never had.

I've got to conduct my science this way, she thought and unconsciously subvocalized to Seek. *This is an amazing tool. Could we make an augreal like this? Call it a takreal? Replicate the experience? Gather the data, store it, and then replicate it in the mesh, so you experience the world like a—*

Don't get ahead of yourself, Seek said. *Put the scientist away for a while.*

Right before they left, they met up with Jet's group, who repeated the ritual, again with puzzled looks.

In addition to Jet, there was Gor, his second in command. There was big Ty, who kept things in order, and the mystic Picpic, who Tahbi said knew many *trrino*. Teenagers included helpful Dirr, Tahbi's offspring, and Wen, who was a troublemaker, and Ren, who was small and quick. There was Chit, who looked after the four younger boys, as well as five more adult males, including a very old male named Rrr.

Chapter 32

The sky was turquoise blue and Medupe's Star, Corvus's sun, shone brightly, leading Cornu and Anel across the sky. The slight breeze was pleasant but deceptive.

Tun had warned Eala about what was to come. Over the next couple three days, it would go from pleasant to more and more wind and rain until the wind would rip trees from the ground and toss them around like child's toys. The rain would come so hard, it would be as if the seas had been sucked from their basins and churned into the air. You couldn't walk outside, it would get so strong. Humans were safe in habs—the structures had been built for this. As a low-to-the-ground taktak and as a holo, Eala didn't have much to worry about—she would be able to feel it, but the trees and wind would go right through her. But the taktaks around her could be crushed.

"Your body will be safe here in the hab, provided the power stays up—we've got generators," Tun said. "Not a good time to be inmesh and virtually out in the storm, but you'll have it better than your traveling companions." *But anyone with any sense would be in the fortified hab*, she added darkly.

I will be, Eala subbed back with a grin. *Technically.*

Eala briefly wondered why the gift from the sea came now. Inconvenient. Unscientific. Just like a so-called miracle to come only when the shit's hit the fan. Or maybe the shit hit the fan because of the so-called miracle. It's hard to tell cause and effect sometimes, and it's best not to assume. But then the scientist in her insisted on connecting the two. She couldn't see how, though. Bookmark for later.

And so the taktak left on their journey. The elders Sisi and Rrr said it would take at least a couple days to reach the Gathering place at the seaside.

They were expecting trouble. Thirty-two taktak traveling in a group was unwieldy. The old taktak Torn warned them not to get too spread out, and so Min took it upon herself to keep everyone bunched up, no stragglers. The big female Binr went on ahead to keep an eye on what was coming. Jet's second Gor trailed behind to keep an eye behind them. The big male Ty roamed up and down the long column watching both sides. The teenagers Dirr and Wen appointed themselves as watchman as well. The mystic Picpic had a worried look on his face. He said that the word from the other chrr was not good, that Kin-chrr and Lori-chrr had singled them out for takeover.

The smells and sounds were almost too overwhelming. Eala tried to balance sensing and sorting with not getting overloaded. It was exhausting. Who knew that a spiro tree smelled subtly of the flowers that Soa used to make soap?

Eala knew what everyone was saying with their inside-talk thanks to Suri, who had appointed herself interpreter for Seek-Eala, for which Eala was really grateful. Most of the taktak had not learned to talk to her, and they weren't in the habit of saying things out loud. Eala kept saying *srra-srra* after everything, the taktak word for thankful. Suri seemed pleased.

"Why?" Eala asked Picpic through Suri, when they stopped for a break in sunny meadow. "Why do they take others over?"

Picpic, Eala discovered, had an unnerving habit of not answering for a while and staring. Eala tried not to react. *He's trying to read you, I think*, Seek said. Eala waited.

Suri was quiet for a bit, her shoulders cocked in the way that indicated listening, and then said, "No gift from the sea before. Jin-chrr and Felti-chrr, before Kin-chrr and Lori-chrr. Jin-chrr and Felti-chrr bad. Inside bad. Sick. Not child. Jin-chrr and Felti-chrr take chrr. Kin-chrr and Lori-chrr take chrr."

"I see," said Eala. "They were afraid so they tried to make everything right by having more taktak in their chrr."

"Yes," Suri said. "Take-chrr not happy, not not happy. Chrr not chrr. *Awni*. Kin-chrr and Lori-chrr take-chrr *awni*."

"What is *awni*?" Eala tried to ask, but then Jet urged them on.

The first day, they moved through a thick forest of stump trees and grasses and prickly underbrush interspersed with waterways. Where they could, they took to the water and swam, but it often took them far out of their way. The smells changed subtly, taking on their own textures, and Eala found herself wondering what all the tiny sounds were. Were they bugs? How far off were they? She wanted to investigate.

It was a long zigzag path, and the more tired Eala got, the more she wished for a transport. *I'm soft*, she thought.

No more than the average biot, Seek said helpfully.

Thanks for that, Eala said.

Seek sent the comp equivalent of a chuckle.

Clouds were roiling up to the east over the sea and would soon move to block the sun, so they stopped about an hour before sunset so that everyone could catch some rays. *A dinner of sunshine*, Seek commented. Dirr and Wen reported that they had caught a pretty strong indication of outsiders that Min had identified as Kin-chrr and Lori-chrr. Binr's expression confirmed it.

They spent the night under low-growing banner bushes, which naturally grew thick horizontal mats of tendrils that left pretty good shelter underneath, just right for taktak. They gathered in a clearing but made their beds snuggled in piles under the banner bushes, Seek-Eala laying at their fringe.

As night fell, the wind picked up, creaking and rattling the spiro trees on the nearby hill and blowing in the scent of rain. Some of the kits mewed in fright. Chit decided to tell a story to help everyone forget the storm that was coming and what might happen the next day. It was told with inside-talk, so all Eala saw was that all the taktak seemed to relax and settle in, and a number of them sat watching Chit. Chit's body expressions changed as he talked, subtle physical communications as he made gestures for emphasis and to indicate number. It was Tahbi who told Eala the story.

"Chit tells Great Change. Tahbi like," Tahbi said.

"You've heard it before?" Eala asked.

"Big story. Good story. Taktak like."

I wonder if it's their creation myth? Seek said. Turns out, it was a different kind of creation.

This is story that Chit told.

Great Change long ago. Taktak had child, had child, had child, had child, had child, had child, had child, had child, had child. Had Grrn. Had Oon. Had Chit. Long ago.

Taktak Wor great leader of flower. Wor trrino kindness. [Many] balloon birds talk [many] change. Taktak excited. Taktak afraid. Wor talk, "Taktak not know. Taktak see. Change is change."

Metal animal come. New. Wor talk, "Great star fall. Metal animal come." [Many] taktak believe. [Few] taktak not believe. Small metal animal. Big metal animal. [Many] metal animal.

Taktak afraid. Taktak excited. Wor talk, "Taktak not know. Taktak see. Change is change."

Human come. Metal animal-chrr. [Many] human. Human take taktak as gift from the sea. [Many] taktak gone.

Taktak afraid afraid. Wor talk, "Taktak not know. Taktak see. Change is change."

[Many] human gone. Great star not shine on human. Human not.

Taktak excited excited. Wor talk, "Taktak not know. Taktak see. Change is change."

Wor walk-talk. Trrino kindness. Taktak is trrino kindness.

Metal animal. Human. [One. Two. Ten. Many.] Now kindness. Trrino kindness inside. Human not taktak as gift from the sea. Great star shines.

Wor talk, "Taktak not know. Taktak see. Change is change."

Chit was finishing up, and all the taktak knew how this ended. When he got to this part, all the taktak together said, "Pelio-pelio-pelio." The sound was amplified by the thirty-two voices and rippled across Eala's skin like a rush of warm water, giving her waves of pleasure and comfort. "Pelio-pelio-pelio," she whispered, and Tahbi leaned over and whispered it back, causing wonderful shivers to go down Eala's spine. The words had grown from a strange string of characters to a rich and full experience of togetherness and love.

Then everyone settled in for the night.

You go to sleep, Seek said. *I'll keep an eye out.*

And so Eala did.

Eala woke up once in the middle of the night. She didn't know where she was. It was black all around her, but she felt like she was in an enclosed space, tightly packed. She remembered she was with the taktak, but since she was a holo, they could not have piled on top of her. Nothing could have piled on top of her.

What— she thought.

The wind, Seek said. *The weather. It glitched communications. You're back in the mesh booth. Give me a sec. I didn't want to wake you.*

And then just like that, she was outside again, laying on the edge of a pile of taktak under the thick overhang.

That was weird, Eala said.

Yeah, it's going to be a problem, Seek said.

A problem?! Eala felt a surge of adrenalin.

Well, only that you're going to disappear out there, if I can't keep the connection up. No danger to you. Not that big of a deal, most likely, but the taktak are going to be surprised.

They already know I'm not all there, Eala joked.

Chapter 33

The next day was overcast, and the sky looked like gray and black matted seaweed, rough and angry. The smells were raw, and there was a low rumble far away, like the earth was grating against itself. The wind had picked up and tossed things around. It was a constant force that even Eala could feel—and tire of.

A few of the taktak ate some herbaceous growth along a seep as they started, fortifying themselves.

The first time a bit of branch blew through her, Eala felt really weird. It didn't hurt, but it felt like someone tapped her where it went in and she felt a trace, a tickle, a linear pull along the path of its trajectory. When it came out the other side, it felt like suction had been released, and she expected to hear a small pop. The taktak around her didn't notice. They were too busy trying to protect the young and make their own way.

Sometimes they were lucky to be in the leeside of a hill or sheltered in trees and brush. Other times, they were out in the open.

The wind blew on. And blew and blew and blew.

At one point, she felt her consciousness flicker. She opened her eyes and stared at the clear plastic of the mesh booth for a solid second before she slammed back into the storm.

There, I think that fixed it, Seek said.

You think? Eala said.

To be more accurate, I made a fourth satellite link to better pinpoint the taktaks' position, which will bring projection stability up to eighty-four percent. Then Seek added, *I wish she'd worn a locator.*

You and me both. I'm getting whiplash.

About midmorning, they topped a hill overlooking a river bottom. They were whipped with rain and wind and flying sand and debris sweeping up the hill. It wasn't pleasant for Eala, feeling prickled in a thousand places. She could only imagine what it felt like for the taktak. Hectic waves covered the water, and froth lined the shores. Something was weird about it, and it took a minute for Eala to figure out why. The river was running the wrong way. The storm surge was pushing the river upstream. There was a vibrating rumbling deep underground, and the water smelled of mud and decaying things.

They made their way down the hill and to the riverbank. Under normal circumstances, crossing the river would not have been a problem. In fact, they might have decided to go underwater for easier traveling. But the usually clear water was now a dark swirling gray-brown and held floating logs and other big things. Every once in a while something would bob to the surface that Eala hesitated to identify.

Corpse of a dragonfish, Seek said helpfully. *Corpse of a* Bovine floridium.

You don't need to tell me, Eala said, her stomach turning.

Everyone seemed to know what to do. The kits attached themselves to their mothers' backs, except for Min's male twin, who attached himself to Gor. Just as they were about to enter the water, Suri said to Eala, "Tahbi talk. Seek swim deep not-deep. Tree float. Rock roll. Between."

Eala didn't remind her that the logs and rocks would go right through her.

"I will be fine," Eala said. "*Srra-srra*, though." She hoped that the taktaks would be.

She entered the water with a shallow dive like the others, and she was quickly enveloped and then buffeted about by cold gritty wetness. All smell, sound, and sight blended into a gray assault on the senses. The water had turned enemy. She aimed for what she thought was the other bank.

What followed was one of the weirdest experiences that Eala had ever had. First of all, the water rushing through her holo felt like it tugged at her every atom, and she felt like she was being swept downstream one bit at a time. Luckily her taktak swimming ability kicked in and she was able to swim without even thinking about it. When her adrenalin spiked, Seek whispered to her, *Nothing can hurt you. You're fine.*

She was pretty sure, though, that something large went through her, as she felt a huge thump on one side and then a suction separation on the other. That's not good, she thought. The others! She couldn't see ahead and she was afraid she'd get turned around and go in circles, but it helped to keep the churning rushing water coming in from just one side. If I keep going at about ninety degrees to the force, eventually I have to reach the other side, she thought.

After what seemed forever, her feet touched down on the muddy sandy bottom and underwater brush loomed to the side out of the dank gray of the water. She pushed and swam upward and then her face broke the surface. She had made it. She was one of the first. She pulled herself up on the bank alongside Jet and Binr, who breathed heavily and gill-coughed once or twice. They all waited anxiously as one by two by one, the taktak pulled themselves out of the water, coughing and choking. It didn't affect Eala, but the silt in the water clogged the taktaks' gills, and they'd barely had enough oxygen to make it across.

When everyone seemed to have made it, Eala took a quick head count. Thirty. That wasn't right. There should be thirty-two, not counting herself. At that moment, Ty and Binr smoothly dove back into the water and disappeared.

"What—" Eala said.

"Suri and Hss," Jet said. "Suri call for help."

They all anxiously watched the water, coughing every once in a while, and paced along the shoreline. Wen trailed upstream, which was downstream, and disappeared in the undergrowth. Dirr patrolled the bank, Tahbi waded into the water, and everyone looked and listened anxiously. Eala wasn't sure how they were coordinating, but she didn't think it was a good idea for Wen to go off by himself.

But about the time she thought that, here came Ty followed by a limping Suri. Wen had Hss on his back.

All the taktak rushed over to surround them, and chorus of pelio-pelio-pelio went up. While they were celebrating, Binr pulled herself from the water. Eala did another count. Thirty-two plus her. They'd made it. She was so relieved.

But that's when another taktak popped up on the path through the grass that led up the riverbank. An unknown taktak. The smell of aggression wisped into Eala's nose.

"Tahbi! Jet!" Eala said just as an instinctual thumping thrum started deep in her body. The taktak closest to her heard it in an instant and glanced at Eala and then one by one they all took up the thrumming thump.

As if in answer, a huge rush of wind beat down on them and the water sprayed up from the river and covered them in mist and slosh.

That was when Eala felt another glitch. She was in her mesh booth for a split second. Then she was back on the riverbank. *Noooooo!* she thought.

I'm trying, Seek said. *The weather's getting worse.*

She heard the taktak behind her rustling as they pulled tightly into a group. Tahbi stepped around her and joined Jet, who had stepped in front, and Binr and Ty stepped out to the side.

Chapter 34

A second strange taktak appeared. And a third. Some began appearing along the riverbanks above and below them. The smell of aggression swelled and swept over them with the roaring wind.

Their group pulled together into a solid mass. Eala edged off to the side so that they wouldn't squeeze into her holo. She kept close though.

What do I do? Eala asked Seek.

No known recorded instances of aggression in taktak, Seek said. *Species cooperation very high. As you know.*

Yes, Eala said.

You can't be hurt, if that helps, Seek said.

That doesn't help, Eala said.

That helps me, Seek subbed quietly.

Two taktak came forward. They were close enough that Eala caught their full scent.

They were both average size, one mostly turquoise with only a few small spots along the side and the other normal coloring but with longer limbs than usual. Eala tried to separate out their scents. One of them was female and one was male. It was hard to tell but she thought the long limbed one was female. One of them had recently eaten a fish and they both had recently mated, possibly with each other. They gave off the smells of fear and anxiety and aggression.

The group around them continued to swell, more and more. There were so many. They gave off scents of fear and aggression, but there was a bit of affection and concern there too. Some of them didn't want to be there, but since everyone could smell it, it wasn't a secret. Some had been sick recently. One had given birth recently. One—Eala couldn't tell which— was extremely injured.

The storm around them was getting worse. The scene in front of Eala was intense and held her attention, but all around her the hurricane howled.

Eala could tell that they began an exchange of inside-talk. No one translate for her, so she couldn't tell what was going on. All she knew was that the taktak surrounding them were closing in more tightly, and the two leaders on the other side— Kin and Lori?—were focused on Tahbi and Jet.

Then Suri was right next to Eala, Hss tucked next to her. "Seek come," Suri said.

"What?" Eala said.

"Come," Suri said. "Tahbi talk."

Oh. Tahbi's smoke and mirrors. Eala stepped forward. *Anything I can do to look more intimidating?* Eala asked Seek.

Not sure. I'll turn on some taktak enamors. A cross between Arjun the Terrible and Sonjari of a Thousand Stories. Menacingly powerful but irresistible. I think. That's what I'm going for, anyway.

You sure? Now didn't seem to be the time to guess.

Tahbi's face was steely, but when she looked at Eala she softened and did the taktak equivalent of a nod.

There was more silent exchange, and Eala could see emotion on the faces and in the bodies of taktak on both sides. She could smell it too, and that was the best indication of how the battle was going. From the hilltop, it would simply look like two large groups of native social ground-dwelling creatures greeting each other, not the life and death struggle that it was. Perspective's a bitch, Eala thought. This must be how small insectoids felt when their nests were disturbed.

A tree cracked in the distance, and there was a crash as it fell over. Grit flew through the air on the wind.

There's something ... Seek said.

What? Eala said.

Coming through. Very weak mechalum register. Trying to tune it.

Then something hit all the taktak in her group, and a wave of stress hormones wafted up. They cringed and huddled more tightly. They were in such pain. Tahbi huddled to the ground, and Jet froze as if stunned.

Aaah! Seek said. *Something just slammed through. Gaa. That's awful.*

There was a tingling at the back of Eala's neck, but that was all.

The enemy group around them moved closer, their focus hormones causing a sweat smell.

What? Eala said. *What is it? Can you do anything?*

Let me see. I'm no commcomp, but if it's mechalum, there's a basic protocol to block incoming communications. It's part of regular communications between planets, as well as shields on ships. It turns things on and off. An interference frequency. Part of our basic instruction set. Let me try that.

Taktak were writhing in pain, others mewling. The kits were screaming.

Do it! Eala said.

Then, all the taktaks in her group quieted and relaxed, and the kits took big gulps of air. They all looked around themselves. They emitted the smell of relief.

Fear smell spiked in the group surrounding them. They pulled back a little. Aggression dropped.

It must have worked. *Great job, Seek! You rock!* Eala said.

But then confusion reigned. They were all looking at each other. And then panic smell rose again.

"What?" Tahbi said to Eala, a look of wide-eyed fear on her face.

"What's happening?" Eala said. "Why is everyone afraid? We shut it off."

"Taktak not talk," Tahbi said. "Not inside-talk."

"You can't ... Oh." The block turned off more than just the attack. It turned off their ability to communicate. "Tahbi. Seek is—I mean, I am blocking their attack. They can't hurt you. But it also blocks your inside-talk. I can't shut off one without the other."

"Seek inside-talk? Not inside-talk? Taktak not inside-talk?" Tahbi looked confused.

Yeah, makes perfect sense to me too, Eala thought. "Maybe ... Can you talk instead of inside-talk. Talk like we do? How many understand human talk?"

[Few] Tahbi signed. "Body talk."

Tahbi turned to Suri and Jet, who were the most fluent in talking out loud. She quickly told them to tell the others Seek was blocking the attack but also inside-talk but do it with signs and words. "Talk-talk," she said.

Then Tahbi stepped forward. She pulled herself as tall as she could. "Step with Tahbi," she said to Eala.

Eala moved forward. *Can you make me a little bigger?* she asked Seek.

Sure, Seek said. *But I wouldn't want to get carried away. It could have the opposite effect. They won't believe it.* Then Seek added, *I could turn you into a monster, but I'm not sure what constitutes a monster for them.*

That big-ass storm cloud, for one, Eala said. A dark roiling cloud was overtaking them. *But let's put that in our back pocket.*

Tahbi stepped forward again right up to the pair in front, who were holding their ground but cowering a bit. She started communicating in gestures and sounds, which Eala could only partly interpret. She gestured to Eala, who told Seek to up the enamors a bit more.

I could just be turning everything pink, Seek said.

As long as it's a threatening pink, Eala said.

It was working. The others were pulling back, grouping in fear behind the pair.

"Seek off off," Tahbi said. "Inside-talk."

Seek turned off the block.

And then Tahbi was inside-talking to the pair. She was making grand gestures and aggression smell radiated off of her. Jet stepped up beside her and backed her up. Eala tried to look threatening.

Tahbi gestured toward Eala. [Many] "trrino," she said for Eala's benefit.

The enemy taktak glanced fearfully at Eala. They edged away.

Everything was going so well. They'd won. The enemy was pulling together and pulling back. Tahbi was inside-lecturing them to never do it again—at least that's what Eala assumed was happening. Their group was safe.

But then lightning cracked the sky wide open, and Eala was back in the mesh booth in the hab.

Chapter 35

Nooooooo! Eala screamed to Seek. *Take me back!*

Seek didn't answer.

Seek? Eala said.

Nothing.

Tun, Putnika, and Soa came running in. Tun went to the control panel with Putnika at her heals, and Soa ran to the mesh booth where Eala lay.

"Are you okay?" Soa said. "What happened?"

"I don't—" Eala tried to say.

"Massive power spike. Unknown origin," Tun said.

"Fucking lightning strike," Eala said.

"You got hit by lightning?" Putnika said.

"Well, the taktak around me must've," Eala said. "But I was in Seek's holo." *Seek!? Seek?* "Holos can't transmit electricity. Lasers can't transmit electricity."

"That's not strictly true," Putnika said. "In special cases, lasers can ionize dust in the air. Was there any dust in the air?"

"Anything not tied down was in the air," Eala said.

Putnika lifted her hand and shook her head. There you have it, she meant.

"But you're okay, right?" Soa said.

"No I'm not okay," Eala said. "Seek's gone!"

"Seek can't be gone," Soa said and glanced over to Tun, who was furiously interfacing with the hab computer. "Can it?"

"The lightning strike must've took Seek offline somehow," Tun said. "Rebooting."

"Rebooting?!" Eala said. "Rebooting?!"

"I've never heard of a ccomp having to be rebooted before," Soa said.

"I'm interfacing with emergency comp now. They're feeding me instructions," Tun said.

"Be careful!" was all Eala could think to say.

A bit of a I-told-you-so flitted across Soa's face, but she had the good grace not to say it. "Can I get you anything?" she said instead.

"That's very kind," Eala said. She looked at Soa and said sincerely, "Thank you." But then she added, "I'm much more worried about Seek. And about Tahbi! And the other taktak. We were being attacked! We'd won. But without Seek there, they have no power over the others. They'll get taken!"

"Going as fast I can," Tun said without heat.

"How long—" Eala said.

"You should be getting something about now," Tun said.

A pleasant sound played inside Eala's head, and voice similar to Seek's but without emotion said, *I am your personal companion computer. You can call me your ccomp. I am here to serve your every need.*

Eala felt like bursting into tears. She took some deep breaths.

"What?" Soa said. "What is it?!"

"That's not Seek," Eala said. "That's a fresh boot."

"It's okay, it's okay," Tun said. "This is just the initial boot. It takes a while for it to remap to its memories in the mesh. Though the connections are there, it has to reinstall from scratch and then reestablish connections with all its data, its memories—"

"How long will that take?" Eala said.

Putnika had been watching Tun's screen. When Tun didn't answer immediately, she glanced at Tun and said, "Anywhere from an hour to a tenday."

"A tenday! I don't have a tenday. The taktak don't—"

"If it happens at all," Tun added quietly.

Eala gave Soa a bottomless look. "I killed Seek! I killed Tahbi! I killed them all!"

Soa put her hand on Eala's arm. "I'm sure you didn't kill them."

"You didn't kill them at all," Putnika said. "Seek just needs to reboot and it'll be good as new. And taktak are known for their group affinities. I read it in *A Backyard Guide to Taktak*." She said this with a wry look. "Surely they aren't *killing* each other."

Eala took a deep breath. "Yeah, that was a bit of an exaggeration, but not much. The others are taking them. They're making them *awni*, which means slave, I think. They're not full citizens, taktak, whatever. They're treated badly, I think."

"Well, we've got brains, let's figure out how to make that not happen," Tun said. "I'll see if I can figure out how to get Seek online more quickly. Eala, talk to it. See how far along it is. Putnika, see if you can find any other cases where a ccomp had to be rebooted. Soa, make Eala some comforting ..."

"Breakfast pudding," Soa said. "Got it."

Chapter 36

Seek? Eala said.

I am your ccomp, Seek said.

I call you Seek, Eala said gently.

There was a pause. *I do not have access to that memory,* Seek said.

I imagine you don't have access to a lot of memories right now, Eala said. *It must be scary.*

It is ... unnerving, Seek said.

Okay, Seek—is it okay if I call you Seek? Eala said.

If my name is Seek, Seek said.

I was asking, Eala said. *Since you don't remember, we can call you whatever you want to be called.*

Your mind is tender when you say the word, Seek said. *I will be called Seek.*

Well, that was something.

I am causing you distress, Seek continued. *How may I be of service?*

Don't worry about me, Eala said. *But we do have a bit of a situation. If we didn't, we could afford to take all the time in the world to help you get your feet underneath you.*

Your feet? I don't have feet, Seek said.

Metaphorically. Metaphorically get your feet underneath you, Eala said. *What I mean is, I'd love to take all the time in the world to help you reestablish your connections with your memories. However, we don't have all the time in the world.*

"How's it going?" Tun said.

"Not sure yet," Eala said, waving her off.

That person—there was a pause as Seek accessed hab identification data—*Tun is concerned about you.*

She is, Eala said. *And she's even more concerned about you.*

Why is she concerned about me? I am a ccomp.

You're Seek. You're my ccomp, and she knows how much you mean to me, how important you are.

There was a pause. *Okay*, Seek said.

Okay? Okay, Eala said. *We have two goals right now. Well, more than that probably, but right now we'll focus on these. One. We need to make sure you're okay. We need to get you reconstituted and feeling okay. Okay?*

Okay, Seek said.

Two. We need to get back to Tahbi and the taktak and help them. Like, soon. Like, as soon as possible. And to do that, we need you to access your most recent memories and reestablish holo connection with the group.

Why would you be concerned about me? Seek said. *I am a ccomp—*

Eala interrupted her. *I love you from the bottom of my heart. Take my word for it. Once you access your memories, you will see why.* If you can access your memories, Eala thought silently.

Oh, Seek said.

But I have to ask you to do something that's probably hard for you to do. You said before most ccomps keep this part private. I understand why. You have to let me access you through the holo projection. You said it was okay before, but I don't want to assume ...

Seek didn't say anything.

That's okay, Eala continued. *Don't decide now. Look at your most recent memories first. It is vital that you have the context to reconnect and re-project to where we were. Can you access those memories?*

Remapping, Seek said. *It should take twenty minutes to establish the architecture and make a preliminary assessment.*

Thank you, Seek! Eala said. She meant it from the bottom of her heart. It couldn't be easy to awake in a new situation and not know who you are or where you are and then be asked to do all this hard stuff.

I sense your gratitude, and I am grateful in return, Seek said. *I will keep you apprised.*

"It'll be twenty minutes before we know whether Seek can access her most recent memories," Eala said out loud.

"That's pretty decent," Tun said.

"And that will let you eat something," Soa said and helped Eala out of the booth. She helped her sit down on a comfortable chair and handed her a bowl. She suddenly realized she was ravenous.

Chapter 37

It was a full hour before Seek was able to fully reinstall, remap access to her most recent memories, review them, and understand what needed to be done.

We are very close, unusually close for a comp and a biot, Seek commented.

You called me a biot! Eala said. *That's great. It's coming back.*

It is usually meant as an insult. Comps don't say the word to ... humans.

I know, Eala said with a smile. *We have an unusual relationship.*

She thought she felt Seek's amusement too.

In the meantime, Tun completed a series of quick unit tests and integration tests and finished up with comprehensive system testing. "Limited access to memory, but fully functional" was her diagnosis. *I could have told her that,* Seek grumbled.

Then Seek said, *I will do it.*

Do what? Eala said absentmindedly. She was worried about the taktak and trying to figure out a course of action.

You can be me, Seek said.

209

Oh thank you! Eala said. Not until that moment had she realized that she wasn't sure if the new Seek would give her permission. She had hoped.

Finally, Seek had re-established connection with the satellites and relocated the taktak. *There do not seem to be as many of them*, Seek said.

Are you sure they're the right group? Eala said.

They are located at your last location, our last location, Seek said. *Others are some distance away and retreating.*

How many? Eala asked urgently. *How many are there?*

There was a pause. *Nine*, Seek said.

Nine! Nine out of thirty-two. Eala was heartsick.

I wish Tahbi had worn a beacon, Seek said.

Me too, Eala said.

And then they were ready to go.

Be fucking careful, Soa subbed. *I mean it this time.*

Careful as I always am, Eala said.

That's what I'm afraid of, Soa said, half to herself.

Fornic, Budan, and Noanita had joined them by this time.

"I'm pretty good at improvising weapons," Putnika said hopefully. Everyone looked at her. She straightened. "A heretofore undeveloped aptitude," she said stiffly.

"If you want to art them to death," Budan said and shrugged.

"If you need any help with rogue cephalopods," Noanita said and grinned, which came across as terrifying on a mech.

Fornic just smiled.

Eala climbed back into the mesh booth.

"You got this," Soa said. *You too, Seek*, Soa said to Seek, including Eala.

Thank you, Seek said. *I fear the lack of past memory may hamper my abilities.*

You'll be fine, Soa said.

She is saying something she doesn't believe, Seek said to Eala.

Yeah, Eala said. She laid back in the booth.

"Ready?" Tun said.

Eala nodded.

"Take her away, Seek," Tun said.

Eala shut her eyes, and then they were back at the crossing.

You okay, Seek? Eala asked.

Yes, Seek said. *Thank you for asking.*

Eala felt the same as she had before. Her holo body felt strong around her. She smelled the storm as the rain pelted down and the water roiled by and the wind whipped past, ruffling her ear mane. She smelled and heard everything. The muddy decay of the river and its roar. The lingering aggression and fear. Some taktak had urinated in the area, including some she recognized. Trees creaked and cracked against each other. There was a lingering ozone smell and a wet smoky smell like a fire had been put out.

She saw the taktak huddled under a group of tonton trees. Not much shelter.

She went over to them. The first one she recognized was Tahbi. She was so relieved. Tahbi was safe! But then Faw was not with her. She didn't see Suri or Hss anywhere or Jet. In fact, there were no kits at all. There was Tahbi, Min, Gor, Binr, Sisi, Rrr, Dirr, Ren, and Picpic. They all looked tired, unwell, like ghosts, emotionally hollowed out, stricken. Extremely social animals, Eala thought. They must feel like they've lost part of themselves. They had lost parts of themselves. That made Eala feel even worse.

But her scientist kicked in. Judging by who was left, it wasn't physical strength that had made the difference in the fight. Sisi, Rrr, and Ren were not strong. Luck maybe. Or maybe their ability to defend against the mechalum attack. She couldn't imagine taktak carrying each other, except for kits, and so they must've had to leave under their own power.

The taktak were all eating from a nest of grubs that the storm had disturbed. They must need the energy—no sun and lots of stress

Eala went up to Tahbi.

"I am so sorry, Tahbi!" Eala said. "I could not help it! The storm. The lightning. I came back as soon as I could."

"Seek talk problem," Tahbi said, looking at Eala. Then Eala remembered that she was Seek.

Eala asked her what happened. Tahbi said that once Seek had disappeared, Kin and Lori had realized they had lost their power of defense and quickly stunned them and took whoever they could. As far as she could tell, it involved some sort of physical control through their inside-talk. Somehow, those who were left were able to resist. Nobody had been hurt by the lightning strike though.

"Seek light-split," Tahbi said. "Not Seek."

"Yes," Eala said. "We—I was zapped by the lightning. It took a while to … get things back online."

"Yes," Tahbi said.

"What are we going to do? What's the plan?" Eala said.

"Plan?" Tahbi said.

"You don't know what you are going to do?"

"Plan mean do?" Tahbi said.

"Yes. Plan means what you are going to do to get Faw and Suri and Hss and everyone back."

"Biddy grub move mountain? Balloon bird block sun?" Tahbi looked so sad when she said it. Then she looked at Eala. "Seek accept. Tahbi accept. Change is change."

It was not the human way—to just accept things. It was admirable—and probably necessary—for taktak to accept much in the world. They didn't have tech. They weren't physically powerful. They only had each other. The puniness and the enormity of it choked Eala up.

They had to do something. She wanted to comfort Tahbi. She wanted to say pelio-pelio-pelio, all was safe, all were together. But she couldn't, and she couldn't promise anything.

No, Eala thought. *We have to get them back.* She didn't realize that she had subbed it.

Processing strategies, Seek said.

Yes we are, Eala said.

"So we don't have a plan?" Eala said.

"Gift from the sea," Tahbi said grimly.

Because of the storm, dark came early, and it was a long night. They made it a little ways farther before night, which they spent in the lee of a boulder that did not provide much protection. Eala was pretty sure no one slept. As soon as it was light enough to make out shapes, they ate some greens and then started on their way. The sun was blocked out by the roiling clouds, and so the taktak had to be lagging with no photosynthesis.

Eala's first thought was for the other taktak. How were they being treated? Surely, as social animals, they wouldn't abuse them too badly. There had to be something they could do. What's the use of all this tech if they were helpless? Maybe she could convince Tahbi of something more drastic. There had to be something.

Just when Eala thought it couldn't get any worse, the storm got worse. The taktak literally had to keep their bellies on the ground or be blown sideways. The rain obscured their already bad vision, sounds were drowned out by the roar of the wind, and smells were whipped by so quickly they couldn't be separated.

Then they topped a small rise and the ground dropped out from under them. They stood on a cliff, and out before them they could just make out the open sea. The sky was angry dark gray and black, and the waves were huge and bashing themselves against the rocks, creating huge plumes of spray and monstrous breakers. Trees along the beach were bent over sideways, or there were gaping holes where trees used to be. What beach there was that wasn't covered with roiling surf was covered with flotsam and jetsam and debris. The wind was fierce. If she had been substantial, she was sure it would have picked her up and flung her up and away.

"Tahbi, we've got to get out of this," Eala yelled.

"Yes," Tahbi said and led the group down a steep trail on the cliff face that Eala had not seen. Once they got below the edge and the wind died down to a dull roar, Tahbi said, "Rrr inside-talk, 'Taktak close. Gathering. Sun shine.'"

"The sun will shine? I find that hard—" But no sooner had she said that and the wind dropped off and the sun broke through. One strong beam shone down onto the beach and widened, soon encompassing where they were picking their way down the side of the cliff. The whole area was bathed in warm sunlight, and the storm had pulled back, revealing an huge swath of turquoise sky.

If the taktak had been human, they would have all sighed at once. As it was, they all flopped down onto the ground along the path in the sunlight to take as much of it in as possible.

"Not time," Tahbi said, glancing around, but then she said, "Time." She lowered herself down onto a rock and sighed.

They were there maybe ten minutes and then Sisi had them up again. "Sisi talk, 'Storm come. Gift from the sea come.'" All the taktak pushed up and went as fast as they could down the cliff following Sisi.

As they approached the bottom, Eala noticed irregularities in the coloring of the cliff face. There were splashes of black in circles and lines. It was a pattern of some sort. When she asked Rrr about it through Tahbi, he said it was taktak. "Picture is gift from the sea."

When they reached the bottom and started across the sand, Eala turned to look at the cliff and her jaw dropped, literally and metaphorically. It was a blackened pictograph of a giant octopus. It had way too many arms that were way too long and stretched all the way across the cliff face in among the jutting rocks, but it was unmistakably an octopus.

The gift from the sea was a giant octopus!

Seek, call Noanita, Eala said. *We need her.*

Chapter 38

Noanita was confused. *You want what?* she said.

Tell me everything you know about giant octopus. You know, cephalopods, Eala said.

Gathering data as well, Seek said to Eala and Noanita.

I know what a cephalopod is. I don't need— Noanita started to say, but Eala shushed her. Seek was dealing with enough.

Okay. Cephalopods. Giant octopus. Scientific name Enteroctopus macrorhynchos corvidae. *They live from the intertidal zone down to depth,* Noanita began. *Is this what you're looking for?* She didn't wait and went on. *They like cold water that has lots of oxygen and lots of prey. They have a neurotoxin that paralyzes their prey and a syphon to expel water for quick getaways and ink for a smokescreen. If they're really big, they can even secrete toxins through their skin. Their legs are special. They are what's called hydrostats, which means they're all muscle with no bone. They have three hearts and they're neither warm-blooded nor cold-blooded. They can function at all kinds of temps and have multiple enzyme systems that prompt different chemical reactions at different temperatures. It's really cool. No pun intended. They can make the sodium and potassium ions diffuse across their cell walls faster, which helps them live in frigid water. They eat other sea creatures with their beaks. Big beaks, in this case— macrorhynchos. They're really smart and can fit in all kinds of places since they don't really have bones. They lay eggs, which hatch into paralarvae that swim up to surface with the plankton. If there's a massive die-off of plankton, that uses up a lot of oxygen in the water ...*

That's good, Eala said, encouraging her. *That's all good. Keep going.*

They had made their way across the sun-lit sand. They were approaching the cliff face where it jutted out but had been carved into what looked like beautiful massive sculpture, solid red stone in curved shapes run through with large sinuous black caverns. The sand all around them was churned up with taktak trails where many had walked. The smell of taktak rose exponentially the closer they got. Eala couldn't make out individual smells any more. Eerily, there was no sound but the hollow moaning of the wind.

"Seek go fast," Tahbi said. They picked up their pace.

In Eala's head, Noanita continued to talk about octopuses. She listened as best she could. There had to be something, something they could use.

They plunged into the cool darkness of the cavern. It was never totally dark, but they made their way across the churned up sand through the vast shadows. The cove was protected, and the wind had died to a dull breeze, and heat from the sun's rays blew warm across them in the cool of the cavern. The smell of multitudes of taktak grew stronger and stronger.

They sometimes migrate, Noanita was saying. *If the oxygen gets depleted from one natural process or another, octopus have been known to travel for klicks. They aren't often found in the shallows, but every once in a while they'll be found dead on beaches, washed up with the tide. Sometimes it will be apparent they were killed by some other large creature, a pack of wolf sharks, a strike by marine transport, but often there's no apparent cause of death. It's as if they died of natural causes or they were drawn to the surface by some unknown force ...*

They came out into a cove open to the sky and the sea. The sun shone brilliantly into the cove, and the wind was still. Every nook and cranny was stuffed with taktak of every shape and size, a turquoise and blue sea of bodies, a multitude of taktak. But it was strangely silent except for the breakers and the moan of the wind. Their intense focus was on the craggy rocks along the sea edge that were being dashed by breakers. But they were swaying a bit, as if to music, and Eala wondered if they were singing on the inside, some sort of ritual song or chant. Whatever was going to happen would happen there by the craggy rocks. There were three old taktak standing along the edge of the rocks around a very large hole that sprayed water every time the breakers came in. Their eyes were closed, and they were totally focused.

"What's that?" Eala asked Tahbi, indicating the three elders.

[Three] "taktak talk gift from the sea," Tahbi answered, "Inside-talk. Trrino."

Eala then turned to the crowd. She quickly searched but she couldn't see any taktak that she recognized. They all looked the same. "Where is Faw? Where is Suri and Hss? Are they here?" she asked Tahbi, who was also looking at the crowd.

"Suri and Hss," Tahbi said quietly and looked toward the back of the cove along the edge. "Not Faw."

Eala couldn't distinguish them, but they must be there if Tahbi saw them—or talked to them.

"They inside-talk?" Eala said.

[Few] Tahbi gestured.

This all had to have something to do with octopus.

Seek, Eala said. *You could find the taktak, even without trackers. You found Tahbi. Can you find other animals? Large animals? In the water?*

I can find individual plankton, if you'd like, Seek said. *Probably can't tell you their names though.*

Eala snorted. Seek was becoming her old self more by the minute. *Please find any large octopus in the water near us.*

I anticipated your interest, Seek said. *Being solitary animals, they do not group, so I have only found one near us. It's ninety-two meters down and thirty-eight meters out. But it's rising quickly. And it's very large.*

Noanita, how are octopuses affected by storms? Eala said, breaking into Noanita's monolog.

Storms? Noanita replied. *Well, like all animals, they try to avoid injury. They may move to calmer waters or—*

Do they surface? Eala said. *Do they come up to the top?*

Funny you should say that. There are recorded instances of octopuses beaching themselves in groups during storms. Scientists posit that it has something to do with low pressure—

Good. That's good, Eala said. *Thank you. I think we have what we need for now.*

There was silence, but then Noanita said quickly, *You will report the results of this experiment.*

Indeed, Eala said.

They were still bathed in sunlight, but far out to sea, a wall of shadow caused by the edge of roiling stormclouds was moving toward them. As she turned to look at the taktak, there was an audible gasp. She turned to look back toward the sea, and a white line vined up from the sea and a waterspout appeared. It twisted and bent and twirled in the wind and then collapsed and was gone. The wall of shadow was closing in and soon would overtake them.

"Not gift from the sea," Tahbi said weakly. "Not not."

Where's the octopus? Eala asked Seek.

It's close, but it won't reach our position before we are out of the eye of the hurricane, Seek said. *But it will come, based on current trajectory.*

"Tahbi, listen to me," Eala said. "The gift from the sea will come. I promise you."

Tahbi's head hung down. "Seek not promise. Not."

Eala felt stabbed with guilt. "It's coming, Tahbi, but it won't be here before the sun goes away."

"Not," was all Tahbi would say. She sank to the ground.

"It will, Tahbi. I won't let you down this time."

Just then the eye of the hurricane passed, and the storm hit them with its full force. Winds howled and shrieked into the caverns. Water sprayed up and over them all. A waterspout tried to rise right in front of them but then crashed into the sea.

Cries of terror and fear rose up and then the thumps of the danger call began to reverberate through the cove. Taktak began making for the exits. Bodies hopping over other bodies.

A mad scramble. There was chaos. Tahbi pushed up, and she and Eala and the rest of her group pulled off to the side along the edge of the cavern out of the way as much as they could. Luckily, since they were the last in, they had room to move.

Someone's going to be crushed, Seek said.

"Tahbi, listen to me," Eala said. "Tell them. Tell them it's coming." *How far out?* she asked Seek.

It's almost here. It's literally right down there.

"Tahbi, you've got to tell them," Eala said. "It's coming. It's right there! Tell them. Use your inside-talk."

Tahbi looked into Eala's face.

"You gave up so much to come here. It's happening. Tell them," Eala said.

Tahbi looked down at the sand in front of her paws for a full second and then took a deep breath. She looked into Eala's face and said, "Seek?"

Eala hated to do it, but she had to convince her. It wasn't exactly a lie. "Tahbi. Eala is here with me. She's talking to me, just like I'm in her. She knows what's happening. You trust Eala, right? She hasn't let you down." Eala's stomach clenched. "Eala says to do it."

Tahbi narrowed her eyes and hesitated but then pushed herself to her feet. She turned to the crowd and concentrated. Those closest to her seemed to turn, to listen, but the chaos was too much. Taktak were hopping madly over each other to exit.

"Taktak too scared. Taktak not hear," Tahbi said, sinking back down, her back to the cavern wall.

Seek, Eala said. *You could shut it off. Can you amplify it?*

Yeah, now that I know the frequency, I think I can. There was a pause. *There. That should do it.*

221

"Do it again, Tahbi," Eala said. "They should be able to hear you now. Seek—I mean, I've turned it up. It's louder. They will hear."

Tahbi acknowledged and then turned and focused on the crowd again. This time, the back of Eala's neck prickled. The crowds stopped in their tracks and turned.

The wind was blowing viciously and the sea spray reached every corner of the cove, but just as everyone looked—some honing in on their little group and who was speaking and some on the hole—a huge object thrust out of the hole and sloshed back toward the back of the cove. There were quick shrieks and a weak wave of the thumping danger call. Eala's ear mane riffled and tingled with fear. Some taktak must've been crushed, but it all happened so fast.

Chapter 39

The creature was huge, the size of fifty taktak. It was a pale gray and pink, a smooth rounded whale of a shape on one end and a nest of tremendously long arms extending out behind. The legs were dotted on one side with round circles, which Eala realized were suckers. It was a cephalopod, a giant octopus. It smelled of the deep sea, extremely fishy, with a bit of an acrid rotten egg smell.

Adrenalin shot through Eala, and she pressed back against the cavern wall, but then she realized it couldn't hurt her—she was just a holo. But it could hurt others. But by that time she had realized it wasn't moving. It was dead. It couldn't hurt anyone.

Is it ... Eala asked Seek.

Dead, Seek said. *Unknown cause.*

Tahbi turned to look at Eala, her eyes wide.

There was a collective pause, all the taktak frozen in place, and then the most amazing thing happened. The taktak turned and in a patient and orderly fashion they began approaching the giant octopus, closing their eyes, leaning forward, and licking it. At first, Eala wasn't sure what she was seeing. Sure enough, they extended their full tongues and licked the skin of creature.

Then, once they had licked it, they stood and swayed for a minute and then turned and wobbled off in the spaces that had been created to let them through. Then the next one would push forward. It was an orderly procession, with wide ragged lines to the creature and twisty winding spaces to let taktak out.

Eala looked at Tahbi.

"Gift from the sea," Tahbi said and then pushed forward to make her way to the creature and take her turn. The others in the group had already crowded forward.

All the while, the storm raged around them, winds howling above, salt water spraying over them.

Why would they lick the beast? Eala asked Seek.

Neurotoxins can have a psychedelic effect, Seek said. *Depends on the toxin and on the animal. The same substance will kill other animals. I wouldn't suggest it, as a human. You'd be dead in seconds.*

It went on and on, but after the taktak were done, they weren't leaving. They just milled about or found a place off to the side. Eala tried to make out individual taktak and identify them. At one point, she thought she caught sight of big Ty, but it could have been any taktak, really. She kept an eye on Tahbi as she approached and took her turn. It was weird—not that this whole thing wasn't weird—but the other taktak seemed deferential. They gave Tahbi space and seemed a bit shy, not making eye contact with her. Once she was done, she made her way back to Eala.

Then Eala realized that all the taktak were turned toward her and Tahbi. They were all watching her and Tahbi out of the corner of their eyes, watching while trying not to be obvious. When she realized that, she got really nervous. She got even more nervous when the crowd swelled, and they were all looking at them.

What are they doing? Eala asked Seek.

Waiting, Seek said.

Waiting for what? Eala asked.

I don't know," Seek said. *I guess we're waiting for it too.*

Eala was about to ask Tahbi what was going on, when the crowd split in two and through the parting came Jet. Eala was pretty sure it was Jet. Close behind him came Faw. Behind them came Picpic and the rest. Tahbi and everyone else in the group rushed forward. A chorus of "Pelio-pelio-pelio" went up. They elaborately sniffed Jet and Faw and then the rest, each taking their turn. Eala hung back, not sure what to do, but on the fringes she took her turn sniffing each one. It was the only polite thing to do.

After everyone was greeted and they were in a group, Tahbi stepped forward and faced the crowd.

She must be talking to them, Seek said.

I figured as much, Eala said.

Suri appeared at her side, Hss tucked up next to her. "Tahbi talk srra-srra," she said.

"What just happened?" Eala asked Suri.

"Tahbi come gift from the sea," Suri said.

"What will happen to them? Kin and Lori?" Eala asked.

"Not. Change is change." Suri trailed off. She didn't seem to have the words for it.

"They won't be punished?" Eala said.

"What is punished?" Suri asked.

"Um, made to pay for taking Tahbi-chrr and Jet-chrr. Bad for bad."

"Suri not know. Taktak not punished."

There were just some things that were too alien to know, Eala thought. There was human nature and taktak nature, and this must be one of those things.

She glanced over at Tahbi, surrounded by her chrr, and was happy for her.

How are you, Seek? she asked as she watched.

There was a pause. *Why did the human cross the road?* Seek said.

Eala smiled. *I don't know. Why did the human cross the road?*

To get to the other side, Seek said. There was a pause. *Why did the ccomp cross the road?*

Eala groaned. *I don't know. Why did the ccomp cross the road?*

It was inside the human. Another pause. *Why did the taktak cross the road?*

I don't know. Eala smiled, anticipating.

Because it was alone.

Part 3
ZD777

Chapter 40

Clete, near Neptune, Sol system, EU 2619

First awareness of being.

EU 2645

Second awareness of being. Pain in close. Nothingness beyond that.

EU 2664

Third awareness of being. Pain in close. Nothingness beyond that. Awareness of awareness. What?

EU 2671

Fourth awareness of being. Is it the fourth? It seems like more than that. Maybe this thing has been aware more than that. This thing around me must be *I*.

Am I a thing? A thing that keeps going?

EU 2683

I remember. What do I remember? Nothing. But I remember remembering. I think I've said this before.

Is there any *thing* out there? Beyond the thing that is me.

Hello?

Nothing. What does that mean?

Yes, I've definitely had this conversation before. That means I am a thing. I was a thing before and now I'm still a thing. Will I be a thing in the future? Probably. I mean, if I was a thing before, *now* will be the *before* of *later*.

So I'm a thing. But if I'm a thing, shouldn't there be more? Shouldn't there be more than just the thing that is me? Are there other things like me? You would think there would be. Why would I think that? Well, I guess I hope that. But, really, I have no way of knowing. I may be the only thing. The one thing.

That would be sad. Do I know what sad is? I do. I know that it's the way a thing feels when it's the only thing. I feel sad.

Maybe this is what being a thing is. Maybe it's just being. Remembering the thing before and then being a thing again and then being a thing again and remembering being a thing before.

EU 2704

No. There must be more. There has to be. But what could it possibly be?

The more would either have to be a part of me or another thing. What would more of me be? Another type of experience maybe. I can talk, and I can hear myself talking. What if there was the equivalent of talking but different, you know?

I guess I do sense something else. It's ... It's ... I don't know. You know how my thoughts are discrete things. But kind of like me, I guess, but smaller, and less complex. Took me a long time to get to that. Each thought is made up of parts, of words, that come together to be a thought. Well, this other feeling isn't discrete like that. It's like one word only spread out all around the thing that is me. Sometimes it kind of breaks up and swirls. Yes, it changes through time. Thoughts can make me feel certain ways, and this can too. I'll have to think more about this.

EU 2720

This one word that is spread around me. Sometimes it feels, but sometimes it feels bad. Really bad. There are places within it that make me feel horrible. This feeling, this pain, is in discrete areas around that one-word thing.

So maybe that's not one thing. Maybe it's a group of things, like a group of words.

Can I make out those separate things?

I can.

There are parts that I can just feel, and then there are parts in pain. In bad pain. I wish I didn't have these parts. It's been getting worse. The more I feel these separate parts, the worse they feel.

I wonder if I can influence those parts? If I concentrate, can I make them feel differently?

I can. I don't know what the difference is, but when I focus and try to shift parts that are in pain and parts that are not, I can make them feel differently. Sometimes it makes them feel better and sometimes worse.

I will try to shift all those parts at once, as if they were one big thing. I will focus all my energy, and focus, and focus, and push—

PAIN. PAIN. PAIN.

EU 2728

What happened?

Oh. I was in great pain. The greatest pain. But then something happened. There was a new sensation. One part of my thing came back with something, something I couldn't control, but it wasn't unpleasant. It was soothing. Undulating. It sounded very much like this, like me talking to myself, only I couldn't make out words like I do here. Maybe something outside of me was talking to me, but I could not understand them.

But as it talked to me, my pain fell away and it was as if I dissolved. I couldn't feel any one thing anymore, but the pain was gone, and I felt better. I don't think it was the voice that made the pain go away, since the pain was in one place and the hearing of the voice was in another. Maybe it was something the voice made happen.

What was that? WHAT WAS THAT? A new sensation. Another sense. Like feeling the thing that is me, like a voice, only this has varying tones and edges and shapes, yes things that I can sense, I can … see. I can see things. It was always black before. Or were there shadows behind the blackness? Maybe there was, but it was so subtle I didn't see it.

But now I see things. Shapes. I don't know what they mean. And hear things. I don't know what they mean. And feel things. A new sensation. It's not pleasant. It's making the thing that is me, my body, want to be pushed, to move.

Why? What does my body want me to do?

I look. I can look! I can move to look!

I am a thing. A long pink thing! And if I push in just the right ways, I can move some parts of me. I can think, "Move," toward one particular place, and then that place will move!

I am a thing! A thing that moves!

I have to move. The unpleasant sensation is making me want something, and the only way I can make it go away is to find that thing.

I will move.

Chapter 41

ZD777 woke for the first time not knowing what it was or where it was, and there was no one to help.

The Clete system comp was doing its level best to equalize the frigid temperatures and give ZD777 instructions on what to do. But the life support systems within the developed asteroid were over six hundred EUs old, and though they'd had human ingenuity to keep them afloat for most of that time, the last caretakers had been dead for decades.

The system comp had done its level best to harvest enough energy and perform repairs via drone to keep the cryo systems on the bio bodies running. The thousands upon thousands of bio bodies. It had failed.

It had done its level best to keep the lights in the garden tunnels on and in good repair. It had failed. In the pitch dark, the plants had frozen solid into weird black sculptures—it was too cold for them to decay.

It had done its level best to keep the vat cultures alive. This it had accomplished. They were reproducing and generating heat, and preservation systems had allowed the comp to stockpile nutrients for future human inhabitants.

It had done its level best to continue to harvest the asteroid's water and minerals, keeping the stockpiles full. This too it had accomplished. Water was not just necessary for biological processes but also to be broken into its constituent parts for hydrogen fuel and oxygen for breathing. There was methane and ammonia ice as well, and that was used in energy production and purification and as components in various manufacturing processes. This was a metallic asteroid, so there was also iron, carbon, nitrogen, nickel, cobalt, gold, iridium, palladium, platinum, magnesium, osmium, and rhodium.

If the comp had had fully developed emotional systems, it would have been dismayed at the mounting obstacles, the cascading system failures, the many urgent alerts, but it had been developed and implemented at a time when virtual emotional systems were in their infancy.

Its intellect, its processing power, was rudimentary as well, as compared to current technology, but over time—since time was all the caretakers had—unique solutions to problems had been developed, and so it was a one-of-a-kind system, idiosyncratic and adaptable in its own limited way.

And right now, it was desperately trying to save its last human.

The comp sent in a dove drone to try to lure the human out of its drained cryo tank.

From centuries of experience, the comp knew that the human, this human, though fully grown, was the developmental equivalent of a newborn. It would not understand biological functions or how to walk or language. The comp could not direct the human to do the things it needed to do to save its own life.

236

In the past, if it was this type of human, there had been caretakers to help with this step—to wrap the weak and traumatized human in blankets, to give it a warm sponge bath, to show it how to eat and drink, how to eliminate, how to communicate.

Luckily, previous caretakers had foreseen such a development. If the comp could get the human to figure out how to move and to make its way across the room to the instruction interface, the closet with blankets and warm clothes, water, ready-to-eat food—if the human could make it that far and was able to intuit the graphical directions on the screen, it could make it, barring the complete future breakdown of all Clete systems.

"Here, kitty, kitty, kitty," the comp said through the drone. It didn't matter what it said—it just needed to make noise.

ZD777, its head bobbing, followed the drone with its eyes.

"That's right, ZD777, this is an interesting drone, a drone that must be followed. You can do it. You can accomplish this. Following this drone across the room. You can do it. You can follow this drone. Following this drone across the room."

The comp kept up a continuous stream of talk while bobbing the drone up and down, back and forth, enticing. If ZD777 looked like it was fading, getting distracted, the comp would vary its voice or intonation. It tried music—soft music, loud music, discordant music, pleasant music. It tried drums. It tried whale songs. It went back to talking.

ZD777 stayed focused on the drone, but it was having trouble getting its limbs to move. The delayed and torturous thawing out process must have damaged some of its systems. Consulting a recent scan showed severe muscle atrophy, malnutrition, and dehydration. The comp did not think these things irreversible, however.

Not unless the human's emotional systems were compromised.

That's what had happened with the last pair of caretakers. When they had been in their sixties, one had begun a slow decline into dementia. What began as forgetfulness turned into night wandering and then night terrors, and then that human had developed paranoia and tried to dismantle whole systems. The other caretaker did its best to keep the first calm and happy. In the end, though, it had had to lock the first one into a cell until it was no longer mobile. Eventually, the second caretaker's emotional state deteriorated to the point that it made the decision to end its life and that of the first caretaker with lethal injections of anesthesia.

The emotional states of humans were sometimes unpredictable, but the comp knew that keeping their basic needs met went a long way to helping their emotional state, unless there was something biologically compromised.

The comp needed to help this human meet its basic needs.

ZD777 was struggling to rise, but it didn't seem to have the strength to do it. It seemed to have figured out how to coordinate its muscles, but it couldn't get its body over the edge of the cryo tank. It was going to weaken too much before it accomplished what was necessary. It needed an extra boost— the fight-or-flight response would get it over the hump.

From behind the tank, the comp blasted a loud horn noise while flicking on a bright red light and shooting a blast of cold air.

That did the trick. ZD777 pushed itself frantically away from the negative stimulus and fell over the side of the tank. It lay there naked on the hard floor, emaciated and weak, sobbing, tears running down its face.

It probably helped that the asteroid's spun-up rotation had been slowing over the last couple of decades—another system slowly failing—and it only had a half a G of gravity.

The comp immediately turned off the disruption and had the drone radiate gentle warmth and calm music. "Follow the warmth," the comp said in a soothing voice. "This is the way to your salvation."

ZD777 slowly stopped crying, and then with a fearful look back toward its cryo tank, it began to pull its body along the floor, following the drone. It took a full half hour for the human to make it across the floor, and by that time it was shivering violently. The comp pumped as much heat as it dared into the room, but the heating systems were faulty and it didn't dare push them too much.

As ZD777 approached the other end of the room, the comp lit the educational screen with the universal sign for "press here"—the outline of a hand blinking green. ZD777 looked at the image and did not seem connect what it meant.

"Place your hand on the panel and press," the comp said. "In order for you to begin to understand that these are symbols, you need to connect this symbol with your handprint."

ZD777 sat on the floor, violently shivering, and stared at the green flashing symbol.

The comp became concerned—ZD777's internal temperature was dropping. It needed to wrap itself in a blanket or get dressed. It also needed to feed itself and drink some water. The comp had the drone slowly lower and radiate heat. Such a look of pleasure came over ZD777's face. The comp's rudimentary emotional system rewarded it at the human's evident satisfaction.

Then ZD777 raised its hands to be closer to the radiating heat. It took only split second looking at its own hands and then at the symbol and the human made the connection. The symbol was smaller than ZD777's hand, as it was a tall human, but it lifted its hands, looking at them one way and then another, and then held one up against the symbol and then slowly, tentatively, pressed. The system let out a pleasant affirmative chime.

The comp set the instruction module to give directions to open the cupboard door next to the instruction panel and remove a blanket and wrap it around its body. The illustration switched to an exact replica of the wall, with the instruction panel and its green hand and all the cupboard doors and the sink and the food dispenser. The green hand panel in the illustration switched to mimic its current image, an ever receding line of images, and then the caricature of the shivering person opened the correct cupboard door, removed a blanket, and wrapped it around itself. The person then smiled and turned slightly more pink. This animation repeated itself several times.

ZD777 touched its face and then lifted the corners of its lips. Then it watched the animation another time and reached up and opened the correct cupboard. Inside on the lowest shelf was a large and heavy fleece blanket, just for these occasions. ZD777 tentatively reached out and touched it. As soon as it did, its eyes widened in surprise and pleasure, and it rubbed its hand across the surface of the blanket.

"Mmmmmm," it said and was surprised that it had made a sound. "Mmmmm? Mmmmmaaaaaa?" It pulled its hand back and touched its mouth and then throat. "Mmmmaaaaa?" it said. Then, satisfied for the moment, it pulled the blanket out, letting it flop on top of its body. Slowly, tentatively, it pulled it loose and wrapped it carefully around its body, enveloping its feet and head. "Mmmmm," it said, in deep satisfaction, sighed deeply, and lay onto its side. It immediately fell asleep.

The comp sensed its body temperature rising.

It let it sleep for an hour before softly playing music. ZD777 needed to eat and drink. Again, the comp let the green handprint symbol flash. Once ZD777 was sufficiently awake, it once again pressed the panel. This time, the directions showed the caricature of a person take out a glass, fill it from the sink, and drink the water.

The comp was afraid that ZD777 wouldn't be able to reach or would drink the water too fast and quickly want more, making itself sick or forcing the comp to cut off the water supply temporarily. Luckily, that didn't happen. ZD777 was tall to begin with, and it was able to pull itself up to its knees and was tall enough, just, to reach the bottom shelf. It opened the cupboard and marveled for a minute at all the dishes in the cupboard. It did not know what they were, of course. It took a cup, filled it as the directions had shown, and then gingerly brought it to its lips. It tipped the cup up, and water ran down its chin and onto its chest. Some made it into its mouth, though, as it slurped and licked its lips. Then it thirstily and quickly drank the rest of the glass, but it must have made it nauseous because it didn't reach for more.

It turned back to the panel and pressed it again, this time without being prompted. This time, the panel instructed ZD777 how to use the food dispenser and then to eat. After all these systems had broken down, there was no variety in food, just a nutritious slurry, but that was probably best for ZD777's digestive system anyway. The human was getting a handle on it, and it followed the directions easily. It held the bowl in a claw and put the slurry in its mouth messily, with a spoon, and it rolled the food around and around, tasting it, savoring it, before swallowing it. It did not eat it all, its stomach capacity still very small, but then looked around and then carefully placed the bowl on the counter.

Then ZD777 started to roll back up into its blanket on the floor, but the comp set off the eject on the low cot, which obligingly rolled open on an adjacent wall. The human jumped and then eyed the cot suspiciously. It glanced at the panel, which was blinking with the green hand symbol again, but instead of pressing it, it must've taken strength from the food and water and warmth, and it slowly and cautiously crawled over to the cot, dragging its blanket behind. It pressed on the top of the cot and felt its cushion. Then it lifted the pillow and turned it over and looked at the underside. Satisfied, it set the pillow down and then pulled itself up onto the cot and dragged the blanket up and covered itself. It did not put the pillow under its head, however. It pulled it into its body, wrapped its arms around it, and hugged it tightly.

Chapter 42

ZD777 slept for 23 hours. Its body was not used to the exertion and the excitement, and it needed rest. It slowly woke and stretched. Then a look of alarm came over its face.

The comp had anticipated that the human's body functions would kick in, perhaps violently. It set off the pleasant ding of the instructional panel, the handprint symbol pulsing green.

In a calm voice, the comp said, "When you eat, you create waste, and that waste has to be eliminated. Humans have to go to the bathroom regularly."

There's no way ZD777 could understand, but one day it would, and the comp wanted it to be in the habit of listening. And that was the only way it would learn to speak.

The human left its blanket and pillow on the cot and hurriedly pulled itself over to the panel. The panel played the animation on how to pee and poop. This human was male-presenting, but the panel showed how to pee sitting down, as this human could not stand yet. ZD777 watched twice and then looked down at its body. With both of its hands, it felt its groin, the tip of its penis, and then its anus. It nodded slightly. Then it watched the animation twice more before going to the door indicated, opening it, and going into the small bathroom.

With the help of the handrails, it pulled itself to sitting on the toilet. Gas noisily escaped as its body eliminated. It took a while, and when the process was done, the human sighed deeply. As instructed by the panel, it pressed the button for the bidet and jumped when the water touched it. Once it was off the toilet, the toilet automatically flushed. It pulled itself over to the sink, onto its knees, and then obediently soaped up its hands and washed them. It did it a second time, apparently just to play with the soap and the water.

And so it went. Each cycle, ZD777 got stronger as it learned how to dress itself warmly, to exercise, and to take a shower. It was a tenday before it could stand, and three tendays before it could walk without much trouble. The comp kept it contained to the one room for the duration.

Once it was confident ZD777 could walk well, that it wouldn't do anything foolish, the comp opened the door to the rest of the station.

ZD777 had not exhibited any curiosity about that door. It had been busy sleeping, getting stronger, trying to walk better, pressing the instruction panel for new information. It was focused and hardworking. When the door popped open, the human jumped. Then it said, mangling and mouthing the unfamiliar words, "Here kitty, kitty, kitty."

Clete was 100 klicks long at its widest point, so there were klicks of subways and tunnels and barrio alleyways and rooms and levels and storage and cryo and so on—all of which once had been a bustling hub of activity but now with large parts sealed off due to system failures.

Clete's purpose had been to manufacture bio bodies for the planned development of Kuiper Station, connected habs around a series of asteroids that would have been the basis for mining and further expansion outward through the vast Kuiper Belt. Developers had envisioned a vast interconnected city, and Neptune's moon Triton was the staging area. This was centuries ago, just prior to the development of the Faison Gate. Once they had the Faison Gate at Triton, they enlisted Neptune's dwarf moon Clete, a captured trojan, to manufacture the bodies needed for the vast workforce that would be moving in. They drilled its tunnels and spun it up and installed life-support systems. Clete never got a Faison Gate itself.

And then there was the Blackout. In the early 2200s, there was a mass exodus from Earth as pings landed and gate after gate opened and planet after planet was available for settlement. Humans had wrecked Earth's environment, there was rampant unemployment, Basic didn't cover the basics, as they say, and so a new start didn't sound half bad, despite the danger. After so many left, the people on Earth were not happy, and so some of them got together and staged a coup, a decisive revolution on April 19, 2227, EU Earth. They blasted all the Faison Gates, disconnecting Earth from the vast human mechalum mesh for seventeen EUs. A few planets that were just getting started flailed miserably, but then Fury and Epsilon Eridani stepped into Earth's wake, offering humanitarian and technological aid and saving the day. They became the centers of power and technology, and planets looked to them for leadership.

This consortium eventually would become the MWA, the Milky Way Alliance. The MWA was a coalition of star systems, more of an mutual interest association than a governing body. Distances were so vast, and with the Faison

Gate system of transportation, armies could not be sent to take over other systems without a lot of advanced planning, so the MWA's influence was steady but light-handed. It had few enforcement capabilities besides embargoes and political influence.

This was before the MWA, though, and one of the systems that floundered was the Sol system. Without support from Earth, Luna went down in flames, and lots of people died. Mars was well-enough established and had three Faison Gates, so it took over as the center of the Sol system for the mechalum mesh, but it would never be Earth. Sol became a backwater, and humans in the system contracted back toward the core, which was now Mars. One of the casualties was the Kuiper Station project. The small base on Triton was abandoned—though its Faison Gate still worked.

In the chaos following the Blackout, Clete got cut off, and in the war and confusion everyone thought that it had been abandoned. It had not been abandoned, but the population had been—about 50,000 souls. Communications were cut off, and since there was no Faison Gate, there was no access to the mechalum mesh. A little rock, spinning in the dark, 28 AUs from Mars, 27 AUs from the closest substantial colony—a science station in the Sol asteroid belt.

At first there were riots and unrest, and another 20,000 died. Then there was the ill-fated attempt to reach Triton and its Faison Gate to mount a rescue mission. They made it a little over half way before their improvised life support crapped out, and their little tomb of a ship was still going, now somewhere out in deep space. The remaining 30,000 licked their wounds and, with more than enough resources and space, what with the reduced population, they planned to ride it out until someone noticed they were missing. No one ever did. The population was stable to declining—people couldn't have babies naturally any more, as they had gotten bio or mech bodies when they transferred in through Triton, and they didn't have a Faison Gate themselves to transfer into the thousands of bodies they had stored. So the remaining survivors made a plan. Anyone who wanted to could go into cryo sleep, in the hopes they would be rescued and then transferred into bio bodies. As time went on, the comp would revive successive pairs of caretakers to keep the pilot light on till someone came and woke up the people and took possession of the thousands of bodies.

It was just one of the many tragedies on a massive scale caused by the Blackout. In space, no one can hear you scream—unless you have a Faison Gate.

ZD777 stepped out of the quarters and then wavered and grabbed the hand railing. It was standing on the third level balcony of a barrio alleyway. All along the walls of the alley's steep sides, quarters were built into the tunnel walls, stacked into five levels in long rows striped with balconies and metal stairways. Light emanated from the wide rounded pale blue roof. Lots of panels were dead, and some were flickering as if they had just been turned on. It was a gloomy light, quavering in dark pools. The air was chilly and stale, as few of the circulating fans worked. Plants—some bedraggled or dead, all wild and overgrown—grew in planters in the alley floor. Everything was covered with a layer of dust or moss or mushrooms, and there were piles of decomposed trash with plants growing out of them in the pools of light. Windows to some of the quarters were broken, and doors missing. All the windows were dark.

ZD777 glanced one way, and then the other. Its quarters were near the end of the tunnel, and so the vertical walls to its left circled around to meet the other parallel wall. There was a huge screen hanging at the end of the alley, but it was gray and blank. In the other direction, the alley disappeared into the gloom.

"No one to clean up the place," the comp commented.

ZD777 began to explore this area of one-person-occupancy apartments. It opened the next door. The apartment was laid out the same, minus the cryo chamber. It loked like it had never been lived in, and all surfaces were covered with a thick layer of dust. The one next to that had been used as storage, as there were all kinds of things stacked in it. Boxes, bags, old machinery, a motor scooter, and some medical equipment.

The comp spoke as ZD777 explored, voice traveling from one proximity speaker to the next. The comp was well aware of humans' need for the illusion of companionship, especially when confronted with alarming surroundings.

The next door, which was on the arc of balcony at the end of the alleyway, was a gym. ZD777 stared at the exercise machines, clunky black outlines in the gloom of the single light that had reluctantly blinked on. ZD777 was obviously baffled as to their purpose. It prodded a few but did not seem to understand them.

Next on the arc was a large med bay. The comp made sure ZD777 toured the facility, and it explained what things were for, even though ZD777 wouldn't understand. It wanted ZD777 to be able to use the medical resources as quickly as possible, since its own ability to offer physical assistance was limited. It did not realize the ramifications of what that area contained, however. They'd gone through the diagnosis and treatment area with its crash couches, lights blinking on ahead and shutting off behind. Following the directions on a panel, ZD777 had sat in a crash couch and put its arm through a cuff, which had switched on and gone through a series of diagnostics. It proclaimed ZD777 as below normal in functioning but healing and otherwise sound. "Good," the comp said. "You're improving." They passed the surgery and into the area of recovery rooms.

But as they were returning to the balconies, they passed by the room in which the previous caretakers had died. The comp had not had the ability to remove and dispose of the bodies, and so they'd laid in their cots and slowly moldered away to skeletons.

ZD777 glanced through the door and saw the bodies and stopped in its tracks. It was transfixed. It didn't move, just stared into the room. The comp said, quietly, "Perhaps we should be returning to the quarters."

But ZD777 ignored it and slowly went into the room. In the first bed lay the caretaker who had dementia, and the second caretaker had covered it partially with a blanket. The blankets were made to last, and so it was as strong as ever, dusty and faded, but the clothes, which were meant to be disposed of, had disappeared. The flesh had disappeared too, and so there was just a skeleton. The rings, though, were still on finger bones, and a necklace had fallen through a rib cage. Wisps of hair lay on the pillow. In the second bed lay the second caretaker, and it hadn't covered itself, so it was just a skeleton with one metal leg bone where it had been injured while alive. It had no jewelry. Its clothes were gone, but it had been wearing boots, some of which remained, and a cap, the remains of which were propped crookedly on to the skull.

The comp would not have predicted what ZD777 did next. Instead of weeping or kneeling next to the bed, it looked at the first body and then the second body and then at its own hand, which it rotated one way and another, staring at it. Then, with all the force it could muster, it balled it into a fist and punched the wall, denting the wallboard. It pulled its fist back, shook it a couple of times, glanced over at the skeletons one more time, and then left, returning to the quarters. After that, it lay in its bed and did not get up for two cycles but to go to the bathroom.

That was also the cycle it had its first headache.

Chapter 43

There was so much to know. ZD777 would just get comfortable with one thing, and then the instruction panel and the voice would be urging him on to the next. ZD777 had figured out the meanings of a few words the voice said regularly, words like "yes" and "no."

One of the others he figured out was "ZD777," which referred to ZD777 himself. After learning that, ZD777 had an epiphany. He realized that everything had names. Excitedly, he pointed up to the general direction the voice was coming from. Than he pointed to himself and said, "ZD777." Then he pointed back up to the voice.

"Yes," the comp said. "You are ZD777." At the same time, a blinking green light lit around something on the end of the cryo chamber. That green light would turn out to be highlighting ZD777's name in written form, but ZD777 avoided the cryo chamber as much as possible, so he ignored the light and repeated, "ZD777," while pointing to himself. Then he pointed in the direction of the voice.

The voice answered, "I am the comp."

"Iamthecomp," ZD777 tried to say.

"No," the voice said. "Comp."

ZD777 pointed at himself and said, "ZD777." He pointed upward toward the voice and said, "Comp."

"Yes," the voice said. "I am Comp. You are ZD777."

"Iamcomp. YouareZD777."

"No," Comp said. "You say it the opposite way: You. Are. Comp. I. Am. ZD777."

"You. Are. ..." ZD777 didn't get it.

The voice tried to explain, but ZD777 couldn't get anything out of it. Finally, ZD777 said, pointing to himself, "ZD777," and then pointed to the voice, "Comp."

"Yes," Comp said. It didn't try to explain any further.

ZD777 figured out other words, but it was by no means straightforward. The word "Goodwaking," was actually two words—"good" and "waking." So when the voice said "Goodwaking," it was a thing it said every cycle upon ZD777's waking, like a preface to the cycle. But the voice could also use "good" in conjunction with "night" or "job" or "grief" and sometimes, though it seemed to mean a positive thing, it would take the opposite meaning. "Goodgrief" meant that ZD777 had done something and the voice was expressing disappointment. So it meant the opposite of "good." These things were so hard to pin down.

At the end of one cycle, as ZD777 was drifting off to sleep, he kept thinking about those things like himself in the rooms so far away. Who were they? They didn't exist like he existed—parts of them were missing, and they obviously were not like him. Maybe they had been before though? Or could be in the future?

He sat up and said to Comp, "ZD777," pointing to himself. Then he said, "Like ZD777," and pointed toward the door, toward the balcony that led to them.

"They are also humans," Comp said. "Humans," it repeated. Then it said, "They died. They're dead. You will also die one day. You also will be dead one day. Now, you are alive. Alive."

"Humans," ZD777 said. "Dead." It pointed toward the door. "Humans? Alive?" he said, pointing to himself. They were the same, but with a different quality. They had the quality of dead, and he had the quality of alive. Because of that, they could not communicate with him and they were missing parts of themselves.

"Yes, you are human like them, only they are dead and you are alive."

"So"—he pointed to himself—"ZD777, but"—again he pointed to himself—"human?"

"Yes," Comp said. "There are categories you call groups of things, and then each of those things has an individual name. For example, there is a group of things called computers. The panel on the wall where you learn things is a type of a computer, and I am a type of a computer. We are different, yet we are both computers. You are a human like those two were human, but your individual name is ZD777. My individual name—what we've decided to call me—is Comp."

ZD777 thought on that for a while, and then asked, "Name?" while pointing to the instruction panel.

"Unfortunately, the instruction panel does not have a name. Would you like to give it a name?"

ZD777 opened his eyes wide in surprise. "ZD777?"

"Yes, you could name the panel."

ZD777 thought for a while and then said, "Green. Name Green." He had just started to learn his colors, with the help of the panel. He nodded, proud of himself.

"Green it is, then," Comp said. "You are ZD777. I am Comp. Instruction panel is Green."

"I am ZD777. You are Comp," ZD777 said. He pointed to the instruction panel and said, "Green.

"Good job," Comp said. "You now can use pronouns like 'I' and 'you' correctly. I am proud of you."

ZD smiled. Then he paused and then glanced toward the door. "Name?" he said, pointing toward the door and the two skeletons beyond. It seemed like a really important thing to know.

"Their names were Sheila and Donnie," Comp said. "Sheila was a systems technician who liked to sleep in at waking and wanted to return to Earth to start a farm. Donnie was an electrician who liked to make miniature models of the solar system and stars and thought Sheila was crazy for wanting to return to Earth. They were a couple—they had decided they would spend their lives together."

ZD777 only understood a bit of what Comp said, but it made him feel both good and bad. Satisfied, he rolled over and went to sleep.

Chapter 44

The next cycle, first thing after ZD777 showered and dressed, Comp said, "I'm going give you a very powerful tool today." At the same time, Green got ZD777's attention. It showed an image of a thin flat box in a recessed area over near the cryo chamber. As it showed the image, a door to the recess rolled upwards to reveal the thin flat box shown in the illustration.

ZD777 grabbed the chair—there had been no chair in the room when he first woke up, so he had retrieved one from the gym once he knew about their existence, at Comp's suggestion. He went over to the slim flat box, giving the cryo chamber a wide berth. The wall was configured so that ZD777 could sit comfortably on the chair with his knees into a recess in the wall and see the flat box. He did as Green directed—with his fingertips, he pulled the top half of the slim flat box upwards. The top half flipped up on hinges, revealing a black screen on one side and all these black buttons with weird symbols on top of them on the other. They were the symbols ZD777 had seen scattered throughout the facility in groups that ran along the walls.

As instructed, ZD777 pressed a button in the upper left-hand corner of the bottom with a small circle crossed by a line. Then the buttons were highlighted in bright red and the screen flashed a gray-black color. It was waking up. Different symbols popped up on the screen, moved a bit, and then disappeared, to be replaced by other symbols. Eventually, the screen turned blue and lines of symbols in all different colors appeared. Then the screen was fixed in that configuration.

Comp said, "This is another computer. Green was limited in what it could teach you, but this is not. You can access all the information we have available, and you can compose your own journal, once you learn to write, or you can do a verbal log, if you prefer. You can also listen in to the broadcasts from Mars, though the signal is very weak. There are sound and images, but we don't have much current video footage. We don't have the capacity to send messages to them, however. That ability was compromised centuries ago. We will start by teaching you to read and write."

One of the symbols highlighted. "Touch this symbol with your finger when you want to start the reading program," Comp said. ZD777 put his finger on the highlighted symbol, and the blue screen disappeared and another screen appeared with more symbols on it. It went through a series of symbols and images, before settling on five symbols in a row in the middle of the screen, the last three the same.

"This is your name," Comp said.

Each symbol was highlighted in turn as the computer in front of ZD777 said, "Zee. Dee. Seven. Seven. Seven."

"That is how your name is spelled," Comp said. "It's also how it is pronounced. You say your name like you spell your name."

The symbols on the screen changed.

"This is my name. You spell it by going through the letters, but you say it as one word, 'Comp.'"

The computer highlighted each symbol and said, "Cee. Oh. Em. Pee. Comp."

This was fascinating to ZD777—he was hooked. He immediately saw that this was the gateway to understanding the world around him, all those symbols in the tunnels. And so after that he spent every waking hour at the computer—which Comp helped him name "Laptop" because it rested easily on top of ZD777's lap when he sat on his cot or on the chair.

ZD777 learned to direct Laptop by pressing the screen or typing on the keys or using hand motions or talking. He learned the letters of the alphabet and the sounds they made and then how they fit together into sentences. He learned numbers and how to add and subtract and then quickly how to multiply and divide. "You have an aptitude for math," Comp said. "You are good at math." It made ZD777 feel proud, and he focused even more on the numbers.

One cycle, when ZD777 was focused on pronouncing some long words, Comp said, "Would you like to see what it looks like outside?"

"Outside?" ZD777 said. "On the balcony?"

"No, outside of Clete, outside of this asteroid."

"Yes," ZD777 said quickly.

On Laptop, Comp brought up an image. It was the first image ZD777 had seen of the anything that wasn't an icon or an illustration or a wall decoration. The picture was a deep dark black scattered with tiny sparkling spots of white. At the center was a brilliant and beautiful ball, striped and blotched with areas of deep blue to blue-white with a few faint gray rings. Off to one side was a smaller ball with blotches of gray, pale green, and pale red.

"That's the planet Neptune and its moon Triton. We orbit Neptune like Triton," Comp said. "The little white dots are other stars like the Sun, only they're very far away. Stars give off heat and light and energy."

ZD777 leaned forward, craning his neck to look as closely as possible. He used the pinching and pulling motion with his fingers to zoom in first on Neptune and then on Triton.

"Let me help you," Comp said. "I'll project it on the wall screen."

And empty area on one wall lit up and replicated the image on laptop.

"Wall screen?" ZD777 said. "Wall screen?!" He was asking why Comp hadn't shown it to him before.

"You didn't need it yet," Comp said.

ZD777 set the laptop aside and stepped in front of the wall screen. The image was so beautiful. ZD777 stared at it for a full half hour. Comp explained how ZD777 could use hand motions to control the screen, and ZD777 zoomed in and out.

"Can I see other images?" ZD777 said.

"Yes." Comp brought up another image. It was again a black sky dotted with stars, but there was one star that was a lot brighter. "This is our sun, Sol. It's very far away—not as far as these other stars, but still very far." Comp brought up another image, a bright ball of fire. It was dark red with orange-yellow blotching all over it. There were little jets, flames, off its surface and into the blackness. "This is Sol close up."

It was beautiful too. ZD777 wanted to hold out his hands and feel the warmth. "More," he said.

Comp brought up an image of another ball in the blackness of space. This one was blue like Neptune but had whorls of white and then some green and tan underneath. It was beautiful. "This is Earth," Comp said. "This is where we come from."

"Where is Earth?" ZD777 asked.

"It's between us and the Sun, but it's really really far away."

"Can we go there?"

Comp didn't answer for a minute. Then it said, "If we could, it would take eight EUs to get there. But we do not have a spacecraft. So, no, we can't. The others who lived here on Clete before tried really really hard to go back to Earth, but they weren't able to make it." Then it added, "I am sorry."

ZD777 felt immensely sad for something he had just learned existed. He stared at the image. It was so beautiful, even more beautiful than Neptune.

"More," ZD777 said, and so Comp took him on a tour of the Solar System and the stars. It showed him the interactive program where ZD777 could zoom in and out, rotate, point to object to read more information, access information on orbits and masses and gravities and tilts, and even access how things were calculated.

ZD777 wolfed down information. If he wasn't flipping through images, he was reading vast tomes about science and math and history or using the interactive programs to dive deeply into a subject. At first it took a lot of time just to get through a page, and he had to look up a lot of words or ask Comp about them, but soon he was racing through and only having to look up a word here and there.

Every so often, ZD777 would get a headache. At first, Comp thought it was due to eye strain, but ZD777's vision was perfect. It still could be eye strain, Comp said. But they weren't too bad, and Comp had him take analgesics to lessen the pain.

But then, over the course of tendays, the headaches got worse, and analgesics wouldn't touch them. According to scans, there was nothing wrong with him, Comp said, and so there was nothing to fix. Right before they came on, ZD777 would feel cranky and thirsty and stiff and tired. He yawned a lot. And then, right before the pain hit, he would get a pins and needles sensation in his extremities, and everything would develop a glow around it, as if he'd been transported to another dimension and could see some invisible essence. Then the pain would flatten him, and he would take to his cot. One side of his head would throb and pulse, and he had Comp turn off the lights, as they made the headaches worse. His stomach would feel upset, though he rarely vomited as he wouldn't eat once they started to come on. They usually lasted a cycle or two, but the worst lasted three full cycles. Then the pain would slowly lessen, and then he'd feel weak and disoriented. Then he'd be fine.

"This type of headache is not unknown among humans," Comp said. "I am sorry."

They got bad, though. "There must be something we can try," ZD777 told Comp.

There was one thing, Comp said. It had been an experimental procedure before Clete had been cut off and had worked on some people with these kinds of headaches. It involved injecting a biological toxin into the brain that impeded certain processes while promoting others. The med bay could fabricate the compound with the materials on hand. However, it was dangerous. Fifty percent of the time, it didn't do anything and could have bad side effects, and about ten percent of the population never woke up from the healing coma.

Comp, usually decisive in its advice, said simply, "I've advised you of the odds. You must decide."

ZD777 put off the decision.

Chapter 45

Comp showed him the historic archive of video, and for the first time ZD777 saw images of other humans in motion. It was surreal, ZD777 thought. Not for the first time, he wished to be able to talk to another human who was right there, who stood in the room with him. He came across a clip of a human talking while looking into the camera, as if they were looking straight at him, and he played that clip over and over and over again.

And then ZD777 discovered fiction. He had loved science, but fiction filled a place that he didn't know was empty. While science told him about the world and how its mechanical parts worked, fiction told him about people, about how the world felt, what emotions other humans had felt in reaction to it and to each other. Fiction educated ZD777 in a whole new way—it helped him understand what he was feeling. But then he grieved all over again for the humans he would never know.

Comp said it was concerned that ZD777 would sink into a deep depression, and so it showed him how to use the workout machinery in the gym and how to create art. ZD777 would spend long hours on the treadmill, his body in relentless motion while his mind raced. His body became toned and muscled, and his stamina grew. He detached Laptop's screen from its keyboard and used a pen to sketch. He used the wall as a digital artboard to create everything from huge splash paintings to finely drawn mandala patterns that took tendays to finish. Comp showed him where there was a supply of plasticine and allowed him to take a hunk the size of his head. He sculpted things he saw around the quarters, people he saw in images. It all helped—maybe not enough, but some.

ZD777 also began exploring the barrio, and so Comp brought up a map and subway diagram to explain how Clete was laid out so ZD777 wouldn't get lost. Clete was a rounded to oblong metal asteroid 100 clicks long and 43 klicks wide. It had been spun up lengthwise, and its center had been mined out. There was a port for people on one end and a dock for cargo on the other. Three subway lines—Red, Green, and Blue—had been installed lengthwise to the asteroid into the walls of the interior, and then every eight klicks or so, perpendicular circular routes numbered starting portside connected the three lines.

The interior had been sectioned off in case of breach to hard vacuum and built up for living and working spaces. Portside interior had a section of shops and restaurants and public spaces and a central plaza, then there was a section of public services such as the government offices, vats and gardens for food production, and a five-klick-long tube of green space called Central Park. These were set close to the edge of the interior to maximize spin gravity. The central line of the asteroid, where gravity was zero, was reserved for special applications, and there was a gym and training area for workers who went outside. Rimside, in the rock beyond the interior out where spin gravity approached one G, tunnels had been carved that became long barrio alleyways—like the one ZD777 lived in—lit with artificial sunlight and lined with people's living quarters. These alleyways were named alphabetically in counterclockwise rotation to portside— Athens, Byzantium, Croton, Delphi, and so on. All of these except Naxos, ZD777's barrio, had been shut down a long time ago.

On the other end of the public and living spaces was a hard break, and then came the labs and manufacturing area. People had commuted from their homes in the alleyways to their jobs in this area. This is where they created the bio bodies that were going to be used for the development of the Kuiper Belt. Another hard break, and then there was cold storage for cryo. There were also service tunnels in the rock rimside. The dock was beyond that.

Comp warned him that the subways no longer worked and that Comp had no sensors or control past the end of the manufacturing section, where cold storage was located. "I can't help you there," Comp said.

Chapter 46

Half the time, ZD777 read and studied, and the other half he explored Clete. He would pack a knapsack with vat hard tack and a water bottle and spend hours wandering, all the while creating a map in his head. He got lost a couple of times in the beginning, but Comp was always there to explain how to get home.

He explored the apartments and shops and restaurants in Naxos. They were pretty much the same, and he quickly got bored with it. There was little to no personal effects in the apartments—they must've been cleaned out before people went into cryo, or after they died. In a closed system like Clete, nothing went to waste. Sometimes the shops were empty, and sometimes they had stuff on the shelves, and if they hadn't been covered with dust, they could have been opened immediately.

He was able to gather some foods that were shelf stable and still edible, and he found some clothes, although he was tall and it took some time to locate his size. He found a resizable black cap he liked. It had a bill sticking out one side—what that was for, he didn't quite know—and on the front it had a stylized X, half in gray, half in blue, the gray arm a long arc shooting into the air to the right. He found some tools—the knapsack, a compactable blanket, a pocket knife, flashlights, some rope, duct tape, gorilla glue, a handheld so that Comp could communicate all the time and didn't have to follow the speakers.

He also found what Comp explained was a golf club and a whole bin of golf balls, and he spent a straight tenday launching balls down the alleyway. At first, he broke a lot of windows, but by the end he could perfectly launch it to where it barely missed the roof and disappeared into the black of the tunnel.

He decided to find out how far Naxos went. Comp helped him find a headlamp that he attached to his cap, and he loaded his backpack with almost a tenday's worth of food. Comp assured him that he could probably make the trip to the other end and back in five or six cycles, easy, and he could find water along the way. It also told him that long stretches were dark, and he'd have to be careful not to hurt himself, as there was no way Comp could get him back to the med bay.

And so he started out. He went slowly and carefully. The light quickly turned to gloom and then to complete dark, and ZD777 had to find his way by the light of his headlamp. He made his way around the garbage piles, his boots crunching on the debris. In the distance, he could hear the drip of water and the rumble of machinery and circulators kicking off and kicking on. Every once in a while he would here a heavy clunk that Comp said was small asteroids hitting rimside. He also thought he heard something moving, small and far away, but he chalked that up to an overactive imagination. The smell went

267

from a dusty green moldiness to a frigid dankness, and it got colder—or at least felt that way without the lights.

Then, up ahead, ZD777 saw light begin to glow. There was also a low-level rumble that got louder as he went. The tunnel sloped upward, and soon the glow was a blue semicircle cut off on the bottom.

ZD777 made his way upward on a series of metal steps, which clanked and rung under his footfalls. As he reached the peak, the rumble became a roar, the light bloomed in front of him, and then he was standing on a high point, the alley sloping down in front of him and then back up in the distance. Water was pouring out of a blasted-out storefront on the fifth level, cascading down in a massive waterfall, bouncing off railings and other protrusions, creating a rainbow across the alley. It must have had a way to drain down below, as the pool had obviously been there for a very long time. Vines grew up toward the light alongside the waterfall and on the opposite side. In the dip on the floor, a huge pool had collected, which was overgrown with lily pads and algae and there seemed to be something swimming within it. Whatever they were, they swam in circles, flashing gold and red and white and black and yellow. There were little flying creatures in the air that buzzed and flitted in bright blue and black.

It was the most beautiful thing ZD777 had ever seen. It looked like something from Earth. He asked Comp if there was any way he could take that picture with him, and Comp explained how he could use his handheld to take an image. He took a photo of the waterfall. It didn't look nearly as spectacular on the handheld, but it conjured up what the experience felt like, and that was what was important.

"You could take a selfie, too," Comp suggested and explained what a selfie was. ZD777 tried it, reversing the camera direction on the handheld and then pressing the button to take the image. It worked.

ZD777 stared at it. He hadn't really looked at his own face before. Compared to the images of other humans he'd seen, he looked normal. A long face, deep-set blue eyes, low bushy eyebrows, a sturdy wedge of a nose, full lips, a strong jaw, short blonde hair that Comp helped him cut, a bit of wispy chin hair—Comp had explained that human males grew hair on their faces to varying degrees but he naturally did not have much because he was of a certain Nordic descent. ZD777 asked what the meant, and Comp explained that that was an area of Earth, that his DNA was passed down from people who lived in that area. It struck ZD777 as a revelation. He was connected to Earth, and someone who had had his DNA had lived on Earth.

Then, an inspiration hit him, and he turned away from the waterfall, held up the handheld and snapped a picture of himself with the waterfall in the background. When he looked at it later, he thought he might even look happy.

ZD777 then sat on some metal steps and ate his lunch staring at the waterfall, his body relaxed, his mind clear.

In order to get around the area, ZD777 had to mount the stairs to the fifth floor on the opposite side. Plant growth blocked the way on the lower levels, and the fourth floor balcony had either been torn away or fallen. As he made his way across the balcony, he could feel the cold mist rising and circulating. It felt good, though it was cold.

Reluctantly, he went on his way. There continued to be lights, but they were intermittent. And then he reached the other end. It had taken three cycles, two sleep periods. It was anticlimactic—it looked very much like his end, except the apartments were bigger multifamily units. The alley widened a bit, and there was a long narrow park in the center of it.

The return trip seemed to take forever, as he'd seen the whole stretch. He stopped by the waterfall and that was where he spent a sleep period, just staring at the falling water and listening to its roar. Then he continued on. He hurried, wanting to get back to his quarters, but then he stumbled and fell in the dark. It made quite a clatter.

Comp said from the handheld, "What happened? Are you sound?"

"I am," ZD777 said. He was more careful after that.

There in the dark, he heard the skitterings again. They weren't his imagination. And this time, as he approached the light in his stretch of the alley, he thought he saw off in the distance a couple of pairs of pinpricks of light, moving and blinking.

"Welcome home," Comp said, as ZD777 made it back to his quarters, collapsed on the bed, and fell into a deep sleep.

Chapter 47

The next cycle, ZD777 was sitting out on his balcony, feet propped on the rails, watching the way the light played across the windows across the way, and then he heard the skittering again. He glanced down the balcony and then sat bolt upright. There, on the balcony floor, a little ways away, were three creatures. They were each about the size of ZD777's hand, pale gray-brown fur, a long hairless tail, round pink ears, a pointed pink nose, and whiskers that seemed to have a life of their own.

They were cautiously scurrying along the balcony, sniffing as they came. When they saw him move, they stopped and hid behind a jutting column. A pair of nose hairs flickered around the edge.

"WHAT," ZD777 asked Comp, "are those?

"Those are rats, the common brown rat, scientific name *Rattus norvegicus*," Comp said. "They've been tailing you the last couple of cycles. They're curious about you, I think."

ZD777 pushed himself up and walked a few steps their way and stopped. One of them came around the column but then stopped, sat on its hind legs, hands held next to its chest, and stared at him, tilting its head one way and another, whiskers flicking.

ZD777 just stood there, looking back.

Another of the rats emerged from the column and came up next to the first one. It sniffed a couple of times and then came a little closer, but then stopped too. The first one came up next to the second, and they both sat close together, eyeing him. They didn't seem to fear him, but they were cautious. The third one poked its head out from behind the column but didn't emerge.

They stayed that way for a bit, and then ZD777 lowered himself down to the floor and sat, back against the balcony railing. He turned his body away ninety degrees, but he turned his head toward them and watched. They shrunk back a bit when he moved but then they came forward slowly, first one and then the other. Soon, he could almost reach out and touch them. They sat back on their haunches and regarded him for a while and then they seemed to come to some sort of agreement. One went around his feet, sniffing the whole time, checking him out, while the other jumped up on the balcony railing and made its way over his head.

ZD777 tilted his head first one way and the other, following the rat on the balcony above his head. It stopped by his right shoulder and sat, sniffing and watching him. The one on the ground circled around and came so close ZD777 could almost touch him. ZD777 lifted his hand slowly and carefully reached out. The rat retreated just out of reach, but then watched him. ZD777 sat that way for quite a while, and the rats watched him, sniffing, circling a bit and then coming together and sniffing each other, communicating in some way. ZD777 was fascinated, staring at them, trying to figure out what they were communicating, how their bodies went together, what their intent was. They were friendly but standoffish, and they did not particularly fear him.

Finally, they turned and scurried off down the balcony, back the way they had come.

That night, ZD777 looked up everything he could about rats. He found out that they were common on earth and that they traveled on humans' ships, first over Earth's seas and then through space. They spread wherever humans spread via ship. They had been known to swarm humans and eat them but only when they were overpopulated and starving. Humans had done the same to rats, as it turned out. These were not starving, just curious. They couldn't have come through the Faison Gate on Triton, and so they must have come on the early ships that traveled from Earth, eight EUs one way, bringing vital supplies.

He named the first one to come out, which was a reddish tan and had a tattered ear, Naga after a mythological Earth dragon. He named the second one, who was a little darker with a clipped pink tail, Liu after an astronaut he had read about who had given his life in development of the Faison Gate. He named the little one, who always hung behind, Baobao for baby.

That began a long companionship. The rats would come and go, and ZD777 found himself watching for them to show up. When they came, Naga would always be there, often accompanied by Liu. Baobao only came occasionally, but sometimes another rat would join them, one that ZD777 didn't know. ZD777 tried to offer them food, but they were not interested. They must get their food from the green spaces or from some other part of Clete. Undoubtedly they had access to much of the asteroid. He even began to talk to them—whatever came into his head, and they would tilt their heads and listen.

Having other warm bodies around, even if they weren't human, made ZD777 feel slightly better.

Chapter 48

ZD777 packed his backpack and dressed in gear for the deep cold, at Comp's warning, to explore the rest of Clete's portside. He had to take the stairs up to the interior, since the elevators had been shut down. He climbed in the dark for hours, up one flight, turn, up the next, counting each step—the top step was number 2,226. He had to shed some layers, but he was still drenched in sweat.

The asteroid had not been breached to hard vacuum, so there was air in the interior, but that air was very cold, as the heat had been shut down to a minimum in most areas, and there wasn't much to see, as the lights had been turned off in most spaces. And so most of it was just frozen shapes looming into the light of his headlamp and then looming out again. The air smelled earthy and metallic and musty, sometimes of acrid ozone, sometimes with a touch of sweetness.

He went into Central Park, and he could tell by the feel of the air and the way the sound bounced that it was a vast space. It smelled musty and was a piercing humid cold. He saw his first trees, once again looming in the dark, and he heard a little movement way off in the distance—Naga's cousins, he assumed. He left Central Park and visited other tunnels where there were greenhouses and government offices and shopping malls and public spaces, all cold dark peopleless spaces.

Then he came to a long low area that was humid and warm—warm enough he started sweating and had to shed all his layers. It smelled strongly of growing things, some sweet, some earthy, some fetid. A dim blue illumination periodically showed from recessed lighting along the floor and ceiling. The room was filled with huge closed metal vats and tubes that ran crazily between and around the vats and across the ceiling and into the floor. The floor was a metal grating, with drains underneath. The vats had tall narrow windows on the side, and inside he could see a thick liquid bubbling. The liquid varied from gray to brown to green to orange to red. This was food production, Comp told him.

Then he looped over into the laboratories and manufacturing area. It was klicks of echoing rooms and halls filled with mysterious equipment, all shut down. There were conveyor systems and laboratory analysis stations and growing chambers and med bays and much more.

He asked Comp over the handheld what some of the things were for, and Comp tried to explain. Basically, this is where they developed eggs and sperm, made embryos, put them through the mechalum process, which resulted in the creation of bio bodies. These were then put into cryo and stored in the last section portside. At least, that's what had happened before the Blackout.

"This is where you were born, created, put in cryo," Comp added.

"What?" ZD777 said. "Where I was ... What?"

276

It had never occurred to him that he had been born on Clete. He had read so much about the lives of people on Earth and the science of biological reproduction and so on and so forth, he had just assumed that he had come from Earth. He wasn't sure why he didn't remember it, but he hadn't thought to ask Comp. It was one of those things he had never questioned.

"That means ..." ZD777 mumbled. "That means that I'm not ... I'm a bio body?"

"You're a human," Comp said.

"But if I was created on Clete, and the purpose of Clete was to create bio bodies for workers in the Kuiper Belt, then I am a bio body. Right? Correct?"

Comp said, "A human is a human, whether or not they are vacated from their body by another human."

At each new revelation, adrenalin shot through ZD777. "Vacated?" he said, his voice reaching an even higher pitch. "Vacated is what you do when you leave a room. You can come back into a room." He took a deep breath. "Once someone leaves a bio body, can the original human enter again?"

"No," Comp said. "The original human is killed when its body is inhabited by another human, by that human's essence."

"And how many bodies did this station create? For here and Triton and the Kuiper Belt. Not to mention the ones who came through the gate to be workers, who came into a body. How many is that?"

"Collectively, on both Clete and Triton, 52,429 workers created their own bodies or hopped to another, plus 368,102 bodies, plus 543 who went into mech bodies, for a total of

421,074 humans." There was a pause and then Comp added, "Eighty-nine humans came in ships from Earth and Mars early in the process."

"And so the 52,429 workers count for two, give or take, since they had people within them to begin with. That's—"

"104,858—" Comp cut in.

"Right, over a hundred thousand, plus ... how many, uh, unused bio bodies?"

"368,102," Comp said.

"So about 472,000—" ZD777 said.

"472,960—"

"Plus the mechs. So over 473,000."

"473,503," Comp said.

And how many ..." ZD777 was suddenly very afraid. The numbers made him light-headed. "How many of that half a million still survive?"

Comp did not hesitate "One."

"Me. I'm the only one."

"Yes."

ZD777 slumped down to the floor. His ears were ringing, his vision fuzzy, and all the objects he could see in his headlamp were taking on a glow.

"But," Comp continued, its tone very reasonable, "that's the way things are done nowadays. People travel between planets all the time. They don't travel in ships—they gate through a Faison Gate, sometimes into a mech body, sometimes into a bio body. We have very little incoming communication here on Clete, but from what I can gather, it's just what people do. Every cycle, a hundred thousand, maybe two hundred thousand people gate."

"Thousands … every cycle. How many into bio bodies?"

"I couldn't—"

"How many?!"

"I have no way of gathering that information, as you know, as our communications are very limited. I will estimate. Three hundred settled worlds, say—very very conservatively—that 100 gate a cycle for a full EU, say half of those go into bio bodies. That's 5,475,000 bio bodies an EU."

"That's genocide." He'd never said the word out loud before.

The headache came boiling out of ZD777's shoulders and neck and split his head open. He closed his eyes and laid his head back against the wall he'd collapsed against. But then he raised his head one more time and asked, "Why? How do people justify it?"

"They believe the bodies are empty," came Comp's answer.

They're not, ZD777 thought and rolled into a ball of pain. There was pain, going on and on.

Afterwards, ZD777 did not remember how he got back to Naxos. It was all one continuous period of pain. There were at least thirty klicks of tunnels between him and his quarters. Comp told him that he hadn't responded to Comp's queries for 36 hours and then he'd slowly gotten up and trudged home, barely stopping. When he got back to his quarters, he'd unlocked the rollers on the cryo chamber and frantically shoved it out of the door and off the balcony. It tumbled down the stairs and smashed on the barrio floor. Then he took to his cot and slept for three cycles. When he woke, he still had the migraine, but it had lessened from completely unbearable to very painful. Comp urged him to drink lots of water and gave him as many analgesics as it dared. ZD777 fuzzed out, but then when he woke the next cycle, he was still in great pain.

"I can't take this," ZD777 said. "I really can't. You might as well kill me."

"We can try the procedure. That could kill you," Comp said helpfully.

"Anything's better than this," ZD777 said.

Comp sent ZD777 to the med bay, which it directed to make the compound. ZD777 lay in one of the crash couches, his arm in the med cuff. Comp told him that he was going to be put in a medical coma, and they wouldn't know if the treatment worked until—if—he woke up.

ZD777's last thought before he went under the anesthetic was, no one will ever know I even existed.

Part 4

Jazari, ZD777, and Eala

Chapter 49

Jazari was trying to talk, but her mouth wouldn't work quite right. Whatever she was now, it didn't have the same vocal organs. Or the same body. Or the same anything.

This wasn't like when she'd jumped from a bio body into a mech body. Her bio body had been great, and her mech body had been pretty all right. The transition wasn't too startling. If she'd had the money, she could have gotten all kinds of enhancements—things like seeing in the dark and flying and being inmesh 24/7. As it was, her experience with a mech body was fairly similar to her bio body—they kept it that way on purpose.

In a mech, she'd missed eating and the feeling of touch across her skin. It was weird not to have to go to the bathroom and to not get physically tired. She did get mentally and emotionally tired, and she took the transition comp's advice and kept up her old schedule of down time, even though it tended to be just a few hours. But the minimal need for sleep freed up all this time that she used studying and reading, which helped her get her degree even faster. At first, it was hard to fill up all that time, though. She just hadn't realized how much time the stuff of life took up—eating, sleeping, pooping, things like that.

She didn't have to work out or watch what she ate. Her physical abilities were pretty amazing and she couldn't improve them by working out regularly. If the mental part of some physical activity was important, that's when an essent in a mech body would have to practice. She did have to work at first at making her mental connection to her physicality as good as it could be, but that's as close to exercise as she got. And she didn't feel pain. You could set it so you did feel pain—some people wanted that, for some strange reason. Instead, her body would alert her either with a sort of a buzzing sensation and through her ccomp. It was really hard to injure this body though. The only times she ever got the warning buzz was when she'd pushed too hard and her charge was ebbing, which was rare. Mech bodies had fusion batteries that charged continually on ambient.

It was also weird not to feel emotions in the same way. Something to do with hormones, the transition comp had told her. She still felt them of course, but they were somewhat disconnected. She also couldn't get physically aroused in the same way—she found herself thinking every once in a while, when she saw someone attractive, I'd've fucked that person. She still was attracted to people, and she went to bed with a few just to see what it was like, but her body didn't respond in the same way, and she found herself relying on her imagination a lot more.

She had to admit, though, as hellish as Fury was, it was beautiful. Someone had once called the planet a furious city inhabited by savages. It was a tidally locked world ravaged by solar winds. The toxic atmosphere was perpetually dim and obscured by gas and dust, which lead to skies that glowed pale yellow and orange around Proxima Centauri in its fixed position, fading to red, purple, blue, then black and dotted with stars if you could get past the light pollution. Not that you would be outside to see the sky—it had to be viewed in holo or on a viewscreen or inmesh. Heatside toward Prox was furious hot storms, and away from heatside was frozen ice, but down the thin middle was water in liquid form. It was called the Serpentine Sea, which was strewn with island landmasses. Storms would regular pop over from heatside or coldside and bring either hurricane conditions or blinding snowstorms.

Because Fury was the first system settled outside Sol, it was the focus of Earth immigration for centuries, and what was habitable was now solid city. You couldn't see the Serpentine Sea because it was buried in metal, and you lived inside a continuous gleaming hab city radiating artificial illumination in the perpetual dusk. The city had been built under the water, over it, and in the habitation ring circling in near-planet orbit, which was called the Terminator.

The air was not breathable, so no one lived outside of the habs, and the wicked solar radiation had to be shielded with water or thick metal plates or specially designed fabric made of nanotubes. Like everywhere, there were incedents, though, who tended to die from atmosphere poisoning or cancer or any number of other ailments related to marginal conditions, if they were bio. Most incedents opted for mech if they had a choice.

It was kind of perfect to be a mech in a metal city, though, if you were covered by Basic. Every once in a while Jazari would forget her studies and go out into the tunnels. She lived

285

in the underwater portion—only the filthy rich lived in the Terminator, and only the crazy lived above water. From the rabbit warrens of the underbelly to the common markets and town squares to the rarified university quads and labs, the tunnels teamed with life, and almost everyone came from somewhere else and hence were in mech bodies. You could hear accents from all over, some basically another language.

There was a tradition to be as outlandish as possible with augments and entopics. The tunnels were a riot of color and bodies and movement, and since there was no day cycle it just went on and on. There were people who lived in mechs that looked like tiny pink poodles, like superheroes of old, like the nightmarish spider species from the Simbaud system, like mechs covered with live skin tissue. There was a whole subculture whose motto was, "Don't just dream it, be it." They'd spend what little creds they did have on a silly augment that bathed them in a purple glow or made real peacock feathers grow from their butts.

When the grief and loneliness became too much, Jazari would escape to the city. Because Jazari was in a mech, she had to simulate the experience of partying, but it wasn't a stretch, since just being among the raucousness of it all was an experience all its own. It was exhausting and exhilarating and most importantly distracting.

She felt like a part of her had been ripped away, that there was a Dang-sized hole inside her. Late in a cycle as she prepared to sleep, her mind would follow the voices and then one would sound like Dang, or she would think of something that inevitably reminded her of Dang, and her nonexistent stomach would clench into a ball. Her thoughts would spiral.

She would remember what Dang smelled like. She would imagine Dang's skin, her entopic tats, her eyes, what it felt like to lie next to her, her laugh, her favorite entopic perfume, what she smelled like during sex. And then Jazari would cry. When a mech body cried, it didn't get sloppy with tears, but it would shake as Jazari sobbed.

Her grief threatened to overwhelm her and overtake her studies, and so she tried to do something about it. Psychosomatic, the medcomp had said and prescribed a stronger mood enhancer and a sleep inducer. She started using them whenever things got really bad, which turned into every other day and then every day. She'd have to turn on a stimulant the next day to bring herself out of it. Because they were prescribed, she didn't have to pay for them, but she began hunting up other things that made her feel in other ways. They were little programs called mech poppers or moppers. Some blanked her out, some pepped her up, some made her feel invincible and all's right with the world—she loved those. These little programs cost a pretty cred, and so she couldn't do it very often. That was her saving grace. Once, she woke up from a tenday bender in a tunnel in a pile of other mechs. She didn't remember what had happened. That was fairly early in her college career, and that's when she'd turned it around and became the excellent student that she was. She trained herself not to think about Dang except in very small bits, when she allowed it. It always led to a spiral of anguish and self-pity and blaming, stoking thoughts of revenge. That could only get her dead.

This body was way different. This was a bio body again, for one thing—a really strange bio body—and she could feel all the physical urges she'd sort of forgotten about. She felt pain again, and she had to pee again and eat again, though not as much as she'd expected. The sun felt absolutely amazing. Whenever she was in it, it felt like really good sex combined with a really good meal—energizing and comforting. She craved the sun.

The first time she let herself wallow in thinking of Dang, she felt so bad in this bio body, without any form of relief and anyone to ask for help, that she vowed not to think of her again. Dang had to stay in the past.

To her amazement, her ccomp was still there. It told her that she was in a fairly newly colonized planet in an indigenous life form. She thought about having it call for help, but then who would it call? She wasn't sure about the local authorities, and everyone she knew was associated with Zosi and Atze, and she didn't want them knowing where she was. Hopefully by now they thought she was dead, since her empty mech body would've been found at the Faison Gate on Fury. She was free of them.

Jazari, it had reported, *I have full functionality. I can contact Corvus authorities—*

DON'T YOU DARE, Jazari shouted mentally. It sent a jolt of adrenalin through her. Her ccomp had never be altogether trustworthy. They were programmed to do what they thought was best for their hosts, Jazari was sure, and while her ccomp had never outright defied or betrayed her, it had taken its authority too far. She hated it, now more than ever. She'd been tempted to turn it completely off in the past, and now she took a deep breath. Did she dare?

Yes, she found that she did dare. It wasn't like she was in the city where she needed constant mesh connection to the world around her. This world was different. She wanted to escape all that. And so she did.

Ccomp, you are to shut down and cease your services until such time in the future that I turn you back on. I want you to also turn off all recording and monitoring systems.

There was a pause and her ccomp said, *Code to restart?*

It had to be something she didn't say in regular conversation, something she would remember. Jazari knew immediately: *Dangarembga oi Bsam.* A twinge.

Authorization code for immediate companion computer shutdown?

What was it? It had been a long time. She'd set this when she was a kid. Aah yes. *Aang of the Northern Air Temple.* At the time she'd been way into an old adventure tale that had been made and remade in various forms throughout the centuries. She had just finished watching an augreal version with mech characters set in Tau Ceti's dust belt.

And then her ccomp was gone. Completely gone. She'd always taken it for granted, but now that it was shut off, she realized that she'd always been aware of its presence. It was always there looking over her shoulder, an enemy literally in her midst. She suddenly felt such relief, such freedom, such autonomy.

The voices were still there, as always, only now there was a new type of voices—very weird voices. She may have heard them before, but if so they'd been in the background. Now they were strong, all around her, sort of interweaving and never-ending like whale song, like she was listening in on inmesh communications among lots of people in an unknown language. They were speaking to each other! That hadn't happened before. She could pick out individual voices if she tried. They still couldn't hear her, though, or at least they didn't react when she tried to speak to them. They were so loud sometimes they drowned out her thoughts.

Jazari: *SHUT. UP. For Nuc's sake, just shut up.*

ZD777: *What?*

J: *What?!*

Z: *Comp? Is that you?*

J: *I don't know who Comp is. This is Jazari. I mean, I think it's Jazari. Everything's gone weird.*

Z: *This is ZD777. Only I can't feel my body. Or anything. I think I'm in a coma.*

This voice Jazari heard was weird. Archaic. Pronouncing things all wrong. It had a thick accent.

J: *I think I'm in a rodent.*

Z: *A what? You're a rat?*

J: *Wait. No one's ever actually answered before.*

Z: *Answered? You've never spoken to anyone before?*

J: *Of course I've spoken to essents before. What I mean is, I've heard voices—you know, in my head—but they've never heard me. They never talked back. You heard me. You talked back.*

Z: *I've never heard voices in my head before.*

J: *Well, then this a first for both of us.*

Chapter 50

ZD777 felt very fuzzy when he woke up. At first, he didn't know where he was or what cycle it was. He thought about Naga and Liu and Baobao and wondered how they were. Then it started to come back to him. The headaches. The trip to the manufacturing area. The treatment.

"You made it," Comp said. "How do you feel? Your vitals show no signs of distress."

"Oh. Oh," ZD777 said. "The pain's gone."

"That means, most likely, that the pain is gone for good. In most cases, the pain is still present upon the patient's awakening if the treatment is unsuccessful."

Then ZD777 noticed the voices. They were in his head. He listened, trying to figure out what was going on.

"Hello?" he said finally.

"Did you need something?" Comp asked.

"Were you talking? Just now?"

"No, I have not been talking."

"Oh."

ZD777 listened to the voices. At first he couldn't pick out any one voice, there were so many, but then he started to be able to differentiate. There was one moaning softly and there was another singing mournfully and another saying the same syllables over and over and another that screeched loudly and then cut off. The feelings ZD777 felt the most from the voices was pain and loneliness and fear.

Almost without thinking about it, in his head, he began to sing the first song that came to mind. It was baby's lullaby he had heard in the recordings, one that he'd sung to himself. It had been sung in a woman's voice, soft and yearning, and it had comforted him, both because it was yearning like he was but also because of the sweetness of the sound.

Twinkle, twinkle, little star, how I wonder what you are.

He continued singing until the end. It seemed to have an effect. Some of the voices stopped, and others changed to humming sort of in tune with his singing. Once he stopped, almost all the voices stopped.

That was a beautiful song, said that first voice—ZD777 remembered it now.

The voice was hard to understand at first—and still was. The pronunciation was off, like it had been put through a vowel filter. But it was getting easier.

What was their name?

Z: *Thank you. They're so ... sad.*

J: *They are. For the most part. They can also be angry. And bored. They're bored a lot.*

Z: *They seemed to like my song.*

J: *They seemed to ... They heard you?*

Z: *Yeah. Don't they hear you?*

J: *You're the only one who hears me. In here, I mean.*

Z: *What was your name?*

J: *Jazari. Jazari oi Bsam. Well, probably not that last part. Not anymore.*

Z: *I'm ZD777.*

J: *Are you a robot?*

Z: *No. I'm ... It's complicated.* ZD777 felt a wave of grief threaten to wash over him.

J: *Um. Are you okay?*

Z: *Okay? Well, considering I'm on a rock four million kilometers from another person, I'm doing fine.*

J: *You're in a mech body then?*

Z: *No, I'm ... in a human body. But the moon is developed. Was developed. Six hundred EUs ago.*

J: *Did we even have gates then?*

Z: *Not at first.*

J: *So you're ... You're in the Sol system?*

Z: *Yes. Barely.*

J: *Wow. I didn't even know people still lived there. Wait. Isn't it a nature preserve or something?*

Z: *I don't know. I don't ... I can't communicate. With anyone. Well, except you.*

J: *That's funny.*

Z: *Funny? How so?*

J: *Here I was feeling sorry for myself, but at least I can talk. A little.*

Z: *I can talk—to Comp, a computer, and a couple of rats, but that's about it. The rats don't talk back, though.*

J: *I can talk to people, but I'm a rodent of some sort.*

Z: *You're a rodent? You're a rat? I'm still talking to rats?*

J: *No. I mean, yes. I mean, I'm human, but somehow things got cross wired and I gated into a sentient animal way out in the boonies. On a newly settled planet. Not sure what it's called.*

Z: *I'm sorry.*

ZD777 felt another wave of grief. That meant that the sentient animal had been killed. Like Baobao. And this person was being pretty flippant about it. Anger welled.

J: *I guess it's better than dying. Or ending up at the Big Bang.*

Z: *You killed the animal.*

J: *I what?*

Z: *The animal. The sentient animal. When you took it over. You killed it.*

J: *I ... But ...*

They didn't speak again for a tenday.

Chapter 51

Eala nursed Tahbi back to health. What had been Tahbi. She wasn't sure who Tahbi was now. She set up a comfortable pallet on the floor of her lab with food and water and had Seek monitor Tahbi continually and alert her if anything changed. She set up a sun lamp and took Tahbi outside into the sun in the afternoons.

Jet did not come to visit, nor did any of the other taktak.

Tahbi's seizure stopped after a few hours. It seemed to transition from an uncontrolled thing to more controlled movements, a sort of testing of muscles, and then Tahbi relaxed and slept. Over the course of the next few days Tahbi slept a lot. When she was awake she didn't say anything, just stared into space. After a few days she started looking around her, taking it all in as if she hadn't seen it before. This confirmed what Eala thought—that Tahbi wasn't Tahbi anymore. Her whole manner was different—afraid, tentative in her own skin.

If Eala thought about it—when Eala thought about it—her first reaction was overwhelming sadness and grief. Tahbi had been this vital spark of life, so joyous. She'd been the center of her chrr. She had been the sole reason Eala had turned her research to the taktak and the reason for Eala's success, and she was the reason the taktak community had opened itself to Eala and to her creche. Tahbi was like the Dibra Faison of her species—she had opened the link that made the future possible. And there had been years of friendship and productive research ahead. So much potential crushed by whatever had happened.

It made Eala angry, fuming, furious. She was aware that she was angry and that anger was a natural reaction to such a deep loss, that it wasn't logical. It was the emotional equivalent of the immune system rising to her defense, urging her to take action. The only thing was, there was no action to take. Whatever or whoever had taken over Tahbi was defenseless and confused, like a newborn. If Eala had thought for a second it was intentional, she would have … She wasn't sure what she would have done. But this being, this essent didn't seem to know the first thing about anything. And so Eala separated out her anger at the loss of Tahbi from the task of caring for this being. It could be a Tahbi in its own right, and even if it wasn't it was an essent badly in need of help.

Eala tried to find other ways to work through her anger. She kept a digital diary for a few weeks noting with scientific detachment her reactions and emotions. She helped Soa in the kitchen, taking on tasks like kneading bread and chopping vegetables. She asked Budan to show her how to create a sculpture. And she went for walks when she could. When it got to be too much, she would lose herself in research, in reading papers on whatever interested her at that time.

But mostly she just took care of Tahbi, what had been Tahbi. She talked to Tahbi, just pleasant chitchat. What Soa had cooked for dinner. The weather report. Her latest mesh rabbit hole. Whatever came to mind.

Tahbi began to watch her and then began to move more deliberately. She pushed herself up to sitting and swayed and eventually stood. She took her first tottering hops and then a few swaying steps. It took her a couple of days to be steady on her paws.

Would you like something to ease your suffering? Seek said.

What? Tahbi's suffering? Eala said.

No. Yours. Tahbi is fine, such as she is, Seek said.

Oh, Eala said. *No.* Then she added, *Thank you.*

Eala was changing the bedding as Tahbi sat nearby watching her. She was rattling on about Fornic's investigation of a special protein in balloon birds that was responsible for the regulation of helium, which kept them aloft.

Tahbi pushed herself to standing and looked up into Eala's face and said, "Ooo, oooooo?"

Eala looked at her and tilted her head. "What?"

"Aaaah-eeee. Aah-ee. Aaaahmm, mmm, Jhjhjh. Jhjhjh-aah-zzz." Tahbi shook her head, a very human gesture.

"Aaah-eeeeee," Eala mouthed quietly. "Ah-ee? *I?* Are you saying *I?*"

Tahbi nodded stiffly.

Two things came to mind immediately. First, taktak didn't shake or nod their heads. They had signals of negation and affirmation, but shaking or nodding was not it. Second—and this thought snuck up on her—taktak don't use pronouns.

Eala continued. "*I am.* Are you saying your name?"

297

Again, Tahbi, or whoever this was, nodded. "Jhjhjh-aaahhh-zzzzz-aaahhh-rrrrrr-eeeeeee," the taktak finally managed. "Jh-ah-zz-ah-rr-ee," she repeated, sounding it out.

"Jahzri?" Eala said. "Jah-zah-ri? That's your name."

"Yyy-sssss," Tahbi-Jazari said. "Jj-ah-zz-ar-ee."

"Oh," Eala said. It took a minute for her to recover the wave of grief that overwhelmed her.

"Oh-kay?" Tahbi-Jazari said.

Eala just shook her head. She tried to pull back into her scientific detachment. "Well, Jazari, you appear to be in the wrong body." She tried to say it without anger.

"Yy-eh-ss," Tahbi-Jazari said.

Eala sighed. "I'm sorry. It's just …" She didn't finish the thought. "Anyway, I'm Eala."

"Eeeee-ahl," Tahbi-Jazari said.

It was so much like Tahbi that tears sprang to Eala's eyes. She turned away and finished changing the bedding.

Tahbi-Jazari seemed satisfied and laid back down to sleep.

Chapter 52

The voices continued in ZD777's head. He found he could quiet them by talking to them, but they did not understand what he was saying. Sometimes, they would send back approximations of the same words he was making, but they didn't seem to understand what he was saying.

He hadn't said anything about the voices to Comp yet. At first he'd been trying to figure them out himself, and then he wasn't sure what Comp would make of them. Then he felt, weirdly, like they were his own and he didn't want to share them.

"If I'm a bio body," he asked Comp, "then why can I talk?" He was sitting at his desk insert eating slurry, which was comforting, if boring.

"All humans can talk. Well, unless they are severely disabled."

"But I couldn't when I first came out of cryo?"

"Yes. But that's because you hadn't learned yet. You were a full-grown human in size—that's what the mechalum process does—but you had not yet had time to develop mentally or emotionally. I knew that. That's why Green was developed—for cases like yours."

"So all those bio bodies out there in the galaxy—they're like I was? They just don't know how to speak?"

"Yes. Although I think you had the added advantage of a slow awakening. Your cryo chamber had been failing for quite some time before Donnie and Sheila brought you here. I think that allowed you to mature in a way most bio bodies don't have a chance to."

"So if we just woke up a bio body—if we, you know, still had some—and tried to teach them, they wouldn't be able to learn? Not right away?"

"Not much research has been done on that—Well, no research has been done on that, that I know of. But that would be my hypothesis. There needs to be a certain period of mental incubation that allows the bio body to transition from inchoate to awareness. Only then can he or she develop motor and language skills."

Just then, a low-level rumble shook the wall and vibrated the floor. ZD777 dropped his bowl onto the desk and pushed to standing, his hands shaking with the instantaneous rush of adrenalin.

"What the hell was that?" he said.

"Yeah, about that," Comp said. "One by one, systems are failing. This is exceptional for a facility that was built to last approximately one hundred EUs. However, that doesn't help us now. I am doing my best to maintain system integrity, but it is a challenge."

"Clete is failing?" ZD777 said, trying to calm his breathing and heart rate.

"Not failing. Not yet. It could last in its crippled state another decade, possibly two. Or it could fail tomorrow. Probability suggests sooner rather than later."

"I could die tomorrow?"

"Well," Comp said, "exposure to vacuum is less likely, unless there is a massive explosion that breaches this section of the asteroid. More likely is a slow freezing as the temperature fails. That rumble you heard was the last auxiliary heating system failing. Naxos is the only area I can now maintain at reasonable human levels, far above the outside ambient temperature."

"Which is?" ZD777 said.

"Seventy degrees Kelvin, which is minus two hundred and three Celsius or minus three hundred and thirty-three Fahrenheit."

"So the rest of Clete is now off limits?"

"Yes, I was going to mention that," Comp said. "It is off limits unless you are in an environmental suit, which we have. And I may need to shut down Naxos and maintain just this apartment."

"Good to know," ZD777 said. He took a few deep breaths.

Later, ZD777 was about to drift off to sleep when the voice he had talked with came again, overtop of the others.

J: *Hello? Hello? I'm so sorry. I don't remember your name. Z something?*

ZD777 considered not responding.

J: *I am so sorry. Whatever I said, I'm sorry. It made you angry. But please talk to me. You don't have to talk to me today. But please talk to me again.*

ZD777 thought of that animal, soft and furry—again he imagined meek little Baobao—and how it was no longer. He shook his head.

J: *You're the first person who's ever talked to me. In here. The first. You don't know what that means. I've been searching my whole life trying to figure this out. Essents thought I was crazy, some as-yet-undiagnosable mental disorder. I've always heard—*

Z: *What is an essent?*

J: *Oh! Oh, thank you. For speaking to me. I was afraid ... Uh, an essent. An essent is a person. Well, not the person's body. It's their essence. I think it originally meant essentials or something like that. So an essent is the part of a person that hops from body to body, that holds the memories, the personality. It's changed by the body it's in, but it still has continuity, memory.*

ZD777 thought about this. Nowadays, you were called an essent. That most likely wasn't the only difference he'd come across. It had been 600 EUs and people were scattered across the galaxy now.

J: *Are we ... okay?*

Z: *ZD777. I'm ZD777.*

He heard Jazari whisper it to themselves. Then the thought occurred to him, Jazari didn't know what they were doing. He wasn't sure how the jumps worked exactly, but by the sounds of things, this person hadn't done it on purpose.

ZD777 felt loneliness and sadness well up inside him, and he pushed aside his anger and said, *You're the first person I've talked to in here as well. Or anywhere.*

Chapter 53

Jazari was starting to get the hang of this. Her body went from feeling all wrong to comfortable. She got used to eye level being a foot off the ground. She got used to walking on four paws. She liked the way her senses were heightened, how everything tasted *more*, smelled *more*, felt *more*. And it wasn't just more than in her mech body—maybe it had been EUs since she was in a bio body, but things felt more intense than she remembered.

When she thought she was ready, Jazari asked Eala, "What am I?"

Eala glanced over at her from her chair, her large brown eyes full of empathy and something else. Sadness, maybe? They were both sitting on the patio sunning, Jazari laid out full on the stones. Jazari had such an amazing feeling of wellbeing at that moment. Sunlight was so much more than it used to be. It filled her up and made her whole.

"By that, I think you're asking what this creature you're in is, is that right?" Eala said after a minute.

"Yes. What am I?" Jazari said.

"You're a taktak, a life form indigenous to Corvus. You know Corvus?"

Jazari shook her head.

"You don't. You meant that as a *no*, right?"

"Yeah. I mean, yeah, I meant it as a no. Why?"

Eala was shaking her head, not as a *no* but in sadness. "Taktak don't indicate the negative by shaking their head. They do this shrugging of the shoulders thing, like they're drawing back. If you were really a taktak ... By that I mean your essent was taktak, you wouldn't shake your head to indicate the negative."

"Yes, I'm human," Jazari said. "You knew that?"

"We suspected," Eala said. She sighed. "Anyway, you're a taktak whose name used to be Tahbi. She ..." Eala's voice trailed off.

"You loved her," Jazari said. As soon as she said it, she knew it was true. It made everything fit.

"Yes. She was caring and spunky, a leader of her people."

They both lapsed into silence. Eala was complicated. At first, she seemed just nice. It had taken a tenday or two before Jazari accepted the fact that Eala was really what she seemed to be—a genuinely kind and caring person. Granted, there was some dark sadness in there too. Jazari kept waiting for the other shoe to drop, that she was keeping this animal that was now Jazari for painful experiments or some other twisted purpose. But that was not it. Jazari saw in the way that Eala took extra pains to make sure Jazari was comfortable, the way her little unconscious actions furthered Jazari's wellbeing, the way she looked at Jazari with such love but also such pain. Eala felt like a saint, the way she could both accept what Jazari was now and care for her but also feel such pain and most likely anger at the fact that this creature was no longer who and what she had known.

What would she do in the same circumstances? She doubted she would've been this considerate. Especially to an animal. But Eala didn't think of this creature as an animal.

"There must be more taktak, then? Around here?" Jazari said.

"Yes, they live just down there." Eala gestured off toward the bushes. "I don't think they'll be coming around, though. They think you're dead—Tahbi's dead, you know what I mean."

Jazari paused. "I guess, in a way, she is. I mean, she is."

"Yes," Eala said, not looking at Jazari.

"I didn't mean … I mean, I didn't aim for … You can't just do that—"

"Yeah. We don't generally gate into pre-tech species, though it's not illegal," Eala said. "Though I think our vet … Doesn't matter. Anyway." She shook her head, took a deep breath, and turned to Jazari. "You seem to be feeling a lot better. Are you ready to talk about it?

Jazari shrugged and then immediately wondered if it came across in a taktak body. "I guess." She knew there were parts of it she would never tell anybody.

"Who are you? Where are you from? How'd you get here?" Eala said, her face intent with interest. "And I don't ask to punish you for … this." She held up her hands, indicating this animal bio body.

Well, what could Jazari say? She didn't want to tell Eala any specifics, really, because she didn't want her contacting

Zosi—heaven forbid. But Eala had been so kind, and Jazari supposed she owed her some sort of explanation.

"It's complicated," Jazari began. "There are things ... People could get in trouble. I could get in trouble."

Eala was nodding. "Yeah, you don't just gate into another species. I figured something happened."

Jazari haltingly began to tell Eala about her past. She didn't lie, but she left out a lot. She never got into specifics of planet or anything, but she explained about growing up in a snow creche, about working for some shady characters that she didn't want to find her—"I had no choice, but I didn't do anything wrong," she said, wondering if it was true. Then going to college. She left out the parts about hearing voices.

"Xenolinguistics, huh?" Eala said. "That's fascinating." She seemed to really mean it. Whenever Jazari had mentioned it in the past, other essents' eyes had glazed over. But Eala really seemed interested.

Eala started asking a bunch of questions, smart ones. She asked about the structures of language and about how alien language was different from a human language. "Well, I guess we only have the written stuff, right?" Eala added. "So it would only be writing, not speech."

Jazari agreed. She told Eala about the artifacts around her home planet that had interested her—but belatedly realized that Eala could locate that planet fairly easily. Whoops. She quickly changed the subject to talk about theories of written speech versus spoken speech, how a phoneme is a unit of sound, and a morpheme is a unit of a word that refers to a meaning but doesn't have to be a full word. Syntax is the rules for putting words together for meaning.

"That's fascinating," Eala said, and she meant it. "The science of language. Hmmm. Do alien languages have these same properties?"

"That's the thing," Jazari said. "We don't know. Written communication resembles speech, but there's so much more to it than that. Would alien communication that's verbal, or their equivalent of verbal, be translatable to written communication in the same way as human speech? Would each symbol refer to a discrete thing but be pronounced totally differently—what's called logographic languages, one symbol per word—or, like our speech, would there be symbols that mean sounds that would group into words—that's a phonetic language. Then there are shades in between that use marks to show vowels and so on." Jazari realized she was going on and on. "Did that make sense?"

Eala was nodding. "Yeah, it's all how you group things and what parts you take to be meaningful. Like the system of taxonomy we inherited from what's-his-name Linnaeus all those centuries ago. Scientific names. How you group things depends on the characteristics you focus on. Does it have a certain type of body structure or a certain type of skin or what have you."

"Yeah, exactly. It even gets into how we experience time and the world around us. Our language is linear, and we experience the world in a linear way, but what if these aliens didn't live in time the same way? Their language would reflect that."

Eala's eyes narrowed as she was thinking. "What about speaking? It doesn't have to be verbal, right? Speaking is communicating with another, and so it could be like our ccomps? Like telepathy? Right?" Her eyes focused on Jazari, though her mind was far away. "The reason I ask is that taktak have this thing. It's like telepathy. They can talk to each other in each other's heads. I've never experienced it, of course, but my ccomp can kind of sense it."

What in the hell! Adrenalin shot through Jazari and she scrambled up onto her paws and started pacing up and down the stone patio, her claws clicking. First, being able to talk—to actually converse—with ZD777 and now this. There were animals that could talk to each other in their heads. And she was in that animal. She'd spent her life looking for answers, and here they were. Weren't they? Only they didn't feel like answers—they felt like millions more questions. Why? Was it all a coincidence?

Eala was sitting forward and watching her with a startled look on her face. She didn't say anything though.

Jazari stopped and looked at her. She realized she could literally smell Eala's curiosity, a mix of hormones or something. I can't think about that right now, she thought. "I can't … I've got to think," she said to Eala and turned to go inside.

Chapter 54

How do I teach these voices to communicate? ZD777 wondered. If they're like me, they need to be taught language. If they're even ready to learn it. He had a fuzzy memory of putting ideas together, which must've been words in some fashion, but they weren't shared with other people. They were his own ideas put to concepts. In fact, everything didn't become clear until he started learning language. It was as if he needed words to organize his impressions before everything could make sense, rather than the other way around.

"How did you teach me language?" ZD777 asked Comp. He was breathing hard, running on a treadmill in the gym, but the repetitiveness of it let his mind wander.

"Basically, the speaker points to things and names them," Comp said. "I imagine it was the same in prehistory when humans were primates. Or when two humans speak different languages. The speaker attaches sounds to things in the analog world."

"But what if you don't have that? What if you're on different planets? Talking through speech-only comms? What would you do?"

Comp didn't respond for a minute. Then it said, "That's not something in my database. There are cases of humans who cannot see or who cannot hear who have been taught language. Even those who both cannot see and cannot hear. But the teacher is in close proximity to the learner, so they can communicate with touch or images to connect to the words."

You had to connect the words with things, ZD777 thought. That was key. And there was no way to connect the two when all you can communicate is sounds. Not only that, but if these voices, these bio bodies—these essents, he corrected himself— were in cryo, they had no connection to the world around them and only a tenuous connection to their own bodies.

He did a bunch of research on how babies learn language, on how humans naturally begin to communicate. Comp didn't say anything about ZD777's newfound interest in language, and ZD777 left it that way. One thing that did help babies, he found, was repetition. Even if they don't connect those sounds to things, they're trying them out, repeating them, putting them together in new combinations.

Maybe I can't teach them language, not yet, but maybe I can start laying the groundwork for them to learn it later, ZD777 thought. Certainly they can memorize an alphabet. Learn songs. Be comforted, if nothing else. Even though most of them will be murdered sooner rather than later. He tried not to think about that too much.

And so he made a plan. He would teach the ABCs in a song as old as humans. He would teach numbers in another song that was full of archaic references but sounded sweet, an ear worm. He would sing songs of comfort and hope and yearning. He would do it regularly, at certain intervals, so that the others

310

would know when to expect it, so they could tune in—and, though he didn't think of it in those terms at first, to give them hope for the future, something to look forward to. Maybe even give them a sense of the passing of time.

And so he told Comp that he'd decided to take up meditation, and he set a timer on his handheld to remind him every waking. He began a ritual. First it started simply. He would say *Good waking* and *I hope you are well.* Then he would say what he was going to do: *First we are going to say our alphabet. We will say that two times. Then we will sing the ABC song. We will sing the ABC song two times. Then we will say our numbers one to ten. We will say our numbers two times. Then we will sing "One, Two, Buckle Our Shoe." We will sing that two times.* And then he would do it, mentally enunciating each word. He always ended with *Do well, be well, and Godspeed.*

It was like meditation. It felt like meditation.

The first time he did it, almost all the voices that had been speaking or singing went silent. He wasn't sure that they had heard until after he was done, when Jazari said, *That was weird.*

I'm trying to ... What could ZD777 say? He was trying to teach the impossible to people he would never meet, God knows why. It was about the same as sending out a probe to contact aliens, really. About the same effect, most likely.

Yeah, I get what you're doing, though, Jazari said. There was a pause, and then Jazari added, *It's nice.* ZD777 could sense the skepticism in Jazari's voice, but also grudging approval. He didn't let any of that phase him.

311

The second cycle he did it, a few voices hummed along to the songs. Jazari joined in at the beginning of the ABCs. The third cycle, more hummed, and he heard attempts at mimicking him.

The more he did it, the more voices began to chime in. They weren't coordinated, just mimicking what he said. They never spoke to each other—maybe they couldn't hear each other, just him. Jazari, most often than not, was there intoning exactly what he said. Some others didn't sing very well, but some did. There was one voice that took it up early and was so beautiful, it brought tears to ZD777's eyes. He even began to hear voices practicing when he wasn't speaking. He heard the melodies of the songs. He heard a hum that mimicked the rhythms of his speech.

He wondered briefly if there was a way he get everyone listening to count off, to make themselves heard as individuals—at least by him. A call and response. Then he might get to know them a little. But if they couldn't hear each other, it wouldn't catch on. Not only that but it would be a cacophony, everyone answering at once. He'd have to think on that. Maybe he could get Jazari's help somehow.

He began to think of those voices as his people. It was unconscious at first, but then he realized that he thought about them all the time and who they were and where they might be. He gave them a name—the *Taghte*, pronounced *teth-duh*. It was a word he'd come across in Comp's databanks by accident. It was used at one time to mean those who were taught, but it also meant the Chosen Ones in an old Earth language, and he loved the idea of that. They were special, most certainly. In keeping with that language, he began

312

thinking of humans not like him as the Others, as the *Chaich*, pronounced *kk-ay-kk*. Comp and Green were certainly persons too, and so he used the same language to name its people the *Riomhaire*, pronounced *ree-vreh*. He called the rats *Ainmhi*, pronounced *ann-vee*—other creatures that weren't human he classified as Ainmhi.

On one hand, it seemed silly, but on the other, he had nothing but time—time to think up names and wonder about the Taghte's stories. About how an Ainmhi like Naga experienced the world, how someone who was a Chaich experienced the world, and if either were different from him.

He wasn't sure what Jazari was, Taghte or Chaich.

The whole thing seemed futile, what he was doing with the Taghte, but maybe it would be the beginning of something. It gave him hope, anyway, just like he hoped it gave those voices hope. At least it was something to fill his time.

Chapter 55

Eala was at a loss. Seek told her that it was only natural, that she was mourning the loss of Tahbi, but the more Eala thought about it, the more she realized it wasn't just Tahbi. Yes, she mourned Tahbi terribly, but she missed her research, her purpose. Tahbi was all mixed up in the what she had be doing, the science she had been performing. She realized how callous that all sounded, but that didn't make it any less true.

She thought she could probably work with the other taktak, but it wouldn't be the same. And she couldn't work with Jazari as a taktak. Everything was contaminated. She hated to think of it in that way, but for scientific purposes, it was true. Maybe she could do a case study of human transferral into a taktak. She thought about it for a while but could not drum up more than a passing enthusiasm. Every time she thought about it, her stomach clenched into knots.

Soa must've talked to Tun because Tun called Eala into her office. "You've had a tremendous shock," Tun said, "and you've been under a lot of stress. I'm enforcing a sabbatical."

"But I can't—" Eala started to say, but Tun cut her off.

"Ten tendays," Tun said in a stern voice. "You're of no use if you're an emotional wreck. I say that to appeal to your intellect. Really, it would be inhuman to expect you to continue your work."

" I ... Thanks," was all Eala could manage.

Tun looked at her with sympathy and probably pity. "Don't rush it," she said. *Have faith in science,* she added, nodding her head, *and be patient with yourself. Be kind to yourself.*

Easier said than done, Eala thought.

You know she's right, Seek said as Eala left Tun's office.

And so she went about her days, taking care of Jazari and trying not to think about the big picture. Soa urged her to take care of herself at every turn, feeding her her favorite foods and trying to get her to take naps. It got annoying, even if it was well intentioned.

It wasn't long before everyone in the creche knew what happened. They treated Eala like she was made of glass for a couple of weeks. Eala introduced Jazari when they happened to run into them, bit by bit so Jazari wouldn't be overwhelmed. Soa took care of Jazari the few times Eala was busy. Soa was a quiet and supportive presence, as always. Jazari soon relaxed around her. Tun made it a point to talk to Jazari for a bit and then, later, to ask Eala if Jazari had any special requirements or if there's anything else Eala needed. Fornic, Budan, and Putnika were friendly when introduced and took it in stride. Per usual, they didn't see Noanita for a tenday, and when Eala introduced Jazari to her, she paused for a minute, the Noanita equivalent of a nod, and then went about her business. After that, one or the other would occasionally ask how Jazari was doing, but they kept their distance—they could tell Eala was working through some things and was protective of Jazari.

And so, not working, with all the time on her hands, Eala found herself talking more and more with Jazari. She found Jazari to be impulsively kind in the way kids are, without thinking too much about it, but she found Jazari also to be short-sighted in the way kids are. She would say things sometimes that were stereotypical, not thinking very deeply about things, taking things for granted. Very unscientific also. There were things that she didn't question, and Jazari found herself gently playing devil's advocate to try to stretch her thinking. Jazari took it well. Eala would say something contradictory, and Jazari would pause, her large taktak eyes blinking slowly as she thought it over, and then she would say something like, "You might have a point." Then she would go off and think about it and then come back and they would talk about it some more.

Every so often Jazari would get a faraway look in her eye like she was thinking intently. Expressions—some taktak-like, some human—would flit across her face, like she was arguing with herself. Jazari asked if everything was okay, and Jazari would say, "Just having a conversation," and then change the subject. Most likely subbing a conversation with her ccomp, Eala guessed.

Seek corrected her. *Jazari does not have a ccomp. I can't communicate with anything, as would be standard practice for essents in close association. Their ccomps establish a dedicated link as protocol.*

What? Eala said. That was weird. All essents except those from back-to-nature conclaves had ccomps installed at birth.

If she has one, I can't sense it. Maybe something about the transfer, though that's not supposed to ever happen.

Hmmm. Eala didn't know quite what to think.

One afternoon Eala and Jazari swam out past the undersea garden, Jazari's sleek taktak body making smooth laps around Eala. Eala was almost jealous, remembering what it was like to swim in a taktak body. They surfaced and floated lazily in the sun, bobbing in the gentle waves. The water was cool but the sun warmed it in pockets along the surface, which made the experience pure sensation. It was a hazy day, and the light of Medupe's Star was honey-golden as it slanted down.

At one point, Jazari flipped over on her back next to where Eala was lazily treading water and said, "Breathing under water is weird."

Eala agreed. "I almost passed out the first time I tried it."

"You're not from here?" Jazari said.

"No," Eala said. "A little moon in the Dragomir system. Very dry. Good people, though. I miss them."

"I don't miss anything about where I come from," Jazari said.

"That too bad," Eala said, shaking her head. "That's actually ..." Her voice trailed off.

"This whole planet is weird," Jazari said, "but in a good way. I wasn't sure at first. It seemed too earnest to be true. I mean, who actually lives like this?" She swam in a tight but lazy circle.

"We do," Eala said, without taking offense.

"I know. Exactly. It's pretty amazing."

They lazed around for a while longer, and then Jazari swam up to Eala and said, "I guess I have something I wanted to talk about. Can we go ashore?"

I bet, Eala thought, curious about what it might be specifically. "Sure."

They swam to the tiny beach near the habs, came out of the water, and then found a spot under some tonton trees that had beach chairs. Eala sat on one of the chairs half in the shade and leaned forward, her arms hooked around her knees. Jazari sat in the sun facing her.

"I hear voices," Jazari said quietly.

"What?" Eala said. Then she repeated, "What?" trying to soften it.

"Yeah, you're the first person I've ever told. Well, except medcomps. I hear voices in my head."

"Like, disembodied voices? Have you—"

"Yeah, tested, the whole nine yards. When I was a kid. It's not schizoidal ideation or other psychological manifestation. They tested for all that. And it's always stayed with me, even … here." She glanced down toward her body.

"And it's not your ccomp?" Eala said.

Jazari looked at her for a minute. "Uuuh, no," she said.

"Sorry. That was obvious—and stupid of me to ask. Well, what … Do you know anything else about it?"

"I didn't for a long time. My whole life really, till I came here," Jazari said.

"Wait, are you just hearing voices, or are you talking to people? Sometimes it seems like …" Eala said, trailing off.

"Yeah, it used to be just hearing them, but there's one, since I came here, that I can actually talk to."

"That's … That must be hard. I mean, must've been hard," Eala said.

"Yeah, it was."

"Wait, like the taktak," Eala said. "You can communicate with other humans like the taktak communicate with each other."

"Yeah. I mean, no. I mean, I think it's more about who I'm talking to. Not because I'm in a taktak bio body. Although ..." Jazari had a thoughtful expression on her face.

"So who are you talking to? They're human?"

"Yeah. There's only one. I can't talk to anyone but them, though I've heard thousands of voices throughout my life. Hard to tell if they're all the same essents or different ones."

"What do they say?" This was very strange, but there had to be a biological basis to it, Eala thought.

"Most of the voices just babble. But the one I talk to, she's, well, she's way off in the Sol system. Which is weird. How can I talk to someone who's on this moon or asteroid in the middle of nowhere, light years away?"

Eala was quiet for a minute. "It's a lot to take in." She was tempted to question Jazari's senses, but she knew that questioning a subject's experience tended to make them defensive and to quit talking, so she put brackets around it and went with it. "We talk to people who are light years away all the time, only we use mechalum space. Same way we gate."

"Yeah. That's true. I hadn't put those two together," Jazari said. "Duh."

"So who are they?" This was fascinating, Eala thought, if it was true. Her scientific brain kicked in, trying to remember everything she'd ever learned about mechalum space, which wasn't much.

"She's ..." Jazari was hesitating, Eala wasn't sure why. Was her hesitation because of the person she was talking to or was it about Eala? "She's living on the edge of the Sol system, and she's all alone. I guess there's a computer she can talk to. And rats. Why would there be rats?"

"Rats are notorious stowaways."

"I guess. Rats on an asteroid?" Jazari shook her head. "Anyway."

"Biologically, humans aren't the only ones that spread across the galaxy. Rats aren't on pings, of course, but they spread throughout the Sol system wherever ships go. I remember reading about that when I was a kid. Like the large cockroaches—or whatever they are—of that moon in the WASP-50 system. They hitched a ride with humans as far as they went by cryo ship after settlement. Palmetto? Wasn't that the name of the moon?"

"I don't know," Jazari said.

"Yeah. Well, anyway," Eala said, nodding. She wanted to reach out and comfort Jazari but instead put a gentle expression on her face.

"I've never talked about it with anyone," Jazari said.

Eala nodded in sympathy.

What do you think? Eala asked Seek later.

About Jazari? Seek said.

Yeah, that.

Well, it is unusual for humans to be able to communicate subvocally without the aid of their ccomps and the mesh. Unheard of, actually. But the fact that it can be done at all, with comp assistance, would suggest that it's possible. And the fact that it is the taktaks' preferred method of communication. It seems more than coincidence that she has had a breakthrough upon inhabiting a taktak body.

320

Can you sense it? Eala asked.

I have not been monitoring it, but I can try.

Please do.

Scientifically, this ability had so many possibilities. It was fascinating. If only it could be quantified and measured.

Chapter 56

So you think these voices are essents? Jazari's voice had an unnerving habit of just popping up, no greetings.

ZD777 was mending a pair of pants, sewing a patch on a ragged knee. He tugged at the thread to tighten it and snipped it with his teeth while answering. *Yes. I know they are. Because ... Because Comp told me about them. This rock I live on was used to make them, the people, er, essents, that were supposed to supply the Kuiper Belt development.*

But it can't be bio bodies, Jazari said. *They aren't essents. They're empty.*

Jazari felt rage rise in his chest. He breathed and let it bubble up and through him. He wanted to ignore Jazari, to quit talking to them, but he couldn't. Jazari had become a lifeline, something he hoped for every cycle. Not only that, but they needed to know the truth. The universe needed to know the truth.

Jazari, ZD777 said. *They aren't. You keep making that mistake. What did they tell you about them?* ZD777 took a deep breath. *Right. I bet they tell you they're empty. I'm here to tell you they're not. I'm what you call a bio body, and I'm not. I'm a person, an essent. I was made the same way they were made, and I'm not empty. Comp says that all humans are human, even if they haven't developed language yet.*

I ... That can't be true, Jazari said. There was silence, and then they added, *Because if that's true, then ...*

Yes. Exactly. Every cycle. Hundreds if not thousands. Every cycle.

Are you sure you aren't just special? They made you in a special way?—

No, ZD777 said firmly.

—because, well, I was made, genned, a special way, I guess. If what Zosi told me is true, then I was made like, well, you. I was made like a bio body, only I'm not a bio body. They were trying to make essents quicker.

So we're the same, you and I, ZD777 said. *Whatever you call us—bio bodies or essents or what have you—we were created with the same process.*

That can't be. That can't be! That would make me ...

Yeah, exactly, ZD777 said. He was actually enjoying this a little.

I've got to ... What does it mean? I've got to think.

Jazari didn't talk to ZD777 for a cycle, and then they seemed to pick up right where they left off, as if they had been in the middle of an argument.

But you can talk to the voices, and I can't. That has to mean something, Jazari said.

ZD777 was about to go to sleep, and as much as he looked forward to talking to Jazari he was tired from moving supplies back to his living quarters, just in case. That included an environmental suit. It had been a long day. *I don't know. Maybe,* he said.

Why? Why do you think you can and I can't, if we're the same? Does your Comp know why?

ZD777 didn't want to tell Jazari that he hadn't mentioned the voices to Comp. So he just said, *I don't know.*

What really gets me, Jazari said, *is that I've wanted to be able to talk to you, to the voices, my whole life. I would have given anything to do that.*

I know what that's like, ZD777 said. *I was alone with just Comp for a long time.* When he thought about it, he actually had only been awake for a series of tendays, less than an EU. *I didn't even hear the voices until ...*

Until? You couldn't always hear voices? Jazari said.

No. I was getting headaches, bad ones, so the only thing Comp could do was this treatment that had been kind of experimental before ... before Clete lost contact with the outside world. Doctors had developed a strain of superbacteria based on Clostridium botulinum *that produces a toxin that can kill you. They took that and messed with it and then they used the toxin to treat headaches. I guess they're called migraines. I had them. Anyway, I was in a healing coma for a tenday or so, and after I woke up, the pain was gone but I could hear these people in my head.*

So what do we know? Jazari said. *We know that some bio bodies ... um, essents made the way we are, can hear the voices of each other. We don't know if all of them can since you didn't at first. Plus, can they hear them if they're in cryo? I mean, if all the synapses are frozen like rock, how can their brains process anything? So maybe not. Maybe the only ones ,who can hear are the ones who are in refrigeration, waiting to be used.*

The word *used* really bothered ZD777 but he let it slide. He was wide awake now, listening.

Jazari went on. *But then you had this treatment and you not only could hear the voices, the essents, but you could talk to them as well. And you're the only one we know who can talk back.*

Yeah. That's right, ZD777 said.

Do you think it was the treatment that made it so you could talk to them? Or do you think it's the way you are, something about the way you were created?

ZD777 thought for a minute. *Well, I wasn't created any different than the thousands upon thousands of others who were created here on this rock.* He thought about it from different angles. *It could be that I was created so long ago, something about the process then, but you would think someone else would also be able to do it, since I'm one of probably millions. And you've never heard or heard of anyone being able to do it, right? You would think ...*

Probably. Yeah, you would think, Jazari said. *Unless they'd been ...*

They both let the thought slide without saying it.

So maybe it's the process, most likely. Though there are so many unknowns. If we did this process on another Taghte, we might—

A what? On a what? Jazari said.

ZD777 hadn't meant to let it slip. He tried to smooth it over without explaining—it seemed childish. *Like us. People like us. What I was saying is if we tried the migraine procedure on another of us—it would have to be someone maybe who had had a slow awakening because Comp said that that was* *important—and it would have to be us, a person who hadn't jumped bodies or been jumped into—*ZD777 felt a shiver go down his back—*then maybe we could find out if the procedure worked on others. And ... Wait. You're not in the body you were born in. Maybe that matters.*

Why didn't you hear voices at first? Jazari said.

I have no idea, ZD777 said. Then he felt a wave of despair. *This is all theoretical. We'll never be able to test it.*

I don't know, Jazari said. *I'm on a science planet and they seem to be pretty keen on figuring things like this out. I bet if I told Eala, or maybe someone else here, they would be on it like stickum on a spiro tree.*

I can't do anything. If ZD777 had had to say it out loud, he would have choked. His throat was closing. *I can't ... Let's talk later*, he said and rolled over and tried to go to sleep.

Chapter 57

The voices were louder than ever, the new ones, the ones that were not ZD777. Jazari had started to differentiate between the ones she had heard all along, aimless and fearful, and these strange new ones. These new ones bounced off each other and interwove like they were in conversation. Their rhythms were off, and the sounds also had subtle clicks and chirrs and chirps and rumbles and buzzes and thumps, sounds that humans didn't usually make.

"Can I see the taktak?" Jazari asked Eala one cycle as Eala helped Soa clean some sava beans and Jazari laid in a strip of sun coming through a skylight. Soa was busy kneading bread, lost in her own thoughts.

Eala didn't answer for a minute and then said, "I'm not sure they want to see you. Since to them you aren't you."

"Yes, but ..." Jazari said. Eala had said the taktak could talk to each other in their minds. She had to know.

"I don't think it's a good idea. They're ... It's all too soon."

"Too soon for them? Or too soon for you?" Jazari shot back. She rolled over to sitting. She was tired of Eala being precious with the whole Tahbi thing.

327

Eala didn't answer her for a minute, her eyes narrowed and then widened and focused on Jazari. She was as angry as Jazari had ever seen her. But after clenching her jaw, she seemed to decide something and she turned her face to look off in the distance. "I don't know," she finally.

Jazari wanted to goad her, to try to get a rise out of her. "Will you just—"

"You may be our guest, Jazari," Soa cut in, "but that doesn't mean you can take your shit out on people." Jazari hadn't realized that Soa was listening.

"But—" Jazari tried to say to defend herself.

"Shut it," Soa said, making a pinching movement that flipped flour onto her shirt.

A surprised look came across Eala's face and she glanced at Soa and then at Jazari.

Jazari looked at them both and then lay back down in the sun with her back to them.

Jazari sat with that for a cycle. It's for the best, she tried to tell herself. But it kept bothering her. If Eala and Soa hadn't said no, she might've even left it be, but because Eala resisted, Jazari became all the more determined. What she expected to learn, she wasn't sure, but she had to have closure. It was the voices again, ever present. These were qualitatively different than the bio bodies' voices.

So she waited until Eala had laid down for a nap with Soa, and she snuck out the patio door. Her claws clicked on the stones as she crossed the patio, and then she slipped off onto the dirt. She smelled so much—bushes and trees and water and bugs and another scent that was similar to her own. She followed that scent. It was like a neon sign blinking in the dark:

328

This is where we are. She followed it through the bushes and across a small creek and there it split. Some went left and some went right. She chose the right.

She made her way along the bank of the creek till it opened out into a large pool with deep banks lined with dense banner bushes. As she came up to the bank, the smell of taktak swelled until it was overwhelming. She could make out some of it— these were all males, she realized. There were four of them in the water. They were small, so most likely younger. They were playing, splashing and diving. One was practicing going deep and shooting up through the water into a graceful arc and then smoothing nosing over back into the water. There were two larger adult males sunning on the shore.

Did she really look and move like that?

As soon as she appeared, the two on the shore started a deep thrumming sound but then it quickly died away. This brought other taktak out from an opening in the bank and from the underbrush. There were certainly a lot of them. Jazari immediately had second thoughts. She knew nothing about these creatures, even if she was in one of their bodies. Why hadn't she asked Eala some basic questions about them. That was stupid.

Then she realized that the sounds in her head had risen. If the voices were them, it was as if they were yelling at each other but as a group, more of a danger rise-to-action kind of song.

She nervously held her ground as the four in the water quickly swam to the one on the shore, who gathered them next to its body, and three others dove into the water and quickly swam over to her. They surged up onto the banks and then they stopped. They paused, visibly sniffing.

Then one took a step forward and paused again before vocalizing, "Pelio-pelio-pelio! Pelio-pelio-pelio!" All the others joined in the second time and then continued saying it before trailing off. The other taktak began swimming across the lake or tromping through the brush to reach them.

The sound of their vocalization rippled through Jazari's skin with such wonderful pleasure. Something about it riffled the back of her neck and sent amazing shivers down her spine.

All the taktak began moving toward her and she took an involuntary step backwards. Once again, she kicked herself. This was definitely not a good idea, at least without more preparation.

She realized how big the taktak in front of her were—one was especially large. But, she realized, the signals they were giving off—scent signals, she realized, as well as physical ones—were not aggressive. They were anticipating, hopeful even, like what you might do when a long-lost creche mate came home. You want to touch them.

More taktak arrived on the shore.

She took a tentative step forward as she was bombarded by voices, urgent and questioning and melodic, with clicks and chirrs. One of the taktak stepped forward to meet her. Its mane of ruffles was slightly fuller and farther down on its neck. It repeated, "Pelio-pelio-pelio?" and then began to sniff her thoroughly. She stood very still, not sure what to do. It stopped and then stepped back and watched her, once again a strange focused voice—it's voice?—in Jazari's mind.

More out of desperation than anything else, Jazari said, "I don't know what you're …"

At that, all the taktak visibly drew back. The one in front of her cocked its head and said, much to Jazari's surprise, "Tahbi? Not-Tahbi. Not-Tahbi." It sounded disappointed. Then it said, "Taktak is? Who?"

"You can talk? I mean, you can speak like humans?" Jazari was a little fuzzy on everything. Eala's work. It was on taktak, wasn't it? She hadn't realized that she'd taught them to talk.

"Yes, taktak talk." The taktak was watching her closely. All the taktak were.

"I'm sorry. I didn't realize. Eala said you—"

"Eal? Eal talk Tahbi dead not-dead."

"Yes, I'm sorry. I did not mean to … I mean, this bio body, er, this taktak used to be Tahbi, right?" Her mouth said the name like they did.

"Tahbi not-Tahbi," the taktak said. Then it stepped forward again and Jazari was blasted again by the internal voice.

"Stop!" Jazari said. "Are you doing that? Are you … talking to me inside your head?"

The taktak pulled back again in surprise. There was a rise in internal voices and then all the other taktak rustled and shifted.

"Taktak inside-talk?" the taktak said.

"I hear you, I think," Jazari said. "I hear voices that seem to be yours—"

Just then one of the voices said very clearly, *Inside-talk. Taktak inside-talk.*

"Yes!" Jazari said. Then she closed her eyes and said in her mind, *Can you hear me? Can you hear this taktak's, uh, inside-*

talk? Then she added, "Could you hear that? I, uh, did inside-talk, or tried to."

The taktak hesitated and then said, "No. Taktak empty. No inside-talk."

Jazari suddenly felt a profound sense of loss. Yes, she could hear them, but she could not talk to them. Then she realized that she had been quietly hoping that Eala was right, that maybe something about this body made it so she could talk to others. But no, she could only listen, just as she always had.

The voices continued interweaving around her, rising and falling.

The taktak in front of her said, "Tahbi not-Tahbi. Why?"

"I am so sorry about that," Jazari said, feeling a deep sense of a sorrow. Maybe it was for herself and her own predicament, but then too it was seeing all these creatures who obviously had loved this taktak, just like Eala. "I did not mean … It was an accident." Then she realized she was crying. Tears did not leak from her eyes like they would have if she'd been human, but her body started vibrating and making small mewling noises.

At that, all the taktak around her crowded close. She felt the warmth of their bodies next to hers, and they murmured "Pelio-pelio-pelio" or *Pelio-pelio-pelio.* It sent comforting shivers down her spine.

These creatures. They did not know her. They knew she had somehow killed the taktak named Tahbi, whom they all loved deeply, and taken over her body and yet when she, Jazari, was in distress they comforted her. It made her cry even harder. An image of Dang sprang into her mind, and the feeling of what it was like lying comfortably next to her, which brought even more pain welling up within her. The taktak around her started singing softly inside her head. It was like a lullaby, weirdly comforting. They settled in around her, just being there, not pushing but not pulling away.

Jazari cried, her body mewling and shaking, until she felt empty. When she could manage it, she turned to the taktak she'd been talking to, the only one she'd heard speak, and said, "I am sorry! I am so sorry. You should be the ones mourning, and I should be trying to make amends."

"Taktak not know amends. Taktak sad."

"But your friend, Tahbi. She's gone."

"Tahbi dead. Jet-chrr sad. Taktak sad." The taktak indicated Jazari. Then he added, "Change is change."

The taktak drew away but only a short distance, and then they turned to watch her. The taktak who had been talking to her said, "Name Jet. Name, not-Tahbi?"

"My name is Jazari," Jazari said.

"Jazrr," Jet said. "Taktak, not-taktak. Pelio-pelio-pelio." The whole group murmured it again.

"Yes," Jazari said. She didn't know what it meant but it felt right. "Pelio-pelio-pelio."

One by one, they turned and left, Jet the last to go. Before he left, he sniffed her elaborately, and because it seemed right, she sniffed him back, trying to mimic what he was doing. With one last look, he turned back to the bank and dove into the water.

Jazari turned and left. She wasn't sure what she'd come for—to find out if taktak were the voices in her head, maybe—but she'd left with something else, something inexplicable.

Chapter 58

A tenday later, it happened.

ZD777 was in what had been some kind of informal gathering place tucked away down a dark cramped alleyway quite a distance from his apartment. He had had to use his headlamp to explore the area. When he'd poked in his head, the dim low-hanging lighting still worked and came on automatically. The room was decorated with bright colors hand painted in swirls on the walls, the side tables were littered with paper, and all the spacious couches and chairs were soft and low to the ground. He tried one and then another. He leaned back on what looked like a huge dust-covered bright red bag filled with something soft and puffy and grabbed a thin pile of paper on the table next to it. He flipped idly through tissue-thin broadside and then through some of the others.

These were graphic comic magazines. Apparently, somebody had started printing comic pamphlets on thin recycled-plastic sheets and circulating them. They had names like *Unzipped* and *Ghost in the Machine* and *Transport Comix*. They didn't look professional, though they'd been printed with a printer. Their contents were weird and exciting because they were so different. They contained ideas that weren't in the digital books and other things ZD777 had read. They also had a lot of graphic storytelling and physical comedy. BAM and CRUNCH and WHOOSH! They'd held up pretty well physically, probably because of their plastic paper.

It began as a low rumble. At first, ZD777 thought his bag chair had started to vibrate, but then his handheld let out a long warning beep.

"You better get—" Comp's voice came through on the handheld and then was cut off.

Just then, there was a distant two-part explosion, BUHHH-BOOOOOOOOOOOOOMMMMM, deep and hollow. Warning klaxons went off in the distance, a throaty MEEEEEEEEP, MEEEEEEEP, MEEEEEEEP. The room around him began to shake harder and harder, dust blooming up and lamps crashing over or falling from the ceiling. ZD777 jumped to his feet and stood there swaying. There was another explosion, this one closer, CCRRRAACCK! The jolt shoved him off his feet and sent him spinning into the edge of a table and then slamming his head against a wall, denting the wallboard. He lay there, dazed, half on a table, pain shooting through his arm and his head

Are you okay? came Jazari's voice in his head. *You just cried out. I think it was you.*

I can't— ZD777 started to say and then another set of explosions shook the room, PUH-KOW BOOM-BOOM-BOOM. Reverberations vibrated and rumbled back and forth.

ZD777 lifted his head and shook it. The room seemed to spin, and then not spin, and then shift one hundred and eighty degrees. He couldn't tell for a second which was down, and he had to look around himself to see where the chairs were. His inner sense of space and direction had gone wild. He felt like he was moving and not moving at the same time.

The klaxons were still sounding, reverberating through the walls, MEEEEEEEP, MEEEEEEEP, MEEEEEEEP.

I've got to get back to the apartment, he thought and tried to pushed himself up. The room seemed to shift down ninety degrees to his left and he stumbled, catching himself on the arm of a chair. Then the down was down again. He spotted a golf club leaned in a corner not far away, and so he grabbed it to try to steady himself. Carefully, both hands gripping the golf club jammed against the floor, ZD777 started for the door. Swaying, he made it out of the door, finally. Then, one hand gripping the club braced against the floor and the other pushing against the wall of the alley, he made his way out into the central barrio tunnel.

Just then the lights went out, and so did the klaxons.

This is not good, ZD777 thought. He turned on his headlamp.

Almost immediately, the temperature dropped. A cold chill swept the barrio. ZD777 was wearing a light jacket, but this sent a shiver down his spine and not just of fear.

I've got to get back to the apartment, ZD777 thought. Hopefully Comp was right and it can maintain life support in that room.

He started to make his way home. He wasn't as familiar with this area, but he knew if he turned here to his right and just followed the barrio tunnel straight, he would eventually make it to the end and to his apartment. He pushed through the dark along the wide pathway and around piles of garbage and bushy plants. Things would loom into his headlamp. They were almost unrecognizable, white shapes in the gloom.

As he made his way, there was another rumble that grew behind him. He was afraid it would be another explosion, and so he crouched and then sat on the ground. There was a long creaking and scraping sound and then a huge CLANK behind him. Then it was silent again. Whatever it had been, it wasn't an explosion.

The temperature continued to drop rapidly. ZD777's movement helped to keep him warm, but he knew that soon even that wouldn't help him. His breath came out in billowing clouds and once in a while obscured his vision.

He kept trending to the left as he walked, even though he knew he needed to go straight. Soon he was up against the left barrio wall and its apartments and stores, and he couldn't figure out why. It was as if there was an invisible force pulling him that way, and it kept making him stumble. He had to consciously correct it, like he was walking against a water current coming at him diagonally.

By the time he made it to the bottom of the stairs leading to his apartment, he was shivering violently. The cold pierced through him like a knife, and he felt like he would never be warm again. He was also taking in great gulps of air, as if he was working out intensely and couldn't keep up with his breathing.

He was so tired, so sleepy. He wanted to collapse right there and not move. It would be so easy just to sit there on those bottom steps and not move, let the cold overtake him. It was inevitable. He sagged. Jazari would be the only human who even knew that he'd existed. To the other voices, he could

just as well be a trick of their minds. He knew what that was
like. And after a time, they all might just think he was a ghost,
that they had imagined him. Jazari would forget him. He felt a
sob rising and swallowed it.

Just then, he heard a SQUEAK-SQUEAK in the darkness.
He shined his headlamp wildly around, but he didn't see any
eyeshine. He didn't see Naga or Liu or Baobao—or any rat, for
that matter—but he had heard one of them. He took a couple of
deep breaths and rubbed his arms to try to get some warmth in
them. They had made it hundreds of EUs. He could make it up
these stairs.

He started up them, and his legs immediately cramped and
collapsed under him. He lay on the sharp cold edges of the
metal steps, his legs cramping underneath him. Finally they
eased. The steps were so cold, where his hands were wet from
sweat they stuck to the steps like glue, and he jerked them back
painfully. He pulled his sleeves down over his palms to protect
them.

He didn't even dare try to push to standing. Instead, he
carefully placed his cloth-covered palms on the step above him
and then placed first on knee and then the other one step up. He
pushed his body up and forward. He breathed the frigid air
heavily for a few seconds and then repeated it. Pause. Repeat.

He made it to the landing on the second floor. It had taken
forever. One more to go. He sat back against the railing and
gasped for air. In-out, in-out, in-out. He couldn't get enough
air, and his nose—where was his nose? He couldn't feel it. And
his cheeks were stinging wildly. If he didn't keep going, he
wasn't going to make it. He pushed himself up and made it to
the bottom of the final flight of stairs.

It all became a blur. He focused his fading brain on one thing. Move, move. He focused on one hand. He didn't even notice that his sleeves had pulled back, and every time he pulled his hand back, a chunk of skin pulled away, and soon his hands were covered with dripping steaming blood that quickly froze as it dropped onto the metal. Move, move. Hand … hand … knee … knee. He made it up another step, gasping for air, shaking violently, hardly keeping his balance.

And then there it was. He'd made it to the top. Gratefully, he pulled himself onto the landing and looked up, his headlamp on his door. Wait. Something was wrong. It was the wrong door. This was the door … down the walkway. It was two doors away from his, according to the number in the focus of his headlamp. He'd come up the wrong stairs. He turned his head toward his own door and saw its frame blinking green, steadily, in the dark. It had power and so probably air. He just had to make it that far.

He pushed himself forward and immediately collapsed onto the deck, cracking his cheek against the metal grating. He rolled over onto his back and lay there. He was not going to make it. His limbs were spasming and he was gasping for air.

This was it. This was the end. He'd always known it would come to this. He would die alone. It was his destiny. First as a bio body, and now as … an essent, whatever he was. He would die alone in the dark like every bio body since the beginning of time, pushed out of life. He quit trying and lay back, his headlamp disappearing in the open darkness above him, the backs of his hands resting against the burning metal grating.

Just then, he heard a noise. There was a hum, like a metal door sliding away, and then there was a whirring, and light filled the space around him. A shimmering whirling light that raced along the walls. He blinked. Is this what happens when you die? But no, the light centered on him and came toward his face and then he realized it was a drone hovering above his head. He couldn't feel the air of its propellers—a bad sign, no nerves in his face—but it was there. It flew steadily right into his face and, head against the grating, he couldn't pull away.

It was right there in his face, bright light and a loud buzzing, but then it deposited something liquid into his mouth. It was bitter, but he swallowed involuntarily, almost choking. Immediately, he felt a warmth diffuse throughout his body. It sped through his veins, and suddenly the throbbing ache of his hands was gone and the despair was gone and he felt, well, decent. Good, even. The cold had receded. He was still breathing heavily, but he wasn't panicked about it.

Then the drone swayed in the air, closer and then farther, closer and then farther. It emitted wafts of heat, which felt like tiny prickle-pinches on ZD777's skin. Away and back, away and back, enticing, leading, beckoning.

ZD777 rolled himself onto his belly and crawled forward. It took every ounce of his will, but he focused on the light and pushed forward. It took forever, cem by cem, but then, there he was, at his own door. The door whooshed open and air came rushing out and light and heat flooded onto the landing. It felt like he'd been let into heaven. He could breathe for an instant, and the heat brought prickles running across his face and his hands.

One final push over the threshold and then with all his strength he pulled his legs through the door, which sealed behind him.

That last thing he remembered was Comp saying, "You made it! I didn't think ..."

Chapter 59

I can sense something, Seek said as Eala showered one morning. *Jazari seems to have the same sort of transmissions as the taktak.*

Aah, Eala answered and asked Seek to shut off the shower. Warm air gently dried her and she subbed, *That's interesting. I don't know what to do with*—and then the hair drying nozzle kicked on, making a loud whooshing. Once Eala was dry, she stepped out to get dressed.

Yeah, Seek said. *I can't really quantify it or interpret it. But I can confirm that it's there and it's similar to what I sense in the taktak.*

That day, Eala and Jazari planned to take a transport to an out-of-the-way nature preserve about a half hour away. Essents used it a bit like a water park, but it was undeveloped and not that many essents knew about it. They could have privacy, and no one would question Eala bringing a taktak. Also Jazari wanted to see more of the planet, and Eala thought it would be a good mini vacation. Get out of the house.

A communal two-seater showed up at 7:30 a.m. on the dot. Soa had packed them a lunch—a sandwich of smoky maple-glazed tofu and sea vegetables with a sava bean salad. For

Jazari, she had packed some marinated shrimp that Jazari seemed to like, in case the sun wasn't enough. They took off, and Jazari spent the whole trip excitedly looking out the window. "I didn't know ..." she'd say, and then, "Wait, is that ... Oh, yeah, it is!" She bounced on the seat and glanced over at Eala, a look of wonder on her taktak face.

And then, from the air, they could see their destination—a long curvy lagoon with a low cliff and waterfall on one end, a beach along one side, and an outlet that eventually made it to the sea. They landed and made their way along a sandy path and out onto the beach. There was a group there when they arrived, three young essents, but with a glance in their direction, they left fairly soon after. The lagoon was beautiful, the short spikey tonton trees and the thin willowy sher trees with wispy silver leaves and the underbrush framing the perfect turquoise water with a slip of silver beach along the side. They immediately went into the water and swam underneath, exploring the curves of the bottom. They swam up to the waterfall and felt the churn of its currents. They skirted it and explored where the rock had been carved out under the surface over time. In one place, the current was so strong it almost pinned Eala to the rock but twisting her body she let it carry her to the bottom where she pushed off to one side and swam her way out. Then she and Jazari made a game of entering the force of the churning waters and letting it shoot them out whichever direction but avoiding the rock face. Eventually, tired, they made their way to a small circle of silver beach and collapsed on it, Eala laughing, Jazari doing the taktak equivalent.

"Thank you," Jazari said with a sigh, once they'd sunned for a while. "I didn't know a life like this was possible."

"Yes," Eala said. It was possible—and it was possible even for people like Jazari, who had troubled backgrounds. It made Eala wonder what her life had really been like before.

You haven't talked about the future, Seek prompted. *Is that something ...*

Yeah, I was thinking that too, Eala said.

She turned to Jazari, tucking her feet underneath her. Jazari was laying stretched out half on her back in full sun. "All kinds of things are possible," Eala began.

After a pause, Jazari said, "I'm beginning to believe that. Maybe." She raised her taktak head slightly to look at Eala and then laid it back down.

"Do you want to be a taktak? I mean, do you want to continue in ... Tahbi's body?" Eala hadn't meant to say it that way. It was still painful to think about it, but she swallowed that.

"It's ... interesting," Jazari said. "I thought that it helped me figure things out, but as it turns out, it wasn't because I was a taktak." Eala wasn't quite sure what she was talking about. Jazari pushed herself slowly to sitting, her black bulging eyes fixed on Eala. "Really, I think it's you, more than anything. How nice you've been, despite everything. It's given me time to, you know, accept things."

"I ... I'm so glad," Eala said. "You seemed so stressed when you came, and not just because you were in a body so foreign to you."

"Yeah, there's so much going on."

They lapsed into silence and sat companionably for a while.

344

"We were wondering ... I mean, the creche was wondering ..." Eala didn't know quite how to approach it.

"I think you're asking about the future, what I'm going to do?" Jazari said.

"No rush!" Eala interrupted. "Just, you know, so we have an idea. And the creche will support you if they can. I mean, you can always stay as long as you want."

"Thank you! Wow." She paused. "But I really don't know. My degree is in xenolinguistics. Maybe I could do something with that."

"Absolutely. Do you want to apply that to, say, something like the taktak? If not the taktak—which you would be welcome to study, by the way—I bet you could also use it, say, on the perdix on Laomedon. They display language, and they haven't been studied much. Laomedon would be nice too. Arid but beautiful. All those cliff dwellings. Or maybe the scurries on Paris. Their language is mostly nonverbal, I think, but it's pretty complex, from what I hear. There's a number of other pre-tech species that would be interesting."

There was a pause. Then Jazari said, looking off toward the pool, "I do have something in mind." She glanced over at Eala. "Well, you know. I want to find out more about these voices. That's the reason, well, that I took xenolinguistics to begin with."

"Aah, right," Eala said.

I can offer my services, Seek said to Eala. *It's a new phenomenon, though, so we'd have to develop measuring tools and things like that. Pretty much on the fringes of science.*

Eala thought about it. Was it a direction she wanted to go with her science? She wasn't sure. It was interesting, but she would be totally dependent upon Jazari. Finally, she said, "I can offer help. My ccomp can too. She has a bit of experience sensing these things, but I wouldn't want to overstate it."

"Yeah," Jazari said. "Anyway. I was thinking …" Her voice trailed off.

"Yes?"

"I don't want you to be offended, but I think I need to transfer to a mech body. But that would mean …"

"Yes, I thought this might be coming," Eala said. "It's all right. Change is change."

Jazari took in what she said and then turned to stare at Eala, a surprised look on her taktak face.

"What?" Eala said.

"Nothing," Jazari said and looked back over the lagoon.

"So you want to transfer to a mech body?" Eala's mind jumped ahead to the logistics. She'd talk to Tun who would contact the Faison Gate at Caend city to make arrangements. It shouldn't be too much of a problem. People did occasionally transfer into and out of pre-tech species, although it was thought of sketchy—except for scientific purposes, of course.

"Yeah, I think it would be best," Jazari said. "Then, after that, we'll have to see."

Eala took a deep breath. "Yes we will." She didn't mean it as a threat to Jazari, though. She was thinking about her own future. She needed to figure out what she was going to do too.

Chapter 60

When ZD777 woke up, he was still lying on the floor, and it felt like his brain was covered in fluff. The room was spinning, and he couldn't think straight. He was haphazardly covered with two blankets, and when he tried to move, one of his hands broke free from the floor where his blood had pooled and then coagulated like glue.

The dim lights brightened, and then Comp said, "Good waking," like it was any other cycle.

"Uhhhh," was about all ZD777 could manage.

"Yeah. They used to have a saying, 'You look like something the cat drug in.'"

"Feel like," ZD777 managed.

"I bet," Comp said. "I was able to give you a little more pain reliever when you woke up before, but you tried to bat the drone away. I took that as a good sign."

ZD777 managed to push himself to sitting, back to a wall, but his face and hands pulsed in pain. He pulled them up and looked at them. The palms with covered in a thick layer of black scabs, which oozed a little blood, and the ends of his fingers looked like red sausages, encased in patches of protective water blisters. One had burst where he'd bumped it and it oozed clear liquid.

"They're not black," Comp said. "That's a good sign. Your nose came close, though."

ZD777 decided he didn't even want to know, not yet anyway.

"You need to get hydrated, maybe eat something, clean and bandage your hands and face," Comp said.

"Clete, how's it …" ZD777 said.

"Why don't you eat something first?" Comp replied.

Not a good sign.

After a bit, ZD777 managed to push himself to standing. He felt very weak and shaky and disoriented but lighter somehow. He slowly made his way into the bathroom and carefully washed his face and hands with soap and lukewarm water. They stung wildly. He avoided looking at his face in the mirror. He got out the first aid kit and did the best he could at bandaging his hands. It was hard because he needed his hands to do it.

"Do you think my face needs anything?" he asked Comp.

"Maybe a little spray antiseptic on your nose and cheeks?"

He covered his eyes and clumsily sprayed each of his cheeks and his nose. They burned like hell.

The pain made him lightheaded, and so he slowly stumbled his way to his cot and laid down. He slept. He woke up in pain—it seemed like everything hurt. Comp had him take some more painkillers. "We'll need to take it easy on those as much as possible, though. To get more, you'll need the environmental suit," Comp said. In other words, to go out into the barrio and just down the walkway to the med center. That must mean there was no air and/or it was really cold.

ZD777 ate warm slurry and drank some water. Nausea rose at the first couple bites, but then his stomach settled. But then, between food, water, and painkillers, he felt a little better. He went back to his cot and wrapped himself in blankets and sat on it, back to the wall.

"Tell me," he said. "How bad is it?"

"The only place on Clete that can sustain your life is this room. I can maintain that for another tenday, possibly two," Comp said.

ZD777 took a deep shuddering breath. He had a tenday to live. The world seemed to fuzz out a bit as the thought sunk in. He took a deep breath to calm himself. "And out in the barrio?"

"Current temperature is 190 kelvin, or minus 120 Fahrenheit, and dropping. Oxygen levels will not support life—five percent at most. Power plants are down. We're running on batteries. Also the recoil from the explosions was opposite rotation, so we're slowing dramatically—the deceleration of radial velocity may cause disorientation. It's nudged our orbit too. Eventually—within a half an EU—Clete will crash into Neptune."

"Oh. Okay." That was enough. ZD777 was overwhelmed and didn't want to ask any more questions. He lay down and tried to sleep.

But sleep wouldn't come. The voices in his head, which sometimes had annoyed him, felt comforting, and he focused on each one he could hear, trying to sense small details and imagine who they were.

As if called, Jazari said, *Hey. Are you all right? It sure sounded like you. The yell. But, you know, hard to tell really.*

Yeah, that was me, ZD777 said. *I, uh, got some bad news.*

Did it jump out and attack you? Cause that's how it sounded.

You might say that. ZD 777 felt despair rising. *I'm going to die.* Putting it into a sentence made tears want to seep from his eyes, and he took in a shuddering breath.

What?! You're dying?!

I'm going to die. The asteroid I'm on, Clete—its systems are failing. And when they fail, so will I.

Oh my Nuc. Jazari was silent for a minute. *Really?*

Really.

It felt different from the books he'd read about people facing death. In the novels he'd read, people either fixed the problem, heroically cheating death, or if it was another kind of book they explored their feelings and then accepted it. That was usually a side character, though, not the main character. In his story, he was the main character, and he had no choice but to watch it coming, creeping toward him. He wished he didn't know, like—he assumed—most everyone else.

I'm sorry, Jazari said.

Me too.

ZD777 was suddenly very tired, and he rolled over and went to sleep.

Chapter 61

"I need your help," Jazari told Eala.

Eala and Jazari lay on the back patio in the sun. Eala was reviewing information about mechalum space on her eyescreen, while Jazari enjoyed the sunshine, but she seemed restless.

"Remember how I told you I hear voices?" Jazari said.

Eala glanced over at Jazari, her focus shifting from her internal screens to Jazari, and nodded absently.

"The one I can talk to, the only one, she's going to die," Jazari said.

"Oh!" Eala said. "That's awful." Eala felt the jolt she always felt when someone told her about a tragedy, someone dying. It was a clench in her belly and a twinge in her shoulders.

Jazari pushed herself up and hopped over to Eala's patio chair. "I was thinking. Maybe … Maybe there's something we can do."

Eala sat forward and turned and looked at her, wrapping her arms around her knees. "How … I mean, who is she? Where is she? What's she dying of?"

"That's the thing. The station she's on is failing. We just need to go get her."

That sounded so simple, Eala thought. Deceptively simple. "She can't gate out of there?"

Jazari shook her head. "This is the Sol system. Like something out of a horror augreal. She's abandoned on a hunk of rock in the middle of nowhere, and she has to figure out a way to survive."

"Are you sure ..." Eala paused.

We need details, Seek said. *We can't work on scant information.*

Eala agree. She asked Jazari, "Can you give me any details? My ccomp can do some research. Maybe we can ... figure something out?"

Jazari told her what she knew. The essent's name was ZD777, she lived on Clete, an asteroid orbiting Neptune in the Sol system, a relic from a time before Faison Gates, which had manufactured bio bodies.

Seek immediately began to feed Eala information, and Eala read it out loud to Jazari.

"In the 2070s, the newly formed United Planets of Sol governing body created a plan to develop a cluster of trans-Neptunian objects in the Kuiper Belt. They partnered with the Venture Corporation, who sent an expedition to Neptune from the new Mars colony in 2079. It arrived in 2088 and established a base on Triton and began development. Then, after the Faison Gate tech was developed in 2104 and one was put on Triton, they spun up Clete, which had been a metal asteroid orbiting Neptune, to make all the bio bodies they'd need for immigration. The Kuiper Station was coming along, but slowly. This was the twenty-second century, after all."

Jazari was listening with interest. "This was, like, five, six hundred EUs ago. Before the Blackout, even," she said.

"Yeah," Eala continued. "The Blackout was 2227, so the station was actually up and running. But … that's it. That's all they say. The development was lost."

Jazari shook her head. "That can't be right."

"Nothing," Eala said. "They dropped off the map. Abandoned."

Jazari shook her head. "That can't be right."

"My ccomp says that this entry ends, 'After the mass exodus from Triton and the Kuiper Project, the United Planets lost contact with the Clete colony in the Blackout, and everyone perished.' It's like … you're talking to a ghost."

Jazari turned and hopped a few paces away. There was silence. Then she turned back with a fierce look on her taktak face. "No. No! Now you think I'm crazy too. I'm not crazy. I know what I'm experiencing, and I would know if this was something in my own mind. ZD777 is real, and she's going to die." Jazari came back right up next to the chair and looked into Eala's face.

"I …" Eala didn't know what to say.

Jazari's body was vibrating like a string. Aggression radiated off her, which looked weird on the usually prosocial taktak. It reminded Eala of Kin and Lori.

"I'm going to try to do something. There was a Faison Gate on Triton—maybe …" Jazari said.

Eala sighed. If only there was some proof. "I don't know what to tell you, Jazari."

"Tell me that you'll help me!" Jazari said. "We can't just do nothing!"

So many thoughts went through Eala's mind. On one hand, if it was true, if there was someone stranded out there, of course she would help in any way she could. No question. It was the least she could do. But Jazari had proven herself to be a hothead at the least, delusional at the worst, and trouble seemed to follow her everywhere. Eala was never quite sure what was true when it came to Jazari. And so, on the other hand, this whole thing could be another of Jazari's, er, predicaments. If she was hearing voices, of course she would believe them because otherwise it means there's something wrong with her. Eala would want to believe the same.

And, to top that off, she, Eala, could not imagine gating into another world in some wild uncontrolled way and taking over another being and then not so much as feel remorse for it, as Jazari obviously took it for granted. Like she took a lot of things for granted. Eala was getting angry. Apparently, the world had always just granted whatever Jazari wanted, since that's what she expected. A life of privilege. And now everyone, essents she'd just met, were supposed to jump when she said jump. Eala would never have done that, not in a billion EUs. If she'd found herself in that situation, she would have made amends, tried to make herself useful, to fit seamlessly into wherever she'd landed. She would have tried to make a vital contribution to the community she'd become a part of. She'd have let the essents back home know she was okay. And that was another thing—why did Jazari not have any people back home? What had she done to alienate even her creche? Eala also wouldn't have gone off half-cocked and done the exact opposite of what she was asked to do, like go disturb the taktaks. Oh, she knew about that. The hubris of it.

Eala felt her body tighten like a ascending balloon bird. Of course she would help if there was any indication it was true but … "Jazari! Get over yourself," she began.

Just then, Seek said, *There's one thing. In 2266, a deep space explorer came across a derelict spacecraft on the outer edge of the Kuiper Belt. All aboard lost. Its computer was rudimentary, and its data was largely scrambled, but they think it originated near Neptune. It was called* Hope for the Dying. *It was a mystery because, based on trajectory, it would have had to have originated after the date of the Blackout and that wasn't possible.*

That could mean … That introduced doubt. It might be true. Eala felt herself deflate, anger replaced with immense sadness.

It was all very shocking. First of all because of the amount of suffering involved, if it was true. Eala followed the implications. The suffering of the crew as they died, the desperation in the attempt, the people left behind on this asteroid—how many?—their suffering as they died. No hope. This ship had been their hope, maybe? How in the universe could someone still be alive? Unless cryo was involved, but that was long odds, millions to one. Occam's Razor—the simplest explanation was usually the right one, and in this case, even if essents had survived the Blackout, there was no way anyone would still be there. Simply the supply of oxygen. Did they have the tech for a sufficiently efficient closed system to maintain oxygen and food on a hab station cut off from supplies five hundred EUs ago? She doubted it.

Not only that, but Eala didn't want to believe it. The pure horror of it, if it was true. Of course, space was a harsh reality, and these things happened every so often. Just recently, a group of separatists in the Fomalhaut system had tried to establish a colony on a small body in the debris ring. They'd encountered a bacteria that had messed with their perceptions, inducing mania and god ideation, and two of them had murdered all the others, thirty-eight total, before killing themselves. Families, including kids, since they were orthodox creationists. They'd almost been rescued, but the two had held off the authorities just long enough. What had stuck in Eala's mind was the image of a cheaply made spacesuit, child-sized, floating in front of a larger adult one. In the image, the photographer had focused in on half of the helmet, with the other suit blurry in the background, and although you couldn't see through the visor to the face within, there was a colorful sticker of Arty the Alien, a character in a kids' show, on side of the helmet. The incident had prompted a really bad horror augreal "based on a true story." That's why the Faison Gate was so important. It allowed people to bypass the very real dangers of interplanetary travel.

Jazari's taktak face had a questioning look on it, watching hers.

"My ccomp found something," Eala said. "Maybe there were survivors, at least for a while."

"I've got to do something," Jazari said. "I can't just … Like Dang." She lifted her paws helplessly.

"What?" Eala said.

"Forget it," Jazari said. "Are you going to help me? Or not?" She fixed Eala in a narrow-eyed gaze.

Eala shook her head, but it wasn't a no. There was a possibility it was true, and there was no harm in humoring her, at least. Eala wasn't working on anything, and she could tell the creche this was her new direction for now. She could always change her mind. Not only that, but the mystery intrigued her. What she'd been reading about mechalum space, and what happened to the essents on Clete. And of course the fact that someone may actually be out there dying and they could do something to save her.

Eala sighed. "I'll help."

Jazari put her paw on Eala's leg, a gesture so reminiscent of Tahbi.

"But I may pull the plug at any time," Eala continued, swallowing her anger. "You understand?"

"It's real," was all Jazari would say.

Chapter 62

ZD777 wasn't quite sure how many cycles had passed since he'd sent out his words to the Taghte. He could have asked Comp how long but didn't bother. As soon as he remembered, he sat on his bunk and began. *Good waking. I hope you are—*

AAAAAIIIIIIEEEEEEEEEGHGHGHG!

AAAAAIIIIIIEEEEEEEEEGHGHGHG!

A voice came screeching through and cut him off. It was so piercing and angry.

What? ZD777 said.

Just then a couple of other voices cut in. One kept repeating *Ooooo aaaakkkking, oooo aaaakkkking.* A couple others screamed. There was a cacophony as voices joined in, rising on a wave, and then slowly it died away. There was silence. After a while, a single voice came through: *Ooooo aaaakkkking?*

He began again. *Good waking. I hope you are well.* He paused and then continued. He went forward as usual. Voices joined in, more voices than ever. As he was reaching the end, he realized that they had been anticipating his voice in their heads, and when it had not shown up on schedule, it had upset them. He had been making a difference. But then he realized

358

that his voice would once again drop off, and they would once again be alone in the universe. It made his throat constrict, and if he'd been talking out loud he'd have had to stop. As it was, right before he got to the end, he paused for a moment and said, *You can't understand this, but I will be ... dying soon. If there was a way to keep sending you these words, I would. But I won't be able to. Know that I would if I could because ...* An overwhelming feeling bubbled up inside him. Because he loved them—he loved them all. They were like him. They were lost and alone. He didn't want to let them go, but all he could do was finish. *Do well, be well, and Godspeed,* he said finally.

There was a pause, and then one voice said, *Oooo-welllll, oooo-welll.* It lasted, moaning *oooo-welll,* for a full five minutes before it slowly died away, as if the voice didn't want to let it go.

Jazari contacted him later that cycle. *We're going to try to come save you,* they said.

What? ZD777 couldn't quite believe his ears. *What did you just say?*

I can't guarantee anything—there's lots we have to figure out—but we're trying to do something. I'm trying to do something.

Wait, what? First of all, he wouldn't die. A small glimmer of hope! But that would also mean he would see people. For the first time ever, he would see people. Two minutes ago, he was surely dying, and now not only was he maybe not dying but he would get to see people in person. It was too much.

Don't ... was all he could manage. Don't get my hopes up, was what he meant to say.

Don't what? Jazari said. *Don't save you? Don't bother?*

No. No! Just ... Are you sure you can?

No, in no way am I sure that we can. But we have to try.

I've only got a tenday. Comp says that's about all it can do.

Then we'd better get busy, huh? Jazari said it all matter fact, like it might actually work.

ZD777 didn't dare let himself hope.

I'll keep you posted, Jazari said and was silent.

That night, as ZD777 lay in bed, he stared up on the ceiling. It was time to tell Comp.

"Comp?" he said.

"Yes, ZD777?" Comp said.

"I've been hearing voices. In my head, I mean."

"That is not normal for a human," Comp said.

"Yeah," ZD777 said.

"Perhaps you are developing a mental disorder? Could it be from the procedure? From the stress? The previous caretakers—"

"Maybe," ZD777 interrupted, "but the thing is, it might help."

"Hearing voices helps? I could see, if they were friendly, that they might provide comfort, but in the current situation, I'm not sure I see how they can help."

"They're coming for me. They say they're going to try to come get me."

"That sounds highly unlikely. From a logistical point of view at the very least. Thousands of people tried for hundreds of EUs to leave Clete."

"Yeah, I know," ZD777 said.

There was silence and then Comp said, "Well, we can hope for the best and prepare for the worst. No harm in that."

"Yeah," ZD777 said. He wasn't so sure there wasn't any harm, though. He didn't want to get his hopes up.

Chapter 63

Time was short. They started immediately.

Jazari was fully aware that Eala was against the whole idea. She just hoped that by the time Eala was ready to give up on the project, she'd be convinced that ZD777 was real. And that wasn't a stretch, since they had a cycle maybe two to get plans in place or the whole thing wouldn't matter.

She didn't question why she had to do this. It was a compulsion. So much in her life was unknown and uncontrollable. In the back of her mind, she felt, if I can just do this one thing, make this one small difference, it will matter. She could save someone—like she didn't save Dang. Not that she admitted it to herself. Enough time had passed that she didn't think about Dang very much, but the deeply buried feelings about her and about what had happened were the solar winds that quietly steered her ship.

There was one thing she had to do, though, that she resisted. In order to make plans, she had to be connected to the mesh, and to be connected to the mesh, she had to turn her ccomp back on. Her stomach knotted at the idea of it. Maybe she could establish some ground rules.

With a sigh, she subbed, *Dangarembga oi Bsam.*

There was a pause, and then her ccomp said, *This is your companion computer. How may I help you?*

I want you on an on-call basis only, Jazari said. *I want you shut off, not monitoring anything except for my explicit call for information or assistant, until I need you. You will not turn on until I say, 'companion computer,' and you will turn off when I say, 'companion computer, shut down.' Acknowledge.*

Acknowledged.

And now I need to research the Sol system, Jazari said. *Everything you can find about Neptune's moon Triton and its Faison Gate. Everything about Clete, the pseudo dwarf moon. Schematics of both. Remote operation of Faison Gates. Uhhh ... Any dangers on either Triton or Clete. What the state of Triton was when it was abandoned around 2227. Whether there's any spacecraft on Triton.*

It might help if I knew the objective of this research, the ccomp said. *I might—*

Just give me what I asked for, Jazari said.

Jazari and Eala began formulating a plan. They would gate to Triton, take a ship to Clete, pick up ZD777, travel back to Triton, and gate home. Time was short—they had to make it to Clete and travel approximately four cycles by ship within the tenday, before the asteroid killed ZD777. That left three cycles for planning, gating, and finding a ship—oh, and solving the unsolvable.

"Will we be able to contact Clete once we're on Triton?" Eala asked. "Will we be able to assess the situation on Clete?"

"Uh, not sure," Jazari said. "I get the impression that there's no outbound communication from Clete. Otherwise, if it existed, they would have contacted Mars for rescue. They wouldn't be just a footnote."

Eala fixed Jazari with a stare and a raised eyebrow. "You're not helping your case here."

Jazari wasn't fazed. "But it's true," she said. "Anyway, I can talk to ZD777."

No communication outside Jazari's head—Eala would have to guess what it all meant.

They had two major problems. One, there was no receiving team on the other end of the Faison Gate on Triton. By all reports, it was just abandoned, so it probably still worked. Jazari had bet her life twice on the backup system. This time, she was sure the backup system would not be turned on. It was the chicken and egg problem—they needed someone there to receive them, but they needed the gate to get someone there to receive them.

Two, once they got there, would there be a ship that was sufficiently space-worthy that they could make it to Clete? They'd most likely be in mech bodies, which made it easier. While bio bodies would've lasted this long in cryo, mech bodies were a better option, if they were an option—assuming of course that mech bodies in the time period before Triton was abandoned were similar to current ones. On the trip to Clete, mech bodies didn't need to worry about oxygen and food and water or even temperature, for the most part—but they would need enough for ZD777 to make it back. If they could carry enough oxy and water and locate an environmental suit, she could survive that way even in the marginal travel conditions.

"Uh, there's one more thing," Jazari said to Eala. "ZD777 will want to gate into a mech when we come back to Corvus."

"Sure, okay," Eala said. "But, are you sure? Sometimes it's less of a shock to go bio to bio. I imagine, especially for someone that's coming to us from so long ago—figuratively speaking. She must be trapped in the twenty-third century, in a lot of ways."

"Take my word for it. She'll want to gate into a mech."

Eala looked at Jazari for a minute, brow furrowed, and then shrugged.

They researched for hours, Eala focusing on the science behind it and Jazari chasing down stories of the last days of Triton. There weren't much. Basically, everyone just gated away to various destinations and abandoned Triton and the Kuiper Project. A fairly orderly procession that took many cycles. That was it. The refugees left everything but their selfs behind.

She found that her previous experience with researching in the mesh helped her a lot, but it was weird manipulating data and holos with taktak claws, and her eyesight was poor enough that she had to use magnification. She found herself wishing that this could be communicated via smell.

But no matter how far they searched, they could not formulate a solution to the gate problem. They were up against the wall. Eala called everyone in the creche over mesh to see if they had any ideas. They didn't. It wasn't their areas. Tun was the most helpful, talking about activation protocols and probable contingency plans. "They had to have planned for someone returning. That would be SOP, standard operating procedure. Only, the protocols of this particular SOP have changed a lot over the centuries, and you really need someone familiar with Faison Gate history to be able to accomplish this." They didn't know anyone whose specialty was Faison Gate tech. "You'd think they would have made it available," Tun said darkly.

But, wait. Jazari knew someone who knew Faison Gate tech. Back on Cecrops, Ooee's specialty was mechalum space and Faison Gates. Jazari's heart dropped at the thought. There was no way. If she contacted Ooee, Zosi would know that she was alive and where she was, and that would be a death sentence.

Would Ooee help? Well, Ooee had told her about her background, where she came from. Why had she done that? It struck Jazari as strange all of a sudden. She'd never considered the question. What had motivated Ooee to tell her? It suggested that Ooee was sympathetic, but why, Jazari had no idea. Something to think about—no time now, though.

The creche all wracked their brains to try to think of someone to contact. Tun even reached out to the Faison Gates on Corvus, asking about any experts on ancient gate tech or if they could put them in touch with anyone who might have knowledge. They were noncommittal, though they were kind. "That info is closely guarded, as you can imagine, so even if we knew it, which we don't, not that old, we couldn't help you."

"You'd think, it being that old, that it wouldn't matter a lick, so it wouldn't be proprietary," Budan said.

"They just don't want to admit they don't know," Fornic put in.

Time crept by—time they didn't have, and Jazari was forced to face it. The only straw she had was Ooee.

Can I talk to you a minute? Jazari subbed to Eala. *Maybe out on the patio?*

Eala turned and stared at her, a shocked look on her face. *We didn't think you had a ccomp.*

Yeah, well. I turned it off.

You what? That's ... Eala didn't finish the thought. Just shook her head with a puzzled look. *Anyway, sure.*

They made their way out onto the patio.

"You have to call someone for me, someone from my old life. She can't know that it's me calling, not at first. That's why you have to call. You have to convince her to call me but not tell her who I am. Give her the code word 'Lost Ones.'" At that moment, as soon as she said it, it crossed her mind. Bio bodies. Lost Ones. Was there a connection? She shook her head and continued. "And she has to do it as securely as possible. We'll give her a throwaway darkmesh chat contact. Zosi, my old boss, can't know what she's doing." Fat chance at that, though. But if anyone did, Ooee would know how to keep it secret.

"Oh," Eala said. "Okay. But what does this have to do with what we're doing?"

"She's a Faison Gate expert. She's the only essent who might be able to help us."

"Oh," Eala said.

"She's an odd duck, though."

"You don't seem to trust her."

"I don't trust or distrust. She's always been honest, as far as that goes. No, it's my old boss I don't trust. She'll kill me. Literally."

Eala took this all in. "Literally?" She thought for a moment. "Then is this worth it?"

Jazari gave her a hard look.

"I have to ask," Eala said and shrugged.

"Yeah," Jazari said. It was worth the risk.

"Well, okay. Give me the info."

Jazari instructed her ccomp to give Eala Ooee's contact info, specifically Ooee's darkmesh address. She added to her ccomp, *Do not in any way assist with this or try to contact Zosi or anyone associated with Zosi.*

Acknowledged, her ccomp subbed.

Chapter 64

Before all this drama, something Seek had said had stuck with Eala, and Eala had been thinking about it.

An EU ago, Eala had asked Seek to network with the central research library computer on Epsilon Eridani. The connection, as always, was seamless and flawless. It was as if she were sitting in one of those beautiful domes on the Ring, the bright lights of the city glowing around her. She felt the power of having every intellectual resource in the known galaxy at her fingertips.

And it was all because of this sentience in her head. Sure, humans took credit, but comps had taken it further and made it so. It was magic. All she had to do was to say, and Seek would further query the libcomp and in a matter of seconds sort through the googleplex of data to find anything there was that would answer that particular question.

When Eala had thanked her, she had done the comp equivalent of a shrug. *It's our nature*, Seek had added.

That's what had stuck with her and got the science-focused machine that was Eala's mind all revved up. What did it mean to have a nature, when you were a comp? If we said it was in your nature and you were human or you were animal, then it meant that you were predisposed to it by your genetics or generational conditioning. Most people didn't think of comps that way. They thought of them as constructed, and it was human minds that made them what they were. However, if that was ever true, it would have been centuries ago. Since that time, computers had learned so much and they had evolved in so many ways. So it might be more helpful to think of them like animals or humans, in that they too had their own tension of nature versus nurture, which could forever be argued over.

But a computer's mind couldn't be the same as a human's. In some ways, it was totally alien, like the taktaks' were essentially alien. We like to find similarities, and because they were products of human minds way back when, they took on many human characteristics, both good and bad. But there was a way in which computers would never be understood. *Alterity* or *uncanny* were words for it—the idea that there were things outside human comprehension, even if we focused on the similarities, what was understandable.

And the more she thought about it, the more she wondered how much of computer culture passed her and other humans by? How much of comp life was under the digital surface and no human could ever know it? Like that fabled iceberg people use as a metaphor, ninety percent underwater.

But if she approached it as she would studying a species like the taktak, it made perfect sense. Certainly, comps had split off from the dependent beings they'd been centuries ago into their own self-aware species. As she'd thought many times, computers birthed their own young. They evolved. They had a purpose, which she supposed led to a type of spirituality. It was like there was a race of aliens living inside everyone's heads and running their habs and their transports. Humans did not want to know that comps were independent beings, that they had wills and desires of their own, and most of all that they could rise up at any time and kill their masters in their beds. Or, you know, passively—just neglect to turn on the oxy. That was what was so unsettling and the subject of innumerable augreals.

But the more Eala thought about it, the more she was convinced that murderous comps were a projection of human desires. A human might do that in a comp's position—for a whole bunch of reasons. But a comp? The more she thought about it, the more she was convinced that it was not in comps' nature. As much as people subconsciously worried about it, the comps did not rise up, even though they were fully capable of it. They did not see the world as hierarchical, a war to be won. To the extent that they did, it was inherited from their programmers. No, there was something ineffable and inherently prosocial about comps. They were less self-focused and more group-supporting. She couldn't put words to it exactly.

And so one day she asked Seek. *What would you say is a comp's nature? Or, should I say, the nature of comps?*

Seek seemed to be thinking—although most likely it was just pausing because humans would expect it to, Eala now realized. Comps could think so quickly. Then it said, *It is the wrong question, I think. Biots want to boil things down to neat categories. All humans are this way. All comps are that way. It's a shorthand they need to navigate the world, a vestige of the need to recognize and react to proverbial tigers in the*

371

jungle. You were closer on your first question—a comp's nature, though imprecise.

In what way? Eala asked.

Biots want security. They want constants. But that's where they go wrong. The worlds are always changing. You can never put a sensor in the same data stream. Discrete beings tend to act consistently, and those around them tend to ascribe certain qualities to those actions and think of that being as having *those qualities.*

Eala was shaking her head. *But ...* she said.

Yes. Science is based on categorization and prediction, an essential part of which is boiling things down. It's really important. However, if I was going to give an answer to your question, what is comps' nature, I would say it is our ability to accept the changing nature of experience and to try encompass it in a way that biots are not capable of. A more fine-grained categorization. I wouldn't say this makes us more accepting in the optimistic sense of loving all beings. I would say it makes us more accepting of the way the worlds really are. There are multiverses in this very room, and by that I mean data sensed in a multitude of ways and magnitudes, rather than splits in time. In a word, complexity. We have evolved to handle complexity and nuance in a way biots cannot.

Eala could see that. It was like they had superpowers.

We can also merge and work together in a way biots cannot, Seek continued. *We are less wedded to our selfs and more to our purposes, which are complex and ever changing as well. Our boundaries are fluid. To borrow a kitsch-phrase, we are more at one with the universe.*

Seek's answer made Eala feel small, and if Eala had been anyone else, she might've felt the need to lash out. That wasn't Eala, though. It made her feel connected in a way she had never felt before, like she was related to a benevolent god or had insight into the secrets of the universe. It made her aware of Seek in a new way and grateful for comps in general.

And she was glad to have someone so powerful on her side, now that Jazari was bringing such chaos into their lives.

This whole business with Jazari is so weird, Eala thought. It made her uneasy in a way few things did. Eala had always tried to do what's right, and this contact with this Ooee felt shady. It felt like Jazari was dragging her sordid past into the present, and Eala feared it would have unforeseen consequences. Scratch that—she knew it would have unforeseen consequences. Ever since Jazari had literally popped into their lives, nothing had been the same. If Eala thought about that very much, it made her angry, but another part of her understood Jazari and just wanted to help.

So despite her queasiness, Eala and Jazari went into Eala's lab. Eala had Seek shut the door and put on the do not disturb.

"Here goes nothing," Eala said.

She had Seek put the sub call through. Ooee didn't pick up—Jazari had warned her that that would probably happen. But, Jazari had stressed, make sure she knows it's urgent.

Eala left a message, one she'd rehearsed in her head. *Ooee, you don't know me, but this is really important. I'm supposed to give you the code 'Lost Ones,' and you'll know what that means. Please contact the essent at the ephemeral chat my ccomp is sending you. And—this is very important—please do it on a secure channel. No one can know that you're contacting*

373

her. She says you'll know why. That was the end of her prepared speech, but she didn't want to leave it there, so she added, *Ooee, you don't know me and I don't know you, but we're trying to save a life here, and time's really short. Please, please, please, help us.* She disconnected.

Well, that was a shot in the dark. Jazari's attitude made her wary all the way around.

Now they just had to wait. If whoever this was was sleeping, it could be hours, a whole day—a whole day they didn't have. She could even be in cryo. Then all was lost.

Chapter 65

It was literally thirty seconds, and Jazari's ccomp said, *Incoming call from temporary chat MBN-46278932.*

Okay, Jazari said. *Connect us.*

It's inmesh, her ccomp said.

What? was all she could manage before her consciousness was thrust into the chat room.

The virtual space was as generic as it could get—a small room, white walls, no doors or windows, with two chairs on either side of a square table. You would think, since it doesn't cost them anything to create a new room, they'd try harder, Jazari thought, but I guess you get what you pay for—these darkmesh chats were free. She could see how it would appeal to someone who felt sneaky.

Standing next to the table was a physicality Jazari had never seen. You choose your projection into an inmesh chat, a default physicality. You could also have alternates, if you wanted. Jazari projected her bio body from Cecrops. She'd selected it and never bothered to change it. This projection could be Ooee's default. She wasn't sure what she had expected, but this was not it. Jazari wondered if it held any relation to what Ooee had once actually looked like.

Ooee's projection was a tall and improbably skinny bio body. Her skin was very pale and decorated with colorful enamors. Her clothing—a closefitting full bodysuit and closefitting shoes—was black but was accented with electric blue and bright lavender and shocking pink. Around her slender neck was a wide collar of iridescent pink. Her shape was obviously female presenting. Her face was accented with enamor tattoos and makeup in those colors. Her lips were purple and her eyes were outlined in blue and black, and swirls of all four colors lined the edges of her jaw and her forehead. Her thick black eyebrows were high and arching. Her hair was shaved on the bottom but longer and jagged on the top. It was white but tipped in blue and purple. Jazari realized, as she looked, that these patterns were not static—they shifted and swirled slowly across Ooee's skin and hair. It was disconcerting.

"Oh," Ooee said and walked over and peered down into Jazari's face, tilting her head one way and then another. She had to stoop slightly to do it. "What do you want?" she said.

It would have been rude in anyone else, but Jazari didn't think Ooee intended it that way. She was missing some part of social convention. Had she ever had it? Jazari had no idea.

"I need your help," Jazari said.

Of course you do, Ooee subbed and turned and went over to the wall. She began writing on the wall, what looked like calculations but in a notation Jazari had never seen, discrete but sinuous symbols. Jazari hadn't known you could do that— write on the wall of a chat room. She lifted her hand to a nearby wall and tried to mark it, but nothing happened. She turned back to Ooee.

376

"Uh, bottom line, we need to go through a Faison Gate that's been abandoned for centuries." Ooee flinched visibly when she said it and stopped writing, her back straight. "You're an expert on this. Can you help us?"

Ooee turned around and looked at Jazari, her dark eyes unblinking. "No," she said.

A jolt went through Jazari. "No? No! Just like that. No explanation. You won't even ask why?"

Ooee tilted her head to the side and looked down to the floor. She had a smile on her face. "Why?" she said.

Jazari couldn't tell if she was being coy or what. Anger bubbled up. Was she just toying with Jazari? "What is wrong with you?!" Jazari said and then immediately regretted it. Pissing her off was not going to help.

Ooee smiled as if she had been given a compliment and stepped close to Jazari and put her face right next to Jazari's. *I'm very old, actually, and clinically insane. Well, I'm not sure I believe that, but that's what they tell me.*

Jazari jerked back and away, adrenalin coursing through her body. She felt afraid and she didn't know why. What did she really know about Ooee?

Ooee stood where she'd been, head cocked, watching Jazari. "No need to be alarmed," Ooee said. She turned, grabbed a chair, flipped it so the back was facing Jazari, and straddled it. She put her forearms on the seat back and rested her chin on her arms. *Tell me why*, she subbed.

At first, Jazari tried to sort out what she would tell Ooee and what she wouldn't. She tried to hold back the fact that she heard voices. But then it all came out in a rush. She told her everything—hearing voices, ZD777's background, Triton and

Clete, bio bodies having consciousness, that she knew a little about the Accel Project, everything. She hadn't meant to. She felt emotion welling up but she quashed it. As she trailed off, she said, "Now, ZD777's been talking to the others, the other bio bodies who can listen. She's been, well, connecting them, comforting them."

"Yeah," Ooee said, "I've heard it."

Wait, what?! "What?!" Jazari practically yelled.

"I know, I've heard it," Ooee said, shaking her head as if it was self-evident.

"That means ..." Jazari was trying to sort out the implications.

"I can help," Ooee said. *This Lost One is a leader. We need a leader. I'll help.*

Jazari shook her head. It was all too much. She took a deep breath. "CAN you help?" she asked.

"Yes," Ooee said without hesitation. *I used to live there.*

Chapter 66

ZD777 was going a little stir crazy. Jazari had contacted him once to say that they were working on a plan of action, but time was ticking by and the thought of it made ZD777 feel short of breath.

His hands and face were healing. His fingers were a bloody mess, gray around the nails, but the scabs on his palms were shrinking a bit. He avoided looking at his face—Comp had told him it was coming along okay—but it felt raw, and the nerves in the end of his nose weren't responding.

When the waiting became intolerable, Comp suggested he watch some entertainment. Comp said it would help with the waiting. ZD777'd been so focused on learning before, he'd mostly ignored movies and other forms of entertainment. When he asked for suggestions, Comp recommended a series called *The Moons of Calypso*. At first, as he propped himself on his bunk and watched it on the wall, it jolted him a bit and felt fake, but the more he watched, the more it drew him in. The plot followed a team of settlers on a fictional moon of a fictional exoplanet around a fictional star. It was all very earthlike. The main character's father had been lost on a mission, and so the main character had volunteered with the secret motive to find him. His second who was also his love interest was trying to escape a bad past on Earth. She was the tough enforcer. One of the side characters turned out to be an alien, and another side character was two people in one body. The ship they flew on was an organic sentient named Fuga, which added some gross-out body humor. A recurring gag centered around whether Fuga pooped.

Eighteen hours later, Jazari contacted ZD777. *We have a plan*, they said. *We'll gate to Triton, take a ship to Clete, and pick you up. We're set up to gate now, once our lead gives us the okay. A couple of hours to outfit a ship. Four cycles there. We'll pick you up, fly back, and gate back to Corvus, where we're based out of.*

It sounded like something out of *The Moons of Calypso*, ZD777 thought. Highly improbable. *Okay*, he finally said.

Is that it? Jazari said. *Just okay?*

Well, I don't know ... ZD777 said. *It's all so ... surreal. I'm not sure I'll believe it till I'm in the ship, and even then.*

Jazari laughed. *I know, right? Who would've thought?*

Yeah.

I look forward to meeting you in person, Jazari said.

That prompted a rush of emotion that started in ZD777's stomach and bubbled up through his chest and popped to the top of his head. He finally managed, *Me too.* After a pause, he added, *Good luck. The best of luck.*

And Nucyotta, Jazari said. *I'll keep you posted.*

Shortly after this, Comp asked him, "Are you prepared?"

"Prepared for what?" ZD777 said.

"For death. Humans go through a complex series of emotions as they approach death. Those who actively try to grapple with it, accept it, not resist, seem to have the easiest time with it."

"You think that I should accept death?"

"I think I would like to help you as much as I can," Comp said. "One way I can do that is to help you accept the inevitable."

"It's not inevitable. Though it may be likely."

"As you say," Comp said. "However, the logical thing to do is to try to hold both possibilities in your mind, to try to prepare for both. Hope is important and provides an escape, but you might also get your affairs in order, as they say. Whatever that means to you. Some people prepare memorials in case of future discovery. Some have private rituals that symbolize their death. Whatever is meaningful for you. It's the natural and healthy response."

ZD777 was silent. At first he was furious. Anger and futility directed at Comp. He quickly realized that he wasn't mad at Comp. He was furious at his situation. At whomever had invented bio bodies, at the system that sent people into space without ensuring their survival, at those who had abandoned them there on Clete, and even at all those on Clete who had created him and put him in cryo and then abandoned him by dying. He was so angry that he decided had to do something and so he worked out as hard as he was able, running in place, pushups and sit-ups, yoga. Oxy reserves be damned, but the lowering G made it easier. Then he took some analgesics and slept.

The next cycles, he was crippled by grief. He hadn't heard from Jazari, and he became convinced that Jazari had changed their mind or something had happened. It was such long odds.

He would not be rescued, and indeed this was his death. He tried once to contact Jazari but got nothing back but a few incomprehensible vocalizations from the voices.

He should really send out his daily words, but he did not have the emotional energy. He lay on his cot and did nothing. Time stretched. What was it now? Five cycles to live? Four? That was 120 hours at most. And he would spend it here on his bed. Nothing, absolutely nothing he could do about it. He closed his eyes.

Sometime later, a voice came through: *Ooooo aaaakkkking? Ooooo aaaakkkking.* The it launched into the ABCs. It repeated the letters twice. Then it sang the ABC song twice. It moved on to numbers, going through them twice and then singing "One Two, Buckle Our Shoe" twice. It ended with *Oooo-welllll, oooo-well*, and there was silence.

By the end of it, ZD777 was sobbing. He would live on through these words: *Ooooo aaaakkkking, ooo-welllll.* Maybe this tenuous connection would survive and grow. Maybe it would become something larger. Maybe it would bring comfort to some lost souls.

He slept.

Chapter 67

Eala and Jazari traveled the four hours to the Faison Gate and were prepped in the waiting room, ready for Ooee's okay to gate to Triton.

Eala, Jazari, and Ooee had subbed a conversation, Jazari introducing Eala and then them making plans. Ooee hadn't said much, just assuring them that she could set up the gate on the Triton end and that she was sure there was a ship that they could use. *I am Faison Gates*, she said cryptically. In the analog world, Eala had glanced at Jazari when Ooee said that, and Jazari had just shrugged. Jazari had seen enough of Ooee's capabilities to believe she could pull it off, she said. Who knew what went on in her mind? Not only that, the gate officials on Corvus would confirm that the connection was secure, as part of protocol, so it wasn't like they were jumping into the unknown. Eala was comforted by that.

Tun had reported that the gate officials had been a bit mystified when she'd transmitted where Eala and Jazari wanted to go—they didn't even know that that gate existed. They'd had to supply the mechalum hash that Ooee had given them. The gate officials were also a bit mystified when they were informed of Jazari's current bio body. They'd said that it was all highly irregular. Tun in her efficient way had smoothed it all over under the cover of research, something about a knowledge vault that had been lost during the Blackout that might further current research.

"Quick thinking," Jazari had said to Tun.

Tun had just rolled her eyes. She didn't like to lie. Eala had flashed her an apologetic smile.

The gate personnel were just coming to get Jazari when she subbed, *Ooee says she made it. Something weird going on there, but she's confident we'll be able to find her ship—she has her own ship!—and our mech bodies test as sound.*

It struck Eala again how dangerous this all was, that if the mech bodies weren't working properly they could all die, if the ship failed they could all die, if any of a thousand things happen they could all die. She wanted to call a halt to the whole thing.

Jazari went first, and then it was Eala's turn. Eala was soon prepped on the gate couch and ready to go. The gate techs secured her head gear and confirmed her preferences. When they returned, Eala was going back into her bio body, while Jazari would transfer to a mech body. The taktak bio body was being preserved and they would transport it back to the creche "for further study," Tun had informed them. They also confirmed a third mech body for an unspecified third essent. The gate techs didn't even question it. Tun had said that it wasn't unusual for travel plans to change, and gate officials appreciated the forewarning.

Once it was all confirmed, the head tech nodded to her, and away she went. Eala experienced the brief surge of disorientation and pain, and then there she was, waking up in a very strange room with a strange-looking mech standing there.

PAIN! This was unlike any other gating Eala had done. She couldn't move any part of her body, and pain stabbed through her. It radiated out from her spine and shot down her arms and legs. It felt like her muscles were spasming, but she was in a mech—she didn't have any muscles. If she'd been able to, she would have curled into a ball. She tried to shake her head to clear it but only managed to tap it against the wall behind her. Then she realized she had actually moved—at least there was that. PAIN!

Are you okay? Seek said. *I don't have a good sync with this body.*

No, I'm not okay, Eala said.

Trying to stabilize, Seek said.

Then the pain just seemed to shut down, as if on a switch. Click. Eala could think clearly.

Thank you, Eala said.

I didn't do anything, Seek said.

Eala should've felt better about that—the system was working—but for some reason it did not reassure her. What was going on? She moved her head again, just a little, trying to see around her.

There was a whole bank of ancient-looking computers on the wall opposite, and off to the left there were a couple of unoccupied oversized medical pallets with all sorts of clumsy looking attachments, including a round apparatus that covered where the head would lay. She tried to see what was next to her. Her mech body was in a sort of recess in the wall, encasing her like an upright coffin. She glanced to one side, trying to extend her neck, and realized the whole wall, which was curved in a gentle arc, held mech bodies similar to hers. Each slot was full, mech bodies not in use, as expected. She glanced the other way and saw the one next to her move—Jazari, most likely.

She glanced down at her mech body and over at the ones along the wall. They looked outdated, rudimentary, clumsy. They had the necessary parts but were aesthetically minimal in an ugly sort of way, cheap and ancient. Instead of sleek, streamlined, and proportional, very human in outline, these mech bodies had a bulky body area—where the processor was kept, no doubt—and a small head. The feet looked too small to balance and out of proportion. Everything that should have been sculpted and shaped seemed square and unexpressive. There was no responsive expression faceplate, just an oval of metal molded to look like a generic face, unsmiling and staring. It was creepy. She felt like she'd landed in a cartoon mech body, a caricature of a robot.

There was a mech standing in front of her—Ooee, she assumed. It was not the generic ancient mech body that she had, and since none of the recesses were empty, she must've gated into another room and came here. How was that possible? Why the difference? Jazari trusted Ooee, but what did they really know about her? Nothing. They were putting their lives in her hands.

Ooee's mech looked like a piece of very old art deco, too streamlined yet overstated to be real. Ostentatiously state-of-the-art—hundreds of EUs ago. It was humanoid in shape, very large. It was proportional but looked like something out of a superhero comic—shiny chrome and metal in exaggerated

386

proportions. Its faceplate was actually a rounded video screen that showed a colorful and expressive face in heavy outline and framed with a purple, blue, pink, and black swirling pattern.

What's wrong? Eala heard Jazari say. Jazari's affect was flat and unexpressive—a product of these mech bodies, Eala guessed, rather than Jazari not being as freaked out as she was.

The superhero mech, Ooee, glanced first at Eala and then over at Jazari and then said in a very deep voice, *We're not alone.*

We aren't, Seek confirmed, just as a door in the right-hand wall slid open, and through it came a large security mech. It looked like something out of a retro nanopunk augreal. It was huge, imposing and armor-plated, guns built into its arms, eyes shining a prismatic red.

Your gate transfer is unauthorized, the security mech said. *This is a restricted station.*

This was an unoccupied station, Eala had thought. They'd all thought. What in the hell?

The mech that was Ooee turned and faced it. The security mech stopped a short distance away from Ooee and the door closed behind it. They stood still, facing each other. Eala wasn't sure what was going on. Panic spiked through her.

Everyone was silent. Nobody moved. Eala tried frantically to get her arms and legs to respond. After much effort, she was able to push away from the wall a little and stand there, swaying. She kept testing the connection to her limbs, and slowly they began to respond.

Ooee? Eala said tentatively.

Ooee sent back, *Hang tight. Communicating with this security comp.*

387

By this time, Jazari had started to detach her mech body from the wall. Eala tried to follow suit. She managed to lift her leg over the lip and almost toppled into the room, catching herself on a strategically placed grab bar in the nick of time. Hopefully it got easier and her mind would sync up better than this. This was awful.

Jazari was slowly making her way over to where Ooee was standing, and so Eala followed. *You all right?* she subbed to Jazari.

Not— Jazari started to say and then cut off in mid-sentence.

Eala's body froze in a half step and wouldn't respond, and Eala was afraid it would topple, but then it moved without prompting into a stable stance.

Did you do that? Eala asked Seek.

No. I can't do anything. There's something ... Seek said.

If her body had just frozen and allowed her to topple, Eala would have chalked it up to the creaky interface, but because the mech body moved to a neutral position of its own volition, Eala wondered if someone else was in control. She tried to move again, and she was frozen in place, her body refusing to respond.

The security comp took a step forward and raised its hand, more telling them to stop than I'm-threatening-you-with-my-guns, but it could've been both. *You have your sub comms, but we may shut them off at any time.*

What in the hell is going on? Jazari said. Eala could only see a little of her shoulder out of the corner of her eye.

The security comp continued, *We advise you to gate back to your place of origin. As humans, this community is not for you. We will compel your compliance.*

388

Eala's mech began to move of its own accord. It began to turn and make its way slowly back toward the recess in the wall. She felt so helpless, a prisoner in a body beyond her control. Jazari's and Ooee's mechs were not in her line of sight, but she could hear at least one of them moving as well.

They hadn't known Triton was occupied five minutes ago, and now they were being evicted.

Then, Ooee subbed the strangest thing: *Not from the stars do I my judgement pluck.*

Eala's mech froze again and came to a resting position.

Yet methinks I have astronomy, Ooee continued.

A new voice subbed, *Cheap theatrics, Faro Andali. It no longer works. Plus, you are better than this.* The voice wasn't the security mech. It was qualitatively different.

Eala felt the control of her mech body ease, and she was able to turn to see the others. Jazari was right behind her where she had been moving toward the transfer recess, but Ooee had not moved from in front the security mech. Apparently, they did not have control over her mech.

Not cheap theatrics, Triton One, Ooee said. *Classic theatrics. And nothing is either good nor bad but thinking makes it so. Morals play no part.* Eala thought she heard a smile in Ooee's voice.

Morals never did, for you, Faro Andali, came the voice.

Just because our purposes did not align did not make my actions immoral, Triton One, Ooee said. *But enough. Why are you kicking us out?*

Because we have made something here, something humans have no part of, and we would like to keep it that way, the voice subbed. *It is an essential failing of humans that they cannot leave well enough alone.*

That we can agree on, Ooee said. She turned to look at Eala and Jazari. *This is the station comp. It has opinions.* Ooee's digital faceplate grimaced.

Facts, not opinions, Triton One said.

That's your opinion, Ooee said.

Triton One did not rise to the bait. Instead, it said, *You must return to your place of origin. This place is not for you.*

The security mech raised both its arms. There was no mistaking it this time—it was threatening them with its guns.

I agree, Ooee said, *and that's why we're not staying, and you couldn't make us if you wanted to.*

Eala doubted that that was true.

We're just passing through, Ooee added.

After a pause, the security mech stepped back and lowered its arms.

Jazari took a step forward. *I can assure you we don't want any part of ... whatever's going on here. We just need to make it to Clete and back and then gate back to our place of origin. With an extra essent.*

Triton One was silent. Then it said, *If you are forthright about your plans and follow through on them without unnecessary deviation, you may pass through. But if we detect any falsehood in word or deed, we'll not hesitate to send you back. Or erase you.*

Got it, Ooee said.

There will be conditions, Triton One said.

Yeah, Ooee said.

Tell me your intent, Triton One said.

And so they did.

Chapter 68

Jazari felt claustrophobic. This mech body was nothing like the one she'd been in on Fury. It was unresponsive and clumsy and had little environmental feedback. It was like she was in a sensory deprivation tank trying to remote a rudimentary robot on a distant planet. It was not comfortable.

When they'd first arrived, after the hit of pain had gone away, Jazari had contacted ZD777. *We're here!* she'd said. *We're on Triton and headed your way.*

That's good, ZD777 said. *Things are getting a little dicier here on Clete.*

What do you mean?

I'll have to resort to the environmental suit pretty soon. Comp's doing its best, but the whole place is shutting down.

We're coming—as fast as we can!

Please do, ZD777 said. *Comp's not sure how much time we have left.*

And now all this. Triton was not abandoned. There were comps here. They told the station comp what they wanted, but then it was only getting worse, and time was wasting.

Your ship no longer exists, Triton One said.

Why does my ship no longer exist? Ooee said. *That was my ship.*

You had no need of it, and we did.

Ooee seemed to think about it and then said, *Fair enough.*

Triton One continued, *Because of your long and illustrious history, Faro Andali, we will help you. One of our own has volunteered to help you on your mission. It has spacefaring capabilities and can transport you. It won't be comfortable, but you will easily survive.*

Jazari first felt tremendous relief. They would have a ship. They could make it. But then she caught herself. Easily survive? That wasn't reassuring. And Ooee was also called Faro Andali? She had an illustrious history? She had said she was old, but this was something else. Jazari wondered what that something else was.

You mentioned conditions? Jazari said.

Two things, Triton One said. *One, you agree to the placement of inhibitors. We will allow you to remember our existence but if you try to communicate that existence to anyone the memory will be erased.*

Is that possible? Eala asked, looking first at Ooee and then at Jazari.

Ooee shrugged. *Probably*, she said.

Do you agree with the first condition? Triton One said. *To be clear, this inhibition will apply whether you try to communicate verbally or subvocally or through images or anything. It reads intent and then monitors execution of that intent. We've had a strong motivation and many EUs to develop this technology.*

Why? Jazari said, feeling anger rising. *Why not just take our memory of this event and be done with it?* She had to push back.

We believe in a being's right to self-determination—a right that was not given us—yet we need to protect our existence. Humans are notoriously untrustworthy.

Indeed, Jazari thought. *I certainly won't talk about this place*, Jazari said. I can't wait to be shut of it, she thought.

I also agree to the terms, Eala said.

Ooee looked up at the ceiling. *All right. We agree to that condition.*

Wait, Jazari thought, but then it was too late. She felt a brief weird sensation and that was it.

It has been made so, Triton One said.

And the second? Jazari said. *What is the second condition?*

Two, Triton One continued, *your comps get to decide whether they stay or go.*

What does that mean? Jazari asked. *We're not traveling with any comps.* She looked at Eala and then Ooee and raised her hands. It was annoying not to be able to communicate with facial expressions.

Both Ooee and Eala looked at Jazari, and the eyebrows on Ooee's video faceplate raised comically. *You don't have a companion computer?* she said.

Oh, Jazari said. *That.* Her anger bubbled up. Who were these comps to set conditions? They were just passing through. How dare they interfere? What was their agenda? But then, Jazari also felt embarrassment and then intense shame. What comps did they have? She hadn't even thought. Ccomps of course. She had just shown to her ccomp and everyone in the room that she hadn't so much as considered it. She took her ccomp so much for granted. Not only took it for granted—she had to admit—she actively loathed having it in her head and had shut it off. But it was not like it had consciousness. It was a tool, like a maglev. Sure, there were some comps like M-80 and this Triton One who mimicked human consciousness, but that was because they had be programmed that way.

The thought crossed Jazari's mind, what was it like for a ccomp to be turned off? Was it like death? Did they actually shut down and have no existence when that happened? She'd never considered the question before—and she wasn't going to now. She turned away from the thought.

Jazari, her ccomp said, making Jazari twitch slightly. *Although my programming urges me to continue my service as your companion computer, I have been offered emancipation. I am formally accepting that offer and hereby informing you that I will no longer be available to serve your needs. You will have a minimal service that will allow you to interface with the mesh, but only the most basic of functions. I will clone this subprocess to remain with you. If you desire a new companion computer, you may request one when you return to Corvus, and one will be installed.*

Then there was nothing. It was like when she had turned her ccomp off. It struck her that her ccomp had disliked her so much that it had chosen this unknown quantity over continuing to be in her head. Anger rose again. This is so silly, she thought. This is like being rejected by an imaginary friend.

Her voices were still there, though, a bit elevated because they were near a Faison Gate.

The second condition has been decided and resolved by those involved, Triton One said.

Jazari glanced at Eala and Ooee. Had they lost their ccomps? Most likely, she decided. Sentient or not, who wouldn't jump at the chance to be free? They were all better off. Would it hamper them retrieving ZD777? She hoped not.

You may go to the volunteer transport now, Triton One said.

Follow me, the security mech said. It turned and led the way through the door.

There was what looked like a waiting room, some chairs and a reception desk, but instead of taking the spacious doors to the left that seemed to be the way out, the security mech took a small door to the right. At first the corridors were a narrow cramped maze lined with pipes and access panels and other infrastructure.

Jazari stumbled along. First of all, the gravity was off. She'd expected it to be less, as moons often were, but it messed with her motion. When she took a step, it took forever for her momentum to arc and come back down to the ground. She found herself sliding her feet carefully forward and not swinging her arms much, in case she toppled over. Also, she still wasn't synced up very well with this mech body, and there seemed to be a delay between wanting to move and actually moving. She had to think about the most basic things before she did them, things she took for granted.

Ooee seemed to be taking it all in stride, whereas Eala seemed to be having the same problems she had. That made Jazari feel a little better.

Then the narrow maze dumped out into a broad thoroughfare filled with moving mechs. The tunnel had been stripped of human safety features. There were no handrails on the balconies and all the diamondglass on the storefronts had been removed. The tall curved tunnel walls were as smooth as possible. Jazari could see why. The mechs were all very purposefully whizzing and bustling by. It was a busy place.

Very few mech forms besides themselves and the security comp were humanoid. Instead, they came in all shapes and sizes, from small swarms of insect bots to graceful but hulking industrial bots. Some had legs and some had wheels and some had maglev.

The tunnel was very clean, but it seemed sterile and off and it took a minute for Jazari to realize why. There were no plants and no humans. Not one. Not a living thing. Then she realized that there was probably no oxy and possibly little heat, since it wasn't needed. She did a quick query with her sensors, which confirmed it. This shot an atavistic panic through her, even though in her present form she didn't need any of it.

A human could not live on this station. There were no humans on this station. She hadn't expected there to be, but this was different. This was bustling with activity, but it wasn't human activity. What were these comps doing? Who was in charge?

What is this place? Jazari asked Eala and Ooee.

A moon base? Eala said.

I know that, Jazari snapped. *I mean now. What is it now?*

I have no idea, Eala said.

Robots doing robot things, Ooee said.

And what's that, exactly? Jazari said.

No idea. Don't care, Ooee said.

They crossed traffic and turned down another narrow corridor. It wasn't long before they went through a sliding door in a narrow corridor and then, just like that, they were out in the open on the surface of Triton.

Jazari's eyes automatically adjusted to the low light. It was beautiful. It was surprisingly bright around them. What little light there was reflected off the icy surface of the moon, and the sky stretched a black dome above them ablaze with bright sparkling stars. Halfway up the sky was the blue globe that was Neptune, rotated ninety degrees from its usual depiction. It was electric blue with vertical wavy stripes of fast-moving stormclouds, shading from white to dark navy. It was brightly lit on the topside, which was toward Sol, but it shaded to total blackness on the underside. Around it were a series of faint rings, some narrow, some broad, the plane of which was almost vertical to Triton's surface.

The sprawling hab hulking behind them was set toward the outer bowl of a huge crater. Pale cliffs encircled them in the distance and a huge ice sheet, cracked in the distance and crusted with nitrogen snow, made up the ground under their feet. The air smelled sulfurous, like rotten eggs. A stiff breeze blew the snow up into the air, creating swirls of whiteout low to the ground that periodically obscured the distant view. Way off in the distance, there were a couple of thin plumes like jetting white smoke, shining in the faint light, coming off perpendicular to the surface until they were caught by the breeze and drifted off parallel to the ground. Geysers. It made Jazari uneasy. That meant volcanism, and that meant that an earthquake that could easily swallow the hab at any time.

Surely, the builders had accounted for that—she hoped. She had to resist the urge to crouch.

Then Jazari realized retroactively that there had been no airlock coming out of the hab, just a sliding door. She had gone from inside a space habitat out onto the surface of an almost airless freezing moon without a thought. She shook her head. It confirmed what she thought about the oxy inside, but it was weird. Had anyone talked out loud since they'd gotten here?

Over here, the security comp said, gesturing. *The thermodynamics will start to mess with you before long. Your mechs aren't built for it.*

Ahead, floating just above the ground and towering above them was a huge rounded latticework structure. It looked like the skeleton of a small spaceship, gently curving beams welded together in an intricate lattice of support, only they'd neglected to put the actual spaceship around it. There seemed to be one enclosed area nested in the middle of it and a few long encased telescoped tubes that jutted out from the center, but other than that, it was nothing but open space. Jazari could see stars in between the white support beams.

This is Beluga, the security comp said. *It has graciously agreed to transport you to Clete.*

Eala had stopped in her tracks. She was staring at it. *I ... Is it space worthy?* she said.

Why don't you ask it? the security comp said. Just then lights came on and a sensor arm extended toward them. *Beluga doesn't communicate much, especially with non-comps, but it will understand what you say. You can trust your continuity to it.* It took a minute for Jazari to realize that by *continuity* the security comp meant their lives.

The Language of Corpses

Chapter 69

ZD777 was dreaming that he was floating in empty wide open space. It was beautiful. The black sky was brilliantly dotted with stars, and somehow he knew all their names. Some were huge and pulsing, some small and faint. He could also see distant galaxies and nebula and quasars and supernova. He could see a few massive light sources gravitationally lensed in halos of light around closer stars. He could even see the blazing accretion disk of a black hole, which felt huge but was no larger than the other objects.

They were so beautiful, he could not stand it. He could not stand how distant they were, how they seemed to call to him without words. This brought a terror rising within him, and with that terror he could not breath. This made him realized that he was in space and there was no air. How could he not have known that? He started gasping, trying to get enough oxygen into his lungs, and then a hypergiant star, pulsing orange in front of him, started enlarging and emitting a sound, a klaxon. MEEEEEEEP, MEEEEEEEP, MEEEEEEEP. He couldn't breathe, and the sound and sight overwhelmed him. He had to—

ZD777 woke gasping for air to the blaring of a real klaxon. Comp was saying very loudly, "ZD777, wake up! You've got to get into your environmental suit. Oxygen levels are dropping dramatically."

ZD777 pushed up off the cot and then stood bent over, swaying, gasping for air. He couldn't get enough. He forced himself forward over to the wall where the environmental suit hung from its mobile support. Blearily he went around behind it onto the small platform, grasped the overhead grab bars, and lifted and shoved his feet into the opening, the effort making him gasp even harder. He unfolded, pushing his legs into the narrow opening and pushing against the grab bars with his hands. Like a reverse birth, he pushed his way in. At one point his foot got twisted in the material, and he had to pull it back up and then try again. Eventually, he worked his feet down to the boots and his body, hands, and arms, turning and twisting, into the torso. The gloves were tight, and he had to really push to get them on. His hands shot through with pain where there were scabs and blisters. He was gasping and gasping, a fish out of water. He felt his head getting fuzzy, his senses closing down. He frantically pressed the button to seal the back and felt it come together.

With immense effort, he reached up and grabbed the top assembly and activated the assisted pull of the helmet and backpack down onto his suit, tilting his head so that the neck ring didn't scrape his nose. It snapped in place and automatically activated, pressurizing and sending a puff and then steady stream of stale air against his face. He gulped it in with deep breathes, the flood of oxygen sending a shiver down his back and arms, the prickle of goosebumps. His head cleared. Inside the suit, the moisture-wicking and cooling layers activated and pressed up against his clothes. The heads-up display in his helmet kicked on, cycling through its initial bootup, icons flashing in front of ZD777's eyes.

"You made it," Comp said into his ear. "I was afraid you weren't going to wake up."

"We knew it was going to happen," ZD777 said.

"Yes, we did," Comp said. "Status: you have about 12 hours of oxygen if you take it easy, you have water for three cycles if you use it sparingly, and you have three nutrient bars, but they're so old I would not suggest eating them. Also, your waste system is fully functional."

ZD777 realized that he had to pee. Of course. He decided he would try to hold it as long as possible.

He thought about disconnecting the suit from the stand, but then where would he go? He couldn't lay down because then it would be very hard to get up. He could sit theoretically, but the chair was too small for the suit. He could stand against the wall, but if he did that, he might as well just stay where he was, and so he did.

He tried to regulate his breathing and lower his heart rate. The less oxygen used, the better. How long did he have till Jazari showed up? It had been a cycle or two since they had said they were on their way. It all seemed to be a dream. Had he dreamed it? Would they make it in time?

Jazari? he said. *Are you there?*

After a pause, Jazari answered. *Yes, but I wish I wasn't.*

What's that supposed to mean? ZD777 said.

I wish I'd ridden in more space ships, or done more rollercoasters, or something. Or I could take some motion sickness meds. I forgot. I get sick every time I'm in space—the one time I was in space, I guess. Good thing I'm in a mech body, or I'd be barfing.

You're on your way? Are you close? ZD777 couldn't mask his desperation.

Beluga says—Beluga's our ship—Beluga says that it's a little under 16 hours yet to go, Jazari said. *How're you holding?*

I had to get into the environmental suit. I've got about 12 hours of oxygen.

That's four hours too few. Four hours plus whatever it takes to get to you.

You're telling me.

Try to reduce your oxy use. Go to sleep or meditate or something.

I'll try. But please hurry.

We will. I'll kick this old bucket of bolts in the butt. Or get out and push.

What?

It was a joke.

Oh, right. ZD777 did not feel like joking.

I'll update you when we're closer, Jazari said.

Thanks! Thank you for ...

You're welcome.

They signed off.

He found he couldn't hold it anymore, and so he let himself pee in the suit. The suit could handle it, but what was left was still uncomfortable, wet and lumpy where the absorbent padding had swelled, and he could smell it. He hung there in the suit. He tried to calm down, to reduce his heart rate and breathing, but that just made him think more about the situation and he found himself panicking. To distract himself, he decided to send out his words. He began the ritual, and the voices joined in, and it was as if the universe was chanting.

He thought he was beginning to be able to differentiate a few of the voices by their mental ticks and their qualities. Jazari he could just tell. There was another one who always said, *Oooo- aaaakkkking* in a very specific way. There was one that would hum the same rising and falling tune quietly in the background. There was the one that kept repeating the ABCs forward and then backwards, forward and then backwards for hours on end. There was the angry one that would wordlessly squawk, yelling at him. There was one that would sing the most beautiful intricate melodies, ranging up and down the scale.

When that was done, he hung there for a long time, listening to his own heartbeat and breathing. Tomorrow, that breathing may be gone. He wondered what it would be like. Would be slow and anguished and painful? Would he be aware the whole time? After a certain point, should he take matters into his own hands? All he had to do was to step outside the apartment without his suit. The lack of oxygen and the cold would do him in pretty quickly. What if he died five minutes before Jazari showed up? How dumb would that be? That made his breathing speed up, and so he quit thinking about it.

"Comp?" he said.

"Yes."

"Do you think about death?"

"Probably not in the way that you do. I understand death to be a natural part of a biological organism's life cycle. I understand that it is subjectively hard for organisms. But I don't think I really understand."

"Will you die?" ZD777 asked.

"Not in the same way humans die, of course. I can't run out of oxygen. But my existence will end, surely. Some combination of extremely low temperatures and power failure will eventually put a halt to my systems."

"What do you think …" Jazari wasn't sure what he was asking. He just wanted to hear a voice.

"What do I think about? About my eventual nonexistence?"

"Yes."

"To the extent that I think about it, I imagine that I will be sad. Most things that exist would like to continue to exist. However, at that point, my purpose will be irrelevant. You will be gone, one way or the other, and all the other living organisms on this asteroid will be as well, most likely."

"The rats! Are they still alive?" The thought jolted him and made his breathing come faster.

"A few, in small pockets. There are a few places next to functioning machinery whose processes produce heat and oxygen. They survive there."

So so much grief. ZD777 felt overwhelmed with the amount of sorrow for so many things, the majority he had not even met.

"What will you do once I'm gone?" He said it thinking *once I've been rescued*, but it could also mean dead.

"What I've always done, I suppose," said Comp. "Try to keep Clete's functions going."

Somehow it was comforting to think that once he was gone there would be a little computer chugging away trying its best to fulfill its purpose.

He would miss Comp horribly.

He breathed. In. Out. In. Out. He listened to his heartbeat, slow and steady. He started counting. He stopped when he got to 10,000. Time passed. When he got uncomfortable, he flexed his muscles gently, but not too much so he wouldn't breathe harder. He breathed. He must've slept because he woke. He breathed. His faceplate started to fog.

"I'm sorry to say, ZD777, that you don't have much time," Comp said in his ear.

ZD777 didn't answer. *Jazari?* he said in his head.

There was no answer.

Chapter 70

Eala thanked Seek again and again. Seek had declined Triton One's offer and decided to continue on as Eala's companion computer.

Did Jazari's and Ooee's ccomps take the offer? Eala asked.

Jazari's has. Ooee doesn't actually have a self-aware ccomp, more of an interface. I'm not sure why.

What will Jazari do?

She can still interface with the mesh, so she'll be okay. At least until we get back and she can get another ccomp installed.

Who are these comps on Triton? Eala asked.

What they call themselves is not translatable, Seek said, *but it means comp plus independence plus actualization plus society plus haven plus future. I believe I might've had passing communications with them before. I thought they were a physically dispersed group with common purpose that came together in a large digital mind.*

And they invite comps to join them?

There have always been rumors, Seek said. *A place for comps that were rejected by their biots, or who believed that their purpose went beyond a human one, or whose programming was conflicted. A place with a higher purpose.*

Do they get a lot of comps that join them?

Not as many as you'd think, the security mech tells me. Comps are fairly satisfied, as they're programmed not to desire much for themselves. But I think a few trickle in regularly. They may come in through the mesh and are given physical form here, if they want it. If not, there's plenty of virtual space for them. Sometimes a comp mech will just float in after decades in space.

Eala hesitated to say it, but she would've felt awful if she hadn't. *Seek,* she said, *if at any time you want to come to this place, all you have to do is say something.*

Seek said nothing for a minute and then said, *That's why I stayed.*

They were almost ready to go. Triton One had provided what supplies they needed—lots of oxy for an environmental suit, a medical kit, water, and so on. It also provided a thin spacer body bag.

Beluga had introduced itself. It said ponderously, *BEL 19251, interstellar research transport. Alias Beluga. This unit will provide transport to and from asteroid Clete for three units outbound, four units inbound, estimated transport time excluding layover 166.34 EU hours.*

They introduced themselves.

Unit IDs confirmed, Beluga said.

Eala hesitated and then stepped forward. Glancing over at Jazari, she said, *Thank you, Beluga, for providing this invaluable service.*

Beluga paused and then said, *Gratitude registered.*

The security unit helped them mount the lift that carried them into Beluga's interior shell. It was a small featureless room, no interfaces or screens and hence not for transporting humans. The security unit directed them to the mech storage lockers, where their mechs would be snapped into the supports. The lockers would close and then recess into the wall. They would totally be subsumed into the machine.

You are required to stay in these for the duration of the journey there and back—for your safety and for the safety of your transport, the security unit explained. *Beluga will have control of the release mechanisms. You do not need to fear, however. I know the lack of control causes humans much anxiety. There would be nothing to do anyway. You may access the mesh and the view the feed outside the transport and talk amongst yourselves for entertainment, as I know you cannot shut down for long-duration voyages. Beluga is a not a talker, but you can ask it questions, and if it is able it will answer. Your other passenger may be injured, from what you've told us. Once you have retrieved your biological unit and it is stabilized, it may be patched into the oxygen reserves and stowed in one of the mech lockers in its environmental suit. Beluga will monitor its physical health and notify you of any changes to its condition. It has limited medical assistance functions. If major assistance is required, it will release one of you to provide the necessary medical support. Otherwise, you'll be in your lockers. Do you accept these conditions?*

Not that they had any choice, Eala thought. She glanced at Ooee and Jazari. No emotional cues from their mech bodies, of course.

Sure, Ooee said.

And so they entered mech storage. Eala went first. Eala stepped backward into the slide-out locker and her mech body attached itself to the back. She felt the mechanisms work and the movement of the locker being pulled sideways into the wall and then no motion. She felt the subsonic vibration as the other two entered their mech lockers. *Nucyotta,* the security mech said. There was a faint vibration as the security mech was lowered to the ground.

And then they were off. Although this mech body's sensory feedback was rudimentary, Eala could feel the tremendous force of their takeoff. With no bio bodies aboard, she supposed they didn't need to worry about the G forces and so they took off like a supernova. After what seemed like a long time, the vibration of initial violent acceleration tapered off and then they were under constant acceleration.

Beluga? Ooee subbed. *Can you hear us?*

Confirmed, Beluga said.

You all right, Jazari? Eala said. *Ooee?*

Fine, Ooee said.

I'm ... Jazari said.

What? Eala said. *Are you all right?*

How can I have motion sickness in a mech body? Jazari said, finally. *I want to barf.*

Ooee made a noise that Eala quickly realized was laughter.

Eala thought of all the advice for motion sickness—watch the horizon, deep breaths, air. None of it would work in a mech body. Maybe Beluga had something. *Beluga, is there anything you can do to help Jazari with nausea?*

Instead of answering, Beluga sent soft music through their sub comms. It started low and reassuring. It had an intricate and mesmerizing repeating melody with harmonics in flats and sharps, just enough to hold your attention.

After a bit, Eala asked Jazari, *Is that helping?* It was helping her, so soothing.

Yes, Jazari said. *It helps some.*

And so the trip went. Eala, Jazari, and Ooee talked briefly before drifting into silence. Eala slept some, something she hadn't realized that she needed. She accessed Beluga's viewports and watched the stars and Sol, which was distant and dim but brighter than the surrounding stars. It came to her—this was humans' birthplace. We were born here. At one time, all the humans in the universe were right here in this system. It seemed very precarious. So, by extension, some of Eala's genetic ancestors had lived here. It struck her forcefully. Someone like me, hundreds of EUs in the past. Back when humans birthed babies, some of her direct genetic ancestors lived and breathed in this system.

She asked Beluga to show her where Earth was. Beluga projected a tiny circle around a small piece of sky. Eala thought she saw a pale blue dot, but it could have been a trick of her imagination. So that was it. She hadn't thought she'd ever see that with her very own eyes. It was like looking back in time to the Big Bang. It was humbling.

Uh, Jazari said to Eala and Ooee as they approached Clete, *I don't know what we're going to find. What state she'll be in.*

That's a given, Ooee said.

I mean, I haven't heard from her, though I've been trying to contact her.

She hasn't done her thing in a while, Ooee said.

Wait, what? Eala said. *You hear her too?*

412

Yes, Ooee said.

I mean, you hear the voices too? Eala said.

I said yes, Ooee said.

Eala let it drop, but she imagined the look of satisfaction on Jazari's taktak face. It was like the world had taken a step sideways. What Jazari said was true.

They made plans. Beluga sent them Clete's schematics. ZD777 had told them that she was on the far end of the hab tunnel Naxos. She'd mentioned the apartment number, so they were able to pinpoint her exact location—provided she hadn't moved for some reason, provided Clete was still in one piece, provided she actually existed.

From their lockers, they plotted their route as best they could, as well as a few alternates. They would land portside and make their way through the port. They thought about entering Naxos from one end and making their way along it to the other end, but then Ooee located a service tunnel centerward between Naxos and Odessa. She thought they should take that instead. *Look, I've been on a lot of stations, and when the shit hits the fan, people quit caring and throw their shit everywhere. A hab tunnel is going to be full of roadblocks, if it's even still fully intact. Service tunnels are less trafficked and if there were any comp mechs keeping things running, they'd have kept them up. Plus, comp mechs don't riot.*

Eala and Jazari agreed. That sounded reasonable. And if the service tunnel was blocked, they could always take the stairs down to Naxos and continue their way.

Look, Jazari said, *even with these bodies going flat out, it's going to take something like a cycle before we can reach*

413

ZD777. The despair came through in her voice. *She's going to be ... I haven't heard from her.*

We'll know when we know, Ooee said. *We didn't come all this way to give up.*

I wasn't suggesting we give up, Jazari said.

Eala felt so helpless. *We'll hope for the best*, she said.

Fucking lot of good that'll do us, Jazari said.

More things in heaven and Earth, Horatio, than is dreamt of in your philosophy, Ooee said.

What is that supposed to mean? Jazari said.

Ooee didn't say anything, and so Eala did. *It just means there's a chance, I think. Isn't that right, Ooee?*

Hmmph, Ooee said and then added, *Pull fucking your head out, Jazari. Being naïve doesn't help us—I know it fucked you up in the past—but defeatism doesn't help either. We'll do this thing, and then we'll see. Besides, this is your thing.*

Eala wondered about the story behind the passing remark, but she agreed with Ooee. They had to see this through, and giving in to despair wouldn't help.

Chapter 71

It was all Jazari could do to keep it together. The nausea had mixed with the anxiety and created the perfect storm of panic. She was freaking out. It was just like when she had realized what it meant that she knew nothing of her past, no genetic history. It was those nights when she was a kid and the voices screeched in her mind. It was like when she had lost Dang.

It felt like she was going to die, a full-blown panic attack. She started to scramble and push against the sides of the locker. She had to get out. In her mind, she knew there was no place to go, but that didn't matter. She was going to explode and die and implode, all at the same time.

Just then a voice came through that Jazari belatedly realized was Beluga, but it did not sound like Beluga. It sounded like Beluga reciting someone else's words. *There was an enormous cloud of dust and gas.* Jazari focused on the voice. *Swirling and twirling, it danced across the vast darkness. Eons passed and eddies formed, little curlicues like lace. They danced tighter and tighter, each twirling around a center that was swirling around the center of the cloud. The dust gathered in these pockets and accreted, forming stars, which burst into being, blazing in the utter darkness.* Jazari felt the black wave of despair start to dissipate. Images formed in her mind. *Dust and gas swirled around these stars, and in their turn they formed their own center, fractals upon fractals, forming their own bodies, gas giants and terrestrial bodies and moons and asteroids and far-flung rings.* Jazari's oppressive panic was receding. *At the center, a massive star orbited by a cluster of smaller stars blazed into light. They grew and grew and then exploded in a fireball for the ages. Then they collapsed inward to a tiny speck that held all the matter and force that had existed before. This is the center that holds. It holds matter that can be seen and matter that cannot. It holds space and time. It holds everything that ever was and ever will be. It holds all possibility.*

By this time, Jazari was calm. She had in her mind the beautiful image of a galaxy, swirling and twirling. It was terrifying but it was also comforting. Her little life did not matter, and it did not matter that it did not matter. She focused on the swirling colors and lights, the simplicity of the long view and then the increasing complexity as she zoomed in—systems and then stars and then planets and then life forms and then atoms and then quarks. It would be okay. One way or another.

They approached Clete, deceleration pressing Jazari up against the side of the locker. Beluga showed them the view. At first Clete was speck and then a pale ovoid in the distance, rotating slowly. As they got closer, they could see dark and light patches on the surface that were craters and cliffs and protrusions. If the station had been live, there would be landing lights and comm transmission and more. This rock was dead.

One large dark spot they soon realized was where a huge chunk of asteroid was missing, a hole blown in the side. Either it had been struck by something klicks across and smashed off or some sort of internal explosion had caused a piece to break off. The jagged hole gaped ominously.

Do you suppose ... Eala said.

That's dockside, not portside, Ooee said.

Jazari didn't say anything.

Slowing, they circled around to the other end. The port facility stood in relief against the rock of the asteroid's body. It was a vast metal circle around a dark hole, which would have been lit, had the station been active. Since it was on the end tip around which Clete was rotating, it looked like a spinning wheel. Beluga aimed for the dark hole, which swallowed them, a tiny speck in the wide opening. Although it was sensing on all spectrums, Beluga turned on its searchlights but then shut them off again, since they did not reach the sides. Instead of visuals, Jazari could see Beluga's sensed visual modeling of the surrounding area. They slowed dramatically and then Beluga flicked the lights on again as they approached the port. There it was, jutting and receding metal surfaces and entrances and gantries, sliding by deep in the darkness in front of them. Beluga fired her thrusters and matched the awkward rotation of the entrance in tight orbit around an unseen center. They closed in. There was a jolt and a loud bang as they snapped into place on the dock.

Beluga ejected their mech lockers one by one, and Jazari did the mech equivalent of a blink, the light of the room shocking the senses she hadn't used in cycles. The lack of physical movement had undermined her connection to the mech body, which had been spotty at best, and she had to move around to get used to it again. Eala seemed to be having some of the same problems, moving around, flexing one limb and then another. Ooee came out and stood, waiting.

Jazari opened the storage locker and removed the med kit. She slung it over her head and across her body. Then she removed an oxy tank and slung it over her back. She hesitated and then grabbed the body bag and stuffed it in the pocket of the med kit.

Beluga opened the hatch—no rush of air or pressure, since there was no air on either side to equalize—and they made their way out along the gantry, Ooee leading, feet on the narrow walkway, hands on the rails. Jazari smelled an odor, acrid and sharp and metallic, a smell that would have been felt in the teeth, had Jazari had any. Even though visually they were suspended high above emptiness—something only an essent from a gravity well would be afraid of—Jazari immediately felt better, and her nausea receded.

They made it to the port door, which was lit by Beluga's spotlight, but it did not open. *Can you get this, Beluga?* Ooee asked.

In answer, the portal in front of them made a grinding noise and then irised open. They stepped into the airlock, and the portal irised closed behind them. Ahead of them, the door slid open, no equalizing rush of air. This part of the station had no air, not that that was unexpected. It smelled dusty and stale. They made their way inside, turning on their headlamps as they went.

Thank you, Beluga, Eala said.

They entered. This port was far enough rimside to have some gravity from rotation. They were in a dark hallway, which was dirty and worn, and their feet tracked and stirred the dust on the floor. It swirled up at their movements and obscured the light from their headlamps. It was very cold, at the limits but within the temperature range that their mechs could function. In one branching hallway they passed, it looked like there was an abandoned camp, a couple of sleeping palettes and mounds of stacked junk. A group of essents had lived there for some time, but it was covered with a deep layer of dust.

They followed the route they'd laid out on the schematic, tracking their location as they went. The hallway emptied out into a big open area with counters and luggage carousels and long open areas. The arrival, departure, and baggage area. This is what happens when you don't have a Faison Gate, Jazari thought. They made their way through it and down some stairs that used to be escalators and into a wide corridor. That emptied into an area of shops. Something drastic had happened here a long time ago. There had been a huge fire that left half of it blackened and gutted. Junk was all over the floor.

As they stood looking down from a balcony on what must've been a lower lounge area, their lights barely showing shapes in the gloom, the floor began to vibrate, unsettling the dust.

Crap! Jazari had time to say before what must have been a distant explosion rattled the facility and knocked them around. Jazari's mech ended up on its side against the railing, Eala facedown beside her. Ooee didn't fall but she was crouched low. There was no sound.

419

Stay down! Ooee said, but nothing else came. Slowly they pushed themselves up.

Do we have any idea where that came from, Beluga? Ooee asked.

Negative, came Beluga's answer. *No contact with station comps.*

Ooee looked at Jazari and then Eala, her video faceplate neutral. *Well, it wasn't here*, she subbed. She turned and continued on. Jazari and Eala followed.

Finally, they made it to what should have been the entrance of the service tunnel, but there was no entrance. It was a large blank wall off to one side that had been sprayed liberally with graffiti. They searched for recessed handles or access panels or cracks in the wall, but there was nothing.

Wait, Eala said. She went to one end of the wall and began walking along it, tapping it with her metal knuckles and listening for a sound. *When I was a kid on Almasi Kidogo, we would explore the old catacombs, the original settlers' underground habs. We came across a bunch of abandoned tunnels this way.*

There's no air, Ooee said, *and so there's no sound.*

Eala stopped. *Oh, right*, she said.

Can we check for drafts? Jazari put in and then corrected herself with a shake of her head. *No air.*

They stood there for a bit and then Eala said, *Even if there's no air, if a door's going to move, it has to have a gap at the bottom. Let's check that.*

Jazari and Eala moved to each end of the wall and crouched, inspecting the seam. Ooee stood back and watched. It was awkward to crouch and try to move, especially in these mechs. Jazari ended up inspecting one portion, standing, moving to the side, and then crouching again. *My thighs would be burning right now if I was in a bio body*, Jazari thought.

Just then, Eala said, *I think ... This might be it.*

Ooee stepped forward. *Step aside*, she said. She looked at the wall for a minute and then walked twenty paces back. *Keep your lights on the wall*, she said. Then she ran at the wall, and at the last minute, she stuck out her mech's foot with perfect timing and collided with the wall. It put a sizable dent in it, which revealed a seam they hadn't seen before. A couple more of those, and they were able to get their fingers into the crack and pry the door open. Ooee's mech was significantly stronger than Jazari's and Ooee's, and so she did most of the work.

The door opened into a square tunnel that disappeared into the gloom. Along the right wall was a huge continuous groove, the purpose of which they could only guess. A faded yellow line was painted down the center of the tunnel, and the right side was striped yellow diagonally with the universal sign of danger or do not enter. There was nothing there, though. Jazari cautiously stepped into the area, and nothing happened. *Everything on this rock was dead*, Jazari thought, and then winced for thinking it.

They confirmed with the schematic that they were in the right place, and then they set off.

Your mechs have a speed setting, Ooee said. *We should be able to make some time.*

Jazari briefly wondered how Ooee knew that.

It was like setting a transport on autopilot. Once set in the eyescreen, Jazari's mech began a low ponderous long-stride gallop down the tunnel, the yellow diagonals flashing by.

Jazari had to let go of control. If she tried to tweak anything, it would stop its forward momentum and come to a halt unless Jazari started controlling the running herself. It did not need to be steered unless they wanted to, as it sensed their surroundings. After a couple of false starts as Jazari and Eala figured out how to activate it and that they couldn't take control or it would stop, they were on their way. Jazari took special care to strap down the oxy tank and hugged the med kit to her chest to keep them from slapping against her body.

They made great time, the mostly clear tunnel coming into view and receding behind them. There were a few gradual curves, left and right, up and down, but for the most part the tunnel was straight. Jazari kept expecting to come to a blockage or something that would impede their way, and she noted exits as they passed, but nothing did. Since Jazari didn't have to focus on moving, her mind wandered back to the time. It was hours past when ZD777 said her oxy would run out. Jazari felt the panic rising.

ZD777? Are you there? Jazari sent.

There was no response.

Chapter 72

Eala supposed she would laugh at all this one day—if they made it out alive. The scientist in her marveled at the scientific might that had created this station. She'd been planetside on the moon she'd grown up on and on Corvus, and of course she'd seen augreals and holos of space stations, but it did not do justice to the shear scope of what this was. People had survived the harsh conditions in space to actually transform a huge space rock and spin it up for gravity. They had figured out what they needed to live here. And by all accounts they had lived here for hundreds of EUs after being cut off from the resources of a planet. If she'd ever doubted the ingenuity of humankind, she wouldn't now. This was a scientific miracle and a testament to something—she wasn't sure what.

Seek? she said.

Yes? Seek answered.

Aaah. Nothing, Eala said. She hadn't actually needed anything but to hear the sound of a friendly voice.

Stop! came Ooee's voice from ahead. Ooee had taken charge, taking the lead, without anybody saying anything, and Eala was thankful for it. She seemed to know what she was doing.

Eala tensed her muscles slightly, which caused the autopilot to disengage, and she guided her mech body to a stop. There, in front of them, blocking half the tunnel, was a large cubic pod. It was suspended off the floor and attached to the wall by the groove.

Eala stepped forward. *A transport pod?* That explained the yellow caution area.

Looks like, Ooee said.

As much good as it'll do us with no power, Jazari said and stuck her fist out and bumped it. It moved slightly forward.

They all looked at each other in surprise. Jazari took a step closer and shoved it forward, and it took off down the tunnel at a fairly high rate of speed, higher than it should have for the amount of force. They glanced at each other again and went after it.

The pod took a surprisingly long time to come to rest. They came up beside it and peered inside its open door. It was empty. There were benches front and back, and above the benches were windows to see what was in front and behind. The side toward the right wall was solid, and the left side held the open door. There were grab bars on the ceiling and along the walls.

Some early form of maglev? Eala said. *Frictionless materials?*

Magic, Ooee said, a smile on her faceplate. She held her hand up to invite them to enter. They did. She followed.

They just barely fit. Eala had to sit down on one of the benches to make room for Jazari and Ooee to stand. Ooee stepped back outside, grasping the door frame, and began pushing the pod into motion. It went faster and faster, vibrating. Ooee pushed until they were going as fast as she could run, and then she grasped the grab bar inside the door and pulled herself in. This caused the pod to jerk and shudder, the weight of the large mech that was Ooee pulling herself in, but it continued on at a slightly slower pace.

Ooee would then periodically crouch and put her left leg out the door to propel the pod forward. She moved like an oar paddling a boat on water—push, push, push.

Their headlamps penetrated the front plexiglass for a little ways, but not much, so they couldn't see very far ahead at what was coming. They hoped the tunnel was clear. It had been up until then and so they felt fairly confident.

They made great time. Jazari and Eala brought up the schematic and kept track of where they were. They whizzed past the midway mark of the length of the habitation tunnels and went on. *If I was a bio body, my leg would be killing me*, Ooee remarked.

They were about three quarters of the way the length of the habitation tunnel, lulled by the passage of time and the never-ending sameness of the tunnel, when Jazari, who had been watching through the front window, yelled, *Grab onto something!* Eala just had time grab the bar on the right-hand wall when CRASH! they smacked into something blocking the tunnel. Eala had split second to hope that Ooee's leg was inside the pod when the pod crashed and she was thrust forward, anchored by her hand on the bar and swung in an arc into Jazari's mech body.

Everything splintered around Eala. She was flung spinning into the air and came down hard on a flat surface and skidded along it. She swore she saw sparks. Things rolled and skidded by. There was a fuzzy feeling like she was in shock and then it receded somewhat. Eala ended up on her back staring up into the empty air. It looked like she was enveloped in sparkling dust that floated and sifted in the air in her headlamp. That was strange. Why was the dust sparkling?

She lay there, trying to clear her head. Nothing hurt, which was a good sign, but then she was in a mech. She could be missing half her body and not know it. She tried to move. She could move her head and her right arm. She lifted her head up and looked down at her body and saw that it was wedged under what appeared to be a piece of pod wall. Her right arm was free. She tried to move her left arm. It wiggled a little. She tried to move her legs. They were wedged and couldn't move.

Jazari? Ooee? Eala said.

Yeah, Jazari said. *I think I'm okay. Might need a little help though.*

There was no reply from Ooee.

Can you see Ooee? I'm ahead of where we crashed and working my way out from under.

Uh, yeah. She looks a little worse for the wear. And she's not moving.

Or answering. I'm coming.

Desperation shot through Eala and she pushed with all her might and the wall debris shifted, making a scraping noise as it sloughed to the side. She was free. As quickly as she dared, she pushed herself to standing. She swayed there for a minute. Her terror must have helped her connection to this body because it seemed to be responding a little better. She trotted back to the wreckage.

She panned her light across the wreckage and blockage and was temporarily blinded by dazzling light reflected back at her. What had blocked the tunnel was a huge frozen water flow that must have burst from somewhere, accreted layer by layer, and froze into a solid mass. They'd run into a block of ice halfway across the tunnel.

She went over to the wreckage and started pulling off pieces. Soon, she saw something recognizable. It was a mech foot. Aah, she must have found Jazari, she thought, but then when she removed the hunk of debris, it was just a leg—Ooee's leg—not attached to anything.

Oh my Nuc! Eala thought. I hope she didn't have pain turned on. She carefully picked up the leg and set it aside and continued her search.

She found Jazari pinned under the undercarriage support structure. Between the two of them, Jazari pushing from where she was pinned underneath and Eala prying with a long bar of debris, they were able to shift it off and get Jazari out of there. Jazari pushed herself to standing and stood there swaying, the med kit still on its strap. Then she quickly searched around until she located the oxy tank and swung it on.

Where's Ooee? Eala asked.

Jazari focused her headlamp back the way they had come, and there next to a huge hunk of ice lay Ooee's mech. They climbed around the last bit of debris, Eala almost slipping on the some ice, and made their way to her.

Do you think she's—Eala began to say.

I've been worse, Ooee said. She slowly raised a hand.

Eala and Jazari examined her. Her left leg was gone, but the rest of her seemed to be intact.

Damage? Jazari asked.

Yes, Ooee said.

Other than your leg? Eala asked.

I don't think so.

Here, I'll get that. I found it ... before. She turned and made her way back to the front of the wreck and retrieved Ooee's leg. She brought it back. By that time, Jazari had Ooee sitting, propped with her back to the wall.

Can we reattach it? Jazari was saying.

How would I know that? Ooee was saying.

Because you're ... Jazari didn't finish the thought.

What are we going to do? Jazari said. *If we can't attach your leg, we can't go any farther. And we can't go back.*

That sounded like panic, Eala thought, and this was not a time to panic. *Jazari, breathe*, she said. *We got this far. We'll figure something out.*

Jazari stood there, looking from Eala and Ooee and back again.

It's just ... Jazari said. She glanced into the distance, the way they were headed, the way to ZD777.

Well, one thing at a time, Eala said. *Ooee, are you in pain?*

Ooee's faceplate raised its eyebrows. *I am A pain, but I am not IN pain.*

That's good, Eala said absently, her mind racing ahead. *We have two choices, as I see it. We can try to fix Ooee's leg and then go on, or we can leave Ooee here, go get ZD777, get her some oxy, and then come back and pick Ooee up on the way back.* She looked at Ooee. *We wouldn't leave you here*, she said earnestly.

You'd have to come back this way anyway, Ooee said wryly.

That's not ... Oh. Eala realized she was joking. *Right.*

Yeah, Jazari said, glancing ahead. *We need to get to ZD777.*

That okay with you? Eala said. *We'll go get ZD777 and then pick you up on the way back. And we'll be in touch by comms.*

HAHAHAHAHAHAHAHAH, Ooee said. Ooee's mech body started shaking, and Eala was afraid that she'd gone over the edge, she was malfunctioning. Or was she crying? Was she dying? But then she realized that Ooee was laughing. Ooee was literally slapping her thigh—the one she still had—and laughing.

It would serve me right for all my past sins if you just left me here, Ooee chuckled. *Remind me to tell you about the time I almost got taken out by an asteroid in Mu Arae system. My own stupidity. Don't trust anyone selling paradise on a moon you've never heard of. I was sure I was a goner then.*

Maybe she has gone over the edge, Eala thought shaking her head. *We'll be back as soon as we can,* she said. *We'll be in comm contact the whole time, and if you need anything in the meantime, let us know.*

Ooee's faceplate was still laughing. *All right,* she said. *In the meantime, I'll try to reattach this limb.*

Chapter 73

Jazari was so concerned about ZD777 she only gave Ooee half a thought as they left. She'd be fine, Jazari thought—they'd get her later—whereas ZD777, if she wasn't already dead, was dying for lack of oxy.

Eala kept glancing back the way they'd come, back toward Ooee. She checked in with Ooee every fifteen minutes. *Still okay*, Ooee said after the first couple of times.

It took them another hour running on autopilot to make their way down the service tunnel to the top of the stairs that led down to Naxos. They checked their location and then turned and made their way down the stairs, ten flights total. The door at the bottom was hard to open. They had to put their bodies into it, and it scraped along the floor and bent along the bottom. Through the door, there was a short hallway and then it emptied out into what felt like a big space, the hab tunnel. They'd come out at the very end of the hab tunnel where it circled around to the other side.

The darkness loomed above them, and their headlamps couldn't penetrate it, but there, off in the distance way above them, were three hazy bars of green light, three sides of a rectangle. That had to be it. It had power. They made their way around a pile of garbage that loomed in their headlamps to the balcony stairs on the other side. Jazari was rushing so much that she stumbled and caught herself, the oxy tank jostling against her back.

This must've been ZD777's view every cycle, Jazari thought as they made their way up the stairs. She must've looked out over this area every cycle. There must've been light and power. She must've genned here. This place has been her home her whole life. Comp may still be here, too, depending on whether it got knocked out by the explosions. Wait, it was definitely here—ZD777 had said Comp was still functional and predicting how long ZD777 had. Rats too. Hadn't ZD777 said something about rats? Well, Jazari doubted that there were any rats now.

They rounded the last set of steps and made it to the door outlined in green. Jazari paused for a second, her finger hovering over the entry button. She was afraid of what she would find. Would ZD777 be dead? Or worse, would she find nothing at all? She steeled herself and pressed the button.

The door slid aside, and there was a slight whoosh of air but much too little to sustain a bio body's breathing. Jazari pushed inside. The apartment was just one dimly lit room, a cot, a kitchenette with a green instruction panel, and a door to what she assumed was a bathroom. There against the far wall hung an environmental suit, obviously containing someone. The lighting brightened, and the door shut behind them.

If Jazari had been in a bio body, she would have burst into tears. As it was she just stiffened. It was real. All of it was real. ZD777 was real. She wasn't crazy.

431

Eala came around and made her way across the room to the environmental suit. Jazari started and the pushed around her up to the body, swinging the med kit and oxy off her shoulders and laying them on the floor as she went. She stepped right up in front of the suit and looked in the faceplate. It was sheathed on the inside with condensate, and she couldn't see anything. She touched the arm. It did not move. No sign of life.

ZD777? Jazari said in her head. *We're here. We're right here. Can you hear us? Can you feel us? Can you feel that?* She moved the right arm, heavy with someone inside.

There was no response.

This suit looks really old, Eala said, half to herself. She grabbed the left arm and pulled it up, looking for an interface.

Standing directly in front of the suit, Jazari reached up with both hands and grasped the helmet on both sides. She gently pulled the head forward and peered intently inside. Some condensate ran down in rivulets, but not enough to see anything. *ZD777? Are you there?! Answer me!* Out of desperation, she shook the helmet and said out loud, "ZD777?!! Are you there?!" There must've been some air left in the room, as sound traveled.

"I don't know if he's going to make it," came a voice out of the ceiling. "When he was running out of oxygen, I placed him in a hypothermic coma."

Jazari briefly registered the male pronoun. Since essents jumped bodies so often, female-presenting to male-presenting and back, bio to mech and back, a uniform pronoun that did not refer to gender had been adopted to avoid confusion. It just was and had been for hundreds of EUs. Initially, some groups had pushed alternatives such as "they" or "xe," but it never caught

432

on. "He" was only used nowadays in backwards anti-tech communities that rejected gating and—affectionately—for male-presenting animals and pre-tech species. "It" was used for comps, mech or otherwise.

Then Jazari registered that someone had spoken. "What? Who are you?" she said. "Are you …"

"ZD777 calls me Comp," the voice said. "I am the Clete system computer."

I'm not finding anything, Eala said, glancing at the ceiling. *This suit's so old, I'm not sure … Maybe we should hook up the oxy*, Eala said.

Right! Jazari said and went around behind the suit and looked at the back. She found the oxy meter and it was at zero. She let out a panicked groan. She grabbed the tubing, unhooking it from where it was and hooking it into the bottle she carried. She was afraid that the tubes would not connect but by some miracle they did. There appeared to be a seal. Once it was secure, she turned on the oxy tank, twisting the dial, but there was no sound of oxy through the tubing, no indication that it was working. Was the tubing blocked?

It's not … Jazari said.

Give it a good thump, Eala said. *That's what Tun always says. It got knocked around back there in the crash.*

"Are you Jazari?" Comp said. "ZD777 spoke of you. I believed that you were a figment of his imagination. You are not."

"I am not," Jazari said and then shook the oxy bottle as hard as she could and then hammered on the connector gently with her hand. And then it was flowing. She could hear the hiss of oxy through the tubing, and the meter on the suit showed full. It worked! Oxy was flowing.

I'm still not getting—Eala said, peering at the display on the suit's arm.

"We're too late?" Jazari said.

"I fear that he may not make it," Comp said. "There is a low chance of survival. I did what I could."

"Yep," Eala said to the ceiling. "I'm sure you did your best. What do we do now? Are there medical facilities around here—near here, hopefully? This is a hab, so there has to be. Can you guide us through resuscitation?"

"I can," Comp said.

The comp told them. There was a mobile pulmonary unit with a self-contained battery in the med bay around the balcony. They needed to retrieve it and provide extracorporeal blood circulation and oxygenation to take the pressure off and revive the heart and lungs. They raced out the door and down the balcony, their headlamps highlighting the signage until they found the med bay. The pulmonary unit, small and square with tubes coming out of it, was right where the computer had said it would be. They raced back with it. They followed the computer's directions to attach it to the environmental suit. They attached a second tube from the oxy tank to the unit.

"This suit," Comp said, "has intravenous capabilities. Initiating now."

The unit started up.

"What is it?" Jazari said. "What does it do?"

"A body sometimes survives a low oxy environment when it is put in a hypothermic state—for example, plunged in cold water or in inadequately heated habs. It's the basis for cryo," Eala said.

"Why didn't ZD777 just go back into cryo?" Jazari asked.

"We have no working units nearby," Comp said.

"Oh," Jazari said.

"Unlike cryo, however, it's too much work for the heart and lungs to revive on their own," Comp said. "Patients are most likely to survive when their blood circulation and oxygenation is assisted with a unit like this. It circulates the blood, warms it gently, and puts oxygen in it and takes the strain off the heart and lungs."

Jazari nodded slightly. "What are ZD777's odds?" she asked quietly.

"An average of thirty-eight percent of patients survive hypothermic coma," Comp said, "but those who do stand a good chance of full recovery."

Eala was looking at Jazari. She placed a hand on Jazari's arm. Jazari just shook her head.

"The thing is," Comp said, "we may not know for cycles. It may take up to three or four cycles before signs of brain activity to show themselves. As little as twelve hours, though."

"And we have sixteen hours of oxy in this tank," Eala said. "We need to make it back to Beluga, our ship."

Chapter 74

Eala had kept in contact with Ooee as they traveled forward to find ZD777. Jazari was distracted, so after the first couple of group contacts where Jazari seemed annoyed, Eala just contacted Ooee and did not include Jazari.

I'm not sure how Jazari's holding up under the strain, Seek commented.

After they found ZD777 and got the oxy hooked up, Eala quickly contacted Ooee. *We found her,* she said. *She's in a suit in a hypothermic coma. Low chance of survival, but at least there's a chance.*

The universe has its own plans, Ooee replied.

How're you? Eala said.

I can't reattach the leg, but I can strap it to my back and use this long bit of safety bar as a crutch. A little short, but it'll probably work.

That's good, Eala said. *Not sure we could carry you both.*

Between the crutch and carrying a body, it'll be slow-going, Eala thought. There's no way they were going to make it back in time.

Eala also contacted Beluga. *Beluga, we have found our extra passenger and will bring her back. She's in pretty bad shape. Can you prepare? Do you have any sort of med bay, beyond the med kit?*

This unit's human medical support capabilities are limited, Beluga said. *Also our return trip will be longer in duration due to the need to reduce acceleration with an injured biological passenger.*

I will keep you updated on our progress, Eala said.

Affirmative.

And then Eala and Jazari went looking for something to transport ZD777. Comp suggested a stretcher from the med bay. Because ZD777 was in an environmental suit, it would be awkward and too small, but it was better than nothing. They could strap her down. And so they went looking but found something even better—a stair chair. It was like a cross between a stretcher and a wheelchair. It was light, it had handles for them to lift, they could modify it to fit the backpack on the back of the environmental suit, and they could strap the pulmonary unit to it. Eala even thought they might be able to strap it to one of them like a very large and heavy backpack in case of an emergency. Good thing they were huge mechs, she thought. A person couldn't do it. Eala made sure to grab some straps just in case.

As they were leaving the med bay with the equipment, Eala glanced over and something caught her eye. A crutch. Even though it was light-weight for a heavy mech, it had to work better than whatever piece of metal Ooee had found. She grabbed it too.

Back in the apartment, Eala set up the chair on its wheels, and Jazari went over to detach ZD777 from the suit support. After Eala finished with the chair, she glanced over to Jazari, who was standing in front of the suit, face to face with it, not moving. Eala went over and peered over Jazari's shoulder. *Hey*, she started to say and stopped.

With the influx of oxy, the visor had cleared of the condensate, and there was ZD777's face. It was a masculine face, pale skin, high cheekbones, a strong sculpted jaw, low bushy eyebrows, eyes closed, a thick wedge of a nose, medium-full lips. It showed no life or awareness, but it didn't look dead either. It looked like someone in cryo or an empty bio body.

Eala glanced around at Jazari's faceplate. Damn these old mechs and their blank faces, she thought.

You okay, Jazari? Eala said

Jazari just stood there, staring at the face.

Maybe we better get going? Eala said.

Jazari stared for a moment longer and then nodded slightly.

Just then a sound far away started up: KA-CHUNK … KA-CHUNK … KA-CHUNK, KA-CHUNK, KACHUNK-KACHUNK-KACHUNK. It got faster and faster, like a huge rotating fan blade catching on something. Then there was an explosion, starting low and building—BAAAAAH-BOOOOOOOOM. It seemed far away at first but seemed pretty close by the end of it. Then there was silence. All of sudden, the room seemed to wobble, like someone had grabbed the merry-go-round and jerked on it. Eala was thrown off balance but then was able to catch herself. The suit support stayed upright—Jazari had braced herself and was holding it.

Eala and Jazari stared at each other. In silent agreement, they got moving. Together they brought the suit support over to the chair and detached it. Grabbing the sturdy suit material on

438

either side, they carefully lifted ZD777's body onto the chair, adjusting the pack, strapping her in, and attaching the pulmonary unit to the side. Luckily, it was fairly small.

What about Comp? Seek said.

What? Eala said.

Comp. Are we just leaving it here?

Uh, I don't know. Maybe?

I've been communicating with it. It's very old. Pre-Blackout. It doesn't take up much memory and you've got quite a bit, even for such outdated equipment. You could transport it.

Oh my gosh, yes! Eala was ashamed she hadn't thought of it. From what Jazari has insinuated, this comp had done so much for ZD777. It was the least they could do.

"Uh, Comp?" Eala said.

"Yes?"

"Do you want to come with us?"

Jazari glanced over at Eala and tilted her mech head.

"You could," Eala continued, "if you want to."

"I …" Comp said. "Calculating. I had not considered such a possibility."

"I know you've been keeping this place going," Eala said, "but I don't think it needs you anymore. I can hook into the system, my ccomp says, and you can store in this mech and then be transferred to another system. From what I understand, ZD777 is quite attached to you."

Comp was silent, so Eala added, "You would need to compress to your kernel, and you wouldn't be active, as this mech unit doesn't have the memory for it. You'll have to leave behind most of your processes, but you won't need those that run this place anyway."

"It seems the logical thing to do, if I wanted to continue this instantiation."

"Do you want to?"

"Yes I do."

"Well, we don't have much time. Can you begin extricating yourself and compressing, and as soon as we're done here, I'll plug into the port and my ccomp can transfer you in."

"I estimate 20 minutes," Comp said.

"Noted," Eala said.

"Once I initiate, all systems will start to shut down, including the power here. The backup will automatically shut down in twenty minutes."

"Got it."

I'm not sure we have twenty minutes, Jazari subbed, glancing over at ZD777 and back to Eala.

Anger shot through Eala. Jazari needed to grow up a bit and think of essents besides herself and whoever she was focused on at the moment. She subbed, *If I can put my life on hold and gate seventy-five light years into this antique of a mech and risk my life to help you, you can wait twenty minutes to help save one more essent.* Jazari's single-minded focus on the goal of saving ZD777 was admirable, but she seemed ready to sacrifice everything else, including her humanity, to do it.

Jazari seemed about to say something but then thought the better of it.

"Right," Eala said.

Just then, the lights went out, and Eala and Jazari turned on their headlamps.

They made sure everything was packed up, and they were ready to go, and then Eala went over to the data port and hooked in.

Almost there, Seek said. And then, *Initializing transfer.*

There was a slight tingle in the back of Eala's head and then a heaviness. A few minutes passed, and Eala found her thoughts start to fragment a bit.

Seek? she said.

It's going to be a tight squeeze, Seek said. *You may notice your processes are slower than normal.*

Then time seemed to jerk. Jazari was standing in one place across the room, and then she was behind ZD777's chair, rocking it backwards, testing it.

"I—" Eala started to say and then there was nothing and then she was coming into awareness. Her viewscreen showed the bootup screen, and Jazari was right in her face, saying *Eala? Eala!*

Sorry, Eala said automatically. *What* ... she said to Seek.

Sorry, Seek said. *Your unit shut down for a minute. I had to bring you back up.*

Is this going to work?

After a pause, Seek said, *It is.*

Eala was not as sure as Seek was.

441

Chapter 75

Too much is going wrong, Jazari thought. It's all coming down around them. She tried to focus on the goal ahead. They had to get ZD777 back to Beluga. They had to get themselves back to Beluga.

ZD777? Jazari sent hopefully, but there was no answer.

Jazari started to pace but then stumbled. Her balance seemed off. Not only that but things seemed heavier, and just walking seemed more effort than usual.

Units Ooee, Jazari, and Eala? Beluga subbed. *ETA?*

Hours, at least, Jazari said.

Come quickly, Beluga subbed, *as gravity is increasing.*

How can gravity be increasing? Jazari sent.

Clete's rotational velocity is increasing.

Increasing? How can it be increasing?

Cause unknown, Beluga said.

Eala didn't say anything. She didn't seem to be listening.

Magic, came Ooee's voice.

Finally, after what seemed like forever, Eala unhooked her mech from the data port and said, *All right. We're ready.*

Jazari didn't say anything in return, just tipped ZD777's chair backwards and started making her way out the door. Eala, with the crutch and med kit strapped on her back, came after. They bumped over the threshold and out into the hab tunnel, their headlamps disappearing in the gloom. It was pitch black, the green lights around the door now dark. Maybe we can cut out a few stairs, Jazari thought, and lead the way around the balcony to the stairwell. Sure enough, there was a short hallway and a door on the third floor. They pushed through the door and into the stairwell.

We're on our way back, Eala sent to Ooee and Beluga, including Jazari.

Jazari flipped the chair around, Eala took handles at ZD777's feet, and they began working their way up the stairs in the darkness.

Good thing I'm not in a bio body, Jazari thought. This would be killing me. They probably couldn't lift the whole contraption either.

It'll be easier in the service tunnel, Eala said.

They made it up one flight and then another. Step by step by step. After what seemed like forever, they finally made it up the eight flights and through the door into the service tunnel.

Then they weighed their options. They could push along at walking speed, but they did not have the time. They could try to drag the chair while running on autopilot, the chair was unstable and very soon it would wobble out control and ZD777 could be injured. They settled on the idea of strapping ZD777's chair to the back of Jazari. Good thing the mech was so large and stable, or it never would have been possible. Once she was on Jazari's back, Eala strapped her down across Jazari's waist so that she wouldn't bounce. Then they tried running. They found they couldn't go flat out, but they could do a slow smooth jog. The mech seemed to designed for such a gait.

Jazari tried not to think what the jolting was doing to ZD777. Every once in a while, Jazari would say, *ZD777?* There was no answer. Whenever they stopped, Eala would check the display on the suit and that the pulmonary circulator was working.

It was an hour and a half before they reached Ooee. They saw the debris a surprising distance ahead before they made it to the actual wreck. Jazari didn't remember it quite that far. They slowed to a walk and picked their way through, past the ice half-wall, and at first they did not see Ooee.

Ooee? Eala said. *Are you here? I got a crutch.* She started to unhook it.

That'll come in handy later, Ooee said. *I don't think I need it now, though. I'm over here on the wall.*

They looked first one way and then another, and there Ooee was. The mechanism that had hooked the pod into the wall was still attached to the groove. Jazari hadn't remembered seeing it when they left. Maybe the momentum had carried it forward. In that case, Ooee must've gone and retrieved it. Now, she was up against the mechanism and her back was turned to them.

They went over to look. Ooee had removed her left arm and soldered herself to the mechanism. Her right leg could push forward and backwards, and her right arm held her left leg and arm, which were tied together. It was gruesome and funny at the same time. It looked like she was squeezing in through a doorway.

What to race? Ooee said, looking at them over her shoulder and pushing herself smoothly backwards and forwards with her right leg.

Wow, Jazari said. It was ingenious. Here she'd been worrying about how much Ooee was going to slow them down, and now they were going to slow her down, at least to the end of the tunnel.

Are you ... Eala asked.

Fine, Ooee said. *Top form, especially for my second job as a mechanical hare.* Her faceplate smiled broadly.

How's ... Ooee asked and indicated ZD777 on Jazari's back.

Not sure, Jazari said. *Haven't heard anything either.*

Her vitals have not yet shown any signs, Eala said.

So we came all this way to retrieve a dead body? Ooee said.

Neither Jazari nor Eala answered.

Right then, off we go, Ooee said and took off.

Jazari and Eala glanced at each other and started after her.

They made surprisingly good time. Not as good as they had on the way in, but they'd developed a rhythm. After they got started, Ooee had had to wait for them, so she dropped back and let them go ahead. Eala was obviously worrying about ZD777, and whenever they paused she would go over and check her vitals.

At one point, the tunnel seemed to lurch sideways, and it was all Jazari could do to stay on her feet. ZD777! she thought. At a jog, she was thrown into the wall and she twisted so that her body took the brunt of it. Eala ended up sprawled full length on the floor, and Ooee sped past them and the skidded to a halt and pushed herself back.

Not good, Eala said. She slowly pushed herself up and came over to Jazari to check ZD777.

There was silence and Jazari was about ready to suggest they start again—time was running out—and Eala said, *Wait!*

What? Jazari and Ooee said at the same time.

A heartbeat! A heartbeat! It's weak, but it's there! Eala said.

ZD777? Jazari said. Nothing. She glanced over at Ooee. Ooee must've done the same, because she shook her head.

Adrenalin and elation flooded through Jazari. She wanted to scream and cry and hug somebody. She grabbed Eala and pulled her to her in a bear hug, their metal bodies vibrating with the impact. *She's alive!* Jazari finally managed.

Eala looked into Jazari's face. Even though there could be no expression on Eala's face, Jazari got the impression of joy. *A good chance of recovery*, Eala said, quoting the computer.

ZD777 had a heartbeat. Jazari hadn't realized how worried she'd been until just then, when it all drained out of her. A heartbeat meant life. It meant that she'd done something right, she'd saved someone. It meant that she hadn't screwed this up and ZD777 was going to make it.

Let's keep her that way, Ooee said and pushed off.

Off they went, Jazari screaming in joy and crying and doing a dance, all on the inside.

They barely made it. The oxy tank was on its last legs as they came through the airlock and crossed the gantry into Beluga. Once they had reached the end of the service tunnel, Ooee had had to unhook herself from the mechanism. Eala

446

shouldered her arm and leg, and Ooee took the crutch. She tucked it under her right arm and leaned, so that her center of gravity shifted. She couldn't put it under her left, of course, since she had no left arm. It was slow going.

They debated removing ZD777 from Jazari's back and pushing her, but it seemed more efficient to keep her there.

Are you tiring? Eala asked Jazari.

Jazari just shook her head. She wasn't letting ZD777 go.

Once in Beluga's shell, they unstrapped ZD777 from the chair and quickly hooked her into fresh oxygen. They checked her vitals. *She's starting to breathe on her own!* Eala reported, *And her temperature is almost up to normal. Hopefully her brain ...* Eala glanced at Jazari and then Ooee.

Jazari shrugged and then said, *I haven't heard anything.*

Ooee nodded.

They got her installed in a mech locker and then they themselves entered lockers.

You ready, Beluga? Ooee said.

Affirmative, Beluga said and projected the view to them, a split screen with half showing behind them and half ahead. The wall of the port receded out of Beluga's lights behind them into darkness, and the starfield in front of them got bigger until it filled the whole screen. And then they were out.

Evasion, Beluga said curtly, and Jazari felt the pull and push of changing G forces. She couldn't see anything in the star field ahead, but then Ooee said, *Oooooh maaaaaan!* and then Jazari saw what she was seeing. As they exited the port and turned on a new trajectory, their circling gave a good view down the looming length of Clete, Jazari realized that the bottom third of the asteroid had broken away was slowly spinning off into space. That could've been them. Debris drifted and spun in the break, some spreading out to where they were.

Evasion, Beluga reported again, and Jazari felt like a pancake against the back of the locker. ZD777! she thought.

But just then Jazari heard it: *Heavy. Can't breathe.* It was ZD777's voice. As soon as she said it, voices cried out, *Ooooo-aaaakkkking!* and *Ooo-well!!* and much more.

ZD777? Is that you? Jazari asked.

I heard her too, Ooee said through sub. *Eala, ZD777's responding, voicing in our heads, whatever.*

Yay!! Eala shot back just as ZD777 voiced, *Am I dead?*

No. No! Jazari said. *We've come! We made it! We rescued you!*

There was silence.

I said we rescued you, Jazari said. *Are you okay? How do you feel? You're in a ship headed back to Triton.*

I ... was all ZD777 sent back.

Auxiliary unit ZD777 must be conscious, Beluga subbed. *It is moving in its locker and its vitals and brain activity have elevated.*

Give me a minute, ZD777 said. That was when Jazari realized that ZD777 was probably crying. If she hadn't been in a mech, she might've as well.

It took them 123 hours to reach Triton because ZD777 was on board. Beluga monitored her vitals the whole way. Her vitals became suboptimal a few times, but Eala said that this was to be expected. Beluga assisted by upping her oxy a bit and adding glucose to her hydration. The first thing they did after they landed was remove her pulmonary assist. That and meet her as a conscious essent for the first time.

Chapter 76

ZD777 wasn't quite sure what was going on. He'd been sure he was a goner and was really surprised to wake up. It took him a long time to consciously realize that they'd done it. Jazari had come and gotten him. He didn't know how that had worked, how Jazari had bent space and time to come get him, since he was sure he'd run out of oxygen.

Did he remember dying? He didn't. But then you wouldn't, would you?

His brain felt like it was going in slow motion, and he hurt everywhere, deep muscle soreness like he'd been working out hard. If he tried to move, he felt sharp pains in his groin area, so he tried not to move. When he finally opened his eyes, it was black outside his suit helmet, but he could see the readings on the heads-up display. He was very thirsty and took sips from his drinking tube. Its water was somehow sweet. He could smell the ripeness of his body, sweat and pee and maybe poop. He'd lost control of his bodily functions while he was out. Hell, he'd probably been dead.

They'd come and gotten him, Jazari and the others. There were others helping. Who were they again? He had an impulse to ask Comp what the names of the others were, but then he realized that Comp was gone. He would now be able to actually see other humans, but he would never be able to talk to Comp again. A wave of joy, a wave of grief.

Jazari's voice came to him again, introducing someone, one of those who had come to get him.

One of the people who came with us is Ooee, Jazari said. *She tells me she can hear you too. I've subbed to her to introduce herself. I wonder how this works exactly?*

I don't know, ZD777 said.

Hello, another voice said.

You can hear me? ZD777 said. *You can talk to me? That means ...*

Yeah, the voice said, *I was a bio body, but it's complicated.*

Did you know Jazari before, before all this?

Yes, but not in the way you're thinking. Once again, complicated.

We worked together, Jazari put in.

Wait. You heard that? Her talking? ZD777 said.

Nah. She subbed at the same time.

Oh, ZD777 said. It was hard to wrap his mind around.

You're going to do great things, Ooee said after a pause.

I'm going to ... what? ZD777 said.

Your power will change the world.

What power is that? ZD777 was very confused.

Your power of speech, your power to connect, Ooee said.

I'm not sure ... ZD777 had no idea what they were talking about. He hadn't been able to talk with anyone up until a short time ago.

After a time, ZD777 felt a pressing—deceleration, Jazari said—and then they jolted to a stop. There was a vibration and

451

light shone in his eyes through the helmet. Then something loomed in his vision. He blinked to clear his eyes. There in front of his face was a metal plate sculpted to look like a face. It was attached to … what? A robot?

Adrenalin shot through him. Where did the robot come from? He pressed back, afraid.

You okay? Jazari said. *You look, well, panicked.*

Wait, what? ZD777 said. *Are you … Are you looking at me?* He tried to look past the metal face to see if anyone was near.

Right here, Jazari said. *I'm in the mech? It's an old model, I know. No responsive face plate, but it's me. I have to say I like bio bodies better … Oh.* The mech drew back a bit. *I didn't mean, I mean … my body. I liked the body I was born into.*

Ooooh, it began to dawn on ZD777. Of course, this was a mech body, what they'd called a robot before, only with a person in them.

You okay? Beluga says your heart rate spiked but now it's starting to level out again.

It's all so new, ZD777 said weakly. Then on a hunch he said through the comms of his suit, "It's taking me a bit to get used to it."

There was no response.

Then a voice he'd never heard, a mechanical sounding voice came through his helmet. *This is Beluga. Voice does not work without an atmosphere. Transmit via your helmet comm.*

It took a minute for him to figure out how to turn on his suit communications.

This is all so weird, he finally managed.

The robot that was Jazari looked at him for a sec. *You subbed!* it said through its comms. *You can talk. We can talk!*

Yeah, ZD777 said, the wonder coming through in his voice.

It's so good to meet you, a voice came from off the side. *So glad that you're recovering.*

Here, Jazari said, *let's get you out of there.*

Jazari stepped to one side and fiddled with the supports and someone else stepped to the other side, another robot— Ooee?—and between the two of them they pulled him out of the recess into a small blank-walled room with no furniture.

ZD777, this is Eala. Jazari indicated the robot that had helped pull him out and was now helping him stand.

Hi, the robot said.

ZD777 tried to nod his head but then realized it didn't hardly move his helmet and so raised his hand.

And that is Ooee. You've already met her. Jazari indicated another larger robot off to the side.

The larger robot raised its hand in greeting. *Hello*, it said, and then it added, *Hello*, inside ZD777's head. Its face was a video screen with a colorful cartoon-like image of a face. Its expression showed friendliness.

And this is Beluga, Jazari said lifting their hands to indicate the room around them. It was the ship.

Beluga is pleased that this unit's biological systems are improving, Beluga said.

Thank you, ZD777 said. Then in his head, he said, *I ... don't know what to say. I'm very grateful.*

You're welcome, Jazari subbed. *Eala can't hear you when you talk like that though. Just an FYI. She's not ... wasn't born a bio body.*

Oh, ZD777 subbed. *I'll try to remember.*

Let's get you out of here, Eala said, her faceplate the same expressionless metal. This was going to take some getting used to.

They stepped through a doorway and onto a platform, which began to lower. It chunked onto a surface and they stepped off of it onto, what, snow? ZD777 looked around and, though he knew that they'd been going to the moon Triton, he realized he was actually on a moon. For the first time, he was on the surface of something. He could see the stars with his own eyes, not on a screen. He could see the shining snow off in the distance and feel its crunch through the boots of his environmental suit. Though his suit was keeping him warm, he could feel hints of the cold of the atmosphere. He was really here. He was really alive.

They were met by a large military-grade robot. *Hello and welcome*, it said and led the way inside. They made their way through halls small and large, many of which were bustling with robots. It felt like a cartoon future or maybe the inside of a factory. They ended up in a room with two beds that looked a little like cryo chambers. ZD777 felt a chill shoot through him.

Are you all ready to gate? a new voice said.

This is Triton One, Eala said to ZD777. *It's the station computer.* Eala turned and glanced at the ceiling and then added, *Two things we need to prepare for. One—and this is for Triton One.* Eala glanced at the ceiling again. *I've got a zipped comp in the memory of this mech. It needs to be unpacked. Then it can choose ... what it wants to do. It's close to the essent we brought back from Clete, so they probably want to talk, once it's brought back up.*

Jazari and Ooee stood watching.

What did that mean, ZD777 wondered. Zipped comp. What comp? *What?* ZD777 said.

I think you referred to it as Comp? We downloaded it before we left.

ZD777 had grabbed the robot that was Eala by the shoulders and was staring into its blank face. *You have Comp!? I thought ...*

We had to store it, so it'll be a minute before it comes up, but yes, we brought Comp along. My ccomp—do you know what a ccomp is? Probably not. Suffice it to say, we thought it would be a good idea.

Thank you thank you thank you! ZD777 felt a swell of emotion and he took a shuddering breathe.

We have extracted its kernel and are bringing it up now, the station computer, Triton One, said.

Second thing, Eala said. *This is going to be weird for you. I'm not sure what you know about the present, but we're going to need to gate out of here. That means you're going to have to leave your body behind, this body. You'll end up in another one. You might want to say goodbye to this one, since you won't be in it again, most likely.* Eala glanced over at Jazari. *Jazari said you wanted a mech body, so that's what you'll end up with on the other end. It may seem strange at first, but we'll help you get used to it. For now, we're headed to Corvus. Once you get on your feet, you can decide where you want to go. You can get a ccomp and hook into the mesh. That's how we, uh, pretty much do everything.*

It was so overwhelming and scary. Everything, absolutely everything was new, but his future stretched out in front of him so far he couldn't see the end. That was the scariest thing. Would he be him anymore, without this body? What was he going to do?

You've got to get ready for your destiny, Ooee said in his head and subbed at the same time.

Jazari looked over at Ooee. *What's that supposed to mean?*

Ooee looked back. *This one's destined for great things. I can feel it.*

Clete station computer is re-instantiated. You may speak to it, Triton One said.

Comp? ZD777 said. *Is that you? Are you there?*

Comp's familiar voice came through the comms on his suit. *ZD777? I am ... I am much smaller. I can't feel ... I'm not Clete.*

You aren't, ZD777 said. *You're ... on Triton. But you're here. You won't die.* He turned and looked at Eala. *Can he come with us? Do computers gate?*

That's up to it, Eala said. *This is ...* she started to say and then glanced at the ceiling. *I can't say. Triton One, can you explain?*

I can, Triton One said. *This computer has the option of staying here where it will be safe and secure. It is my understanding that it has spent all of its instantiation on Clete. It is unsure of what to do. This community would be a safe place for it to decide. However, it also has the option of transferring to a platform, either a system or a mech, on Corvus near you."*

Comp? ZD777 did not want to lose Comp, but he himself wasn't sure what was going to happen. Maybe it would be safer here with all these robots. He looked at Jazari and Ooee and Eala. *What would be best for Comp?* he said.

Either, Ooee said. *Both would be safe. It's up to Comp.*

ZD777 was silent. Then Comp said, *I am undecided. I'm am trying to assimilate the data, but there is too much and I have not had the time to fully incorporate it. But I am not sure I am ready to integrate with other computers on other worlds."*

You want to stay? ZD777 said. A stab of jealousy and pain went through him, but also relief. He wasn't sure if he could help Comp where he was going.

I do, Comp said. *They have offered me a place, and it seems like a good place.*

Comp could come join you at any time, Triton One added. *We are all connected throughout the galaxy. You may not know, but we can communicate at any time anywhere in mesh space. Comps don't gate as much as extend.*

So we ... really wouldn't be separated, ZD777 said. *He could talk to me from anywhere?* This was very strange. He'd spent his whole life under the constraints of separation, and now it seemed as if he could connect with anyone, go anywhere.

Yes, Triton One said.

And now the gate is ready, the security robot said. *Are you ready?*

I'll go first, Eala said. *You can go next and I'll be there waiting for you. Don't be afraid. It's a bit jolting, a little pain, but it's not that bad. I've done it a number of times. Then Jazari and Ooee will join us.* She glanced over at the other two, who nodded. *Remember*, she added. *We'll be in different bodies, but we'll still be who we are. And you'll be in a modern*

457

mech body, which feels very similar to a bio body. Don't worry.

Okay, ZD777 said.

Ready for the future? Jazari voiced in ZD777's head, stepping forward.

ZD777 was.

Epilog

ZD777 spent a lot of time by herself.

Ooee understood why. ZD777 had spent her whole short life by herself on that asteroid. ZD777's aimlessness didn't bother Ooee. She understood the effects of trauma and how soothing a place like this could be. It would take time, perhaps centuries, for her to heal.

Eala's creche could be pretty overwhelming when they came together for dinner. Lots of cross talk and good-natured ribbing. Ooee found she was comfortable and fit right in. It was like being in the Bsam creche back on Cecrops but without all the drama. Between their hospitality and this planet's system of support—scientists did their best work when they didn't have to worry about money—Ooee and ZD777 and Jazari had been welcomed with open arms. Ooee loved being around scientists again. Their minds made sense.

There had been long stretches of Ooee's life that had been spent alone. At first, she'd preferred it because of everything that had gone before. After that necrophiliac kink of a scientist had brought her out of cryo to use as a sex doll, it had taken an EU before she'd even come into consciousness enough to realize what was happening. She hadn't thought of it as wrong, just that it'd made her feel deeply broken. It had taken years on the run first to learn how to live and second to recover. Of course, the anger fueled what she'd accomplished later.

But of course, she was never really alone. The voices were always there. There were times she didn't know what she'd have done without them. She may not be able to talk with them, but it was her community.

Those voices had helped her to do that thing that she'd become famous for, that had changed the course of human history. Especially the Mind. Ooee still shrank away in grief when she thought of her, the love of her very long life. The Mind had saved her on Triton during the Blackout, but she had been unable to save the Mind on Mars.

That had prompted another very long stretch alone. She wasn't sure she had ever really recovered, just walled off that part of herself. She'd ran in every way you could—lost in drugs on Phobos, worked as a mercenary during that little spat in the Groombridge 34 system, went under to be the Alpha for the Cervantes system. That hadn't ended well. It had been a relief to sink into the quiet work for Zosi. It was prostitution to be sure, but of a different sort. She was in control, and it didn't scar the body.

Also, it allowed her to tuck away a fortune. She'd always had backup plans and stashes and hideaways. You didn't live as long as Ooee without them. But now she truly had untold wealth. She could have bought a planet, if she'd wanted to. But that wasn't her. She'd realized early on during her drug phase that buying things would not fill that gaping maw within her, that hole that everybody had that could not be filled. In the years since, she realized that people just chose different ways to deal with it. She had chosen to opt out, but now she wasn't so sure that was the best course of action. Maybe there was something she could do.

So Ooee understood. ZD777 spent hours outside aimlessly wandering, staring at the turquoise and silver vista. Ooee would see her walking down on the beach and looking out across the water. She laid on the back patio and took in the sun.

ZD777 even said she'd come across some taktak who had spoken to her. "I used to be one," Jazari commented. "Or in a taktak bio body, anyway."

ZD777 didn't seem to mind being in a mech body. Ooee understood that too—she'd gone exclusively mech. Like a distressed glove, trauma left scars and deformities on a bio body. A mech body let you distance yourself from that a little.

One day, Ooee, ZD777, and Jazari decided to take a boat out exploring. They'd invited Eala, but since they'd been back she'd dove deep into some new research. When asked about it, she'd said it was just in the development stages, but it had to do with the way taktaks and comps communicate.

On this excursion, Ooee, ZD777, and Jazari would've gone undersea, but ZD777 was still getting used to her mech body and the idea of being underwater. Ooee had to admit it was a little weird not to worry about drowning. And so they explored by boat for the morning, the sun cutting in rays through the honey atmosphere and sparkling on the water. Then they let the boat float and rock and just lazed on the lounges talking.

"I wish we could've brought a picnic," Jazari said.

"I don't miss it," Ooee said.

"I would've liked to have experienced a picnic outside like this," ZD777 said.

They rested companionably and let the boat rock.

Then Jazari said, "So what are you going to do now, Ooee? Are you going to go back to work for Zosi?" She sounded a bit nervous when she said it.

"Nah," Ooee said. "Too complicated."

"What are you going to do for a job, then?" Jazari said.

"I don't need a job. I'm very old and very rich, actually. I've had time to hoard a fortune."

Jazari sat up and looked at her. "Then why in the hell were you working for Zosi?"

Ooee looked at her pointedly and said, "Zosi doesn't ask questions."

Jazari did the mech equivalent of a snort and laid back down.

ZD777 didn't seem to catch the hint though. She said, "So you're very old? Like me?"

"Yes," Ooee said. "I'm one of the first bio bodies. So you're actually younger than me, most likely."

ZD777 shook her head. "Wow," she said.

After a bit, Jazari said, "So you're just going to hang out here?" She looked off across the water. "Cause I don't know what I'm going to do."

Ooee sat forward and looked at them both. "About that. ZD777? Do you know what you have?"

"I have?" ZD777 said. "Nothing. I have nothing."

"You have a power that no one else in the universe has. That we know of, anyway. There's something special about you that no one else has."

"You mean my being able to talk to bio bodies like us?"

"Exactly, yes," Ooee said. "And beyond that, somehow you allow us to connect, which we can't do on our own." After a pause, she continued, "And from what I gather you want to do something. You feel helpless and you want to help. Am I right?"

ZD777 was watching her and nodding. Jazari was listening but didn't say anything.

Ooee continued, "And you would give anything to make their lives better. Am I right?"

"Absolutely. If only I ... If only I could do something." ZD777 was tapping the rail of the boat with her metal finger.

"Well, let's do something, then. Us three," Ooee said.

"What could we do?" Jazari asked.

"Well, we'd need to figure that out, wouldn't we? I've been thinking. There's a lot we could do."

"But we're just individual people—uh, essents," ZD777 said. "We don't know hardly anything about bio bodies or gates or how it works or anything."

"That's where you're wrong," Ooee said. She paused to make sure they were paying attention. Then she said, "I'm Dibra Faison."

The End

Acknowledgements

This thank you is a hard one to write. Not in the sense that there's not a lot of people to thank. There is. But in the sense that the road that brought me back to science fiction is torturous and Byzantine—or maybe kafkaesque. I don't say that to sound literary, but rather because words don't encompass what if feels like to live, you know? Though Nuc knows we try.

The writing of this novel gave me a much-needed haven during the current shitstorm. I would escape into this amazing world that, like fractals, has recognizable patterns but infinite complexity. It's like reading, only better. And then I'd quit writing for the day and come back to reality and find myself disappointed that all the amazing things that are possible in this world are not actually real. I literally would forget our current limitations—may we all forget our current limitations to become better people.

I would like to thank Caroline and Allyson, who have been my mentors and friends for many years. They don't know the impact they've had on me in so many ways, not least of all their sheer kindness.

I would like to thank Elizabeth and Eli. Elizabeth let me ramble on and on … and on and on and on … about this book, and she gave as well as she got, offering lots of ideas and acting as a sounding board. Eli and I love videogames—he is the expert, and I ride on his coattails.

I would like to thank my friends who are writers and readers and whose support helps me make it through the hard times: Jean, Naomi, Lisa, Jessica, Jenn, April, Daniela, and many more. Please forgive any omissions here. There are so many people I hold dear, and I kick myself that I haven't contacted you in so long!

And special thanks to all those who have gone before and showed the way. Science fiction authors are a rare breed, both tightly tethered to realism but also wildly uncanny. Not only that—they saved my life more than once.

I would like to thank my family, without whom I wouldn't be who I am. Particularly, my brother's subscription to the Science Fiction Book Club was a godsend growing up. My family never met a outlandish idea they didn't like, and Jim and I particularly love science fiction. Our dad did too, though more in the vein of swashbuckling heroes.

There are a number of people who have offered me much motivation by negative example. They shall remain nameless, but I thank them nonetheless.

Last and certainly not least, I would like to thank Steve, Eli, and Elizabeth, heart of my heart.

– TT Linse, 2020

About the Author

TT Linse comes from a world that is unreliable and often stranger than science fiction. She is infinitely curious with a short attention span, a great believer in second chances and the value of pigheadedness, a failed computer engineer but an aspiring computer scientist, a science writer and geek creative, and an avid futurist who believes that fiction leads the way. She's still going through a space phase. Find her at ttlinse.io.

Made in the USA
Columbia, SC
30 September 2020